The Ship's Communicator Beeped . . .

"McCoy to Kirk."

"Kirk here. Come in, Bones."

McCoy's face had been haggard before, but they were all unprepared for the terrible look that appeared in the viewscreen.

"Bones!" Jim Kirk reacted instinctively to that look. *"What's happened?"*

McCoy drew a long and shuddering breath. "Nurse Chapel—Christine—she's got ADF syndrome."

"My god, Bones, are you sure?"

"Would I be telling you that if I weren't? What do you think I am, some kind of damn fool?" McCoy snapped back. "Tell Starfleet the damn disease is communicable to humans, and they've got to quarantine anybody who's been in contact with a Eeiauoan in the past *six months*. And clean your own house, Jim. We've got a real plague on our hands now. McCoy out." The screen went dark. . . .

Look for *Star Trek* fiction
from Pocket books

UHURA'S SONG

JANET KAGAN

A STAR TREK® NOVEL

PUBLISHED BY POCKET BOOKS NEW YORK

Another *Original* publication of POCKET BOOKS

POCKET BOOKS, a division of Simon & Schuster, Inc.
1230 Avenue of the Americas, New York, N.Y. 10020

ISBN: 0-671-54730-5

First Pocket Books Science Fiction printing January, 1985

10 9 8 7 6 5 4 3 2 1

For Ricky,
who can out-Spock Spock,
and for
the one, the only,
Tail-Kinker to-Ennien,
who taught me
"Diamonds and dynamite come in small packages."

Chapter One

Captain's Log, Stardate 2950.3:

The *Enterprise* continues in orbit around Eeiauo, on the outermost fringe of Federation space. At McCoy's recommendation, Starfleet has placed the world under quarantine. The *Enterprise* will remain here to enforce that quarantine until the arrival of a Federation task force, specialists in epidemiology and in enforcement.

Dr. McCoy and Nurse Chapel have elected to beam down with the medical team we transported to aid the Eeiauoans in their desperate fight against the plague that is devastating their world—a plague they call "The Long Death."

Personal Log, James T. Kirk, Stardate 2950.3:

Bones, at least, has something useful to do. The rest of us can only sit and listen, as more and more Eeiauoans are struck down. Over a quarter of the population now has ADF syndrome. If only the Eeiauoans had asked for help sooner!

I told Bones of our frustration. His response was predictable. . . .

"*You're* frustrated! By God, Jim!" McCoy let his exasperated words hang for a moment, then he stepped slightly to one side.

1

"Bozhe moi," breathed Pavel Chekov as he watched the viewscreen; it was nothing less than a prayer. To Kirk's right, Lieutenant Uhura gave a small wordless gasp.

Even a clinical knowledge of ADF syndrome left Jim Kirk unprepared for the view behind McCoy. Consciously, he knew the miles that separated him from the scene, but he was still hard put not to take an involuntary step backward.

He saw row after row after row of the circular Eeiauoan hospital beds, each one occupied. The victims of ADF were no longer recognizably Eeiauoan: they lay as if dead, their furless bodies covered with raw, oozing lesions. From Bones's briefing, Jim Kirk knew that, given adequate intravenous feeding and similar maintenance, they could survive in this state for years. *If you call this survival,* he thought. Seeing them, he didn't.

Those in the early, ambulatory stage of the disease hunched in their pain, brushed away their loosening fur and carried on the work of maintaining the others.

The Eeiauoans had not asked the Federation for assistance until they no longer had the power to help themselves.

McCoy blocked the view again.

"Sorry, Bones," Kirk said, when he found his voice. "That was a stupid thing for me to say."

McCoy shook his head. "The Eeiauoan doctors have dealt with two previous outbreaks of ADF syndrome and never bothered to call in Federation help before. It wasn't bad enough, they tell me. Wasn't bad enough! Jim, they lost twenty thousand people in the last one!" He himself looked on the verge of collapse, but Kirk was relieved to see that he still had the energy for righteous indignation.

"Are you making any progress, Bones?"

McCoy snorted. " 'Progress.' If that's a polite way of askin' have we found a cure yet, the answer is no. Nor have we cobbled together a vaccine in our copious spare time. Give me all the time in the world and the greatest scientists and doctors in history and even then I couldn't promise you results, dammit. I can't *command* a scientific breakthrough."

He drew a long breath, his shoulders slumped. "I wish to hell I could. They're good people." With a flash of his old humor, he added, "—for overgrown house cats."

"Is there anything we can do, anything at all?"

"You're supposed to be enforcin' the quarantine, not breakin' it. No, I don't want anyone else down here. The best you could do is carry bedpans, and robots do that well enough. And they, at least, are immune to ADF syndrome."

"Bones, when was the last time you heard of a disease that affects two species as different as humans and Eeiauoans?"

"Rabies," said McCoy curtly. At Kirk's questioning look, he added, by way of explanation, "An ancient Earth disease —it did indeed affect two species as different as . . ." He waved his hand. "The planet's under quarantine, Jim, and I don't want to hear any more about it."

A tall Eeiauoan tapped McCoy lightly on the shoulder with a claw tip. He turned. "Yes, Quickfoot?"

Quickfoot of Srallansre, the Eeiauoan doctor McCoy had been working with since their arrival, was obviously in the first stage of ADF syndrome. Each movement she made was stiff with pain. Her gray-striped fur was already thinning and dingy. Her nictitating membranes, discolored and swollen, partially obstructed her vision. Although she did not yet have the characteristic pained hunched posture, Kirk suspected it was from force of will only.

McCoy accepted a sheaf of papers from her. "Get some rest, dammit, Quickfoot," he said irritably. "Finish that later."

Quickfoot shook her head stiffly. "Too ssoon, too much resst, McCCoy. Work *now*. There is no *later*." She limped away.

McCoy wiped his face and eyes. "Damn cat hair," he muttered, "gets in everything." Kirk nodded, accepting the fiction. After a pause, McCoy straightened and said, "I have some more information for Mr. Spock."

Casting a quick, puzzled glance at his chief science officer, Kirk said, "I thought we transhipped a hold full of medical computers?"

McCoy muttered a response.

"How's that, Bones?" Jim Kirk was quite sure he had heard McCoy correctly—but baiting McCoy was a habit of long standing and seemed to restore a measure of normality even in such grotesque circumstances as these.

3

McCoy scowled. "I said," and this time he enunciated each word clearly, "I'd rather trust Spock."

At Spock's raised eyebrow, McCoy scowled again. Then, very rapidly, to change the subject, he said, "How's Sulu?"

The forced inaction these past few weeks had given everyone time to return to hobbies or create new ones from sheer desperation. Sulu had found McCoy's substitute, Dr. Evan Wilson, a fencing partner his equal—or better. Hard-pressed during a recent match with her, he had tripped and, against all odds, broken his ankle.

The thought of Wilson touched a nerve. Privately, Jim Kirk resented her presence on behalf of the *Enterprise*'s own medical staff. It was not the first time Starfleet Command had shown such a lack of judgment however, and he was not about to mention his feelings in public. Morale was low enough already; it would not do to have his crew questioning their acting chief medical officer. He said, "Sulu's fine. Dr. Wilson says he'll be up and around in no time."

"'Up and around'? How did she get him to stay down?"

Until Bones's question, it hadn't occurred to him to wonder. Jim Kirk spread his hands and glanced at his chief science officer inquiringly.

Spock said, "I believe she learned her bedside manner from you, Doctor."

"What d'you mean by that, Spock?"

"I mean, Dr. McCoy, that she used a purely emotional approach." Spock's features were innocent of expression.

Now openly suspicious, McCoy growled, "I'm waiting, Mr. Spock."

Spock raised an eyebrow, presumably at McCoy's display of impatience, then said, "Dr. Wilson was heard to tell Mr. Sulu that if he did not stay off his injured leg, she would—I quote—break the other one for him."

Jim Kirk gave an inward cheer. He could not have delivered the tale half so well himself, and for the life of him, he couldn't tell if Spock had done it intentionally.

Intentional or not, the story, or Spock's delivery, actually brought a surprised chuckle from McCoy. He gave Spock a wary look, then turned back to Kirk, and said, "Feisty little thing, isn't she? Keep your eye on her, Jim. What she lacks in height, she makes up in brass. Get her to tell you how Scotty and I met her. Might give you a laugh and, God knows, we could all use a few."

Then his brief smile faded and there was a long moment's silence. Kirk could see McCoy's mind turning back to the desperateness of the problem he faced. McCoy, silent, told him more than any of McCoy's outbursts would have.

"I'll turn you over to Spock, Bones, and let you get on with it."

"No, Jim. I have to speak to Uhura first."

Kirk glanced at his communications officer. "Lieutenant?"

"I'm here, Dr. McCoy." Lieutenant Uhura stiffened, as if bracing herself for a blow. "Were you able to reach Sunfall of Ennien?"

McCoy said, "Quickfoot located her. She's alive, Uhura, but—I'm sorry—she has it."

Uhura nodded. She must have spent a long time preparing herself to hear that, Kirk thought, or she's in shock.

Finally, Uhura said, her usually gentle voice roughened by emotion, "How—far along—"

"She's in a first-stage coma, Uhura. I'm sorry," McCoy repeated, "We'll do everything we can."

Uhura nodded again. "I know you will, Dr. McCoy. Thank you." She turned quickly to face her communications panel, but her back spoke eloquently of her distress.

Spock turned to his computers. "Ready to receive your information, Dr. McCoy."

McCoy gave a meaningful nod at Uhura's back. "Yes," Kirk said, in answer to the screen, "we'll speak later, Bones." He stepped to Uhura's side and spoke softly to her. "Lieutenant Uhura, I'd like a word with you."

Uhura turned, her face expressionless. "Captain?"

"In private," he added. He motioned a nearby ensign to take her place and said, "Mr. Spock, you have command." Spock nodded without taking his eyes from his screens, and Kirk gestured Uhura to the lift.

As the doors hissed closed, Uhura squared her shoulders. Oddly, the action seemed to make her more vulnerable. "Yes, Captain. What did you want to see me about?"

"Do you want to talk, Uhura?" he asked, gently. "That's a question, not an order."

"Thank you, Captain. Yes, I g—guess I would." But she was silent as he escorted her to her cabin.

She offered him a chair, and he sat. She poured herself a glass of water and offered him something stronger, which he declined. He decided it was best to wait for her to speak.

At last, she went to the wall and took down a small picture in a gilt frame. For a long moment, she stood looking at it, then she handed it to him. She sat down. "That's Sunfall," she said.

It was an old-fashioned two-dimensional photograph—but there was nothing static about Sunfall of Ennien. Jim Kirk saw an Eeiauoan dancer, as black as velvet, poised in mid-leap. Her long supple body and tail curved ecstatically, her great pointed ears swept up to catch some music he could almost hear by looking at her. . . . He realized he was holding his breath and let it out. "Beautiful," he said.

"Yes." There were tears trembling on Uhura's lashes now. "And that was what she was like inside, too. All that beauty and energy—Captain, I can't bear the thought of her—of her—"

"The doctors are doing everything they can." He knew it was no consolation. The Eeiauoan hospital and its horrors flashed back into his mind, and he thought of Sunfall in the same state. He thrust the thought from him. If he could feel that way just seeing the photo, what must Uhura be feeling?

Uhura picked up her Charellian *joyeuse,* the delicate little stringed instrument she had just recently learned to play, and cradled it, as if to draw comfort from the prospect of music. "Dr. McCoy is a good man, Captain," she said. "I know he's doing everything he can, and more. I just don't know if it'll be *enough.*"

There was nothing to say, no comfort he could give. Kirk looked again at the picture. "How did you meet?" he asked, at last.

Uhura wiped her eyes. "A long time ago. It was my first post, Two Dawns. Sunfall was a junior diplomat with the Eeiauoan mission."

"A diplomat?" he said in astonishment. "Not a dancer?"

She almost smiled at that. "A dancer, a singer *and* a diplomat," she said. "Sunfall of Ennien was all of that. She thought all diplomats should be. She said—she said it would g—give them more flexibility."

"It would," Kirk said, knowingly. He thought of the number of pompous diplomats he'd dealt with and the interminable diplomatic occasions he'd been forced to sit through. What he wouldn't have given for the presence of Sunfall of Ennien!

Uhura went on, "She and I traded songs. In the two years we spent together I think we went through every song we ever knew. She even taught me some of the old ballads of Eeiauo."

"Have I heard any?" Uhura often sang for her entertainment and the crew's; Kirk tried to recall anything he could identify as Eeiauoan.

" 'The Ballad of CloudShape to-Ennien'?" she suggested.

The title jogged his memory. When he smiled at the thought, Uhura smiled wanly back and said, "Yes, I see you remember it."

"The con artist," he said, "the Eeiauoan version of Harry Mudd!" A thought struck him. "Why 'to-Ennien'?" he asked. "All the names I've heard are 'of' something or other."

"I can't answer that, Captain. The Eeiauoans have a hundred or more songs about CloudShape—and some of them call her 'to-Ennien' and some call her 'of Ennien.' That was one of the few I could translate properly. Most of them, and not just the CloudShape songs, deal with such a different culture that they make no sense to a human unless she knows an Eeiauoan. I sometimes sing the others in Eeiauoan because the tunes are so lovely." She hummed a snatch of song and Kirk nodded; he'd heard that one, too, and she didn't exaggerate its beauty.

"Do you speak it? Eeiauoan, I mean?"

"I learned it from Sunfall and kept it up so I could talk to her the next time we met. . . ." She spread her hands in dismay. "We did speak now and again, and I was so *happy* when we were ordered to Eeiauo. I wish—I wish—"

"So do I."

"Captain, couldn't there be just one exception to the quarantine? I'd—like to be there with her."

Her expression was so hopeful Kirk hated to deny her that consolation—but orders were orders, and it would do her no good to see Sunfall as she must be now. He shook his head. "If there were something I could do," he said.

"I know. If there were something *any* of us could do . . ." Her voice trailed off. She wiped her eyes again. "I should return to the bridge."

"Ensign Azuela can handle that for now," Kirk said.

"Thank you, Captain. I guess I would like some time to be alone."

Kirk took that as a dismissal. He clasped her hand in wordless sympathy and left. Behind him, he heard the first glasslike sounds of the *joyeuse,* and then the words of an alien song, that might have been Eeiauoan, that might have been a plea to the gods for the life of Sunfall of Ennien.

The door hissed closed. Adding his own silent plea to hers, Kirk returned to the bridge.

Chapter Two

Spock completed the data run for McCoy and, having finished his watch, retired to his quarters to meditate on this newly revealed facet of McCoy's behavior. Logically, there was no reason for the doctor to insist that he, Spock, run data that could be run as easily and as accurately by any medical technician. Not that McCoy was known for his logic, any more so than any of the humans aboard the *Enterprise,* but Spock did find the question of sufficient interest to devote some little time to its consideration.

There was also the more pressing problem of the crew's deteriorating morale. It seemed to him that their irrationality was increasing by the hour. McCoy would have diagnosed it, in his own peculiar fashion, as "working themselves into a state."

Perhaps the two were not separate problems, he thought; perhaps McCoy's request might be interpreted as a symptom of the doctor's low morale: a desire to do something for the sake of doing it and for no other reason. He had known humans to behave in such fashion before.

Indeed, such symptoms might be widespread, given the magnitude of the Eeiauoans' plight. Even Starfleet Command had chosen to transfer Dr. Evan Wilson to the *Enterprise,* a step that while not completely without precedent, was unusual enough to perplex.

A voice at his door pulled him from his thoughts.

"Mr. Spock? It's Lieutenant Uhura, sir. May I please speak with you?"

"Come in, Lieutenant," he said, curious.

She entered only far enough into the room to allow the doors to slide closed behind her.

He had admired her behavior on the bridge a few hours ago. Under circumstances that would have elicited from most humans a conspicuous display of emotion, she had conducted herself with almost Vulcan reserve. Even now, she kept that same calm.

He beckoned her to a chair. She sat. He pulled a second chair to the small table and sat down to face her. She watched him for a moment.

"Mr. Spock, may I ask that you keep this conversation in confidence?" Before he could object, she added, rapidly, "I assure you, sir, it does not involve the safety of the *Enterprise* or of anyone aboard her."

"In that case, I would have no reason to speak of it to anyone else."

That seemed to satisfy her. She added, "I promise you a logical reason for my behavior, after you answer a question for me."

Fascinating, thought Spock. "Please continue, Lieutenant."

"Is it possible that Eeiauo is *not* the planet of origin of the Eeiauoans? Is it possible that they're colonists from another world?"

"Their histories state—" He stopped abruptly as she shook her head.

"I mean," she said, "aside from what the Eeiauoans claim, is there any *external* proof that Eeiauo is their planet of origin?"

"An answer of any degree of reliability will take time, Lieutenant."

She clasped her hands together in the first sign of emotion he'd seen from her, then immediately stopped the gesture and carefully composed herself. "If you say it's possible, sir, that would be enough."

He realized that she was quite deliberately holding back

her emotions out of deference to him. "That will take several hours, at the very least," he said. "Do you wish to wait?"

"If I will not disturb you."

"You will not."

The answer to Uhura's question came more quickly, and with more certainty, than Spock had expected.

An hour later, he turned from his computer to Uhura. She stared into the attunement flame—light flickered on her dark, unreadable face. Most humans reacted unfavorably to the higher ambient temperature he maintained in his cabin. Uhura looked chilled.

He said, "A cursory examination of Eeiauoan science shows a number of anomalies. There is, for example, no species of vertebrate now living on Eeiauo that resembles the Eeiauoans themselves. In Earth analogy, there is no creature on Eeiauo related to the Eeiauoans as chimpanzees or gorillas are related to humans. It would be as if your closest relative were a lizard.

"In addition, while the Eeiauoans have a highly developed science of paleontology, there is nothing in the fossil record that bears a family resemblance to the Eeiauoans. Under those circumstances, I find it highly unlikely that they could have developed a theory of evolution, yet they did, independent of Federation science.

"There are other anomalies as well, but every one of them could be accounted for if the Eeiauoans did not originate here."

"Mr. Spock?"

"Simply put, Lieutenant, there is indeed a high probability that the Eeiauoans are not native to this world. Is that sufficient for your purpose?"

Her eyes held a look he'd seen in McCoy's often—one that preceded a bellowing cheer. She blinked, clamped her jaw and took a single sharp breath. "Thank you."

She stood as if a sudden weight had been released from her shoulders. "You see, the source of my information also suggests that the Eeiauoans' homeworld knows a cure for ADF syndrome. Your confirmation of the one means that the other has some chance of being true."

11

"An interesting possibility," said Spock. "Although one does not necessarily follow the other as fact, it would be worth pursuing."

"Yes." She nodded. "Any possibility—thank you, sir. I'll tell the captain now."

"I do not understand, Lieutenant, why you chose to tell me, in confidence, and not the captain, as you now intend to inform him. . . ."

Her head ducked briefly, but not before he saw embarrassment in her face. "I've taken advantage of your background, Mr. Spock. *Your* hopes would not be dashed if there were no possibility. I knew you would wait for facts."

"Ah," he said, "your 'logical reason.' "

She nodded.

"Admirable," he said. "I shall accompany you."

Jim Kirk sat in the briefing room with Uhura and Spock to either side of him. Behind him, Chief Engineer Montgomery Scott watched the viewscreen over his shoulder and shifted restlessly. *The inaction's getting to Scotty, too,* Kirk thought.

McCoy was as voluble from a distance as he was in person, but his words came as a disappointment.

"No way, Jim," he said. "I even talked to the World Coordinator—she's down the hall bein' treated. She's in the early stage of ADF syndrome. If there's a cure, she'd have every stake in findin' it, even on this hypothetical homeworld. She says all her generations were born here. I don't know where you got your information, but everybody here denies it."

Kirk said, "Denies it how, Bones? As if it were a fable, a fantasy?"

"How d'you expect me to know what goes on in their furry heads? They have all the emotional expression of Spock there. What on earth gives you the idea this isn't their planet of origin, anyway?"

Spock intervened. "Aside from their histories, there is no physical evidence, either in their paleontology or their archeology, to suggest they originated on Eeiauo."

"In other words," McCoy snapped, "we have only their

word for it. Why should they lie about a thing like that, dammit? It doesn't make sense, Spock."

"I am hardly accountable for the illogical behavior of the Eeiauoans, Dr. McCoy. Other beings have been known to distort their histories."

"To the point of self-destruction? That's crazy!"

Spock said, "I agree, but also highly probable in this instance."

"Gentlemen, enough." Kirk had no intention of letting Spock and McCoy get out of hand. "Lieutenant Uhura, you seem to know this culture quite well. Why don't you ask one of the Eeiauoans?"

"I'll get Quickfoot," McCoy said. He vanished momentarily offscreen, though not before Kirk caught a glimpse of his expression and knew he was being humored, as far as his chief medical officer was concerned.

"One moment, Captain."

"Yes, Mr. Spock?"

"I believe the lieutenant would prefer that you act on my information rather than her own." To Uhura, Spock added, "It was a logical deduction from your behavior, Lieutenant."

"Is that true, Uhura?" Kirk asked. He need not have: her trapped expression told him clearly enough that Spock's assessment was correct. He thought for a moment. "All right, Lieutenant. Is your Eeiauoan good enough to translate for me?" At her nod, he said, "Perhaps you'll have some questions of your own for Quickfoot." Kirk hoped she understood his suggestion. He had no time to make himself plainer; McCoy had returned with Quickfoot.

"Quickfoot," he said, "This is Lieutenant Uhura, my chief communications officer. She has agreed to translate for us." He smiled and added, "In a situation like this, I prefer not to rely upon mechanical translation—that may cause more problems than it solves."

Uhura translated. The sound of it was so unexpected, he turned to stare at her. It was as if she'd taken a random assortment of snarls, hisses and yowls and set them all to music, sweetening them somehow in the process.

Quickfoot responded in kind. "Yes," said Uhura, "she

understands the problem. Dr. McCoy has recently been trying to ask something that is so bizarre everyone—everyone is wondering about his sanity!"

"Thanks a lot," McCoy muttered from a corner of the screen.

"My science officer, Mr. Spock," Kirk continued and indicated the Vulcan, "has been studying your world and its history. He seems to think your people left their homeworld some two thousand years ago to settle Eeiauo—"

He paused to let Uhura begin her translation, but he got no further. As Uhura finished, Quickfoot bristled and laid back her ears. Her pupils dilated to twice their size. Her claws splayed at the screen.

Uhura translated her angry response, hard put to keep up. "She says Spock is crazy, too. The Eeiauoans have always lived on this world. *This* is their homeworld. They have never known any other, they *will* never know any other!"

Quickfoot spat, turned abruptly from the screen and stamped away, her hind claws clicking loudly on the hospital floor.

Uhura finished, awkwardly, "That last was a very strong obscenity."

Kirk took a deep breath. "Methinks the lady doth protest too much."

Scotty nodded, "Aye. Dr. McCoy, dinna ye recognize an angry cat when ye see one?!"

McCoy snorted at him. "Let me know when you've got something more than an angry cat. I have work to do . . . McCoy, out." The screen went dark.

"So," said Jim Kirk to his staff, "we have a hypothetical planet—"

"Real enough to gi' Quickfoot a catfit," interjected Scotty, scornfully.

Kirk chose to ignore that. "—with a hypothetical cure for ADF. Any suggestions? Spock, Scotty?" He turned pointedly to Uhura. "Lieutenant Uhura?"

She made no answer.

"Lieutenant Uhura," said Spock, "I should like to point out that a people capable of denying its own origin in the face

14

of such need might well be capable of denying a betrayal of that origin, if such were to their advantage and if no open acknowledgment of the betrayal were made. I see no reason to inform the Eeiauoans of the source of our information."

Kirk caught on instantly. "Of course we'll keep Sunfall out of it," he said; and, just as swiftly, Scott added, "Aye, lassie, we wouldna hurt your friend."

Unable to keep the urgency out of his voice, Kirk went on, "Uhura, these people are going to die. Every day that passes their chances get slimmer and slimmer. If you know *anything* that can help, you must tell us. I'll make that an order, if you prefer."

Uhura shook her head. "Thank you, Captain, but it is my responsibility. Sunfall is *dying*. I'll tell you what little I know."

She began so softly Kirk had to strain to hear her. "Sunfall and I were very close friends, Captain. It was as if we were sisters, except that we shared more interests than most sisters. I told you how we traded songs. . . .

"One evening, very late at night, I taught her a dozen or so of my favorite"—she glanced away, embarrassed—"bawdy songs. You must understand that to her there was nothing the least bit impolite about those songs: Eeiauoan children learn songs twice as ribald, and in school."

"Infinite diversity," said Kirk, quoting the Vulcan credo. "Go on."

"I was careful to explain that the songs I taught her were taboo in many cultures, including mine, and not to be sung in polite company. I wanted her to hear them because they were wonderful songs." She shifted uncomfortably, as if she expected someone to chastise her for creating an interplanetary incident. Her eyes came to rest on Scott.

"Dinna look at me," said Scotty with a grin, "I'd give ennathing ta hear ye sing them, wi' your voice. I canna do more than croak them."

"Lieutenant," Kirk prompted.

Uhura went on, "A few days later, she came to see me, bristling with excitement. She said she'd make me a fair trade for my tabooed songs. She knew some ballads from the old days of her world—full of heroic deeds and incredible journeys. She would teach me, for the sake of the songs. She would teach me because they were beautiful."

Kirk made a puzzled gesture. "The point, Lieutenant, the point."

"I believe that *is* the point, Captain," Spock said.

Uhura nodded. "She told me the taboo was stronger than the one I meant. No Eeiauoan would ever sing any of them in public. In another generation, she told me sadly, they might be forgotten altogether. She didn't want that to happen, so she sang them all on tape for me.

"And she cautioned me that no Eeiauoan must ever know that I had heard them. I thought she was speaking of a religious taboo, Captain, but it may be that Sunfall committed treason for the sake of those songs."

Kirk said, "I don't follow you, Uhura. Do you mean that Sunfall told you the Eeiauoans were colonists?"

"No, no. In fact, Sunfall implied that the songs were fiction. But the songs themselves imply that the Eeiauoans are colonists. In those early songs, 'Eeiauo' doesn't mean 'beautiful'—it means *'outcast'*."

She looked directly at him with a sudden intensity. "You asked why CloudShape was called 'to-Ennien' and not 'of Ennien,' sir. In those early songs, people often travel to and from Ennien—but there's no place on Eeiauo called Ennien."

"Ah," said Spock, "nor is there a Srallansre." He nodded thoughtfully. "And what of the cure for ADF syndrome? How much evidence have you for its existence?"

"One song tells of a man who falls ill. . . . Captain, I always thought it was a bard's disease, one of those things that people in old ballads succumb to whenever their love is unrequited. You know the sort I mean."

Kirk smiled; he did indeed. "Fascinating," said Spock, largely in reaction to Kirk's comprehension.

Uhura said, "It wasn't that at all. It was ADF syndrome, stage by stage. Dr. McCoy would have diagnosed it by the second verse." She turned again to Spock. "The final verse tells how a woman named Thunderstroke restores the man to life."

"A teaching song," said Spock.

16

And Kirk said, "Do you mean, a song to help you remember—not only the symptoms—but the *cure* for the disease? You *know* the cure for ADF?"

It was as if he had struck her, but she only said, "There is no cure on Eeiauo, Captain. The last verse is missing. Sunfall ended the song there, and her ears drooped and her tail . . . I can't describe it, sir. She looked at me in despair, and she told me it was a song for another world, not hers."

"Then we're back where we started." Kirk slammed his hand down on the table. "We can't even get them to admit that Eeiauo isn't their homeworld. How can we get them to tell us where it *is?*"

"I suggest we contact Starfleet Command," Spock said. "Quite possibly a Federation diplomat might succeed where we have failed."

"Those pen-pushers!" Scotty was outraged. "They'll be talkin' till doomsday, and not a word will they be gettin' for their pains. And all the time, Uhura's friend'll be dyin' by inches. Isna there enna way we could find the world oursel's, Mr. Spock?"

"The universe is infinite, Mr. Scott. To find one world with no clue to its location . . ."

"He's right, Scotty. We haven't a clue, unless the Eeiauoans are willing to give it to us. We'll try through Star Fleet—at least that's something." Kirk rose.

Scotty would not be so easily put off. As Uhura rose from her chair, he leveled his finger at her. "Your songs, Lieutenant. There's the truth in your songs. 'Incredible journeys,' ye said. D'they tell o' the star that shone on that world? Th' length o' th' journey? Ennathin' Mr. Spock here c'ld feed his computers Is it possible, Mr. Spock?"

"Possible, Mr. Scott, but not probable."

"Well, Uhura . . . ?" Scott had not moved from his position.

"Yes, yes, Mr. Scott." Uhura's face lit with sudden hope. "They do sing about the journey! There must be something that would—!" She broke off and composed herself with effort. "If you would be willing, Mr. Spock . . . ?"

The ship's communicator whistled. "McCoy to Kirk."

"Kirk here. Come in, Bones."

McCoy's face had been haggard before, but they were all unprepared for the terrible look that appeared in the viewscreen.

"Bones!" Jim Kirk reacted instinctively to that look. *"What's happened?"*

McCoy drew a long and shuddering breath. "Christine—she's got ADF syndrome."

"My God, Bones, are you sure?"

"Would I be telling you that if I weren't? What do you think I am, some kind of damn fool?" McCoy snapped back. "Tell Starfleet the damn disease is communicable to humans, and they've got to quarantine anybody who's been in contact with any Eeiauoan in the past *six months.* And clean your own house, Jim. We've got a galaxy full of trouble on our hands now. McCoy out." The screen went dark.

Kirk looked up. "I'll contact Starfleet.—Spock, Uhura, find me that planet!"

Spock looked at Uhura. "Possible, but not probable," he repeated.

Montgomery Scott laid his hand on Uhura's shoulder and squeezed it reassuringly. "Dinna ye worry. If ennaone can do it, Mr. Spock can. Ye just let me know and the *Enterprise*'ll take ye there."

Chapter Three

After six days of listening to Eeiauoan songs for references that might give some clue to the location of their homeworld, Uhura was exhausted and discouraged—afraid that, in her weariness, she might miss something crucial. She wished she had Mr. Spock's ability to do without sleep. Mr. Scott had been right: the diplomats were not succeeding. Sunfall's songs were the only possibility they had.

A week ago (it seemed a lifetime), she had seen an off-duty engineer, Marie-Therese Orsay, draw a huge audience in the rec room by building a house of cards. It was no ordinary house of cards: it covered an entire table and rose eight stories before Orsay tired of her sport and toppled it with a sweep of her hand and a delighted laugh.

Afterward, Spock, who had watched from beginning to end, pronounced it, "Fascinating."

When Captain Kirk, amused, pressed him on the subject, Spock had responded, "I was referring, Captain, to the dexterity and the concentration Ensign Orsay devotes to the pursuit of a singularly insubstantial result."

Now, thought Uhura, Mr. Spock is building his own house of cards: the information Spock fed to his computers was so flimsy a single breath might topple it all. Yet he kept on . . .

Assumption: a number drawn from among those songs Sunfall had called "The Journey Songs" that they took to be the original number of colonists—or outcasts. From that and from statistical data on the reproduction rate, deaths from outbreaks of ADF syndrome, and population records of Eeiauo, Mr. Spock had set the date of their arrival on Eeiauo approximately two thousand five hundred years in the past.

Assumption: the technological capabilities and range of the ship that brought them—based on the earliest known space drive of the Eeiauoans, tentatively confirmed by Chief Engineer Scott. That also assumed that the Eeiauoans had made only minor improvements on the drive, had not lost the technology altogether and invented something new.

Assumption: the length of the journey—again drawn from song, not from fact.

Assumption: that this world had been the Eeiauoans' original destination, not their third or fourth try for an inhabitable world.

Assumption after assumption after assumption. The only hard facts were that Eeiauoan after Eeiauoan curled up to die—kept alive only by elaborate medical intervention—and that the Long Death now spread through human worlds.

Uhura realized she had listened to an entire song without hearing it. Angrily, she stopped the tape and rewound it. Without thinking, she yanked the earplug from her ear, buried her face in her hands and said, "Oh, *damn!*"

Spock turned from his computers. Uhura hastily composed herself, made her thoughts and face a blank. "I apologize, Mr. Spock. It will not happen again."

"Computer, hold," he said. The machine cut off in mid-squeak, freezing an image on the screen. Giving Uhura his full attention, Spock said, "The apology is unnecessary, Lieutenant. I assure you I am quite accustomed to the display of emotion from members of this crew. I could hardly be otherwise, given the circumstances under which I work and live."

"Yes, I know." Impulsively, she added, "And no one ever thinks to protect your feelings."

One of his eyebrows arched up. "Dr. McCoy would tell you I have none."

Uhura gave a delicate snort. "That's nonsense, Mr. Spock.

Everyone has feelings. Not everyone chooses to express them quite as loudly as Dr. McCoy."

"Am I to understand that you have been behaving in this unusual—I might even say 'abnormal'—fashion to protect my . . . feelings?" he asked. His slight emphasis made the word hers rather than any admission on his part.

Uhura felt her cheeks warm, as if she were a small child who'd been caught at something, yet she wanted him to understand. "After all these years of working with you, sir, and listening to everyone else who did, it seems to me that we all demand that you be more and more human. But you're not human, Mr. Spock, any more than Sunfall is. You're unique. If I sometimes find your behavior shocking, I've come to realize that even the shock can be valuable. You make us stop and reconsider and sometimes take a fresh view of things.

"You're the only one aboard the *Enterprise* who hasn't spent the past weeks worrying himself into complete uselessness. I felt I would be more useful to Sunfall—and to you as we worked together—if I could approach the problem from your perspective."

She raised a finely drawn brow in deliberate imitation of him. "At the very least," she finished, "I had hoped not to disturb your concentration with any emotional display. That's why I've been behaving 'abnormally,' Mr. Spock. I hope I have not offended you."

"By no means," he said. "I am honored by your attempt." He considered her thoughtfully, then he added, "But I must point out the flaw in your reasoning. Given our present task, your emotional response could be of considerable value."

"Mr. Spock?" She could not hide her astonishment.

"We have no reliable data. With each assumption we make we lower the probability of an accurate result. I have often noticed in humans the ability to extrapolate accurately from just such data. Captain Kirk has frequently demonstrated the validity of this approach."

"Do you mean hunches?"

"Precisely, Lieutenant Uhura." He gave her a piercing look.

21

"In that case, I'll do my best, sir."

He continued to consider her. Suddenly embarrassed, Uhura said, "Is that all, sir?" She meant to return to her tapes; she found herself at a loss for words under his open scrutiny.

"No, Lieutenant," he said at last. "That is not all. You, too, are unique. And, quite illogically, I find I prefer the unique Uhura to the counterfeit Vulcan. May we agree each to behave as our uniqueness dictates?"

Uhura found herself blinking back stinging tears. "Oh, yes, of course we may!" She stretched out her hand, wishing she could touch him. "And thank you, Mr. Spock. That's the nicest compliment I've ever been paid."

His look was totally uncomprehending, and she did not know whether to laugh or to cry her exasperation. At last, she did neither—she moved her outstretched hand to point at the frozen image on the computer screen. With effort, she said, "What *is* that, Mr. Spock?"

To her relief, he turned. "That is a computer simulation of the night sky of Eeiauo in the era in which we believe the Eeiauoans arrived on this world," he said.

Black stars against a white sky . . . Curious, Uhura stepped to his side to look more closely. So many stars! To find just one out of so many stars! "Is that what they'd have seen?" She shook her head at the impossibility of the task.

"No, this is the view without atmospheric interference." Spock gave a command to the computer and a large number of stars vanished. He said, "Given atmospheric interference and the average visual acuity of the Eeiauoan, this is what the first colonists would have seen, had they landed in the northern hemisphere." At her questioning look, he added, "From the pattern of their city development, a northern hemisphere landing would seem indicated."

She nodded and looked again at the screen. Too many stars remained.

At his second command, the stars moved, slowly wheeling past the screen. "You are seeing the seasonal changes in star position."

Something caught her attention. She tried to bring it into

22

conscious focus but could not. "Mr. Spock, could you reverse the colors? I can't—see it properly."

If he thought the request illogical, he made no comment. At his touch on the console, the stars went white against a black field. They continued to wheel across the "horizon" but one formation stayed always in the sky. It resembled an open eye, its iris the edge-on view of a nebula that gave it the Eeiauoan catlike slit.

"This," she said, and touched the screen.

"The gaseous remnants of a supernova that took place within a few hundred years of the time of the Eeiauoans' arrival here. The computer extrapolates from the archeoastronomy of several nearby civilizations and from the faint indications that still linger."

Uhura gripped the edge of the console. "They watch us still, and disapprove," she quoted softly. "A refrain from one of the earliest ballads, as nearly as I can translate it. . . . I have that hunch for you, Mr. Spock."

"Indeed?"

She nodded. "The Eeiauoan homeworld *has* to be somewhere in that constellation."

"That would be consistent with my calculations. However, that is still a great deal of area to cover. Let us attempt to refine your hunch."

Jim Kirk watched the main screen from the bridge of the *Enterprise* as the Federation medship *Dr. Margaret Flinn* and her escort of four destroyers assumed orbit around Eeiauo. The destroyers told him just how serious Starfleet considered the situation.

As if a destroyer could stop the Long Death! He drummed his knuckles impatiently against the cold metal arm of the command chair, ignoring the concerned glance Lieutenant Vuong shot in his direction from nav. *What the Eeiauoans need most from us is the one thing we can't give them—speed! I can no more hurry Spock and Uhura than Bones can command a breakthrough.*

From the communications console, Ensign Azuela cut through his angry thoughts. "Captain? Captain's regards from the *Flinn,* sir, and Chief Medical Officer Mickiewicz requests that we make ready to have those personnel who may have been exposed to ADF beamed aboard without delay."

He must have scowled, for Azuela added, "Orders from Starfleet, sir."

"Acknowledge," he said, curtly. "Request coordinates and relay them to the quarantine transporter room. Inform Dr. McCoy—and Dr. Wilson." He rose abruptly. "Lieutenant Vuong, you have the conn; I'll be in sick bay if anybody needs me." He doubted anybody would and that did little to improve his mood.

By the time he reached sick bay, he had fine-tuned his resentment from Starfleet Command in general to Dr. Evan Wilson in particular for the implied slur against the *Enterprise's* medical facilities and personnel.

The door to Bones's office was open. Of course, he told himself, the senior medical officer would use Bones's office in his absence—but it made Wilson's presence seem that much more of an intrusion.

Time to do some intruding of my own, he thought with some satisfaction, but the sound of an angry voice stopped him on the threshold.

Her back to Kirk, Dr. Evan Wilson bent ominously over her communication screen, McCoy's image before her. "The *Enterprise* has the best quarantine facilities I've seen anywhere," she said sharply, "and Starfleet Command has the unmitigated gall to ask us to transfer her crew to some other ship, state of facilities unknown? Dammit, Leonard, there's no excuse for it!"

She takes it personally, too, Kirk thought with some surprise. He liked her for that. *Still . . .*

McCoy said it for him: "That's the pot callin' the kettle black, Evan."

She cocked her head to one side, clearly puzzled, for McCoy elucidated, "Starfleet sent you, madam, in case you'd forgotten." He said it without the acidity he customarily reserved for Starfleet orders not to his liking, and Kirk realized that McCoy did not object to Wilson nearly as much as he.

Wilson seemed to scrutinize the image. After a moment, she gave a merry laugh and leaned back, shaking her head. "Don't 'madam' me, Leonard. And don't take offense at me—I cut my own orders for the *Enterprise*. I expected to be working with you, not filling in!"

"Ask for a second opinion and get an invasion," McCoy said.

She laughed again and leaned forward, this time with an air of conspiracy. "I leave it to you. I can stay where I am, or I can shift the invasion to give you a hand planetside."

"You've been exposed to ADF?"

"No, but Starfleet doesn't know that." Her voice was light, almost mischievous, but from Bones's expression Jim Kirk knew her offer was genuine. He also knew he was not about to find out how easily his senior officer could be subverted.

"You'll do nothing of the sort, Dr. Wilson," he said firmly, stepping into the office as he spoke.

He had been off watch when Evan Wilson arrived and, aside from a perfunctory greeting via ship's intercom, he had not spoken to her. He got his first good look at his acting chief medical officer—as she swung her chair toward the sound of his voice, rose and advanced on him, all in one smooth motion.

She had a shock of short chestnut hair that would ordinarily have been described as "wavy," although in her case it conjured an image of a wave breaking against rocks with force enough to shatter them. Her eyes were the blue of a very hot flame. *Striking,* he thought, then added, *in more ways than one!* But by the time he realized he had braced to defend himself, she had stopped, only inches away, to look up at him. She stood barely as high as the insignia on the breast of his tunic.

An impish smile crossed her face. "Well," she said, putting her hands on her hips, "just the man I wanted to see. . . ."

Her manner was pure impudence, but the words pricked Jim Kirk's conscience. "I must apologize for my behavior, Dr. Wilson. I see the past few weeks have affected my morale as adversely as that of the rest of the crew."

"I beg your pardon?"

"My snubbing you," he explained, "Childish of me, I

know." He shook his head and gave her his best boyish grin. "In this case, not welcoming you in person entailed its own punishment."

She grinned back. "Business first, Captain, flattery later. There is no reason to transfer *Enterprise* crew to the *Flinn*."

"I'm afraid there is, Dr. Wilson: Starfleet orders. If the decision had been left to me . . ."

She returned immediately to the screen. "How about a formal complaint to Starfleet?" she suggested.

"They'd accept it. They *might* even read it. But they won't countermand the orders. Now before you go flyin' off the handle again, Evan"—this was McCoy at his country-doctor best—"and you too, Jim, Micky Mickiewicz is the best there is. If I needed a doctor, I'd call her."

"High praise indeed, Bones."

"And every word of it true, I assure you," McCoy said. "Now, is there anything else?"

Evan Wilson nodded. "Yes . . . about that help I offered you."

"I thought we'd had the final word on that subject," McCoy said, giving Kirk a significant look. It was clear, however, that her continued impudence amused McCoy.

Equally amused, she glanced up at Kirk and said, "Once I deal myself in, Captain, I play by the rules. Though I sometimes regret it. . . . No, Leonard, not me. Of the sixteen people we've got suspected to have been exposed to ADF, eleven request permission to beam down to Eeiauo rather than to the *Flinn*."

"Suspected to have been exposed is not the same thing as exposed. If they beam down here, they damn well *will* be exposed." McCoy shook his head with some vehemence. "No, Evan, absolutely not."

She threw up her hands in resignation. "Well, can't say I didn't try. Call me if you turn up anything new."

A moment later, she was still staring into the darkened screen. At last she rose, frowning absently, then turned her attention back to him. "Captain," she said, "as long as you're not doing anything, come with me. If they must go, we'll give them a proper send-off. It's not much, but it's something. When it comes to morale, even little things are important."

Looking down at her, Kirk could have said the same thing but decided not to risk it. Since he had fully intended to be present when his crew members were transferred to the *Flinn*, he simply nodded and followed her with a smile.

He'd have shaken hands with each in turn had quarantine procedures permitted it, but the best he could do was acknowledge each with a salute and his best wishes via the intercom.

"Captain," said Yeoman Jaramillo of Science Division, "we did request permission to join Dr. McCoy—"

"Permission denied," said Evan Wilson before Kirk could answer. "I'm sorry, Yeoman, but that's not medically advisable."

"But Dr. McCoy—"

"Dr. McCoy is not here," she said. "*I'm* acting Chief Medical Officer. Since you've volunteered to be of assistance, I'm appointing you my liaison officer with Dr. Mickiewicz. I'll need daily reports from her on anything she learns about ADF, and the same from each of you. If you have an itch, I want to hear about it; we're dealing with a complete unknown and anything could be everything."

Jaramillo's resentment softened—a useful task often did that. "Yes, sir," he said and, snapping a salute, he stepped onto the transporter.

When the last of the party had vanished into the beam, Kirk turned. "You didn't have to take the rap for Bones, Dr. Wilson."

"No," she said, "but since they resent my being here—you did, Captain—it'll do them good to have a reason."

Abruptly she gave a shrug and, with a complete change of tone, she said, "I guess I'll have to make my own fun. What are my chances of getting Snnanagfashtalli assigned as my guinea cat? If *she'll* agree, of course." Kirk had never heard any human crew member pronounce the security officer's real name. Most called her Snarl, though never to her face. Kirk found that even he *thought* of her as Snarl. "Snarl," said Wilson, as if prompting his memory.

"I do *know* her given name," he said, somewhat testily. "I was just thinking I don't often hear it used."

"Sorry, Captain." She touched his hand lightly. "I didn't

think you'd be as peeved as I am about *that.*" She gestured with her chin at the empty transporter. "I should have known better. . . . I think people ought to be called what they want to be called, even if it gives me a sore throat for a week to do it."

"Physician, heal—"

She laughed aloud. "Oh, Elath, you sound like Leonard!"

"What do you want with Snnanagfashtalli?" It was not easy but he made it. She was right about what it did to your throat.

"She's felinoid, too, and genetically much closer to the Eeiauoans than a human. I want to know why humans are contracting ADF syndrome but her people aren't, despite similar contact."

"Yes, by all means, if she'll agree to it. Tell her it's strictly voluntary, though. I'll clear it with Security."

"Thank you, sir!" She led the way to the door. Reluctant to see her go, Jim Kirk outpaced her and stretched an arm nonchalantly across the passage. It was a miscalculation, he found, for she merely ducked her head marginally and was under his arm and into the corridor before he had time to say another word. *I wonder if that's what she did to Sulu,* he thought and followed. He said, "Would you mind a personal question, Dr. Wilson?"

She stopped. "Call me Evan," she said, "if it's a personal question."

"Why would a doctor take up saber, Evan?"

She gave him one of the wickedest grins he'd ever seen on a human being. "I took up saber for the same reason I took up quarterstaff and eating with chopsticks."

She vanished around the corner without another word. Startled into laughter, he did not follow. Even as he heard the soft sound of the turbolift, he knew instinctively that she would not explain even if he caught up with her, and that somehow made it all the funnier.

It wasn't until Chekov found him there and asked, "Are you all right, Keptain?" that he realized fully what she'd done.

"Yes, Mr. Chekov, I'm fine. Our resident doctor just jolted me out of a severe depression. She's given me a riddle."

"A riddle, sair?"

"Yes. Tell me, what do saber, quarterstaff and chopsticks have in common?"

"I heven't any idea, sair." Chekov still did not seem convinced of his sanity. "Perheps if you esk Mr. Spock?"

"That is a wonderful suggestion, Mr. Chekov. I'll do it at the earliest opportunity." If only, he thought to himself, to see Spock's reaction.

Like the Eeiauoans, Nurse Chapel continued her work even as her ADF syndrome worsened. McCoy was worried. The disease seemed to be progressing more rapidly in her than it did in an Eeiauoan. And according to the epidemiological reports he'd gotten, the same was true for other human victims as well.

He could not conceal the reports from her; he needed her help, and she needed to be helpful. He hid his concern in work, as she hid hers.

Even now, it cost her enormous effort to stand erect. Each movement she made was stiff with pain. McCoy could see the strain of it on her face.

Most of her hair was gone. She covered her head with a brightly colored scarf she'd found god knows where; McCoy knew he'd never seen it before. She'd asked and received his permission to exchange her uniform for a loose-fitting caftan that did less to irritate the raw patches of skin that were appearing all over her body.

She slid a rack of culture plates from the incubator and said, "Still no sign of ADF." Bringing them into better light, she inspected them again. "The human and Eeiauoan tissue cultures are already beginning to show signs of the increased toxin production indicative of ADF, but not Snarl's. And there are still no reports of any of her people contracting the syndrome. Snarl may have a natural immunity that we can take advantage of—if we can find out what factor causes it. I did a complete biochemical workup of a sample to compare with human and Eeiauoan workups, but it'll be a few hours before the computer is done with the correlations."

Biochemistry was Chapel's field, and McCoy was never so glad of it as he had been the past few months. "Good girl," he said. "You might be on to something there. Now why don't you get some rest while you're waitin' for that mechanical monster to gobble your data, Christine?"

She shook her head and gave him Quickfoot's reply. "That will come all too soon, Doctor."

McCoy said, "That's an order, Nurse Chapel. We may not know how ADF affects humans, but we do know that lack of rest lowers the resistance to any disease."

"Resistance," she said, almost absently.

"We're going to beat it, Christine." He said it with a conviction he did not feel. It might have convinced a layman but not a trained professional.

"Thanks for the bedside manner, Dr. McCoy." She smiled wanly at him. Then she began to process the tissue samples. "Leonard, I want to say something. I've enjoyed working with you all these years; you've been a good friend. . . ."

Abruptly, she braced herself against the lab table. McCoy caught her elbow. *"Christine!"*

She said, very distinctly, as if it were the most important thing in the world, "Don't let me break those samples. You need them."

He took the single sample from her hand and laid it carefully on the lab bench. She nodded approvingly . . . then she slumped backward.

McCoy caught her and eased her to the floor, to check her with his sensors. "Quickfoot! *Quickfoot!*" The Eeiauoan was beside him with an awkward leap, her eyes round.

"First-stage coma," McCoy snapped, "help me get her onto that bench. I want a complete workup of her vital signs. . . . Don't argue with me, you damn fur-brained idiot! This hospital hasn't any facilities to handle a human in a coma—we'll have to send her up to the *Flinn.*"

"Too ssoon," said Quickfoot; her accent made it sound like a wail. "Too ssoon for first-stage ccoma!"

"Too *damn* soon. God only knows how fast ADF works in a human. Pull your claws in, dammit, and help me!"

Together, they carried Christine Chapel to the bench. McCoy did his work swiftly, then transmitted her coordinates to the medship. As Christine Chapel vanished in the cold twinkling light of the transporter beam, McCoy felt a shudder run through his body—he knew he might never see her again. He reached a hand toward her in parting, but it was an empty gesture. She was gone.

Quickfoot had her tail in her hands. Bare of fur, almost ratlike, it was the most glaring evidence of the progression of ADF syndrome in Quickfoot's body.

As McCoy watched, she began to twist it viciously. "I gave her sscarf to cover head fur," said Quickfoot with a hissing wail. "She was asshamed, asshamed to have disease. I am asshamed."

"It's not your fault, Quickfoot," said McCoy in a weary voice. "We're doing all we can do." He sighed. "I'll have to call the *Enterprise* and tell Jim. Is there someplace private I can . . . ?"

"You come," said Quickfoot, "*Is* my fault. I talk to your captain and transslator, private too. Come, musst hurry."

Having relieved both Spock and Uhura of their duties on the bridge to search for the location of the Eeiauoan homeworld, Jim Kirk felt it his duty to check their progress from time to time. He thought of it as giving them encouragement but he knew perfectly well that he sought rather than gave it.

So far, he had been disappointed. Now, however, he sensed that something had changed. Uhura's face was drawn with exhaustion but there was a spark in her eyes that had not been there before. She listened to her tapes with the sharpened concentration of a stalking cat.

Kirk couldn't put his finger on it, but Spock too seemed to be searching his data for something in particular.

"Any luck, Mr. Spock?"

Spock did not look up from his task. "*Luck,* Captain?"

"Have you *found* it?" He knew he shouldn't have mentioned luck to a Vulcan.

"Captain, making certain assumptions as to the date of the Eeiauoans' arrival on this world, the level of their interstellar technology and its possible range at that time, the direction and duration of their journey, we can place the homeworld of the Eeiauoans somewhere within the quadrant you are now seeing on the display screen."

"A *quadrant*, Mr. Spock! It would take years to search a quadrant for a single planet!"

"Precisely. And I must remind you that even this conclusion is based upon highly questionable data."

"Meaning, Mr. Spock?"

"Meaning, Captain, that should one of our assumptions be faulty, we would be searching the wrong quadrant."

"You've got to do better than that, Spock. You've got to!"

"Lieutenant Uhura"—at Spock's mention of her name, Uhura looked up at him inquiringly; he gave a quick negative shake of his head and she turned her back to them both and placed a slender hand to the ear receiver to shut out their presence—"is endeavoring to refine those results. She hopes to find reference to some . . . *landmark,* as she terms it, some distinctive cosmic formation visible from the Eeiauoans' homeworld or perhaps noted by them on their journey. I believe your presence is distracting her from this task."

Kirk was properly chastened. "I can take a hint, Spock."

" 'Hint,' Captain?"

"Never mind . . . I'll get out and leave you to your job."

A whistle from the ship's intercom halted him before he reached the door. He acknowledged quietly, not wishing to disturb Uhura further, then listened. His face must have shown his horror, for Spock said, "What has happened, Captain?"

"Nurse Chapel is in a first-stage coma," he said softly; then, realizing that he already had Uhura's full attention, he added, in as normal a voice as he could muster, "ADF syndrome hits humans harder and faster than it does Eeiauoans. . . . Lieutenant."

Uhura removed her earphone. "Sir?"

"Quickfoot wants to talk to us. I think we'd better listen." Into the communicator, he said, "Put it on the screen here."

Bones appeared, behind him Quickfoot. He gestured Quickfoot forward.

"I sspeak to ccaptain and transslator," she said, her eyes narrowing at Spock. "No other to hear."

Kirk said, "Mr. Spock is my chief science officer and Dr. McCoy my chief medical officer; I must insist that they

32

remain. I promise you, Quickfoot, nothing you say will go beyond my senior officers. . . . Tell her, Uhura."

Uhura translated.

Quickfoot bristled—it made her fur loss all the more grotesque—and flattened her ears. "You will be sorry for that promise, Captain Kirk, for I will tell you the truth. Your science officer is correct: Eeiauo is not our homeworld. But we are not colonists, we are criminals."

Uhura translated this. Kirk said, "Criminals? This is a prison planet? You mean you have regular contact with your homeworld?"

"No, we left Sivao two thousand five hundred and three years ago. We have not been there since. For many years we could not have returned, now we *would* not. But I will not be so criminal as to let your people die with us. *You* must go, to save your people."

"We'll go, Quickfoot. Tell us where it is."

Quickfoot crouched. Without warning, she let out a long agonized wail. McCoy jumped at the sound, recovered and came forward to see if she needed his help. She waved him away.

"I do not know where it is. When you asked about it, I thought you knew everything!"

"Is there anyone who could tell us?"

"No one *would* tell you. No one else on my world is capable of such treason. We are all criminals, yet I alone—I—I—" She keened her despair.

"Quickfoot," said Kirk earnestly, and he heard the same tone in Uhura's translation, "unless you are two thousand years old, you are *not* a criminal. The Federation does not hold the crimes of one generation against another!"

He waited until Uhura's translation caught up with him, then went on, "You must help us to help you, Quickfoot. Can you tell us anything at all about the homeworld that might help us find it? Can you see its primary in your sky? What did your ancestors see when the skies above their homeworld darkened? Think, Quickfoot! Anything might help!"

Quickfoot looked at him, unblinking. She shook her head. "There was only the Mad Star's light the year my people were—exiled." Uhura hesitated over the final word although her translation came as no surprise. As unaccustomed as he was to the Eeiauoan tongue, even Jim Kirk could hear its similarity to "Eeiauo."

Seemingly puzzled, Uhura asked another question of the Eeiauoan, translated the answer. "The star that cast shadows, the guest star—oh!" she said suddenly. "She means a nova or a supernova, Mr. Spock." A second query to Quickfoot brought a reply that made her nod once at him in confirmation.

Quickfoot went on, as if unaware of Uhura's pause. Softly, but rapidly, Uhura picked up and relayed her words: "They sent us from camp—and the camp was Sivao. We should have died in space. We should never have been born. The same Mad Star bloomed in this sky the year of our arrival—and, as we brought death to Sivao, we have brought death to your innocent worlds. My life will be my apolo—"

Uhura suddenly broke off her translation. She flung her hand at the screen. "Dr. McCoy!" she shouted desperately, "Stop her! *Suicide!*"

As Jim Kirk and his officers watched in horror—unable to help, unable to look away—Quickfoot raised a hand to her throat. McCoy sprang toward her.

Even though Quickfoot had no wish to injure McCoy, the doctor would have had no chance against her wiry strength if Quickfoot had not been well into ADF syndrome.

He grabbed fiercely for her wrists and threw his full weight against her. She went down beneath him. For a moment, they both disappeared from view, then Quickfoot struggled to her feet.

McCoy clung to her back. He had her right arm pinned and was trying desperately to reach the hypo that lay on the table just beyond his fingertips.

Quickfoot threw him from her. He struck the wall and reeled. Quickfoot reached again for her throat—this time Kirk saw the claws splay. McCoy staggered toward her, and Quickfoot slowly collapsed. McCoy reached her in time to keep her head from hitting the table.

He stood gasping for a moment, then he looked up at the

screen. "First-stage coma," he said, hoarsely. "She didn't need to commit suicide, dammit. She's dying *now.*"

"Not necessarily, Dr. McCoy," said Spock.

"What d'ya mean, Spock?" McCoy growled. "And, by god, this better be good."

"Spock?" Kirk said, overlapping McCoy. "If you've got something, give!"

But it was to Uhura that Spock turned. "You do understand, Lieutenant, that many of our assumptions remain assumptions."

She nodded—Jim Kirk realized that she did not trust herself to speak—but her dark eyes were full of entreaty.

Spock said, "I believe Quickfoot has given us your landmark."

"Are you tellin' me you can find this home world, Spock?" McCoy looked down. Quickfoot's form was hidden from them by the table, but no one had any doubt about what he saw: his face was gray.

"No, Doctor. I can give you no such assurance. I can only state that there is now a possibility of doing so, given Lieutenant Uhura's information and Quickfoot's. If my calculations are correct, they serve only to narrow the area of search. And, should we find the Eeiauoans' planet of origin, we have no guarantee that the Eeiauoans' distant relatives can deal any more efficaciously with ADF syndrome—"

"—Than I can, is that what you're sayin', Spock?"

"I had intended no aspersion, Dr. McCoy. You are hardly the only doctor trying to contend with the situation."

The anger washed from McCoy's face. "I know, Spock, I know. . . . God, I'm tired." He looked down again and rubbed his hands over his eyes. "So you're grasping at straws, too."

"If I recall my Terran proverbs correctly," Spock said, "we are looking for a needle in a haystack."

"And Quickfoot told you which haystack."

Spock gave this thoughtful consideration, then said, "Affirmative."

That seemed to satisfy McCoy. He turned his attention back to Kirk. "I'd appreciate it if you'd brief Evan Wilson while I see to Quickfoot and tell her I'll get back to her with Chapel's results later today. A full briefing, Jim—haystack and all."

"Haystack and all, Bones."

"Thanks—and good luck, for all our sakes. McCoy out."

Lieutenant Uhura turned from her station. "Message from Starfleet Command, sir." Her voice was level, but Kirk could see the effort it cost her.

"Put it on the screen, Lieutenant," he said. She flashed him a look of immense gratitude and did.

"Kirk here," he said and found himself speaking to Starfleet's commander-in-chief and the president of the Federation Council. His back straightened and he had to force himself not to salute twice. He wasn't the only one—he could hear backbones snapping erect all over the bridge. *Well,* he thought, *it's not often you see that much brass all in one place!*

Aloud, he said, *"Sir!"* and to the tall, slender woman, "Ms. President. This is an honor."

She shook her head grimly and corrected, "This is an emergency." She gestured to the commander, who said, "The *Enterprise* is hereby ordered to begin a search for Sivao, the Eeiauoan homeworld. Follow your own calculations and proceed with all possible speed. . . . The president has further instructions for you."

"Thank you, Commander." The president gave him a long, steady look, then she said, "Extraordinary circumstances require an extraordinary response, Captain Kirk. When you find the Eeiauoan homeworld, you are to make immediate and open contact with the inhabitants. The Federal Council has agreed to waive the Non-Interference Directive. We will have to rely on your judgment, Captain—make it good."

Kirk nodded.

"That's all, Captain Kirk," said the commander-in-chief. "You will prepare for immediate departure. Starfleet Command out." The image vanished.

There was a moment of dead silence on the bridge, then abruptly everyone seemed to be talking at once. Kirk allowed the babble to continue for a space—it not only provided a safety valve, but it gave him time to consider the implications himself—then he said, "People, please! You heard the orders. I suggest we stop gossiping and get to work."

He got back an enthusiastic chorus of "Aye, Captain!" from all sides.

Kirk rose and positioned himself to look over his science officer's shoulder. It did him no good; he couldn't decipher the data on Spock's screen. "How soon can we have those coordinates?"

"Within the hour, I should estimate. I wish to make one final check." Spock held him with a glance.

"What is it, Spock?" he asked in a low tone.

"In my report to Starfleet, I did, to the best of my ability, emphasize the unreliable nature of our data. Our orders, however—from both Starfleet and the Council—seem remarkably optimistic."

Jim Kirk shook his head. "Quite the contrary, Mr. Spock. I'd say our orders mean the situation is much worse than we know."

"Ah," said Spock, lifting an eyebrow. "You think they, too, are grasping at straws."

"That's exactly what I think."

Spock returned to his calculations without further comment. Kirk raised his voice. "Lieutenant Uhura, will you ask Dr. Wilson to meet me in the briefing room on the double? Mr. Chekov, Mr. Spock is not to be disturbed for less than an impending nova—"

Spock, visibly startled, said, "That is hardly possible in this system, Captain."

"A manner of emphasis, Mr. Spock."

"Of course, Captain," said Spock.

Jim Kirk was sure for once that Spock had told a social lie. He said with a grin, *"You* understand me, Mr. Chekov."

"Aye, sair," said Chekov, grinning back.

"Let me know as soon as you've finished, Spock."

"Lieutenant Uhura will inform you, sir."

Evan Wilson heard him through without interruption. When he had finished, she gave him a long, speculative look that made him acutely conscious of the fact that he had been grinning since he'd received the go-ahead from Starfleet. He added, "Perhaps you should put the whole crew on tranquilizers, Doctor. We're looking for a planet on the strength of a song. It's crazy, I know, but it's the only chance we have to do something useful."

The admission was not simply sobering, it was disheartening; but before the full force of it struck him, Evan Wilson said gravely, "I think you're as crazy as Heinrich Schliemann —and you know what happened to *him!*"

"What?" he said, disconcerted.

"You *don't* know what happened to him?" she asked, her blue eyes widening in mild astonishment. "Ever read Homer's *Iliad,* Captain?"

Taken aback by the seeming irrelevancy, Jim Kirk frowned slightly; but there was something in the intensity of her gaze that reminded him of Spock about to offer an observation. *I'll bite,* he thought, *if only to find out who this is I'm as crazy as.* He said, "I don't know what translation you read, Doctor, but there was no Heinrich Schliemann in mine—or in the *Odyssey.*"

"That depends on how you look at it." Smiling, she settled back into her chair and went on, "Heinrich Schliemann was from Earth, pre-Federation days, and *he* read Homer too. No, not just read him, believed him. So he set out at his own expense—mind you, I doubt he could have found anyone else to fund such a crazy endeavor—to find Troy, a city that most of the educated people of his time considered pure invention on Homer's part."

"And?"

"And he found it. Next time you're on Earth, stop by the Troy Museum. The artifacts are magnificent, and every one of them was found on the strength of a song."

While Kirk absorbed that, she rose and added, "If you have no objection, I'll give Mr. Sulu a hand down to the bridge. Broken ankle or no, he can still compute a course."

Feeling too good to resist the temptation, he said, "Is that medically advisable, Doctor?"

Oh, yes!" She gave him that wicked smile again. "It's the

best thing in the world for my health—he'd never forgive me
if he missed this!"

Jim Kirk could feel the excitement on all sides. "Ready,
Mr. Spock?"

"One moment, Captain." Spock watched the display
screen; of all the bridge personnel, only he seemed unaffected
by the charged atmosphere. "The data transfer is not yet
complete."

Lieutenant Uhura turned in her seat. "What's taking so
long, Mr. Spock?" she asked.

Spock straightened. "I assure you, Lieutenant, that your
feeling of delay is just that—a feeling."

"I'm sorry, Mr. Spock." She said it with such a complete
lack of expression that Kirk wondered for a moment if she'd
suddenly turned Vulcan.

"As we agreed," Spock responded, "there is no apology
necessary."

Uhura smiled, suddenly and brilliantly. "As we agreed,
Mr. Spock," she said.

"Data transfer complete, Captain," said Spock. "The
navigational computer now has the coordinates." The announcement was completely unnecessary—Sulu's burst of
activity was sufficient evidence of the fact.

"Mr. Scott, stand by for warp three. Ready when you are,
Mr. Sulu," said Kirk.

Sulu did not take the time from his calculations to acknowledge. Seconds later, Sulu said, "Course laid in, Captain."

"Then what are we waiting for, Mr. Sulu?"

"Aye, *aye*, Captain." Sulu grinned and touched his con-
trols. "We're on our way."

Chapter Four

Leonard McCoy gulped a last mouthful of the tasteless stuff the Eeiauoans called food, followed it with a handful of vitamins and washed the whole mess down with a slug of coffee. For the fourth or fifth time that day, he considered prescribing a stimulant shot for himself. What little time he could snatch for sleep was being torn from him in nightmares that only repeated the horrors of his waking hours. Once again, he rejected the idea. Stimulants had a way of disrupting mental processes, and that was one thing he could ill afford.

What he needed most, he thought, was someone to talk to. With Jim and Scotty and—he hated to admit it—Spock chasing all over the galaxy after wild geese, he had no one to check his figures, or to cheer him along on his own wild goose chase.

He settled for a shot of scotch. The bottle had been a parting gift from Evan Wilson, a happy result of all his complaints about the Eeiauoans' dislike of alcohol in any form.

Then he returned to the computers and examined his results for the third time. He had built on the work Evan and Christine had done, following up the apparent immunity of Snnanagfashtalli's people.

He had found something, but *what*, he was not sure. At best, it was a palliative, not a cure. At worst . . .

He had to be sure before he went on that it would do no harm to the victims of ADF syndrome.

As the Eeiauoan doctors had predicted, the Eeiauoan victims of the disease still lived—as long as they were massively supported by intravenous feeding and all the rest that Federation personnel and equipment could supply. The deaths in previous outbreaks of the plague had all occurred when the victims finally outnumbered those who could care for them.

Humans were another story: two of the earliest known cases had already died, others were sure to follow. That was the last information he had been able to transmit to Evan Wilson before the *Enterprise* had passed out of range of a Federation relay beacon.

He thought of Christine Chapel and the risks she faced, and he knew he had to go ahead. *She* could not wait for surety. He took a deep breath and placed a call to Dr. Mickiewicz aboard the *Flinn*. It took the ship's communications officer a moment to locate her. When she appeared, she was alone in her office.

"Hi, Micky," he said. "Good god, you look terrible!"

"Your bedside manner's shot to hell, Leonard, and you're no raving beauty yourself. You look like you haven't slept in a month. . . . Chapel's still holding." She shook her head heavily. "Hell," she said, and that was all.

They looked at each other for a long while. Then she said, "I'm glad you called, though. I could use somebody to talk to, just for a minute." She smiled wanly and added, "What's the latest update on coronary infarction?"

McCoy smiled back. "You still don't get it from a sword blade," he said immediately. It was an old joke between two schoolmates, and it made him feel infinitely better.

"Thanks," she said, "I needed that." Her smile this time seemed genuine.

McCoy said, "I've got something for you." At the sudden sharpening of her expression, he added hastily, "Now don't, dammit, *don't* get all worked up until you hear me out."

He laid it all out, transmitted the data for her to check and

41

waited. She looked through it all. Finally she looked up. "It might work, Leonard."

"It might not."

"I see that, but if it does work we could slow the progress of the disease in humans. And anything that gives us time. . . !"

"The ethics—" McCoy cut himself short at the expression on her face. She knew every argument he'd had with himself; she knew what he'd given her was a long shot.

"Leonard," she said, very quietly, "I have a volunteer for your treatment: one who can give informed consent."

"Who. . . ?" As he looked at her, he suddenly knew who she meant. "You, Micky?" He could not keep the anger out of his voice. "Goddammit, woman. . . !"

"Watch your goddam mouth, McCoy!" she shot back.

He was so surprised at her anger that he snapped his mouth shut. She glared at him.

"See here, Micky," he began again, "trying something like this on a terminal patient is one thing—" He broke off in horror.

She nodded. Her voice was very soft, and now he could see the fear in her eyes. "I am a terminal patient, Leonard. I have ADF syndrome; I confirmed the diagnosis myself a few minutes ago. You've just given me the only chance I have. I thank you for it—however it turns out."

"Micky . . ."

She shook herself and gave him a fierce smile. "Now bug off, will you? We've both got a lot of work to do today. I'll keep you posted." She gave him no chance to say good-bye.

He was glad for that. He had no wish to say anything that sounded so final.

Captain's Log, Stardate 1573.4:

Mr. Spock's coordinates have brought us to an area of space uncharted by the Federation. Mr. Spock and the entire Astronomy Division are making a brief but exhaustive survey for solar systems that fit the necessary parameters.

Personal Log, James T. Kirk, Stardate 1573.4:

Three weeks to reach Spock's haystack and another spent sitting here in the middle of nowhere while Astronomy takes pictures. . . .

Every time I think this is impossible, I think of Heinrich Schliemann. I'm not the only one. Like Starfleet Command, the crew has been told only that we're following certain leads Spock has found in Eeiauoan literature, and Dr. Wilson has been dispensing her prescription with a liberal hand. "Heinrich Schliemann" has become a catch phrase all over the *Enterprise.* I've heard it in a dozen different contexts in the past few days. Spock even found it deserving of comment—"baffling."

"Ah, Captain," said Spock, as he stepped into the turbolift to find Jim Kirk already there. "I believe we now have sufficient information to begin a closer scrutiny."

"Good, Mr. Spock. *Very* good." Having spent so much time twiddling his thumbs, Kirk was not about to waste another moment. He activated the intercom and said, "Lieutenant Uhura, please have all senior personnel meet me in the briefing room immediately." As an afterthought, he added, "Mr. Spock is ready."

"Thank you, sir," said Uhura's voice. He could hear the relief in it. "Uhura out."

"Kirk out." He turned again to Spock. "Just what are our chances of finding Sivao?"

"They depend largely upon Lieutenant Uhura, as she is the only one of us with any knowledge of the world we seek."

"Well, she's gotten us this far. Let's hope she can keep it up."

Spock nodded once but said nothing further. Jim Kirk knew better than to press him on the subject. At most, he'd get an estimate of the odds against them, and he was not sure he wanted one.

The turbolift doors hissed, momentarily framing Evan Wilson in the opening. Spock raised an eyebrow at the picture she presented; Kirk said, "Good Lord!"

She wore heavily padded fencing garb that had been slashed in several places as if by enormous claws. Sweat shone on her forehead, her hair was in total disarray, she was openly bleeding from two parallel cuts across her left cheek—and she was grinning from ear to ear.

She stepped into the lift, carrying a wooden staff a few inches taller than she was high, and saluted triumphantly. "Mr. Spock, Captain," she said. "Do I have five minutes to clean up, or can the briefing room take it?"

"You have five minutes, Dr. Wilson. I won't have my ship's doctor running around looking like . . ." Kirk found himself hard put to say what she did look like.

"Like something the cat dragged in?" she suggested. "I'll have you know, Captain, Snnanagfashtalli looks like something the doc dragged in."

"Are we to understand, Dr. Wilson, that you have been engaged in combat with Snnanagfashtalli?" Spock had no trouble with the name; the Vulcan language had more than its share of throat-twisting sounds.

"It was something of an experiment, Mr. Spock. Quarterstaff against teeth and claws. The results were inconclusive. I think I gave as good as I got, but then, Snnanagfashtalli kept her temper, so I'm not sure if she was pulling her pounces. I may just have been pummeled like a kitten." She daubed at her cheek ruefully.

Spock contemplated her weapon and, without a word, she handed it to him. He lifted it, testing the weight. "I have never seen one used."

"Pick your time, Mr. Spock, and I'll be happy to further your education. The quarterstaff is one of the finest weapons ever invented." She took the staff back and smiled. "It might be interesting to try it against the Vulcan disciplines. But that's a separate offer and I wouldn't push you into anything."

The turbolift doors opened. "My stop," she said. She stepped out and saluted, "Heinrich Schliemann, Captain." The doors closed and the turbolift shifted sideways.

"Remarkable . . ." Spock began.

"I'll say," Kirk agreed, but the Vulcan's expression seemed to call for further comment. "Something wrong, Spock?"

"Wrong, Captain? No, I should say rather 'anomalous.' "

"Anomalous? In what way?"

"In both her presence and her behavior."

"I wouldn't worry about it, Spock—her presence, at least. Unless you want to wonder who she knows. She told Bones she cut her own orders and I'm inclined to believe she could. Dr. Wilson is most certainly not shy."

The turbolift came to a halt. As they walked down the corridor to the briefing room, Kirk went on, "You know Snnanagfashtalli, Spock"—the name got easier with practice —"do you suppose she pulled her punches?"

"Doubtful, Captain. If Dr. Wilson wished to test her abilities, it would do neither of them honor for Snnanagfashtalli to do less than her best. However, as Dr. Wilson herself seems quite aware, her best need not and did not include a killing frenzy."

"Let's be thankful for small favors," Kirk said. "Going to take her up on her challenge, Spock?"

"I shall consider it, Captain."

Kirk was taken aback. "I was joking, Spock!"

"I was not."

They entered the briefing room to find Scott and Uhura waiting.

"Lieutenant Uhura," said Spock, without preamble, "I shall require your assistance." He gestured her to the computers.

After a moment of preparation, he said, "We have found twelve planetary systems that meet our general specifications. On the assumption that the Eeiauoans would have chosen a world as similar in type and position to their home world as possible, I have narrowed this to three. I have prepared computer simulations of skies of those three worlds. Logic can do no more."

The day's full of surprises, thought Kirk. *Bones would have a field day with that.*

He got still another surprise when he looked over Uhura's shoulder at the display screens. The starfields were reversed —white stars on black backgrounds—certainly not standard issue from the Astronomy Divison.

He wasn't sure exactly what Spock expected of Uhura, but he kept quiet while she did whatever it was.

When Sulu hobbled in with Chekov's support, the Russian chattering excitedly, Kirk silenced them with a glance. Dr. Wilson entered a few moments later, damp and still triumphant. From the look of awe given her by Sulu and Chekov, Kirk could guess the content of the conversation he'd interrupted.

She grinned at them and settled herself silently to watch the screens, craning forward. Her absorption was complete and encompassed not only the display but Spock and Uhura as well.

At last, Uhura shook her head. "I can't help, Mr. Spock. I'm sorry." From her tone of dismay, she was more than sorry.

Wilson touched her hand lightly to Uhura's arm. "I seem to be missing something, Nyota. What *are* you up to?" Her eyes held a child's grave and intense curiosity, and they drew from Uhura a small, almost embarrassed, smile in return. "Mr. Spock hoped I would have a hunch," Uhura said.

"Oh." Wilson managed to pack the single monosyllable with both comprehension and exasperation. With a comic shrug of her shoulders, she said, "That's not how hunches work, Mr. Spock. Captain, I appeal to you! Explain to him!"

"Captain?" said Spock, clearly expecting him to do so.

Kirk did his best. "Spock, hunches aren't something a person has on command—and certainly not under this kind of pressure!"

"I have observed this human ability to function under conditions of extreme pressure. You yourself, Captain . . ."

"I'm not the one we're talking about. You make no allowance for individual response." Even as he said it, Kirk knew he had made the matter no clearer to Spock. He tried another tactic. "Dr. Wilson, perhaps you have a prescription?"

"Talk, Mr. Spock. Tell us everything you know about what's on those screens. Who knows? That might trigger something for someone, maybe even you."

"Go ahead, Spock." Kirk nodded.

The rest of his senior officers gathered closer, drawn in by the possibility that they too might be of help. Wilson relinquished her chair to Sulu. Kirk found himself watching the screens over her head while Spock took them on a guided tour of this region of space.

Red giants, white dwarfs, double stars, globular clusters that would be seen as single stars, X ray sources that would be invisible to the Eeiauoan or human eye . . . Spock's long slender finger indicated each in turn but his focus of attention remained on Uhura. *That's hardly what I call taking the pressure off*, Kirk thought. *Perhaps it's time I created a little diversion.*

Spock was saying, "This is a visible pulsar."

"Pulsar?" said Wilson. At Sulu's look of horror, she said, "Medicine I know. You tell me what a pulsar is and I'll tell you whatever you need to know about the organ of Zuckerkandl."

Sulu made a polite scoffing noise but explained anyway, "It's a neutron star that seems to blink, sometimes in visible wavelengths, sometimes in X rays. Small but massive. It spins very fast and each time the magnetic pole sweeps by, it shows up as a burst of X rays." He flipped his hand to demonstrate. "Think of it as a lighthouse." He looked at her slyly and inquired, "Lighthouse?" She nodded, and Sulu grinned and said, "Just checking. Anybody who doesn't know what a pulsar is . . ." He left the thought unfinished but Kirk could see Wilson wasn't going to hear the end of this for some time.

Sulu went on, more seriously. "Each has its own very specific rate of spin. They're so regular, you could set your watch by them."

Chekov put in, "They are very useful to a nevigator."

"I'll bet they are!—Go on, Mr. Spock, I apologize for the interruption. What's its pulse rate?"

Sulu laughed. Spock said merely, "The periodicity of this particular pulsar is ninety-five flashes to the minute."

"Normal," she pronounced, in a tone of satisfaction.

"Dr. Wilson, the normal pulse for the human adult is between seventy and ninety beats a minute." Spock had evidently caught the joke but was treating it with his usual literal-mindedness. "Unless, of course, you refer to the normal heartbeat of a human child."

47

"Normal for an adult Eeiauoan, Mr. Spock. I told you: medicine, I know. If there were any justice in the universe, that would be *our* lighthouse, too."

Uhura turned suddenly to stare at Wilson. "Evan? What's the pulse rate for an Eeiauoan child?"

"Somewhere between 120 and 125 beats a minute, Nyota. Is that any help?"

Instead of answering, Uhura turned sharply back to Spock. "Mr. Spock, is there a visible pulsar of that periodicity—one that the Eeiauoan eye could see from any of these worlds?"

"If you will permit me . . ." He took the chair from her and made some few movements at the computer console. After a moment the display changed, although the stars still showed white on a black field. Spock pointed. "This," he said, "would be visible to an unassisted Eeiauoan eye from three worlds in this quadrant."

Uhura took a deep breath. "Can you tell me, Mr. Spock— two thousand years ago, when the Eeiauoans left their homeworld, was that star the north star for any of the three?"

"One moment, Lieutenant." Spock focused his attention on his computers.

Uhura seemed to hold her breath in anticipation. Kirk found himself doing the same; he knew he was not the only one.

Spock said, "Affirmative, Lieutenant." A single image flashed and froze on the screen.

"Sivao!" said Uhura, rising with her excitement. *"Sivao,* Mr. Spock!" The words tumbled out in a joyous flood. "I thought of all the ancient songs but never the everyday songs the children sing. Their equivalent of 'Once upon a time' is"—she spoke a few words in Eeiauoan, startling those who had not previously heard the language, and then translated— "'Sivao, *where the North Star beat like the heart of a child.* . . .' Mr. Spock, that's their world! Oh, Evan, there *is* justice in the universe!" Impulsively, she put her arms around the smaller woman. Evan Wilson returned her hug with enthusiasm.

Kirk was beginning to get that very heady feeling again, but this time the thought of Heinrich Schliemann was sobering.

"All right, people, I suggest we get to work: we still have a good deal of digging ahead of us."

"Isn't that the prettiest sight you've seen in months," said Sulu from the helm. The satisfaction in his voice left no room for disagreement. Not that he'd have had any from James Kirk—the world hung in the viewscreen of the bridge like a single Christmas tree ornament, shining with promise.

The sight might even have encouraged Bones. Had the *Enterprise* been within range of a Federation relay beacon, Kirk would certainly have tried.

Spock said, from behind him, "Sensors indicate presence of life forms, Captain, but I see no evidence of ground-based space ports or, for that matter, cities of the type associated with a space-going culture."

"Is it possible they've progressed beyond our technology?"

"Given the size and diversity of the universe, it is difficult to rule out any possibility, Captain. However, the sensors detect none of the orbital debris common to a world that has passed through the traditional historical phases."

"Perhaps they're just very neat."

"Perhaps."

"Well, we're not going to learn anything sitting up here. Pick us a good spot, Mr. Spock, and we'll go down and have a look." Kirk turned in his seat. "Lieutenant Uhura, will you join the landing party, please."

Uhura was surprised. "Captain?"

"You know more about the Eeiauoans than anyone on board. We need your expertise, Lieutenant. . . . And notify Dr. Wilson to meet us in the transporter room."

Spock's head came up, and his eyebrow lifted simultaneously, "A word with you, Captain," he said.

"Problem, Spock?" Kirk rose and joined him, peering at the monitor over his shoulder. "Looks like a perfectly good Earth-type world to me. I know you prefer Vulcan-type but . . ."

"Doctor Wilson," Spock said.

Puzzled, Kirk said, "What have you got against Wilson, aside from the fact that she's anomalous?"

"She has had no previous experience at first contact."

49

"It's her medical experience I'm after, Spock. We'll just have to remember to keep an eye on her."

Spock nodded and, without further comment, returned to his task at the computer. A moment later, he raised his head to signal that he had finished.

At last, Kirk thought, *something I can do to help Bones and the Eeiauoans!* "Mr. Scott, you have command." He started for the turbolift, with Uhura and Chekov immediately behind. Spock lingered for a moment, then followed.

"A good spot, Mr. Spock?" Kirk inquired with a smile.

"I have no doubt it will suit your somewhat vague criteria, Captain."

Kirk was in too good a mood to allow Spock's oblique criticism to rankle him. "Very good, Mr. Spock," he said, and left it at that.

Chapter Five

The transporter room vanished and, in its place, the landing party found a small clearing. All around them ancient trees rose to heights she had seen only in wilderness preserves, but—Uhura blinked back tears of relief—they were familiar. She laid her hand on the trunk before her and its very solidity warmed her: she *knew* this place. CloudShape to-Ennien had once cloaked herself in mist and climbed a tree like this one . . . to where the storm clouds had been at play with their lightnings. Fooled by the mist, the storm clouds invited CloudShape to join their game. They tossed a lightning to her—and CloudShape caught it with her tail and scurried down as fast as she could climb, leaving the storm clouds to boom their anger.

Once Sunfall had burst into laughter at the sight of a barbecue. When Uhura had asked her why, Sunfall said, "To see a cooking fire is to see the singe marks on CloudShape's tail."

"Mr. Spock?" Captain Kirk's puzzled voice broke into her thoughts and drew her back to the business at hand.

Spock took a reading from his tricorder and said, "The inhabited area is about three hundred yards in that direction, Captain. As these people have, in all probability, seen neither a human nor a Vulcan, I did not wish to add to their surprise with a materialization."

"Good thinking, Mr. Spock." Kirk gestured. "Let's go

51

then. . . . Set phasers on stun and stay alert, people." With him in the lead, the party began to move warily through the forest.

Before her, Mr. Chekov took quick suspicious steps, matching his pace to Captain Kirk's. Slightly to her right, Evan Wilson crept swiftly along; the rapt concentration on her face made Uhura think of a child at play but her steps made no sound. Behind her, she could sense Spock's reassuring presence.

The captain stopped, raised his hand to motion them forward. They approached cautiously. "We hev found a trail, Mr. Spock," said Chekov, somewhat unnecessarily; he kept his voice low.

The trail was not broad—two might walk abreast—but it was hardpacked from frequent use. Kirk looked inquiringly at Spock, who said quietly, "We do not come as enemies, Captain. A straightforward approach would seem most appropriate."

"My thought exactly." Captain Kirk spoke in a normal tone of voice.

A single shriek of wordless anger stabbed through the forest.

"Down!" shouted Kirk, diving for cover himself, as the branches high above them came alive with furious movement and a chorus of chilling cries.

Uhura found herself sheltering beneath a partially fallen tree trunk as a hail of small round objects struck and bounced. She lifted her phaser and scanned the trees. At first, all she could make out were flapping branches, then she caught a glimpse of one of the creatures: it was small and brightly furred. Its feet and long tail were definitely prehensile. Another bounced suddenly into view; it too was screaming, but Uhura could see that the teeth it bared so threateningly were the flat teeth of leaf-eaters.

"Nuts!" said Evan Wilson from just beneath Uhura's left elbow. "They're throwing nuts at us!" The announcement brought a second hail down on them.

That stirred the memory of one of Sunfall's songs. Uhura twisted to look at Evan, but found herself face to face with Captain Kirk. Evan was wedged beneath the two of them,

staring down at her tricorder. "They're *welcome-homes,*
Captain," Uhura said. "That's all they do—make noise, wave
branches and throw things."

Kirk nodded at her and emerged cautiously from cover.
Spock followed suit. The welcome-homes kept to the safety
of their perches; farther up the trail, another group took up
the raucous cries. "All bark and no bite," he said to Spock
and winced as a shower of pellets bounced off his head.

"If I understand your meaning, sir, yes. These creatures
would be herbivorous. Shall we go on?"

"Yes, Mr. Spock. The Sivaoans can hardly have failed to
notice our presence. I suggest we go meet them before they
come looking for us." A mischievous expression touched the
corners of his mouth as he watched Evan crawl from cover
and dust twigs from her trousers. "You can stop sneaking, Dr.
Wilson."

"Begging the captain's pardon, but I wasn't sneaking."

"What would you call it?"

Evan straightened and, as if surprised he should ask, said,
"Pussyfooting, sir."

Captain Kirk laughed. "All right. Don't."

The party set off down the trail to ever louder squawks and
rustlings as the welcome-homes leapt from branch to branch
to keep pace with them. The path veered abruptly to the left
and down and spilled into a wide opening between the ancient
trees. In the clearing beyond, gigantic flowers of a dozen
shapes and colors bloomed in the sudden sunlight.

Kirk spread a hand, silently commanding a halt. Spock
took a single pace more. His action was perhaps deliberate,
for it gave Uhura an unobstructed view; what she had thought
flowers were brightly colored tents.

Emerging from doorways, tending cooking fires, rising
from open-air looms, startled Eeiauoans—*no,* Uhura
thought, correcting herself immediately, *Sivaoans!*—froze
and stared at the *Enterprise* crew members.

There were about three dozen of them that she could see,
but she had the uncanny feeling the number was considerably
larger. This was confirmed by Chekov, who said in a whisper,
"They're in the trees, too, sair."

The captain nodded and said, "Keep still and make no

threatening gestures." With exaggerated slowness, he holstered his phaser, spread his empty hands out at waist level and took two cautious steps forward. "We come in peace," he said. "On behalf of the United Federation of Planets, my people greet your people."

Uhura could tell the universal translator was doing its job. The Sivaoans' ears pricked forward to listen. Half a dozen children of varying ages drew close to adults for security, but they did not take their eyes off Captain Kirk.

"I am Captain Kirk of the U.S.S. *Enterprise,* a Federation starship currently orbiting your world. These are members of my crew." He introduced each in turn and each stepped forward slowly and calmly, to the same unblinking scrutiny. Spock, for once, got no second look. That didn't surprise Uhura—Sunfall would have considered Spock well within the range of human variation.

When he was finished, Kirk stepped back and waited. Save for the continued stares, there was no response. "Suggestions, Spock?" he said, at last, sotto voce.

"Perhaps Lieutenant Uhura might be of some assistance."

"Yes. Lieutenant?"

"I'll try, sir."

"Lieutenant," said Spock, "may I suggest you try the oldest form of the language you know well?"

Uhura was puzzled. "That would be like speaking Latin, Mr. Spock."

"Indeed," he said, "and another scholar might well be able to converse with you, despite the fact that neither of you knew the other's contemporary tongue. In two thousand years, this people's language has surely diverged from a common root."

"I see," she said.

However much she might remind herself that these were Sivaoans and should not be judged on Eeiauoan terms, she had little else to go on. So, as she stepped forward, she focused on the one that seemed to her most friendly—a Sivaoan that, in all but coloring and youth, might have been Sunfall's twin sister.

The Sivaoan's tail and legs were longer than average. Her fur was short; a beautiful silver gray on her back, ears, and tail; a striking white down her chest and belly. Her face bore a triangle of white reaching from between the eyes, over the nose, and down across the lower half of the cheeks and muzzle, giving her the appearance of wearing a silver gray mask over her copper eyes.

As Uhura advanced toward her, the two youngest children started to back away. Uhura stopped. Very slowly, she knelt . . . and the two little ones stopped backing and instantly regained their curiosity.

Scholarly language wouldn't mean much to someone that young, but she knew something they might understand. She rather hoped the captain would understand as well; she couldn't leave children frightened by their first sight of humans and Vulcans. She began to sing an old, old lullaby she'd learned from Sunfall.

If they did not understand the words of the song, the Sivaoans clearly understood her intention. All around her, eyes widened, whiskers and ears quivered.

Uhura let the last note of her song trail away and bowed her head slightly to each of the little ones, then slowly she rose. This time, the two children did not move away.

Once more, Uhura turned her attention to the masked Sivaoan. She stretched out her arms, her hands just slightly above shoulder height, one hand extended an inch or two beyond the other, and curved her fingers as if displaying claws; then, without lowering her arms, she relaxed her hands, as if drawing in those same claws. It was a formal greeting described in ballad after ballad.

The Sivaoan, after a moment's consideration, returned the gesture. Uhura saw the gleam of real claws displayed then withdrawn into silky gray fingers.

Drawing her words from the same old ballads, Uhura asked, "Can you understand me if I speak this tongue?"

The Sivaoan's ears flicked back in surprise. "Yes," she said, "your accent is a bit odd but I understand you." She turned briefly and seemed to receive agreement from several others —*at least*, thought Uhura, *that would be agreement from a Eeiauoan.* "Most of us are able to understand you—do you understand me?"

Uhura nodded. "With some difficulty," she admitted. "If

you would speak more slowly, I think it would be easier; and I would be pleased if you would correct any errors I might make."

"If you wish it," she said. The delight in her eyes warred with the formality of the Old Tongue words and for a brief moment she reminded Uhura so much of Sunfall that, quite without meaning to, Uhura asked, "Are you of Ennien?"

"*To*-Ennien. Forgive me, you may call me Jinx to-Ennien. You are called StarFreedom to-Enterprise? Is that correct?"

This took a moment's interpretation on Uhura's part. The universal translator must have rendered "Nyota Uhura" as "StarFreedom" and Jinx added "to-Enterprise" to conform to local custom. *To*-Ennien" was obviously a language correction; Captain Kirk had been right to question the different versions of CloudShape's name.

"Essentially correct," she said, "Jinx *to*-Ennien." Uhura took a deep breath and went on, choosing her words with care, "I bring sad news of kin of yours on a distant world. . . ."

Jinx's whiskers quivered with excitement. "Kin of mine? On another world?—Please try again, StarFreedom, perhaps I misunderstand you!"

Very slowly, Uhura began again, "Your distant relatives, your kin on another world, are in great danger. I believe—I pray—your people may be able to help them." She got no further.

A second Sivaoan, gray-striped of fur and somewhat older and larger than Jinx, stepped aggressively between the two of them. He said a few terse words to Jinx, who bristled and began what seemed to be an explanation, for it involved pointing to Uhura with her tail.

With no warning, he struck Jinx a stunning blow to the side of the head; she rocked with the force of it, but made no attempt to strike back. Then he said something more, this time with the air of an adult jollying a child, but Jinx made no reply. Her tail drooped perceptibly and she backed away.

The striped Sivaoan turned to Uhura. She tensed, ready to duck a blow, but instead he said something. Again, it was in the contemporary language and she did not understand. She told him so in the Old Tongue.

He made a gesture of greeting and replied in kind. "I am Winding Path to-Srallansre. You do not understand, Star-Freedom, yet your companion spoke our language well."

"Captain Kirk used the universal translator, sir. It would make it easier. May I?" Uhura turned on her universal translator again.

"Do you understand me now?" he said.

"Yes," said Uhura. "As I tried to tell Jinx, we believe your people may be able to help your relatives—"

Winding Path flicked one ear back—in Sunfall it would have been a gesture of disdain—then he said, "Have you walked far?"

Puzzled by his change of subject, Uhura said, "No. As Captain Kirk told you, we come from the *Enterprise,* which is now orbiting your world. . . ."

"You and your friends are welcome to stay under our protection until someone comes for you. You will speak to Stiff Tail," he said firmly before she could repeat her plea for help. "I will tell her how it happened."

There was nothing further to say for the moment. "Thank you," said Uhura, searching her memory for something more formal. But before she found it, Winding Path had already walked away. All her urgent questions would have to await Stiff Tail. Dismayed as she was by her failure, she had only duty to fall back on. She returned to Captain Kirk and Mr. Spock to make a full report of what little she had learned.

Jim Kirk had understood only the last few words of the exchange but Uhura's expression told him plainly that she had found no instant answers to the Eeiauoans'—the *Federation's* —plight. Not that he had honestly expected them, but one could always hope—and hope ran high in a desperate situation.

At least the Sivaoans seemed to accept them as guests. That was certainly useful. The acceptance seemed so complete, in fact, that the camp resumed normal business, or as normal as could be when each of the Sivaoans wanted a closer look at the strange new arrivals to their camp.

By the time Uhura returned to them, the landing party was encircled by curiosity seekers, all staring with that same unblinking intensity. Tails and whiskers seemed in constant motion with excitement. From the trees around the edge of the clearing, half a dozen more Sivaoans scrambled down; the claws were still used for climbing, Kirk noted.

"Captain, I'm sorry," Uhura began. She had turned off her universal translator to give them some privacy.

"For not going by the book?" Kirk suggested. "There is no 'book' on a first contact. What works, works. You did just fine, Uhura."

"Indeed," said Spock. "It would seem your human qualities were a considerable asset."

Kirk would have taken this as quite a compliment, and Bones would have done twenty minutes at least on an "admission" of this sort from Spock. Uhura only seemed further dismayed.

"It didn't help, Mr. Spock," she said. "They didn't listen. We still haven't any help for Sunfall and Christine and all the others. He just changed the subject and walked away!"

"Lieutenant," said Spock, "it took Heinrich Schliemann most of his lifetime to find Troy. He was not seeking specific information from its inhabitants."

I see Spock has finally puzzled out the use of "Heinrich Schliemann," Jim Kirk thought to himself with amusement. Aloud, he said, "Yes, Uhura, give us a few days. We're ahead of schedule."

She shook her head. *Meaning,* he thought, *not as far as Sunfall and Christine are concerned.* He agreed with the sentiment, but he also knew how difficult a task they had actually set themselves.

Uhura went on, "I chose Jinx"—she indicated the masked Sivaoan who stood defiantly close—"to speak to because . . ."

Her voice faltered and Kirk finished for her, "Because she looks like Sunfall, yes. Go on."

He listened carefully as she gave a full report of the exchange in Old Tongue.

"—I'm sorry I can't explain the rest," she said finally. "Mr. Spock was right about the change in the language. I hardly understood a word of what Winding Path to-Srallansre said to

Jinx. If they were Sunfall's people, I'd say Winding Path scolded Jinx like a child. Have you ever seen an adult very angry at something children have done, but not angry at the children themselves?"

"Yes," said Kirk, "I understand."

"But Jinx is not a child, Captain. And she was angry in a different way—as angry and as resentful as if she were being patronized and knew it."

"Class differences, Mr. Spock?"

"A possibility, Captain. As yet, we know very little about this culture."

"Then let's start learning. . . ." Kirk glanced again at Uhura. "If the rest of us do as well as you have, Lieutenant, we'll get our answers."

He snapped on his universal translator.

"Oh," breathed Evan Wilson—she stood face-to-face with a Sivaoan, the two of them regarding each other with undisguised wonder—"I am ambitious for a motley coat!" Her voice rang with delight and no little envy.

This one was about the same height as Wilson, although the ears made the Sivaoan appear taller. Her coat was predominantly white, patched at random with orange and black. Her face too was mostly white but looked as if someone had taken a sooty thumb and drawn a broad black smudge down the bridge of her nose. It gave her an odd, pleasantly clownish look that was all the more striking in combination with the grace of her movements.

Wilson copied the greeting she had seen Uhura give, and the Sivaoan returned it in kind. As if this had broken the ice, another Sivaoan approached Chekov and made the same gesture.

"Well, Mr. Chekov," Kirk said, "aren't you going to say hello?"

"I feel silly, Keptain," said Chekov, eying the Sivaoan with misgiving.

"Then why don't you greet Mr. Spock with a hearty handshake?"

"Sair!" Chekov was appalled at the suggestion. "Thet would be rude—Mr. Spock is a Wulcan!"

59

"Exactly, Mr. Chekov. Don't be rude to our hosts." Having put it that way, Kirk had to set a good example. Chekov gave him a hangdog look but displayed his claws.

The Sivaoan with the smudged nose still stared round-eyed at Wilson. "You—you like my coat?" she asked, as if she'd never heard such a thing.

"I think it's wonderful!" said Wilson.

"Compared to hers, it is!" said a voice from the crowd, and the Sivaoan with the smudged nose turned to hiss in its general direction, her tail twitching.

Evan Wilson frowned slightly in the same direction, then turned back. Pushing up her sleeve, she held out a bare arm for inspection.

"It's all right," she said, "I'm as curious as you are. If you wish to touch, you may." She glanced at Spock, who was being subjected to the same curiosity, and she added, "Please do not touch Mr. Spock. Mr. Spock is part Vulcan—you can tell by the shape of his ears—and to touch a Vulcan may cause him distress." Those closest to Spock considered his ears, and Wilson tucked back her hair to give a clear view of the difference.

Then she held out her arm again. The Sivaoan with the smudged nose reached out very hesitantly and touched Wilson's bare arm. Her ears flicked back and she snatched her hand back instantly. "No fur!" she said, clearly distressed.

"Look closer," said Wilson. "I admit it's skimpy compared to yours, but it's normal for a human. Mr. Chekov has a bit more." She beckoned Chekov and said to the slightly bristled Sivaoan, "In our culture, we should at least introduce ourselves. May I ask your name? Is that polite on this world?"

One of the others—Kirk saw it was the same one who had made the snide comment about Wilson's coat—said, "Sure. She just doesn't like her name. She's Brightspot to-Srallansre."

Brightspot hissed at the other a second time and said, "Some day you will call me something else, Fetchstorm. When I have *my* name . . ." Her tail lashed a promise.

Evan Wilson considered her thoughtfully. "I did not ask

him your name," she said, at last, "I asked you. What do you wish me to call you?"

Again, the Sivaoan's ears flicked sharply back. Kirk decided that it must be their expression of astonishment; given Brightspot's facial markings, it was equally astonishing.

"You will call me Brightspot," she said. Her ears pricked up, returning an air of dignity to her bearing. "When I have *my* name, I will tell you first."

"Thank you," said Wilson, gravely. Without being able to say why, Kirk had the feeling she had been paid a great compliment, and she had responded in precisely the right manner.

"You will call me Evan Wilson. And this is Mr. Chekov. Your arm, Pavel, if you please."

"Certainly, sair." Chekov seemed to have lost his embarrassment; perhaps it was because Brightspot was so obviously young. He pushed up his sleeve to show the thick black hair on his forearm. Brightspot looked up at Chekov's ears, matched them to Wilson's, then hesitantly touched Chekov's arm.

This time she did not pull away immediately; her hand stayed long enough to get the feel of both Chekov's "fur" and the skin beneath it. "Still feels like palms all over!" she pronounced. "There's not *enough* fur."

"Enough for a human," said Kirk, risking a smile. Brightspot did not seem to take it as a threatening expression.

"But don't you get cold at night?"

"We wear clothing," he said. Brightspot blinked at him uncomprehendingly; it was apparent her language did not contain the concept.

Wilson tugged at his sleeve and said, "Artificial fur, the captain means. Here, feel it. We have different kinds to suit various conditions of weather and temperature."

Brightspot checked his ears, patted the sleeve cautiously. The texture of the braid surprised her considerably but when she was done, she seemed relieved, if still a little sorry for their obvious deficiencies. "Is that artificial too?" She pointed to Wilson's hair with the tip of her tail.

Wilson bent her head forward. "No, that's as much me as your fur is you. Give it a tug, but not too hard. It is attached."

After a bit more patting, Brightspot gained the courage to tug. Wilson grunted. One of the adults, black-furred and very elegant, said, "Sounds like you pulled her tail, Brightspot."

"You have no tail!" said Brightspot. Her own whipped suddenly forward; she stared, first at it, then at Wilson. "How do you manage?!"

"I'm not sure how to answer that. I've *never* had a tail, so I wouldn't really know what to do with one if, by some magic, I suddenly acquired one. What do you do with your tail, Brightspot?"

"She sticks it into things," Fetchstorm said, and Brightspot bristled in his direction.

Wilson asked, "Is that an expression, Brightspot?"

Still glowering at Fetchstorm, Brightspot said, "It's what babies do when they want to find out about something."

"Ah," said Wilson, "you're curious!"

"That's not how he means it."

"I can guess," said Wilson, "and I sympathize. . . . People are always telling me I have a long nose"—she tapped the end of it—"and that I'm always sticking it in where I shouldn't."

Brightspot considered Wilson's nose, then those of the other members of the landing party. "But you *all* have long noses!" she protested.

"Right," said Wilson, "but I'm the one who asked about your tail!"

Brightspot's tail curled suddenly into a tight helix. She was not the only one—all around them, the Sivaoans coiled their tails like so many corkscrews—and Jim Kirk could not suppress a chuckle.

Wilson gave her a look that was pure admiration. "I'm *impressed*," she said.

Seeing that Wilson referred to her curled tail, Brightspot said, "That's if I'm happy. If I'm angry . . . well." She glared at Fetchstorm. "If I'm a little bit angry, I can do this." She flicked the very tip of her tail. "And if I'm *very* angry, I can do this." Again she glared at Fetchstorm—apparently she needed motivation for her demonstration—and this time her whole tail lashed twice. "How do you do that without a tail?"

"For a little bit angry . . ." Wilson too looked at Fetchstorm; she folded her arms, gave an exaggerated sigh and tapped her foot. "For very angry, I yell. I won't because I don't want to scare any of the youngsters and, besides, it's hard to do when I'm not angry. As he is Vulcan by philosophy, Mr. Spock does neither."

Several of the Sivaoans flicked their ears back, and one or two tails stiffened. The black one said, "You mean he gives no warning?!"

"No," said Wilson with great emphasis, "I mean he does not get angry. Not a little bit, not very, *not at all.*"

"Why not?" Brightspot asked this directly of Spock.

"Anger is illogical and serves no purpose," Spock said.

Brightspot's wide-eyed stare said she'd think about that for a long while. She checked his ears again, to make sure she had the right one.

"I think I envy you that tail, though," Evan Wilson went on, "now that I've seen how useful it is. You can let people know how you feel all the way across the clearing."

"When I want to be nice," Brightspot continued, "I can do this." Her tail snaked forward cautiously and curled itself neatly around Evan's wrist. *Prehensile!* thought Kirk, surprised. He'd never gotten that impression watching Quickfoot—and neither McCoy nor Uhura had mentioned it.

"That *is* nice," said Wilson. "May I touch?"

"Distant Smoke?" said Brightspot to the elegant black one. Distant Smoke pricked his whiskers forward; evidently that was a nod, for Brightspot told Wilson, "Yes."

Evan Wilson stroked the tail tip. "Soft," she said, "Are you all so soft?"

It was Distant Smoke who answered, "The fur coarsens as we grow older. Brightspot is young."

"Old enough to walk!" said Brightspot, sharply and defiantly.

Distant Smoke pushed his way closer and looped his tail about Wilson's arm, just above Brightspot's. "I am Distant Smoke to-Srallansre, Evan Wilson. You may touch," he said.

Wilson did, comparing the two with gentle strokes. "I see what you mean. Brightspot's is softer than yours—but, to my sense of touch, your fur is also extremely soft, Distant Smoke."

Distant Smoke preened. *That's it, Evan,* thought Kirk, *tell him how young he looks for his age. I've seldom seen a world where that's not a compliment.*

Wilson grinned at Brightspot. "My terrible skimpy fur gives me an advantage: I can feel how soft your tail is all over my skin, not just on my palms."

Brightspot said, "Really?"

"Really. You can stop feeling sorry for me. I suspect our various advantages and disadvantages work out about evenly —except maybe the tail. I must admit I see no advantage to not having a tail."

"Maybe," said Distant Smoke, "the advantage is that nobody can pull it."

"You have a point." Wilson chuckled. "Having your tail pulled sounds very unpleasant."

"It *is,*" said Brightspot with vehemence and, as she glared again at Fetchstorm, the tail wrapping Wilson's arm twitched. There was a longstanding grievance if Kirk had ever seen one.

"What do you do when you want to be nice?" The question came from Distant Smoke and seemed partially designed to distract Brightspot.

"I hold hands," said Evan promptly, "or, in this case, tails." She moved the tip of Brightspot's tail gently into her hand and gave a slight squeeze. "The squeeze is not to hurt but to let you know I feel good and I like you. When I feel very good, I hug."

The universal translator garbled that: another not-word in the Sivaoan tongue. "I'll show you," Wilson said, "but you have to let go for a minute. I don't want to pull your tails, not even by accident." She gave each tail a final reassuring brush as the Sivaoans drew away. Neither knew what to expect, and Distant Smoke eased Brightspot just beyond Wilson's reach.

For fear she did not see Distant Smoke's concern, Jim Kirk said, "Dr. Wilson—"

She turned and cocked her head to one side, her eyes bright with mischief. "Hug, Captain?" she said, catching him completely by surprise. "For demonstration purposes, of course."

"Of course," he said and immediately regretted the words. They made it sound as if demonstration could be his only possible motive—and he could think of a dozen better reasons for hugging Evan. He hoped she wouldn't hold a remark made in surprise against him.

Smiling, she put her arms around his waist and squeezed with all her might. His first discovery was that she was even smaller than he had originally thought; his second, that she was shaking. His arms closed around her shoulders purely to comfort—and remained for all those better reasons. After a moment, he became acutely aware of the eyes on them, Sivaoan, human and Vulcan. . . . He released her.

"Thank you, Captain," she said.

"Any time, Dr. Wilson," he replied.

She blushed and turned back to Distant Smoke. "That's a hug," she said. "May I give you a hug, Distant Smoke?"

"Odd," he said. "It does seem affectionate for such a gesture. For us, that would be a fighting position, but you have no claws and no teeth to speak of, so you pose no threat. Yes, please . . ."

Evan Wilson cautiously enfolded his torso and hugged; Distant Smoke kept his arms raised, well away from her body. She tipped her head back but could not make eye contact in that position. "Distant Smoke? Are you all right?"

"Yes," he said, then added hesitantly, "I should like to experiment . . . may I return the 'hug'? I will pledge in Old Tongue to keep my claws sheathed and my teeth from your throat."

"I don't understand your Old Tongue, Distant Smoke, but I'll accept your word. It takes two to make a good hug; I'd be disappointed if you didn't at least try."

Still he hesitated. "You seem very fragile. You will tell me instantly if I am too rough with you. There is no dishonor in that."

"We humans and Vulcans are tougher than we look, but I'll let you know if you're about to break anything."

Distant Smoke very cautiously put his arms around her, enveloping her completely.

"*Bozhe moi,*" said Chekov, in an awed undertone, "if I hedn't seen her playing with Snarl . . ." His voice trailed off.

'*Playing*!' thought Kirk, and his mind added, with almost involuntary humor, '*Bozhe moi*' is right! He could not tear his eyes away. Although his nerves screamed the necessity to do something to protect Wilson, Distant Smoke was good to his word: his claws remained sheathed, his mouth closed.

"That's it," Wilson said, "now squeeze." Kirk could see Wilson's arms tighten again. Distant Smoke squeezed, then instantly relaxed his grip. "Try again," said Wilson, "a little harder." Distant Smoke did, again releasing very quickly.

"Perfect," said Wilson. "Once more, with feeling—and hold on a little bit longer."

This time their arms tightened in unison, and Jim Kirk caught a glimpse of Wilson's face, half concealed in fur. She had the contented smile of a small child who has been given the world's greatest stuffed toy.

They broke away, Evan Wilson chuckling happily. Distant Smoke, in a burst of identical humor, wrapped his tail about her waist. Not only did Kirk's nerves stop their jangle, but he too found himself chuckling. *And that,* he thought, *is one of the reasons I joined Starfleet—to see that kind of sight.*

Something entwined itself around his right wrist. Startled by the strength of the snakelike grip, he looked down. It was Brightspot's tail. "Hello, Brightspot," he said, "I'm Captain Kirk." He stroked the tip of the tail.

Evan Wilson said, "That's what I call a successful experiment."

Distant Smoke pricked his whiskers forward then laid them back—a nod followed by a more serious expression. "Don't experiment with the very young ones, Evan Wilson, or with Brightspot—even if she is old enough to walk."

Brightspot drooped a little, Kirk thought, and he stroked her tail tip again. "Why not?" he asked on the youngster's behalf, and she brightened in his direction.

"Reflexes, Captain," Wilson answered. "I could feel Distant Smoke fighting his own. Brightspot *needs* her reflexes to survive in this society; she can't afford to fight her training or her instincts."

"Distant Smoke can't hug Mr. Spock either," Brightspot said, "Mr. Spock is a Vulcan." She looked up at Kirk for confirmation; he nodded and, in case the gesture was not understood, said, "Yes, that's exactly right, Brightspot." Brightspot looked pleased with herself.

66

Distant Smoke said to Wilson, "You and your pack will eat with us. You are too many to share our tent but the to-Srallansres will help you with your own shelter. . . . Come, Brightspot."

Brightspot gave Kirk's arm an amiable squeeze with her tail and a quick tug before she unlooped it. Jim Kirk grinned at her. "Yes, Brightspot, I'm coming." To the rest of the landing party, he said, "People, we've been invited to lunch. Shall we go?"

Spock, he saw, was staring after Evan Wilson with an expression he normally reserved for complex computations. "Mr. Spock?"

He received no explanation. With a final glance at Wilson, Spock said only, "Coming, Captain."

Chapter Six

"It's been a long time since anyone asked me on a picnic," Kirk said to Spock between bites. The food was good—not just by the standards of Evan Wilson's tricorder—and the excited distractions merely added to the festive atmosphere of the outdoor meal.

At first, it was a toss-up whether the tricorder or Uhura's gold hoop earrings were of most interest to the Sivaoans. At the moment, Wilson's tricorder was the favorite. The principle rubberneckers were Brightspot and a female called Settlesand to-Vensre, whose fur was dark brown shading to cream at chest and belly. They followed Evan Wilson about the camp, elbowing aside half a dozen other Sivaoans for the privilege of peering over Evan's shoulders as she demonstrated her instruments.

"It would seem, Mr. Spock, that your worries were unfounded—about Dr. Wilson's lack of experience in these matters," he added, when Spock raised a brow. "She's managing quite well."

The brow remained aloft. "I would almost say too well, Captain."

Spock at his stubborn best, thought Kirk. He grinned and said, "You can't have it both ways, Mr. Spock . . ."

He left it there, for Wilson and her rubberneckers had returned to the fireside. Brightspot delightedly insisted that Wilson check her readings, *and* Kirk's *and* Spock's.

"Captain," Wilson said, "would it be against regulations for Brightspot to use the tricorder herself?"

"Could I?" said Brightspot excitedly. "I'll be very careful with it. I'll promise in Old Tongue . . . !"

Kirk looked at Spock, who said, "It would be an interesting experiment, Captain. I should like to know if she understands the use of the tricorder."

Kirk said, "Go ahead, Doctor. We've got a lot of leeway on this mission." He smiled at Brightspot and added, "Just make sure she doesn't take it apart." Brightspot flicked her tail, and Kirk said instantly, "I didn't mean to insult you, Brightspot. I was only teasing." He reached for her hand. "I like you, and I have a bad habit of teasing people I like."

She wrapped her tail neatly around his extended hand; its tip came, tickling, into his palm. "It's okay," she said, "I'm not angry. You pull tails but you don't pull hard—just to get attention. I'll know that next time."

Evan Wilson draped the strap across Brightspot's shoulder and placed the tricorder in her hands. Gingerly, Brightspot aimed it first at Kirk, then at Spock. Her whiskers quivered with her concentration. Giving Kirk's wrist a little squeeze with her tail before loosing her hold, she moved off to take readings on the nearby undergrowth. Evan Wilson and the troop of rubberneckers were right behind her.

"I thought she was a child," Kirk said to Spock. "Now I haven't any way of judging their ages."

"Age is not necessarily an indication of intelligence, Captain. We have no way of knowing what is average or expected in this culture. Lieutenant Uhura might be of assistance with her—specialized—knowledge, but we are still dealing with two thousand years of divergence."

On the far side of the cooking fire, Uhura was speaking to Distant Smoke. Kirk beckoned to her. As she rose to join them, Kirk noticed that Jinx, who had been sitting unobtrusively behind the two, also shifted position to follow Uhura. Unlike the others in the camp, Jinx seemed almost as if she dragged her tail behind her. The sight reminded Kirk of another question. "Spock, could they have developed prehensile tails in two thousand years?"

"Unlikely, Captain. That is an extremely short period on

an evolutionary time scale. They might, however, have learned to exploit a prehensile tail in that period of time."

"Or Sunfall's people might have developed some taboo . . ."

"Not exactly a taboo, Captain," Uhura said. She crossed her ankles and sat on the ground near Kirk's small camp stool. "Sunfall considered using her tail"—she frowned slightly, searching for the proper term—"uncivilized. I only learned that her tail was prehensile by accident: I tripped going down a flight of stairs and she caught me with it. I was very surprised."

"I can imagine," said Kirk, remembering his own thoughts the first time Brightspot had wrapped her tail around his wrist.

Uhura went on, "—and Sunfall *apologized,* sir. For having been so vulgar as to use her tail." Uhura smiled suddenly. "It didn't take me long to find out the hard way that babies stick their tails in everything. They were constantly being scolded for it. Forgive me, Captain, but the only analogy I can think of is a small child picking its nose in public."

Kirk smiled back. "That obviously isn't the attitude here."

"Captain," said Spock, calling his attention to the return of Brightspot, Wilson, and the rest. Brightspot, triumphant, carried a tuft of dark, striated leaves. Drawing close, she suddenly stopped and her tail rose like a bar between them.

"Don't touch, Captain Kirk," she said. "You can touch, Mr. Spock—maybe that's the Vulcan part? But humans must not: sweetstripes will make their skin burn."

"She's right, Captain," said Wilson, as pleased as Brightspot, "and she did all the readings. Everybody take a good look, it could save you a lot of trouble later." Brightspot offered the branch to Spock, who accepted it with great interest to make some readings of his own.

Kirk bent to take a closer look and found Brightspot's cautioning tail still interposed between him and the specimen. Amused, he said, "Trust me not to pull it, Brightspot?"

She looked startled; then her ears peaked again and she said, "Oh—you just did!" Her parti-colored tail looped in amusement but she did not remove it from his reach.

When she was at last satisfied that she had alerted all the humans to the danger, Brightspot carefully disposed of the leaves. Then she was off again, to see what other wonders she could find with the tricorder. Evan Wilson smiled at Kirk and followed.

"Captain," said Uhura, keeping her voice low, "have you seen the . . . temple, sir?" She made a small gesture and he and Spock turned to look across the clearing.

Even with her quiet directions, it was a moment before he saw it. Hidden in the forest beyond the edge of the clearing, a low building laced through the ancient trees. It blended so beautifully with its surroundings that Kirk knew instantly the design of the architect had been not camouflage but harmony.

"Fascinating," said Spock. "It is clearly a permanent structure."

"Extremely fascinating," Kirk agreed. "Why would a people of such obvious sophistication choose to live in tents when they can build something as beautiful as that? Do you suppose we've stumbled on an outdoor festival of some sort, Mr. Spock?"

"That is an unlikely explanation, Captain. If you will recall, my orbital readings showed no indication of cities. I believe what we are seeing is characteristic of this culture."

"The tents are just as beautiful, Keptain," Chekov put in. "Hev you looked et them closely, sair? Each one is a work of art."

"Mr. Chekov is right, Captain. The tents show as much design sophistication as that structure." Spock indicated the low building.

Kirk shook his head in puzzlement. "You called it a temple, Uhura?"

"Only because I don't know what else to call it, sir," Uhura said.

As Kirk contemplated the structure, Winding Path emerged from within, accompanied by a female Sivaoan who was marked like a jester, half-orange, half-black. Deep in conversation, the two walked toward the clearing.

Distant Smoke rose, stepped to Uhura's side and said, "That's Stiff Tail to-Srallansre."

This was the Sivaoan to whom Winding Path had referred them. Kirk rose and gestured the rest of them up. Perhaps Stiff Tail was the leader in this community. "Heads up, people," he said. "Now maybe we can get some answers." He raised a hand to wave Wilson back, but Brightspot wrapped her tail around the doctor's wrist and tugged her straight to Stiff Tail to show her off.

Brightspot's tail still twined about her wrist, Evan Wilson displayed her claws to Stiff Tail. Stiff Tail returned the greeting and Brightspot, chattering excitedly, released her hold on Wilson to coil her tail about Stiff Tail's waist. Fetchstorm, Brightspot's nemesis, also joined them. Kirk could see the family resemblance. *A little sibling rivalry there?* he thought.

Stiff Tail was putting Evan Wilson once more through the poke-and-prod-and-tug routine when, without warning, Fetchstorm reached around Stiff Tail, grabbed the end of Brightspot's tail and yanked hard.

Hissing, Brightspot leapt free; her tail lashed furiously. With great care, she removed the tricorder from her shoulder and handed it to Evan Wilson, then—before Kirk even had time for exclamation—Brightspot sprang at Fetchstorm and knocked him to the ground.

Over and over they rolled, thrashing wildly. Stiff Tail drew Wilson out of the range of their flailing claws but, aside from that, she and the other Sivaoans stood calmly by and watched.

Kirk watched too, not nearly so calmly. He was getting a rapid education in just what Wilson had risked when she stepped into Distant Smoke's embrace. Although Fetchstorm and Brightspot ran through every other fighting position they knew, belly-to-belly was clearly the one they preferred. Foreclaws sunk into each other's back and teeth bared at each other's throat, they pounded each other in the belly with rapid-fire, pistonlike kicks—and Kirk could see that their hind claws were out and ripping. Fur flew.

Beside him, Spock said, "Their style of combat bears many similarities to that of Snnanagfashtalli." Uhura had her hand to her mouth.

As the fight rolled closer, there was a sudden squawk from

one of the antagonists—it was impossible to guess from which. Stiff Tail moved so quickly Kirk almost missed it. Stepping into the middle of the fight, she said, "Enough!" and slapped them each soundly across the side of the head.

They stopped. For a long moment they both lay there blinking up at her, then they rose to their feet, tails still lashing angrily. They shook themselves off and, with one last glower, retired to opposite sides of Stiff Tail.

The next thing Kirk knew, Brightspot was once again telling the adult everything she knew about humans and Vulcans and tricorders and tails and head fur. It was as if nothing had happened. "Kids will be kids?" he ventured.

"I believe so, Captain," said Spock. "The attitude of the others would suggest little need for concern."

"Mr. Spock!" Uhura said, "Surely you can't think that was only two children fighting over a pulled tail!"

"I think 'spat' would be a good description, Lieutenant," Kirk said, laughing his relief, "and Mr. Spock's Vulcan childhood would seem equally violent to many of us."

"I'm gled I'm not a kid," said Chekov fervently, "here, or on Wulcan."

Brightspot was explaining the tricorder at great length and in remarkable detail, but she stopped in mid-sentence as the group reached Kirk and the others. "It is polite to make introductions," she announced and did so with all the formality of a diplomatic envoy. Diplomacy broke down only when she deliberately omitted her antagonist. He hissed at her; and Stiff Tail said, without fuss, "This is Fetchstorm to-Srallansre."

To Uhura, Stiff Tail said, "I seem to have missed all the excitement. And dinner. Will it offend your customs if I eat while you are not?"

Uhura shook her head. "No," said Kirk, "of course not."

"There is very little 'of course' when it comes to custom, Captain Kirk." Her whiskers seemed to quiver amusement, but she sat down and took up a bowl of stew that Distant Smoke offered.

Again addressing herself to Uhura, Stiff Tail said, "Where are your children?"

The question clearly took Uhura by surprise but she said only, "I don't have any—yet."

That seemed to satisfy Stiff Tail. She curled her tail affectionately around Distant Smoke, who sat down shoulder to shoulder with her, and she began to eat. After a moment or so, she looked at Uhura. Uhura made a slight deferential motion in Kirk's direction, so it was to him Stiff Tail said, "You have shared our food. Will you share your news? It is our custom."

"Ours are very similar," said Kirk.

Stiff Tail said, "Then will you tell us of your trail?"

"Yes," he said. This was exactly the kind of opening he'd been hoping for. He gave her a brief discourse on the United Federation of Planets and of the job the *Enterprise* normally performed.

When he finished, she nodded. Not only did she accept the concepts of other worlds and of starflight but she had already learned to use the human gesture of assent appropriately!

Encouraged, Kirk went on, "We came to ask your help for the people of Eeiauo—your distant relatives. They are dying of a disease for which you may have the cure."

He got no further. Stiff Tail rose to her full height, the fur about the back of her neck bristled, the tip of her tail twitched in suppressed anger. "Enough!" she said.

The single word sent a small child scrambling hastily away to vanish into a nearby tent; Brightspot, Jinx, and Fetchstorm shrank a few steps back, as if to present as little target as possible.

"Stupid!" said Winding Path to-Srallansre. His tail lashing wildly, he rounded on Kirk and dropped into a menacing crouch.

Kirk tensed; he did not wish to complicate the issue by drawing his phaser, but he had seen the children fight and knew he would be no match for a full-grown adult. He waited, nerves crawling.

Stiff Tail solved his dilemma by matter-of-factly slapping Winding Path across the side of the head. Winding Path rocked with the blow. "That will be enough from you too, Winding Path," said Stiff Tail, and he too shrank and drew away, muttering apologies.

The slap seemed to have relieved much of Stiff Tail's anger. Except for a small ridge along her spine, most of her fur was smoothed down. Still, she stared balefully at Kirk and said, "There is very little 'of course' when it comes to custom, Captain Kirk. This is custom: You will not speak of this again."

Kirk took a deep breath and said, "I must, Stiff Tail— Eeiauoans and humans are dying."

He saw her hand come up, tried to duck the blow . . . Through a terrible clangor of bells, he heard Uhura exclaim, "Captain!"—and then there was nothing.

Jim Kirk came to with an ache in his head the like of which he hadn't felt since an exuberant shore leave with Scott and McCoy. He struggled to sit up and clear his vision but something small and strong pushed him down again. "Lie still, Captain, and give me a chance to do my job," Evan Wilson said. As her face came into focus, she smiled and added, "Or I'll let Catchclaw do it for me." She gave a brief nod to one side.

From the corner of his eye, Kirk could see Jinx standing a short distance away. Beside her was a second, taller Sivaoan, brown shading to cream and, at first glance, identical in every way to Settlesand to-Vensre. Then he realized this Sivaoan was a nursing mother: she had breasts.

Catchclaw flicked her tail impatiently, and Wilson said, "I practically had to fight her off. She's the local doctor." Wilson peered into his eyes, rotated his head and peered into his ears, and said, "The medical sensors say you're fine, Captain. I prefer to make my own assessment as well . . . How many fingers do you see?"

"Two," he grunted.

"Terrific," she said, "no concussion—you're a lucky man. How do you *feel?*"

"Like the fourth day of a three-day pass."

She chuckled. "You'll get over it. I want you to lie there and take it easy for a while."

That seemed a good idea to Kirk. He looked around, trying not to move his aching head. He was inside one of the tents and he had not been unconscious for long: sunlight streamed through brightly colored designs as if they were stained glass. Wilson knelt beside him. Catchclaw glared at her and she glared back.

"In case you're interested, Stiff Tail pulled her slap. She's very apologetic—this is her tent—and assures Uhura it won't happen again."

"I'm very glad to hear that," said Kirk wryly. His head still throbbed.

Wilson grinned at him. "I thought you'd be. The bad news is that she *means* that we're not to speak of the Eeiauoans." He started and she said hastily, "Don't worry, the translator's off . . . If we do, we get thrown out of the camp."

Kirk groaned; she gave him a piercing look and said, "Is that a physical complaint or a psychological one?"

"Ninety-nine percent psychological," he said; and to Spock, who had entered just in time to hear his groan, he added, "I'm fine, Spock."

"I am most gratified to hear that, Captain. The doctor refused to have you beamed aboard the *Enterprise*."

Evan Wilson shrugged. "He was in no danger, Mr. Spock, and you yourself suggested we avoid magical effects around the natives."

"Very true, Doctor. I commend your logic."

"I'm sorry to disappoint you, Mr. Spock. There was no logic involved; it was a gut reaction. . . . I've told the captain about Stiff Tail's edict. May I make a suggestion? I think we should stay the night, or the week if necessary. In camp, I mean, not beaming back to the *Enterprise* and our comfortable bunks."

Kirk nodded; this time his head didn't ache so much. "I agree, Evan. There must be some way to reach these people, but we've got to know more about them to do it. Mr. Spock, your opinion?"

"As your medical condition is satisfactory, I would advise the same. Further study is indicated, and I see no logical alternative."

"All right, then, notify Mr. Scott. And, Spock—this is voluntary. Not everyone is quite as prepared to rough it as we are."

"I shall see to it, Captain. Dr. Wilson?"

76

"Count me in, Mr. Spock. I have an invitation to join Brightspot in her swagger-lair for the night, pending Stiff Tail's approval, and I'd hate like hell to miss that."

Kirk said, "Swagger-lair?"

"Something like a cross between a tree house and a hammock. From what Brightspot tells me, it sounds like a clever way to get your adolescent out of your tent. . . . Don't worry, you'll get a good look later."

Kirk closed his eyes briefly. The throb in his head was beginning to ease. When he reopened his eyes, Evan Wilson was watching him. He smiled and said, "Tree house, Dr. Wilson? Why, I believe you made your suggestion purely out of self-interest. What do you think, Spock?"

"I have no idea, Captain, but may I point out that Dr. Wilson's 'gut reaction' bears a remarkable resemblance to well-considered logic? Perhaps her expressed desire to spend the night in a tree falls into the same category."

"Perhaps it does, Mr. Spock," said Kirk. He looked at Evan Wilson for her reaction, expecting to find that wicked grin. He was disappointed only as long as it took him to catch on. Evan Wilson deadpanned at Spock, raised a single eyebrow, and said, "A fascinating theory, Mr. Spock, but one based on very little data."

Spock's brow shot up as if in conspiracy. "Indeed, Dr. Wilson . . . I shall, of course, continue to my observations. With your permission, Captain?"

Kirk said, stunned, "Dismissed." He was still looking at Wilson—and suddenly *there* was that wicked grin.

She glanced to see that Spock had gone and, still grinning, said, "I think I just got my tail pulled." She shook her head, and the grin was gone, replaced by a more serious mien. "Captain, with your permission, I'd like to let Catchclaw to-Ennien look you over. I'm sure she thinks I'm committing malpractice all over the place."

"And you'd like me to save your reputation," Kirk suggested.

"A little more than that. If she looks you over, I can look her over. Sivaoan or not, she's a colleague. And colleagues are sometimes able to discuss things that might ordinarily be left undiscussed. If nothing else, it's professional courtesy."

Kirk understood; it was a very good idea. "I'll vouch for your medical skills, Doctor, and more."

She gave him a look of deep concern and said, "You do realize—I can't guarantee—"

"None of us can, Evan. Do your best."

"All right," she said, and she seemed relieved. "I warn you, Catchclaw will probably want to take you apart to see what makes you tick. I understand these urges; Mr. Spock hits me the same way, and so does Catchclaw. Out of loyalty to my captain, however, I'll stick around and see that she doesn't."

"I would appreciate it, Dr. Wilson," Kirk said, returning her smile. "For all I know, she may be a witch doctor."

"Take care, Captain. Some of my best friends are witch doctors—and I'd be happy to know the local equivalents for digitalis, penicillin, and acupuncture. I never argue with a technique that works just because it wasn't arrived at by scientific method."

"You're right," he said. "Let's hope she knows the proper spells against ADF syndrome."

Uhura, Chekov, and Brightspot waited in a small anxious knot a few yards from Stiff Tail's tent.

"The captain is uninjured," Spock said. He waited out the small storm of emotion his statement produced, then went on, "In order that we may gain the necessary data with which to act, the captain feels it imperative that we remain in camp for an indefinite amount of time. Those wishing to return to the *Enterprise* will, however, be permitted to do so . . ."

Lieutenant Uhura said, very softly, "I'd like to stay, Mr. Spock, if it's all right with you."

"Your presence would be greatly appreciated, Lieutenant. Your knowledge of the Old Tongue may be of considerable use." In the presence of Brightspot, Spock did not allude to her knowledge of the Eeiauoans.

"I'll stey, too, sair."

"Thank you, Mr. Chekov. If you will excuse us, Brightspot, we have preparations to make."

"I'll help," said Brightspot. Her eagerness made him hesitate to send her away, but he needed privacy to contact the *Enterprise* and have the necessary equipment beamed down.

Chekov said, "Mr. Spock? I tek it the keptain wants us to live like these people?"

"For the time being—yes, Mr. Chekov."

"Then perhaps we should build our own shelter, not use one menufactured by supply."

Spock raised an eyebrow. "Your suggestion is a good one, Mr. Chekov. However, we have no materials with which to do so."

"Thet is no problem, sair. Let me take the tricorder and Brightspot"—Brightspot curled her tail approvingly around his wrist and Chekov grinned at her—"and we'll find meterials." He pointed, still entangled, in the general direction of the forest.

"Permission granted, Mr. Chekov. I shall assist you; I should very much like to see what you intend to do." Spock glanced at Uhura. "Lieutenant Uhura will remain here to establish further rapport with the Sivaoans."

For the next fifteen minutes or so, Chekov described to Brightspot the types of plants he had in mind. Shortly thereafter, Brightspot called to Distant Smoke, Settlesand, and a female Sivaoan named Left Ear; and Chekov repeated his descriptions with Brightspot adding occasional comment.

"Oh," said Settlesand, "maybe you mean lash-reed and giant's ear?"

"I don't hev the slightest idea," Chekov confessed. "Mr. Spock?"

"I am no more familiar with the local flora than you, Mr. Chekov; nor have I more understanding of your requirements than Brightspot." He turned to Settlesand. "Perhaps if Mr. Chekov were to see a specimen of each—"

"That sounds easiest," said Settlesand, her whiskers arched forward. "Come." She led the way into the forest.

High in the trees, welcome-homes set up a clamor and, without warning, Brightspot began to jump up and down, waving her arms and tail. "Fuzz-brain!" she shouted, "Yah! Fuzz-brain!"

Her attention, Spock saw, was directed up at one of the small shrieking creatures. Her actions were a passable imitation of its own, and they sent the creature into a renewed frenzy. It tore a branch from the tree to emphasize its threats and, when it shook the branch at Brightspot, it showered small hard objects on them all.

Brightspot immediately lost interest in the welcome-home and gathered up the objects.

"Tail-kinkers," Settlesand told Spock, "a spice we use for our food. Some people like to chew on them." Brightspot and Chekov subjected them to the scrutiny of Chekov's tricorder and shortly pronounced them safe for both human and Vulcan.

Spock accepted one and examined it thoughtfully. It was about the size of a ball bearing, almost as hard, and a dark shiny green in color. Spock recalled the human proverb— "When in Rome . . ."—and cautiously tasted it. To his surprise, it had a very sharp but distinctly pleasant flavor.

Chekov, taking his cue from Spock, also put one in his mouth. He bit down—and gasped. *"Bozhe moi!"* he said, hardly able to get the words out. His eyes streamed tears.

Spock had never seen a toxin take effect so quickly, nor one that did not register on the tricorder. "Dr. Wilson!" he said and turned to race back to the camp for medical assistance.

"Mr. Spock, no!" Chekov spoke between gulps of air. "It's not—necessary, sair. *Hhhot!"* He aspirated the *h* with great passion. "Spicy hot! I just—wasn't—prepared!" He wiped at his eyes and took a few more gulps of air.

Spock watched him warily. He knew the human sense of taste was more sensitive than his own but he had never before seen such a graphic demonstration of the phenomenon.

Chekov saw his concern. He wiped his eyes again, drew himself together and said, "I heven't been poisoned, Mr. Spock. I hev eaten peppers hotter then this. I hev no need of a doctor." He sniffed loudly and said to Brightspot with a rueful grin, "You should hev warned me."

"I'm sorry." This was from Left Ear. "I didn't think it would have so strong an effect. The children often hide whole tail-kinkers in each other's food for the joke—and Brightspot really does chew them all the time."

" 'Tail-kinkers,' " said Chekov. "Well, if I hed a tail, it would hev a kink by now!"

"Not angry?" said Brightspot. Her tail bristled with concern.

Chekov shook his head. "Not angry. This is not the only world where I hev hed such a joke played on me."

Brightspot seemed relieved.

Spock knew *he* was. "It would appear," he said, "that the Sivaoan and human concepts of humor are similar in nature. I doubt that I shall ever grasp either. However, if you are quite recovered, Mr. Chekov, let us proceed."

Captain James T. Kirk was beginning to develop a great sympathy for guinea pigs, and he was forced to remind himself that for once the guinea pig was learning as much as the doctor.

Catchclaw had begun by examining him with her own instruments. More than anything he'd seen so far, those instruments told him there was nothing primitive about this society. Functionally, they seemed identical to the Federation-designed tricorder and sensors that Bones used; but there was nothing functional about their design—nothing *purely* functional about their design, he corrected himself. As much effort had been expended to make them beautiful as to make them useful.

Catchclaw turned her instruments on Evan Wilson for comparison; Jinx watched in silence but did not miss a thing. Evan offered her the use of her own sensors; Catchclaw accepted and, again, compared Wilson to him.

Like Wilson, however, Catchclaw seemed unsatisfied to trust the instruments—hers or Federation-issue. Having asked Kirk's permission to touch him, she ran through the same set of manual tests that Wilson had so recently performed on him. Clearly, the indications for concussion were very similar between human and Sivaoan.

"No tail," said Catchclaw to Jinx. It was a complaint; in fact, her manner reminded Kirk very much of Bones's usual reaction to Vulcan physiology. Catchclaw glared at Evan Wilson and said, "Where the"—the universal translator failed miserably, producing a McCoy-like sputter—"do I find his pulse?"

Wilson pushed back her sleeve and demonstrated. After a

moment, Catchclaw verified that she could find Kirk's pulse as well. Then she sat back and grunted, her tail twitching. "You seem fine, but what do I know?"

"He is fine," said Wilson, "and I *do* know."

Catchclaw grunted at her again and began to thrust her instruments back into her belt. "In any case, the blow did knock him unconscious. I recommend rest and continued observation."

In the interest of Wilson's reputation, Kirk said, "Yes, that's exactly what Dr. Wilson recommended."

Catchclaw rose. Staring down at Wilson, she repeated, "Doctor . . . Where are your children?"

Wilson said, "Human females develop breasts at puberty and keep them even when they're not nursing children. One child at a time being the usual, only two breasts at that." She gave a slight nod of acknowledgment at Catchclaw's own eight, and Catchclaw's tail spiraled her amusement.

"I see," Catchclaw said. "Jinx, you'll stay here. Call me if there's any change." At the tent flap, she gave one last look at Kirk, at Wilson; her tail flicked once, then she made a kind of chuffing sound and said with unmistakable exasperation, "Stiff Tail!"

Evan Wilson sighed—a long, drawn-out sigh of disappointment—then she turned to Jinx to-Ennien and said, "Well. And just where would I find your pulse?"

With any luck, thought Kirk, *they'll be so busy prodding each other they won't have time for me!*

Lieutenant Uhura had no idea how to carry out Mr. Spock's order to establish further rapport with the Sivaoans. *To come all this way and not be able to get help!* she thought. To find the world had been a miracle itself, but it was not miracle enough and she knew it. She sat on a small camp stool near the cooking fire, watching the Sivaoans as they went about the everyday business of living, and thought of Sunfall of Ennien, dying. *Surely these people could not deny her help, surely they couldn't be so cruel!*

Without conscious thought, she reached into her utility pouch and withdrew the Charellian *joyeuse*. In a way, it was Mr. Spock's doing that she had brought it—and Sunfall's picture. Readying herself for the landing party, she had deliberately chosen these nonregulation items for luck, because it was something Mr. Spock couldn't do. Perhaps even the captain couldn't have—but she could and she did. Mr. Spock would certainly have raised an eyebrow at that, but she knew in his own way he would approve.

Almost of themselves, her fingers began to pick out a tune on the *joyeuse*, a song she'd learned from one of the children at the Eeiauoan embassy on Two Dawns. She had asked the child to teach it to her; and the child, in turn, had introduced her to Sunfall.

For luck, Sunfall. For luck Christine, she thought and began to sing.

Chapter Seven

After some two hours flat on his back with nothing to do but watch Evan Wilson and Jinx to-Ennien poke and prod one another, Jim Kirk was getting restless. Now the two of them stood at the tent flap to see what all the commotion was—and that was entirely too much for him.

As if she sensed this, Wilson turned and said, "Captain, I think I'll release you from observation." She gestured out. "*They* need more observation than you do!" Jinx stared at him for a moment and then arched her whiskers forward. He took this to mean she released him as well, and he got to his feet and joined them at the opening.

Across the clearing, his crew had once again attracted a crowd. Wilson stepped through the opening and rose on tiptoe, as if the extra inch and a half would give her a clear view. "I suggest we take a closer look," Kirk said. "Even *I* can't see over those ears."

Together they made for the crowd and eased their way through. Uhura sat on a camp stool, her *joyeuse* in her lap, singing an old Earth tune. She was surrounded by Sivaoans of all ages, sizes, and markings who were joining in on the chorus. Kirk had never heard anything like it in his life; what the Sivaoans lacked in pronunciation, they made up in enthusiasm. Punctuating this joyous cacophony were bellowed instructions from Chekov, who seemed to have become boss of a construction gang that included Spock and another handful of Sivaoans, equally assorted.

Chekov appeared to be supervising the construction of an upside-down openweave basket; it was made of long saplings thrust into the ground, bent over, and interlaced, and it was huge. Kirk said to Evan Wilson, "Are you sure I'm all right?"

"You are if I am," she said with a chuckle.

"Keptain!" Chekov came bounding over, as full of enthusiasm as his workers. "Gled to see you! How are you, sair?"

"I'm fine, Mr. Chekov. . . . What is this thing?"

Spock said, "Mr. Chekov is constructing a shelter, Captain."

"Fine, Mr. Spock," said Kirk, still somewhat bemused. "As you were, Mr. Chekov. Don't let me interrupt."

"Yes, sair!" Chekov saluted and bounded back to a pile of saplings. He chose six more and picked up a large rock.

Uhura had finished her song. Chekov shouted across to her, "Lieutenant, pley something for heavy pounding." Uhura thought for a moment, then struck up a new tune and began to sing. Chekov, if it was possible, brightened further. "Pairfect!" he called. Kirk knew he'd heard the tune but did not place it until he realized that Pavel Chekov was caroling at the top of his lungs in Russian . . . "The Song of the Volga Boatmen."

The Sivaoans took up the chorus the second time it came around and before the song ended, Chekov had his saplings driven into the ground in two parallel rows coming from one side of the latticework structure. He deftly wove their tops together to create a long, narrow entranceway.

Then he called for an armload of leaves. These he somehow laced over the framework of saplings. His crew caught on to the technique as quickly as they caught on to song choruses, and a waterproof covering began to crawl up the sides of the structure to the highest point Chekov could reach. Some of the Sivaoans could reach higher but seemed unwilling to——perhaps they didn't wish to outdo Chekov, or perhaps they simply thought that was the right way. *Maybe it is!* Kirk thought suddenly. He'd never seen one of these shelters built; why should he assume they had?

Brightspot brought a second armload of leaves and said to Spock, "Do Vulcans have songs, too?" *Oh, god,* thought Kirk, *here's where we get expelled from camp.* He had heard Spock sing once, and once was enough.

"Yes, Brightspot, we do," said Spock. "I regret, however, that I did not bring my harp."

"Mr. Spock," said Uhura, "I know a few Vulcan songs, if you'll forgive my accent. I don't understand Vulcan, so I sing them by rote."

Spock considered her thoughtfully. "By all means, Lieutenant."

"Please forgive my accent," she said again, shyly. She concentrated a moment on the *joyeuse,* tuning it to Vulcan mode, then she played a long, sweet introductory passage and began to sing.

When she finished, there was silence. She looked again at Spock, more shyly than before, and opened her mouth to say something. Spock anticipated her: "You have no need to apologize, Lieutenant. If you are concerned about your accent, I shall be most happy to help you perfect it—but your singing cannot be improved upon."

"How about that?" Kirk muttered—not quite to himself, for Evan Wilson cast him a questioning glance. He explained very softly, "I always thought Vulcan songs were unbearable to human ears."

Just as quietly, she said, "You mean, it's not Vulcan songs but a certain Vulcan's voice?" When he nodded, she said, "Well, Kagan's Law . . ." It was his turn to question. "Kagan's Law of First Contact," she quoted, " 'You'll surprise you more than they will.' "

Kirk nodded. Chekov was certainly proving the truth of that. Having just finished weaving a circular construction of the large leaves, he enlisted the aid of Brightspot and two of the larger Sivaoans. Chekov and Brightspot were hoisted aloft, and together—with an enormous *flap!*—they dropped the "roof" into position. A cheer went up from the crowd as the large Sivaoans lowered the two of them back to earth.

"There, Keptain," said Chekov, reporting with a salute. "A shelter."

"I see that, Mr. Chekov. Where on Earth did you learn that?"

"Volgograd, sair. Et school."

"What kind of courses do they teach in Volgograd?" Kirk allowed himself to be led inside the structure. He was fascinated; apparently, it was all held together by interweaving . . . no string, no bailing wire. Kirk couldn't imagine a high school course on primitive shelters.

"Enthropology, sair. Hends-on. Wery good professor. She said if we hed to do it, we would learn that primitive does not mean stupid."

"She was right, Mr. Chekov. I'm impressed."

"Thank you, sair." Chekov managed to look proud and bashful at the same time.

Spock, too, seemed impressed. He was intent on examining every inch of the structure and recording its details on his tricorder. Evan Wilson grinned at Chekov and said, "Mr. Chekov, you must teach me how to do that!"

"Of course, sair," he said, flushing with pleasure.

Uhura ducked gracefully through the entranceway. "Captain, the Sivaoans would like to see the inside."

"Of course, Lieutenant. Bring them in—in small groups." While there seemed ample room for the landing party, Kirk did not know exactly how many Sivaoans she meant. He added, "Mr. Chekov will give them a guided tour." Again to Chekov, he said, "Good work, Mr. Chekov."

He gestured to Spock and Wilson to follow him outside. As they stepped to one side to allow a trio of Sivaoans entrance, Kirk found himself face-to-face with Stiff Tail to-Srallansre.

She looked him up and down. Then her tail spiraled. "I apologize Captain Kirk," she said. "I had no idea human heads were so soft. It did occur to me as I struck, but I did not ease off *enough*. Catchclaw has informed the others, so it should not happen again."

"I appreciate it, Stiff Tail."

There was an awkward silence. Stiff Tail examined the leafy covering of Chekov's shelter, prodding it absently with her tail. At last, she said, "We have much to learn from each other. Come, I have finished my work. We will sit and talk, and I will remember that you have soft heads."

"After you," Kirk gestured. To Spock, he added the rueful aside, "And I always thought I was hardheaded."

"Indeed, Captain. So Dr. McCoy has always led me to believe."

When Kirk and Spock rejoined the rest of the landing party, they found the interior of Chekov's shelter lit by a small fire. A cooking pot, tended by Chekov, bubbled cheerfully over it on a tripod of green twigs. Smoke rose through the open hole in the leaf roof.

Brightly colored mats, rugs and camp stools added to the festive air; heads lifted eagerly to greet him. Jim Kirk had no wish to disappoint them but he had nothing encouraging to say. He gave a quick negative shake of his head.

"No use talking about it on an empty stomach, then," Wilson said. "Eat first. Pavel makes a mean stew, Captain. Vegetarian, Mr. Spock; you need not worry—but watch out for the tail-kinkers."

"Tail-kinkers?" said Kirk.

"A form of local humor, I believe," Spock said. "I shall be interested to see if the captain also finds it amusing."

Evan Wilson cocked her head at Spock and, while Chekov ladled stew into ornate bowls and handed one to each, she said, "It might interest you to know, Mr. Spock, that Jinx tells me they're also a fairly potent stimulant—to a Sivaoan."

Whatever a tail-kinker was, it smelled good, and Kirk realized how hungry he was. The stew, though very spicy, tasted as good as it smelled; he gave it the attention it deserved. He had only taken a few mouthfuls when he bit into something round and hard; the resulting burst of spice very nearly brought tears to his eyes. " 'Mean' is right!" he said, gasping. "Your stew bites back, Mr. Chekov."

"Yes, sair," said Chekov. He took it as a compliment, as Kirk had intended it.

Wilson passed him a chunk of bread and grinned, "Doctor's prescription. Water only spreads the fire." The bread did seem to help.

"A fairly potent stimulant to a human, too!" he told her, between bites.

At last he laid his empty bowl aside and stared into the fire.

When he looked up, he found them all waiting for him to speak. "There's not much to tell," he admitted, "Mr. Spock and I had hoped that Stiff Tail would be willing to speak about the Eeiauoans in private. Stiff Tail was willing to talk about everything *but*."

"Oh, Captain!" Uhura said. The terrible disappointment in her voice instantly sharpened his resolve.

"We have to keep trying, Uhura," he said. "We'll find a way to get the information we need, I promise you! We're *not* giving up."

"Captain," said Spock, "may I respectfully point out that these people are of the same species as the Eeiauoans—"

Kirk interrupted, more harshly than he intended, "I know that, Mr. Spock, that's why we're here."

Unperturbed, Spock continued, "—The Eeiauoans refused to speak of their homeworld despite the extreme urgency of their own situation."

Kirk suddenly caught his point. "You mean these people might be as suicidally stubborn as the Eeiauoans?"

"Exactly, Captain. Perhaps more so, as *they* do not have an urgent motive for action."

"I'm stubborn, too, Mr. Spock."

"Indeed, Captain." Spock inclined his head, almost as if in tribute.

"Captain?" Evan Wilson said. "Stubbornness, as you so aptly point out, is a function of individual personality—and not just in humans. All we have to do is find the least stubborn person in camp"—she grinned impishly—"and lock him in a small room with you!"

Chekov coughed and turned his head discreetly to one side.

"I'm not sure I appreciate the way you put that, Dr. Wilson," he said, although he did for the smile he saw Uhura trying her best to suppress. "But, yes, that's all we have to do." He turned to Spock, his own enthusiasm renewed, and said, "If Stiff Tail won't talk about the Eeiauoans, let's find someone who will."

"Such a plan does entail a certain amount of risk, Captain."

"But it's worth a try, Mr. Spock. We'll mingle with the Sivaoans, get to know them, share information. Use your own

89

judgment, people, but if you find a way to mention the Eeiauoans without getting your head knocked off, do it! If someone drops a hint, however slight, that he's willing to speak on the subject, I want to hear about it immediately. . . . Swap songs with them, Uhura. Even a song might tell us something. . . . We've learned that much already. Don't miss anything, however subtle. There are a lot of people counting on us."

"Yes, sir," said Uhura, and this time there was eagerness in her voice.

Something nudged Jim Kirk gently in the small of the back. He spun defensively. The tip of a tail protruded some six inches into the shelter; it poked him a second time, just below the rib cage. He recognized the markings and relaxed. "Not easy to knock on a tent, is it?" he said with a laugh. "Come in, Brightspot."

The tail tip disappeared as Brightspot doubled smoothly around to enter head first. "This long doorway makes it hard to be polite, Mr. Chekov," she said.

"I shell mek the entrance shorter," said Chekov. "I did not know your custom."

She sniffed the air and her tail spiraled. "You cooked with tail-kinkers!" she said, apparently pleased by the discovery.

Chekov nodded and, with an angelic expression, added, "Keptain Kirk was somewhat unprepared. . . ."

Brightspot's tail coiled tighter. "I'm sorry I missed it. Mr. Chekov pulled your tail the way you pulled mine, Captain Kirk." She brushed Jim Kirk's cheek affectionately with her tail. It tickled, and Kirk snatched for it as he'd have snatched to stop tickling fingers.

She flicked it away. "Oh, no!" she said, though her tail still curled happily.

Kirk chuckled in spite of himself. "I had no intention of pulling it, Brightspot. I may tease, but I don't think I could actually bring myself to yank your tail. I never got into the habit." She was quick to see the truth of this and her tail snaked back into reach. He caught and stroked it.

This settled, Brightspot stared across the fire at Uhura. "I have a message for you," she said. "Rushlight to-Vensre invites you to stay with him while you're in camp. He would offer to trade songs, but he does not know your customs, and he would be content with your company."

"Brightspot," said Uhura, "I don't know your customs, either. What would you do in my place?"

"I'd trade! Rushlight makes wonderful songs! Distant Smoke hopes—well, I shouldn't tell you this, but Distant Smoke says he's never seen Rushlight so impressed— Rushlight might make you his inheritor." The prospect clearly excited Brightspot and, when Uhura said nothing, Brightspot said, "Rushlight hasn't chosen one. If he died, all his songs would be lost, and that would be terrible!"

Uhura said, carefully, "Brightspot, I don't understand. Wait—let me explain how it is among my people. I may speak of taboo subjects; I want you to know that if I do it is from ignorance only."

Brightspot arched her whiskers forward, but Kirk felt her tail tip quiver.

Uhura went on, "Among our people, anyone may sing a song. If Mr. Chekov teaches me a song, I am free to sing it where and when I please."

The quiver in the tail tip was stronger now, threatening to become a flick of anger. Kirk tried to soothe it.

"And if Mr. Chekov created the song?" Brightspot demanded.

"*I* would ask his permission before I sang it to others," Uhura said, "but many of our people would not, and Mr. Chekov would be neither surprised nor angry."

In a much softer voice, she added, "If a song is not sung, it dies, Brightspot. Many of the songs I love most survived because just one person heard and remembered—and passed them on. This is *our* custom. Yours must be very different. Please tell me about it. . . . I have no wish to cause harm through my ignorance."

The ridge of fur that had risen around Brightspot's neck slowly began to subside. Kirk could feel her tail relax as well, and at last she gave a long sigh and said, "No one—*no one*—but Rushlight would sing one of his songs without his permission! He's given a great many of them away— Fetchstorm says those he's tired of—but if he gave them all away, what would he have to trade?"

"Did I 'give away' the songs I sang, Brightspot?" Uhura asked, still puzzled. "Everyone sang the choruses with me."

Brightspot bristled again. "We wouldn't steal from you, Lieutenant Uhura!"

"Please, Brightspot," Kirk interjected, "Uhura had no intention of insulting you or anyone else. I had the same question myself—do you mean it's all right to sing the choruses as long as the song is sung by someone who has permission?"

"Yes, that's so," said Brightspot, calming herself again. "No one would sing the choruses without you, Lieutenant Uhura."

"So if I were to teach a song to Rushlight, he wouldn't sing it without my permission," Uhura said. She considered this for a moment, then she asked, "Do you mean *not sing it* or do you mean not sing it in public?"

It was Brightspot's turn to be thoughtful. "Not sing it in public, I know," she said, "but what bards do among themselves, you'd have to ask Rushlight."

Kirk could foresee further trouble. "Brightspot," he said, "we need your advice. If Lieutenant Uhura accepts Rushlight's invitation, she'll feel obligated to tell him of our custom. You were very angry. How angry will Rushlight be?"

"Catchclaw says you all have soft heads and nobody's to cuff you."

Kirk smiled. "Even with the best of intentions, Brightspot . . . even *I* have been known to lose my temper. Mr. Spock is the only one I know who wouldn't." Kirk was not about to go into the circumstances under which Spock might lose control of his emotions.

"Well," said Brightspot, "if *I* had a soft head . . ." She addressed Uhura again: "I'd tell Rushlight, in Old Tongue, that I wouldn't sing his songs without his permission, and *then* I'd tell him my people had very different customs."

"Thank you, Brightspot, I will," Uhura said. "Is there anything else I should know about being a guest?"

Brightspot gave a great sigh of exasperation. "I don't *know!*" she said—her tail twitched away from Jim Kirk's grasp—"I didn't know you didn't know *that!*"

Evan Wilson, surprisingly, chuckled. "I know a trick for it,

Brightspot, one I guarantee will work on any world where you can find someone who's trying as hard to help as you are." She pointed. "Pretend the captain there is Rushlight and show us what you'd do if *you* were coming to accept his invitation."

Brightspot's ears perked up, her whiskers arched forward. Without another word, she ducked into the shelter's entrance.

Jim Kirk had to admire her flexibility—both tail tip and nose poked through the opening. "I stick my tail in," she told him. "Everybody recognizes *my* tail, so I don't have to call my name. Catchclaw would say, 'Catchclaw to-Ennien.' I only call my name if no one invites me in."

Wilson grinned at her. "Since we don't have such distinctive tails, maybe we'd better just call our names."

"I think so," said Brightspot. She looked again at Kirk and said, "Now you say 'come in.'"

"Come in, Brightspot," he said obligingly.

Brightspot entered, then froze. "To Catchclaw, you would say, 'Come in, Catchclaw to-Ennien.'"

"Then I should say 'Come in, Brightspot to-Srallansre.'?"

She raised her head slightly and the tip of her tail switched. "You don't have to. Catchclaw has *her* name. I don't have *my* name yet. If you don't know, do what I do: use the *to-*. It's better to be safe than clawed."

"Brightspot," said Spock, "does Jinx to-Ennien have *her* name?" Spock gave the possessive the same emphasis Brightspot had used.

"Don't be silly. Who'd choose a name like 'Jinx'? That's the only name I know that's worse than mine." Her hand went up, as if of its own accord, to cover the black smudge along her nose.

In that instant, Jim Kirk saw suddenly a shy teenager, embarrassed by her imagined unattractiveness. "Where I come from," he said, "to call someone a bright spot in your life is a compliment." At her ears-back startled look, he explained, "Think of a cloudy day, with just one small break in the clouds. Think of standing in the middle of that little patch of sunshine. How does that make you feel?"

"Warm all over," she said and stretched as if she could feel it as he spoke.

"That," Kirk smiled, "is what we mean by *bright spot*. I'd say it suits you admirably."

"Really? *Bright spot* makes you think of sunshine through the clouds?"

"*You* make me think of sunshine through the clouds, Brightspot."

She curled her tail around his upper arm. "I wish I could 'hug' you," she said.

He stroked the tail. "I wish I could hug you too, Brightspot, but I think we'd better abide by the rules Distant Smoke laid down."

She arched her whiskers and nodded. "Some day, though," she said, "when I have *my* name . . ." She had the wistful look of a small child saying, "When I'm grown up . . ." Maybe, thought Kirk, that's what she *is* saying.

"Captain," said Spock, "I believe you have interrupted Brightspot's demonstration."

"Yes, yes, Spock. Go on, Brightspot. I'm sorry I sidetracked you."

"I'm not," said Brightspot, with a curious look at Spock. "You don't get angry. Does that mean you don't get happy, either?"

"In the sense which I believe you mean, no, I do not. I do, however, find a pleasurable sensation in the solution to an intellectual problem."

Kirk said, conspiratorially, to Brightspot, "Let's go on with the demonstration. Perhaps that will give Mr. Spock his 'pleasurable sensation.'"

When Brightspot had finished, the landing party knew all she knew about being a guest in someone's tent. It did not differ much from normal etiquette aboard the *Enterprise,* but Kirk was grateful that Brightspot had saved them from a few social gaffes.

In complete innocence, Brightspot then turned to Spock. "Have I given you a pleasurable sensation?"

Spock raised his eyebrow. "Indeed, Brightspot, I believe you have. Would you be so kind as to satisfy my curiosity on another point as well?"

She nodded, and Spock continued, "I do not understand your use of the *to-* names. They would seem to indicate blood relationship, as between you and Fetchstorm, yet Catchclaw and Settlesand—who give every indication of being twins—do not share the same *to-*. May I ask the reason for this?"

Brightspot's eyes went round with wonder. "You don't know *anything!*" she said, when at last she found her voice.

Jim Kirk leapt to the defense of his science officer. "Mr. Spock knows a great deal about a great many worlds, Brightspot—more than the rest of us put together, in fact—but even Mr. Spock knows less about your world than a baby does."

"Correction, Captain. There are certain scientific laws that apply to all worlds."

"Correction noted, Mr. Spock. We have that advantage over a baby. But," he continued to Brightspot, "we have a baby's ignorance of language and custom. And we have no way of finding out unless we ask." He spread his hands and gave her his most charming smile. "We may even have to ask stupid questions. . . ."

"I see, I think. All the things I learned when I was little are all the things you *don't* know, but you know the periodic table?" This was addressed to Spock.

"I am familiar with the periodic table," he assured her. "But I have been unable to ascertain whether your name is a matter of blood relationship or of some other factor that is unknown to me."

"Then it's not a stupid question," Brightspot said. "It's a baby question." She gave a sidelong glance at Evan Wilson and said, "I can pretend you're Grabfoot, Mr. Spock. If Grabfoot asked me . . . I guess I'd say that *to-* is where I go to celebrate Festival. I'm to-Srallansrc because Stiff Tail is my mother, just like Grabfoot is to-Ennien because Catchclaw is his mother. That part is blood relationship."

She paused. When Spock nodded his understanding, she went on, "Catchclaw and Settlesand are both born to-Ennien, but Catchclaw is also to-Ennien by choice. Fetchstorm says the only thing crazier than born to-Ennien is chosen to-Ennien, and that Catchclaw is twice to-Ennion." She added, scathingly, "He would," and her tail flicked once in Fetchstorm's honor. "I think Catchclaw is nice. She's like you, Captain Kirk; she only pulls your tail if she likes you. There is one thing, though. . . ." Brightspot lowered her voice. "I don't know for sure, because I've only been to this camp twice, but from things I've heard some people say I think Catchclaw *stays* here!" Her manner made it abundantly clear that this was the most scandalous thing she could say about anyone. She added, hastily but just as quietly, "Don't tell her I said so! And don't ask her about it, not even baby questions!"

Spock said, "Such behavior would be considered exceptional, even abnormal, in a nomadic culture, Captain."

Brightspot nodded emphatically at him, whiskers forward. Kirk couldn't help but smile and say, "I'm willing to bet that my behavior would seem stranger than that, even to Fetchstorm."

"Oh, but you don't know any better!" Brightspot told him; a flick of her tail dismissed the entire idea. Then she looked at the universal translator and added, "I think it would be easier, though, if your machine didn't translate so well. You *seem* to speak our language, so we think you know other things, too."

"A point well taken, Brightspot," Kirk said. "However, our mission to your world is an urgent one. Without the universal translator, it would take us weeks, even months, perhaps, to learn enough to ask even stupid questions, let alone the urgent ones."

"Why not start with the urgent ones, then?"

Kirk rubbed the side of his head ruefully. "I did."

"Oh," she said. "Ask me. Even if I lose my temper too, I can't hit as hard as Stiff Tail. I'll remember you ask baby questions, I promise. And if I don't know the answer, *I'll* ask Stiff Tail. *I* have a very hard head."

From any other Sivaoan in camp, Jim Kirk would have considered the offer a godsend. Instead, he held up his hands and shook his head. "Thank you, Brightspot, but we can't do that. We're guests in your mother's camp and, by my custom, it wouldn't be right to cause trouble between you and your mother."

She drooped from ear tip to tail tip. "I think I understand," she said sadly. "I'm not angry at you, but I'm sorry I can't help."

"You have helped—a great deal. And you can help us still more," Kirk assured her and saw her tail straighten with pride. "Keep answering our baby questions."

"All right," she said. She gave his cheek a last feathery caress. Glancing at the smoke hole, she said, "It's getting dark . . . time for bed. Evan Wilson, do you still want to spend the night with me?"

"Do I?" said Wilson. She leapt to her feet. "Lead the way, Brightspot—nothing short of Stiff Tail could stop me!"

"Stiff Tail says it's okay. You should bring some usefuls, though; it gets cold. And you really don't have much fur," Brightspot finished apologetically.

Wilson grinned. "I know. . . . Usefuls?"

Brightspot pointed at the pile of brightly colored fabrics Wilson had been sitting on. Wilson snatched twice and flourished the results. One "useful" bore a design of stylized flowers in blue and gold, the other a geometric pattern of intertwined helices. Both shone in the firelight. Wilson looked down at them and said, "I do like a world where something that beautiful is called a useful!"

A wrinkle twitched through the fur along Brightspot's side; it seemed to be her equivalent of a shrug. "Useful for making a swagger-lair," she said, "or a tent, or for keeping you warm at night." But she seemed pleased by Wilson's delight. Then she uncurled her tail to gesture Wilson away.

Kirk rose to follow. "A swagger-lair," he said to Brightspot. "This I have to see." The rest of the landing crew were not far behind.

They walked to the edge of the clearing. The sky was darkening rapidly now, and the light of campfires twinkled cheerfully in the dusk. A song, as sweet as the smell of the wood fires, drifted on the wind. Brightspot pointed with her tail. "Rushlight camps outside the clearing," she said. "That way—turn left at the stream and follow the song."

Uhura nodded at her, then she said, "Oh, look, Captain! How beautiful!"

He followed her gesture. Some half dozen of the tents were lit from within; they glowed a rich profusion of color, like pavilions in a fairy tale.

"Remarkable," said Spock, "It would seem they have a form of artificial lighting."

Jim Kirk frowned slightly at his first officer, then looked again. Spock was right: the interior lighting did not have the flicker of candles or firelight. Spock was also, all too often, unnecessarily pragmatic.

"This way, Evan Wilson," said Brightspot.

Her voice came from somewhere above his head; he looked up to find her ten feet up the side of a tree and still climbing. Her claws sent tiny shreds of bark down on them all. Jim Kirk shielded his eyes and peered into the deepening darkness. Brightspot's swagger-lair, some thirty feet from the ground, was little more than a hammock: one useful stretched from branch to branch of two adjacent trees. And the trees rose straight and slender for twenty feet before they branched. "Evan," he said, "how do you propose to climb that without claws?"

Brightspot clung to the lowest branch and looked down, tail twitching. "Oh, Evan Wilson! You don't have *claws!*"

"Keep going, Brightspot," Wilson said, as she shook out her usefuls and tied them at her throat. "I may not have claws, but I come from a long line of the best tree climbers nature ever invented—and I haven't forgotten their techniques." With a sidelong smile at Kirk, she wrapped her arms and legs about the trunk and began to shinny up.

Brightspot stared. "That's neat!" she said. "*I* couldn't do that!"

"You couldn't?" said Wilson in surprise. Like a double cape, the two usefuls billowed out behind her in the soft night breeze.

Brightspot had resumed her climb. Now she reached the level of her swagger-lair and sprang in; it bulged from her weight and swung precariously back and forth. Just as Wilson reached the first of the branches, Brightspot peered over the edge at her. "No," said Brightspot, "my legs don't bend that way."

"Oh, I see," said Wilson, now hanging upside down from

the branch that supported one side of the shelter. She made a quick swing and brought herself to a sitting position, perched on the tree limb. She sat for a moment and caught her breath. Then she said, "Now comes the tricky part. . . . How much sudden shock of weight can that take, Brightspot?"

Brightspot said, "If it won't take four of us jumping into it at once, I didn't do it right."

"Good enough," said Wilson. "Any etiquette I should know?"

Brightspot thought, then she said, "No, you just come in."

"Easier said than done," Kirk observed.

"Tsk, tsk, Captain," Wilson said, "you have no faith. Watch and wonder!" She straightened suddenly, snatched the branch above her for balance, and slowly walked toward the swagger-lair. "Move a little to the right, Brightspot, if you will; I don't want to bash my host for my first act as a guest." As Brightspot shifted, Wilson stretched out her other hand, leaning dangerously, to grasp a branch from the adjacent tree. She tugged it for a moment and then swung abruptly into midair.

Jim Kirk's stomach lurched.

She landed in a great sprawl; the swagger-lair rocked with her impact and Brightspot shifted hastily to steady it. A moment later, Evan Wilson's face, almost luminous with delight, appeared at the edge. "Lieutenant Uhura," she called, "do you know the old lullabye 'Rockabye Baby'?"

Uhura smiled up at her, equally radiant. "Yes, Doctor, I do."

"Then I give you something to remember me by: I promise you'll think of me every time you sing it. Good night, Captain, all."

Kirk laughed. "Good night. And Evan—don't fall out of bed!"

"Don't pull my tail, Captain."

Evan Wilson found herself chortling. The whole experience seemed so unreal, yet even the sway of the swagger-lair was pleasant in an odd, dreamlike way. When Brightspot stretched out her tail and drew a second useful arching over their heads to form a roof, it only added to the sensation, making her feel like a clam in a clamshell. *Happy as a clam,* she thought, and she chortled again.

Brightspot said, "You're all loops! You *like* this!" Her voice in the darkness carried a note of surprise.

She means, thought Evan, '*all smiles.*' She said, "Yes, I do. I've never slept in a tree before, and I *like* new things."

"Me too," admitted Brightspot. "Distant Smoke says I have a to-Ennien tail, but Stiff Tail says I should be more cautious."

"But she didn't mind my sharing your swagger-lair," said Wilson. "I wonder why?"

"I *know* why," said Brightspot. "She thinks you'll talk more to me than you would to her."

"Then what would you like to know? I'll answer almost anything I can."

"Answer a baby question. I don't understand *your* names: you each seem to have several and you never fight about what someone calls you."

"Quite honestly, Brightspot, I'd say it's a lot easier for someone to shame his name than for the name to shame him. But I think you mean customary use of names, and that varies from culture to culture. I can give you the short course that'll work with most of the *Enterprise* personnel. . . ."

Using Captain Kirk for example, she talked long into the darkness, carefully explaining the possible variations of his name and the social occasions in which they occurred. She followed up with an explanation of rank structure. At last she finished, "I'd be pleased, Brightspot, if you'd call me Evan."

"You mean, to be your friend?"

"Yes."

"Thank you." There was a small hesitation. "I don't have a name to give you in return, but I'll try to help you. That's our friendship, Evan." She pronounced the name with extreme care.

"Ours too," said Evan Wilson.

"Then we'll sleep like friends and be warmed by it."

By this, Evan learned, she meant spoon-fashion. Brightspot took the inner spoon for fear she might stir in her sleep and accidently claw. With much shifting and, on Wilson's part, giggling, they nestled in for the night.

But for the sounds of their breathing and the stirrings of night creatures in the forest, the dark was silent. Then Brightspot said softly, "Evan? What's so funny about a lullabye?"

Evan Wilson, wrapped in usefuls and pressed against the soft warmth of Brightspot's body, chuckled once more and quietly began to sing, "Rockabye baby, on the treetop . . ." When she finished, Brightspot's tail curled happily around her ankle. She took a deep, contented breath, smelling the sweet scent of Brightspot's fur, and drifted off to sleep.

Chapter Eight

Kirk woke, sweating, from a nightmare of the Eeia-uoan hospital. He sat up, trusting the movement to shake away the horror. It did not—unfamiliar shapes and shadows assaulted his senses. He fixed on an image beside the fire and found the reassuring form of Spock.

Spock stared into the fire as if into his attunement flame. Perhaps any fire could serve the purpose, thought Kirk; he did not wish to disturb the Vulcan.

"Captain," said Spock softly. Taking the acknowledgment as an invitation, Kirk threw off the light, warm usefuls and moved quietly to the fireside. "Standing guard, Mr. Spock?" he said, low enough not to wake Chekov. "These people seem friendly enough." He had not ordered a guard, for fear of insulting their hosts, though he had set a sensor to wake them if anyone entered.

"Thinking, Captain." Spock's voice was as quiet as his own.

"Any conclusions, Mr. Spock?"

"I regret to say I have only theories. It is my hope that Lieutenant Uhura and Dr. Wilson will be able to supply further data."

"Mine too, though I admit I'm not happy about leaving either of them—unprotected—in an alien environment about which we know so little."

"I do not believe you would have been able to keep either

of them from undertaking the risk, short of a direct order to return to the *Enterprise.*"

"You're probably right, Spock. And I'm not sure a direct order would have done it either. Certainly not in Wilson's case: she's just wild enough to pull medical rank on me."

"Indeed," said Spock, "that is my impression also. And there is a high probability that the lieutenant would have disobeyed such an order as well."

"Mutiny? Uhura? You must be joking, Spock."

"No, Captain. My conclusion was based upon considerable observation of your species. You yourself have disobeyed Starfleet Command—for a friend." It was something they seldom mentioned but that was a part of their own long friendship. "Lieutenant Uhura has not one friend, but several, at risk of their lives. To spend the night in a dangerous situation to gain the information we seek is a logical risk. Had you ordered her to return to the *Enterprise,* her logical response would have been to disobey that order."

"In other words, I would have been illogical to order her back to the *Enterprise.*"

"Precisely, Captain."

"Thanks, Spock, you make me feel better about it—I think." He smiled.

They sat side by side, human and Vulcan, staring into the fire. The night was filled with unfamiliar sounds. At last, Kirk said, "Find us a way, Spock. You found this world, and the odds against that . . ."

"With the information Lieutenant Uhura provided," Spock said.

"Correction noted, Mr. Spock. We need all the help we can get." A vivid image of the Eeiauoan hospital flashed in his mind once more. "Bones and Christine need all the help we can get."

As he stared into the fire once more, he thought of the last image he'd seen of Leonard McCoy, haggard and beaten. *Hold on!* he thought. *Hold on, Bones! We're working as fast as we can!*

Leonard McCoy found it increasingly difficult to keep his mind on his research. He was more and more conscious of the overpowering smell of the Eeiauoan hospital wards—the sweetish alien smell of lingering death. Try as he might to avoid it, his mind kept returning to Christine, to Micky, miles above his head; to Sunfall, whom he had never met, half a continent away. He tended Quickfoot daily and saw the progress of their disease in the body of his new friend—and knew that for Christine and Micky, he was being optimistic.

He focused his eyes with difficulty. He hated what he saw, and he knew that the hardest thing to deal with was the magnitude of the disaster. The sheer volume of cases made him helpless with rage.

This morning one of his Eeiauoan staff, discovering in himself the first symptoms of ADF syndrome, had attempted to commit suicide. McCoy had managed to talk him out of it, but even Spock might have found Patterner of Vensre's reasoning logical. His entire family was in second-stage coma—when Patterner reached that stage he would no longer be of help—he would be an additional burden that might prevent his family from receiving full care. McCoy had only gotten through to him by pointing out that they needed his help as long as he could give it.

How long that would be, neither of them knew.

Two others had been admitted to the hospital not for ADF syndrome but for—hopelessness. One, a mother who had lost three of her children to ADF syndrome, had simply stopped nursing the fourth. The other was in physical shock, brought on by severe depression.

How many have to die, McCoy wondered, before the rest of the living begin to envy the dead?

"Dr. McCoy!" Patterner's voice cut through his grim thoughts.

"Yes, Patterner?" He started to rise. He'd been sitting too long in one position—his knee had stiffened. He flexed and rubbed it to restore circulation.

"On the communications screen. It's Chief Medical Officer Mickiewicz."

"Micky!" Forgetting his knee, McCoy hurried in and leaned on the lab table to look at her image. There were half a dozen doctors and nurses crowded in behind her.

"Hello, Leonard," she said happily. "My staff and I would like to bring you a heartfelt message." She turned and raised her hands to the group. "Ready?" With this, she dropped her hands and the group burst into applause, whistles and cheers.

"It works!" said McCoy.

Micky nodded. She shooed the rest of the group back to work and said, "It works. You've bought us time, Leonard— and God knows, we need it."

Her face turned solemn. "Now here's the drill. You're right—it's only a palliative. There's no remission—no *reversal* of symptoms. But it either slows the progress of ADF or maybe, just maybe, stops it—we won't know that for days, possibly weeks.

"We're synthesizing buckets of the stuff. All terminal cases are receiving massive doses *every* day. Now, and this is the important part, we're also using it on everyone with a diagnosed case of ADF. The longer we can hold off the final stages of the disease, the longer we have to work."

McCoy shook his head. "So what it all boils down to is condemning thousands to excruciating pain. I've seen the way these people move even in the early stages. That's not good enough, dammit."

"Agreed, agreed," she said. The lines of weariness reappeared on her face. "But that's what we have. I'll transmit all our results—maybe you can find something in them we've missed." She made ready to send and he to receive. "We'll also need coordinates. You get the first batch of McCoy serum—where do you want it beamed to?"

He gave her the coordinates, then he said, "Micky, for the record, it's Wilson-Chapel serum. I only followed their lead. . . ." He let his voice trail off.

Despite the seeming good news, he found himself afraid to ask about Christine. Micky had not forgotten, however. "Nurse Chapel seems to be responding well to treatment," she said. "You'll find the details in the reports. In brief, she's not getting any better, but she's not getting any worse, *thanks to you.*"

He and Patterner were very busy for the next few hours. They managed to find enough people who could handle a hypo (or learn in a few minutes) to see that all the patients in the hospital were injected with the new serum. McCoy himself gave Patterner his shot.

Patterner rubbed his shoulder, then wiped the loose fur from his palm. "Dr. McCoy," he said, "thank you. I'm sorry about this morning. I promise you I won't try again."

McCoy found himself both angry and saddened by Patterner's gratitude. With an effort at control, he said, "Is the pain very bad, Patterner? I could—"

Patterner interrupted, shaking his head stiffly. "The pain is sometimes bad, Dr. McCoy, but I prefer the pain to the relief of pain that my family feels. I *thank* you for the pain I feel."

He left McCoy to return to his family's ward where he had a great deal of work to perform. McCoy watched him go. After a long moment, McCoy wiped his eyes—and began to read through Micky's reports.

It took him longer than it might have. The lack of sleep was making him bleary-eyed and he almost asked the computers for hard copy rather than continue to read from the screen. In the end, he didn't.

The final report was a communique from Starfleet on the spread of ADF syndrome through the galaxy. The incubation period is killing us, he thought. People can spread ADF without ever showing a symptom, until it's too late to track down all the people they've been in contact with. Hera Four had been quarantined, he saw. Fifteen deaths—all humanoid —and five *thousand* diagnosed cases. A second Starfleet team had been dispatched to handle it. *Handle* it, he thought, with an angry snort.

He recalled the data on Wilson-Chapel serum. It was working much as he'd hoped. A small hope, that was what he'd had.

He poured himself a shot of ethanol (the scotch was gone) and downed it, wishing he could afford to relax for a day. *Shore leave with Scotty would be nice right about now,* he thought. *An alphabetic drunk—been a long time since we've done that: absinthe, Bacardi, Cold Duck, Devil's Downfall—* he indulged himself with the thought. It was the closest he could come to a break in the overwhelming routine of the hospital. *Ethanol,* he added, disgusted that he could think of nothing else for "e." *Gin and tonic. That was better*—it was an old Earth drink much favored by med students in his day because the tonic was historically a medicine used to prevent and alleviate the symptoms of malaria. Or did it actually cure it? He'd forgotten.

He put down the glass so suddenly that he missed the edge of the table and had to snatch for it. *Tonic!* He skimmed rapidly through Micky's reports once again.

Why not? he said to himself. *If the serum can keep the symptoms from progressing, a regular dose might just prevent infection!*

He laid out his plans hastily. He'd have to take the serum himself for several days, then he'd have to deliberately infect himself with ADF. Since they still couldn't isolate the cause, he'd have to inject himself with blood from one of the victims. *Good thing Jim's off chasing rainbows. He'd have a conniption fit,* he thought wryly.

He prepared a hypo with a dose of the serum. *Dammit,* he thought, *Micky'll have my head if I don't do this right.* He laid the hypo aside and, instead, took a blood sample from his own arm and placed it in the analyzer. *Proper procedure all the way—first prove that the subject is not already infected with ADF—for the record.*

He waited for the results of the analysis, drumming his fingers on the lab table. In his impatience, his fingers felt stiff and out of rhythm. It made him so irritable he stopped.

He read the results, blinked to clear his eyes, and read the results again. They did not change—he too had contracted ADF syndrome. The stiffness, the blurring of vision, the heightened sense of smell—all were symptoms of the disease in humans—he'd been fooled by the fact that he'd seen no loss of body hair. Or he'd been fooling himself.

"Well," he said aloud, "you knew it could happen, you old fraud. Might as well tell Micky. Maybe she can find a volunteer who *hasn't* got it yet." Picking up the prepared hypo, he injected himself with the serum. "I told you I'd hold the fort, Jim, but I'd like it a damn sight better if I believed you were goin' for the cavalry."

Evan Wilson woke with a start. The shelter rocked violently and the sound of shrieks and squawks were everywhere around her. Brightspot stirred and stretched luxuriously. Wilson relaxed: if Brightspot took no alarm, she need not either.

"Good morning, Evan," said Brightspot. She preened her fur. "Did they startle you? They're just announcing new arrivals. These are the people we expected yesterday—we were surprised when you came instead."

"Oh, perimeter guards?" She took her cue from Brightspot and ran a comb through her tangled hair.

"Yes," said Brightspot, thoughtfully. "I guess they would warn us if anything dangerous was coming. It doesn't happen often though. Even slashbacks avoid the camps."

She stretched a second time, combining it with a yawn that displayed fearsome teeth. Evan Wilson watched her with delight—one seldom saw anyone take such full pleasure in such a simple action. It was contagious; Wilson too stretched and yawned.

Brightspot looked at her curiously. "Are you herbivorous?"

"No," she said, shaking her head. "Omnivorous. Mr. Spock, however, is vegetarian by choice, by philosophy; that's another Vulcan trait for your collection, Brightspot."

"You are very different from a Vulcan?"

"That's hard to answer, Brightspot. Physiologically, yes, and often psychologically. But the range of variation within the human species is so wide that Spock is often not as alien to me as some members of my own species."

"Good," she said.

"Good?"

"I think this is a baby reaction. I was afraid you would all be exactly alike because you're not Sivaoan. I'm beginning to see you as different people with different reactions."

"Brightspot, I'm proud to have you as a friend. Some people never learn that . . . or are too lazy to learn it. And those people cause no end of trouble in the universe."

Brightspot looped her tail. Something bounced along the upper part of the shelter, screeching. Brightspot yelled "Fuzz-brain!" and thumped the underside, tumbling it off.

"Is that what they're called?"

"When they annoy you, it is. If you're being polite, they're welcome-homes. Are you hungry?"

Wilson nodded. Brightspot did something and the two halves of the shelter popped open. She crawled toward the access branch. Then she stopped. "You are all different. . . . I will ask you what I asked Captain Kirk last night." This time, Wilson could hear her using the *captain* as a title, rather than as a name. "What is your urgent question?"

"I am under the same restrictions as Captain Kirk, Brightspot. I want to do nothing that will cause trouble between you and your close kin, and nothing that might get us expelled from camp."

Brightspot's shoulder fur rippled. It might have been a shrug. "We could always go to another camp," she said.

Wilson, sitting cross-legged, folded her hands and breathed on them. "You make this difficult for me, Brightspot—oh, no, not deliberately! But I know so little of your world, I *must* walk softly. As much as possible, I must obey *your* rules of behavior. I will try all the legitimate ways of gaining the information I seek first, before I risk your friendship. . . . What I do here may affect relations between my people and yours for all time."

Brightspot nodded. "That makes sense. But I think, Evan, that you would disobey your captain to save a life. . . ."

Giving Wilson no chance to reply to this, Brightspot sprang from the shelter to the branch, scrambled a few feet up the tree and held out her hand. Wilson leapt, caught the hand, and found herself supported by Brightspot's tail as well. "Thanks," she said, "I was wondering how I would manage that."

"Let me go down first," said Brightspot, "I want to see how you climb."

She scrambled down and Wilson followed. "I wish I could do that," said Brightspot.

Wilson grinned. "I wish I had a tail." Each regarded the other with sympathy.

"Let's go eat," said Brightspot.

"Let's," Wilson agreed. "Waiting for magic makes me hungry."

Carefully skirting a large stand of sweetstripes, Brightspot led her into the forest. After a few hundred yards, they came to a small stream where they drank. Evan took the opportunity to wash her face, much to Brightspot's surprise.

"Can you swim, Brightspot?" The universal translator seemed to manage that, so it was at least a possibility.

"Rushlight can swim. He likes water. Most of us hate it so we don't." Brightspot shivered with evident distaste.

"Ah," said Wilson. "What's for breakfast? I should warn you: I'm good at swimming but lousy at hunting."

Brightspot looked surprised. "Winding Path takes a hunting party for tonight's food. Fruit for breakfast—see, here—" She led Wilson farther along the stream. A tree drooped over the water, heavy with fruit.

"Funny," said Wilson, "I would have thought, with your teeth, you'd be exclusively a meat-eater."

It was the same fruit that had gone into Chekov's stew. Wilson picked one and bit into it without hesitation. Brightspot tossed one into her mouth whole, gave one chomp, and swallowed. "No problem with teeth," she said.

"So I see."

They lingered over breakfast. When they returned to camp, Evan Wilson saw a great many changes. Half a dozen tents had been struck, two more were in the process of going down. A structure identical to Chekov's shelter was going up, under Chekov's direction and with a great many sidewalk superintendents. The erection of two new Sivaoan tents gave Wilson an appreciation of just how useful a "useful" could be.

Brightspot's tail thumped twice against Wilson's calf; nonetheless she offered a cheery "Good morning!" Wilson too turned to greet Fetchstorm and Stiff Tail. Fetchstorm glared back, said nothing. To Stiff Tail, he said, "The fuzz-brains are noisy this morning." Stiff Tail slapped him, without malice but with sufficient force to send him tumbling. With a last glower at Wilson and Brightspot, he stalked away.

Wilson said, "What's between you and Fetchstorm, Brightspot? I thought he was your brother."

"He *is* her brother," Stiff Tail said. "We have a saying, 'To fight like brother and sister.' This doesn't happen in your culture?"

"Some," admitted Wilson, "but not enough to have a saying about it."

"And Fetchstorm likes to make trouble," Brightspot said. "Couldn't you tell from his name?"

"Most of our names are pleasing syllables, not descriptions," Wilson said, "so I didn't honestly think about it. We call people like that troublemakers." She added, "Not a name, just an expression." She saw Kirk across the clearing and waved, "Captain! Good morning!"

Brightspot watched, then imitated, her gesture. Kirk waved back and started toward them. Before he reached them, Stiff Tail said, "Come, Brightspot. I wish to hear how it happened." Brightspot, torn, hesitated. Wilson said, "It's all right, Brightspot. Go ahead. You can say hello to the captain later. We're not going away just yet."

Brightspot gave another wave in Kirk's direction and loped off, tail streaming behind her, to Stiff Tail's tent.

"Good morning, Dr. Wilson," said Kirk as he reached her side. "Did you sleep well?" He asked in such a mischievous manner that she had to laugh.

"Yes, Captain, very well," she said.

He shook his head. "I had no idea you were a champion tree climber. I think you even surprised Spock."

"Now that surprises *me*. Mr. Spock doesn't seem given to making assumptions about the range and variation of human abilities—or peculiarities. Are you pulling my tail again?"

"Partly," he admitted. "But Spock did seem surprised. I wonder why? It usually takes a conspicuous emotional display to get a rise out of Spock—and that's only his eyebrow."

"You know him better than I do." She shrugged. "So far the only thing useful I've learned is that Stiff Tail *wants* Brightspot to talk to us. The rest is all YNK."

"Inc," he said, "For incomplete?"

"Y N. K,," she explained, "For 'You Never Know'—they might be useful." She ticked them off on her fingers, "Most Sivaoans can't swim, names are not to be taken lightly, slashbacks seldom attack camps, and Brightspot is the quickest study I've come across in years."

"Bright for her age?"

"Hard to tell. She's the only one I've talked to for any length of time. All the kids seem to be indulged; by the standards of some cultures, they're downright spoiled. If they go too far, they get whopped, but that *ends* the matter."

"Meaning?"

"Meaning Stiff Tail has forgotten all about the fight between Brightspot and Fetchstorm yesterday. Brightspot hasn't, but that's another matter. Morning, Mr. Spock," she added, tilting her head to smile up at him as he drew close.

Kirk acknowledged Spock with a nod, then resumed his conversation with Evan. "Sibling rivalry," he said, and for Spock's benefit, "—Brightspot and Fetchstorm."

"Yes," said Wilson, "and apparently to be expected." She quoted Stiff Tail's proverb, adding, "At a guess, though, I'd say that only applies to twins, triplets, quadruplets, etc. Remember Brightspot identified Distant Smoke not as her brother but as her mother's son? And her relationship with him is quite affectionate. I think the expected sibling rivalry only applies to kids born at the same time."

"That would accord with my observations, Dr. Wilson," said Spock. "It would appear that Distant Smoke and Fetchstorm are only half-brothers. Lieutenant Uhura informs me that the contemporary language contains no word for marriage."

"All kids are legitimate?" Wilson smiled. "I like that, Mr. Spock; they don't take the sins of the parents out on the kids."

"On the contrary, Dr. Wilson. It would appear that, after two thousand years, the local population still bears a grudge —I believe that is the phrase—against the Eeiauoans, who are descendants of theirs."

"Point taken, Mr. Spock," Kirk said. "You've seen Uhura?"

"I have. The lieutenant has nothing to report as yet."

Wilson considered him. "That's easy for you to say, Mr. Spock. Not so easy for Nyota, I'll bet." She frowned slightly. "And not so easy to hear either."

"Troy wasn't found in a day, Evan," Kirk said.

She grinned at that. "A dose of my own medicine, Captain? Right. We keep digging." She turned to Spock and added, *"After* I fill in Mr. Spock . . ."

The report she gave Spock of her conversations with Brightspot was considerably more detailed than that she had given Kirk, and she studied him as she spoke. His undivided attention was disconcerting. More than once, she felt her face grow warm and quickly joked aside to Kirk for the sake of her own composure. When she had finished, she felt something akin to relief.

Spock said, "Would you permit a personal question, Dr. Wilson?"

You're digging too, she thought. *I wonder what I did to deserve that?* Matching his formality with precision and no little curiosity of her own, she said, "I would, Mr. Spock."

"Your display of physical expertise last night was remarkable. . . ."

"Thank you." She sketched a bow to him and caught Kirk's smile out of the corner of her eye.

"When Brightspot became concerned over your lack of claws, you made reference to having 'come from a long line of tree climbers'—I believe that was your phrase."

"Close enough," she said, and he went on, "It has been my experience that most humans prefer to deny their evolutionary antecedents. Yet you seemed proud to claim relationship. May I ask why?"

"Why not?" She instantly thought better of her response. "I'm sorry, Mr. Spock. I don't mean to be flippant, but I have no patience with the kind of person who thinks he's so much better than other creatures, animal *or* human, that he must have been created fully formed and wearing the latest style hat. The universe wastes nothing, so why should I waste a perfectly good talent for tree climbing just because others think it . . . uncivilized? It would be as silly as not using a perfectly good prehensile tail." She knew he would understand her reference to the Eeiauoans without explanation.

"Indeed," said Spock. "May I be permitted to point out to the doctor that once again her 'gut reaction' bears a remarkable resemblance to logic?"

"You may—but I'll probably go down denying it to my last breath."

"*That* is highly illogical."

"I rest my case."

If nothing else, Wilson thought, that was worth it for the expression on Kirk's face: double takes that good came few and far between. Time to make a tactical retreat. She shouldered an imaginary shovel, saluted them both briskly, and about-faced and marched away.

Kirk watched her go. At last he had it, the key to Evan Wilson's style. He laughed abruptly. "Mr. Spock, there is a person who refuses to be taken for granted—even by you."

"Captain?"

That might not be so clear to the Vulcan mind. "I mean that she won't have anyone make assumptions about her. If you must continue to observe her, Spock, remember Heisenberg. Dr. Wilson will go out of her way to skew your data. She enjoys being unpredictable."

"Then she is, as she claims, as illogical in her behavior as most humans. That is most interesting."

So is your reaction to the doctor, Kirk thought, but he said only, "Well, Mr. Spock, everyone seems to be digging. Would you care to choose a site for us?"

Spock indicated the permanent building set among the trees. "I should very much like to see the interior of that structure."

"Then let's go, Mr. Spock."

"May I inquire, Captain, as to the state of your recent injury?"

"If that's a warning, Spock, I take your point." Kirk gazed around the encampment to see Brightspot emerging from Stiff Tail's tent. He waved and motioned her to join them. "We'll ask Brightspot. She says she can't hit as hard as Stiff Tail—let's hope she's right."

Brightspot loped over. "Good morning, Captain. Good morning, Mr. Spock."

"Good morning, Brightspot. I have another baby question; and Mr. Spock reminds me that my ears are still ringing from Stiff Tail's response to my last."

114

Brightspot shook her head: not a negative shake, but a shake as if to clear it. "Mine too," she said. She rubbed the side of her face.

"What did you do to deserve that?"

She hesitated. "Nothing," she said but she turned her head away in an embarrassed fashion.

A typical answer from a typical kid, he thought, then, *Typical nosy adult.* "Sorry, Brightspot. It's none of my business. As long as you're all right?"

"Oh, sure. Head is harder than hand." That was indisputably a proverb. She clasped her hands, wound her tail to bind her own wrists together, then said, "What's the question?"

Kirk smiled at her elaborate precautions. "We'd like a look inside that building. Is that permitted?"

With an air of relief, Brightspot unbound herself. Her whiskers arched forward. "Oh, sure," she said, "come on—I'll show you." She turned, then stopped abruptly. "Wait. I have to think it through." Her tail twitched with her own impatience.

"There is a problem," she said at last. "I think. Lieutenant Uhura said your people feel free to sing what they have heard. Is that true about other things as well?"

"I'm not sure I understand, Brightspot."

"Would you feel free to make what you have seen made?"

Kirk looked at Spock. "I believe, Captain, that Brightspot wishes to know if we indulge in industrial espionage." The universal translator made hash of that, from Brightspot's reaction. Spock found it simplest to give her a brief description of Federation patent law, followed almost immediately by a more elaborate description of the concept of "law" and how it differed from scientific law.

When he had finished, Brightspot said, "Maybe you'd better tell Winding Path and Stiff Tail in Old Tongue that you won't use their information without their permission."

Kirk said, "We don't speak the Old Tongue, Brightspot. Lieutenant Uhura is the only one who does. But I will give your friends my word, by my law. Will that do?"

"I don't know. It can't hurt to ask."

"You're sure about that . . .?" Kirk rubbed the side of his

head suggestively. Brightspot's tail looped in delight. "I'll ask," she said.

She led them to the building and stuck her tail in. Stiff Tail appeared at the door. Brightspot, to Kirk's amazement, gave Stiff Tail a verbatim account of their conversation—and Spock's involved explanation word for word. When she was done, Stiff Tail looked them over carefully.

"Your Evan Wilson does not understand the Old Tongue, but she was willing to accept Distant Smoke's *word* that he would not harm her in a 'hug.' Is this a similar usage?"

"It is," Kirk told her, "I give you my word that neither Mr. Spock nor I will divulge any information we receive here without your permission. With one exception: if it's needed to save a life—"

"I accept your *word*," Stiff Tail said. "Come in. Please don't disturb Winding Path for the moment; if you have any questions, ask me."

They followed. Two steps beyond the threshold, Jim Kirk stopped and stared, disbelieving. "Not quite what I expected," he said at last, when he found his voice. He was not entirely sure what he *had* expected, a temple perhaps.

This was a temple of science. Not in any religious sense, but in its beauty: like Catchclaw's medical sensors, everything here had been designed with an eye to esthetics as well as to function. The walls were hung with calligraphy—it took him a moment to realize that they were simple charts and graphs. Flasks and retorts were etched or imprinted with designs. The desk at which Winding Path worked was carved and polished wood. Kirk could not imagine a more beautiful environment in which to work, certainly not a more beautiful chemistry lab.

Spock, examining a stack of petrie dishes, said, "You'll notice, Captain, that they do appear to be mass produced."

Stiff Tail seemed amused at this. "They must often be destroyed," she said. "If they were unique, that would be difficult."

"I see. What I do not see, however, is the logical reason for the inclusion of a design on a purely functional item."

"Of what purpose are the designs on the petals of flowers?"

Spock took Stiff Tail's question literally. "On most worlds, they serve in some way to attract or even assist a symbiotic creature that pollinates the plant, providing a broad mix of genetic possibilities, which self-pollination alone would not allow."

Lifting a particularly beautiful retort into a bar of sunlight, Stiff Tail nodded and said, "Precisely. These too serve to attract: Who would prefer to remain indoors for any purpose were the beauty not equivalent to that of the outdoors?"

"There is, of course, the intellectual beauty of the problem itself," Spock said.

From the position of her ears, Stiff Tail seemed to find his suggestion remarkable—no, Kirk thought, not that the suggestion was remarkable, but that Spock should suggest it. "Oh, yes," she agreed. "Come with me, Mr. Spock. I'll show you a beauty of a problem."

Before long, the two of them were engrossed in conversation that left Kirk, who had only a starship captain's knowledge of chemistry, to his appreciation of Sivaoan artistry.

Brightspot puttered about the lab, careful not to disturb anything. For a while, she peered over Winding Path's shoulder and he wrapped his tail affectionately around her, though he neither looked up nor spoke.

At last she wandered back to Kirk and said, in a quiet voice, "You understand that?" Her tail flicked toward Spock and Stiff Tail.

"I'm afraid it's beyond me," he admitted. "You?"

She shook her head, and this time she meant the gesture for a negative. "I like to put things together—or take them apart. Especially tricorders," she added, giving him an impish look. "I'm going to find Evan. Do you want to come?"

It might be a good idea to leave Spock to his rapport with Stiff Tail. He nodded. As he turned to say his good-byes, Brightspot raised the tip of her tail to bar her mouth, a silencing gesture as clear as any human laying an index finger to her lips for silence. Trusting her knowledge of local etiquette, Kirk followed without another word.

Stepping into the dappled sunlight, Jim Kirk found himself face-to- . . . face? with a large creature that looked something like a cross between a donkey and a moss-covered rock outcrop beside a stream. He must have startled it as much as

117

it did him, for it took a single four-footed hop backward, stared at him balefully through long tufts of shaggy green fur, and began to hiccup loudly.

"Oh, don't be a dope," Brightspot said to it. "You'd think he was a slashback." She made shooing motions. "Go on, go. Run home before he eats you."

The creature gave three more hiccups and dashed across the clearing to hiccup urgently to a Sivaoan. The Sivaoan patted it absentmindedly and continued with the business of striking her tent.

"Did it scare you?" Brightspot asked. "Oh, but you've never seen one before! It's a quickens. They're not too bright but they're fast, especially if something scares them. They run straight home, right into your tent if you're not careful, so you can protect them from shadows."

Kirk laughed. The creature's hiccups made keeping a straight face impossible—made keeping a straight tail impossible, too, to judge from Brightspot's reaction. Another Sivaoan led a second quickens from the wood; it followed the first's baleful glances in Kirk's direction and added its own intermittent hiccups to those of the first. Two Sivaoans paused in their packing to reassure the beasts, then loaded them with tents and goods and mounted.

"Where are they going, Brightspot?"

"I don't know. They were angry at Stiff Tail and didn't tell her. HotSpring to-Allanien left this morning too. Better to leave than fight," she finished, "at least with Stiff Tail." She glanced at him uncertainly, as if unsure whether to be proud or ashamed of her mother's reputation, then glanced away, as if she had decided against Stiff Tail in this instance.

Before he could make up his mind to inquire further, she said sharply, "He's doing it again! This time he's going to make real trouble!"

He was Fetchstorm. Not twenty feet away from them, he stood glaring down at the seated Wilson, the tip of his tail shivering.

"Human," she said. It was without doubt a correction to something Fetchstorm had just said.

Kirk and Brightspot were just close enough for the universal translator to catch the remainder of the exchange. *"Head fur,"* said Fetchstorm in an acid tone.

Evan Wilson rose to her feet; it brought her to equal height with the top of his skull. With exaggerated care, she folded her arms across her chest and tapped her foot. Fetchstorm thumped the ground with his tail. *"Head fur,"* he repeated.

Wilson said, very clearly and very loudly, "You have the manners of a fuzz-brain."

Fetchstorm pounced. Wilson went down beneath him, knocking the camp stool aside.

"Stiff Tail!" yelled Brightspot and turned and ran back the way they'd come, still calling for her mother.

Kirk reached for his phaser but froze. He did not dare use his weapon on a member of the camp. He raced forward, hoping to pull Fetchstorm off Wilson before he could hurt her.

Fetchstorm and Wilson rolled on the ground. Fetchstorm had caught her in the local fighting hug. He had his claws sunk into her back. But Wilson caught his head and thrust it down, pushing it into his chest with both her arms. The maneuver kept the vicious teeth trapped between their bodies, well away from her throat.

Her legs were longer than Fetchstorm's, and she kicked him hard in the stomach, keeping his hind claws well away from her own body.

Kirk reached for them just as Wilson managed to roll them over. She knelt on Fetchstorm's belly as his hind legs flailed wildly. "For Elath, stay out, Captain!" she panted at him. "He's a kid!"

He had no doubt she meant it, but how could he stand by and let her be mauled?

The pair rolled away from him. Fetchstorm, unable to bite, flung his hindquarters back to try to bring his feet up inside hers. Wilson followed, swung and wrapped her legs around his belly and hung on as she had to the tree. Fetchstorm kicked air wildly

Wilson gave another sudden thrust, pushed his head further down, and bit his ear—hard.

Fetchstorm squawked, released his claws and thrust away

from her. She released just as quickly and rolled backward, coming up in ready position.

Kirk stepped between the two, steeling himself to take the brunt of Fetchstorm's next assault.

Nothing happened. Fetchstorm turned his back on the two of them and began to preen his fur.

Wilson went limp, took an enormous breath. Without taking his eyes off Fetchstorm, Kirk caught her by the shoulders. She grinned up at him, closed her eyes briefly and exhaled.

Fetchstorm started toward them, and Kirk tensed, but there was no threat in the youngster's approach. He stood before them and looked Wilson up and down. "Human," he said, and he offered her his tail.

"Thanks, Fetchstorm," said Wilson. "You put up a good fight, but it was important to me."

"Yes," he said. "Shall I wash you? Stiff Tail says your customs are very different from ours. Your fighting is!"

"From what I've seen of your tongue, it'd probably be rougher on me than your fighting, but I appreciate the offer. I'll just go down to the stream and splash a little water on to take off the dust. You'd better see to your own pelt, though. You look a mess." She drew clawlike fingers through her dusty hair. "I should talk." She pulled out a comb, as Fetchstorm twisted to preen his shoulder again. There was a snag in his fur he could not quite reach, and Wilson said, "Here, let me get that for you, Fetchstorm, if it's okay." He nodded, combining the human gesture with the Sivaoan ears-back surprise. She stepped away from Kirk's supporting arm to run her comb through the snag. Fetchstorm remained twisted to watch.

Kirk felt damp with relief, then glanced at his arm. His sleeve was matted with blood. "Evan, your back!"

"Hurts like hell," she admitted, still combing Fetchstorm. "How bad is it?"

"How should I know? You're the doctor!" He drew her away from Fetchstorm to look. The back of her uniform was ripped nearly in two. Two long deep sets of slash marks stretched from the base of her neck outward to her shoulders. They oozed blood.

"Evan!" It was Brightspot. "I'll get Catchclaw." And she was gone again.

Kirk righted the camp stool with one hand and pushed her onto it with the other. "Tell me what to do," he said.

"Unless it's bleeding badly, we might as well wait for the doctor. And stop making such a fuss. I've been hurt worse in saber practice."

"Is that wise?"

"What—Catchclaw? You let her work on you."

This was not the best of times to discuss the abilities of the local doctors Kirk realized. The fight had drawn a crowd.

Stiff Tail pushed him aside to examine Wilson's back and shoulders. With her tail, she snatched at Fetchstorm and made him look as well. Then she cuffed him soundly.

Wilson half rose in indignation. "It was a fair fight, Stiff Tail, and it was between the two of us. The matter is settled."

"Fetchstorm was told not to fight because you are fragile creatures and because your customs are unknown. He disobeyed." She stared and Wilson sat down again, resigned to her logic. Stiff Tail went on, "Is it your custom to fight in this fashion?"

"We sometimes brawl for fun but we ordinarily take precautions like padded clothing." She chuckled, "As Fetchstorm noticed, we don't have a layer of fur to protect us from claws."

"You have no claws and no teeth—"

"I have teeth. Check Fetchstorm's ear."

Stiff Tail did. "You left no marks."

"I didn't think I had to."

The crowd parted to let Catchclaw through. *Even McCoy's growl couldn't compete with that,* thought Kirk, especially when she saw the wounds on Evan's back. Then with much tut-tutting in softer tones to Evan, she set to work; Jinx handed her various items without comment.

Stiff Tail gave one last wary look at Wilson, then turned to Spock, "Your companion is no longer in danger—shall we continue our conversation?"

"Go ahead, Spock. I'll keep an eye on her." Kirk meant Catchclaw, but Spock's nod was at Wilson.

Wilson grunted; whether in response to Spock's eye or the salve Catchclaw spread on her wounds, Kirk couldn't tell.

Catchclaw said, "Keep it clean. Stay out of fights. I doubt *CloudShape* would know what to do if you break a bone. And see me after evening meal." She growled a few additional comments that seemed to have to do with Wilson's anatomy but which the universal translator refused to translate and stamped away.

The excitement was over. The others went back to their business, and Kirk found himself alone with Wilson. "Well, Dr. Wilson," he began.

"Fetchstorm started it," she said immediately. Then, in a more serious tone, she added, "Captain, I apologize, but I could not let a general slur on humans pass without note. Here, names *mean* something."

"I won't have my ship's doctor picking fights with the natives."

She lifted her chin with an expression of injured pride. "Yes, Captain. I shall consider myself cuffed."

He smiled. "Good," he said, and only then did he let himself express the concern he felt. "Dammit, Evan, you could have been killed!"

She shook her head. "No, Captain. When kids fight, they break away if anybody squawks. Remember yesterday—the fight between Fetchstorm and Brightspot? They were supposed to break it up when one of the two squawked. When they didn't, an adult stepped in and cuffed them both for overstepping the bounds of polite combat."

"You mean to say that Stiff Tail hit them not for fighting but for fighting dirty?"

"Something like that, yes." She shrugged her shoulders stiffly. "Ow," she said, "Catchclaw doesn't believe in painkillers." She pulled a hypo out of her medical kit and loaded it. The hypo hissed against her shoulder and she sighed deeply. "When it's my back, *I* do," she said, putting her equipment away.

"She probably thinks it serves you right. . . ."

She smiled ruefully. "Probably. Were you and Spock able to learn anything in there?"

Kirk found another camp stool and pulled it up beside hers. "Mostly YNK," he said, but he told her what they'd found.

As he finished, Fetchstorm returned, carrying with him a long blue and silver useful. "Dr. Wilson," he said, unable to meet her eyes, "please don't be angry with me for mentioning it, but you have so little fur for protection and your 'clothing' is ruined. . . . You need something to replace it." He thrust the fluttering bundle of fabric into her hands. "A gift," he finished quickly.

Evan cocked her head at him. "From you, or from Stiff Tail?"

"From me," he said, his ears showing surprise at the question.

"Then I accept," Evan said. She drew the useful through reverent fingers. "So very beautiful. . . ." Her voice was soft but there was no mistaking her admiration, and Fetchstorm straightened and looked at her directly.

"Thank you," he said, brightening visibly, "I made it."

"I think you must be some kind of magician, Fetchstorm. I couldn't do that."

"You couldn't?" He bent to sniff at her, and Jim Kirk realized he suspected her of tail pulling.

Evan said, "I couldn't: no one ever taught me to weave."

"I could," he said.

"You're on," said Evan, rising from the stool. "Give me a few moments to change and then I'll come be your apprentice." He waited, and Evan added, "It is the custom of my people to change clothing in private."

"Oh!" he said in amazement and darted away.

Kirk chuckled. "I don't know what you're going to do with that useful, Evan, but you'd better think of something."

Evan looked down at the silky fabric, then up at him. "Stitchit 9-10, Captain," she said. "You'd be amazed what I can do with surgical glue," and left him staring after her, trying to figure that one out.

As she disappeared into Chekov's shelter, Jim Kirk turned to find Brightspot beside him, watching disconsolately, tail and whiskers drooping. "What's wrong?" he asked and, when she made no reply, his concern deepened. "Please tell me. I'd like to be your friend. Isn't a friend someone you can tell your troubles to?" He stooped to pick up her limp tail and stroke its tip.

"You can't tell your troubles to *me,"* she said. "Oh, I'm not angry with you about that. Evan explained it to me. But I wanted to help anyway. Last night, I asked some people, and this morning I asked Stiff Tail about the . . . You-Know-Whos."

He stiffened, and Brightspot said defensively, "You asked Stiff Tail! I'm allowed to be curious!" Her tail twitched briefly within his grasp.

"Is that why she cuffed you?" he asked sympathetically.

Brightspot nodded. "And then she told me I was a kid and I shouldn't stick my tail into adult matters. So I didn't learn anything at all. . . ." Her whiskers drooped again.

"Thank you for trying, Brightspot. It was very kind of you."

She shook her head. "I didn't help, and I made things worse. I asked Fetchstorm because he's really nosy and sometimes he knows things he's not supposed to."

"How could that hurt?"

"I had to trade him. I had to tell him all about Evan and your names—that's why he miscalled her. He hurt her, and it's my fault." She glared and added, "And he didn't even know the answer to my question!"

"No, Brightspot!" She blinked at his vehemence and he said, more softly, but just as firmly, "Dr. Wilson fights her own battles. You are not to blame for what happened. In fact, Dr. Wilson seems inordinately proud of herself for having fought Fetchstorm. *She* thinks she won."

"She was hurt!"

"So was Fetchstorm," he pointed out. "From the squawk he made, I venture to guess that his ear will be sore for a week. *And* he apologized to her for his behavior."

Brightspot nodded. "We aren't supposed to fight with you."

"Wilson was not supposed to fight with Fetchstorm either..I 'cuffed' her for her behavior the way Stiff Tail cuffed Fetchstorm."

She cocked her ears at him. "I didn't see . . ."

"Because I cuffed her with words, Brightspot. Among my people that has the same effect as your mother's slap has on you."

Brightspot's tail began to curl again. "Then she's not angry at me?"

He shook his head firmly. "Not at all. Ask her if you doubt me."

That shocked her. "I wouldn't doubt you, Captain!"

"Good," he said and smiled. "Now I could use your help with some more baby questions. . . ." She instantly clasped her hands, while her tail looped cheerfully around his wrist and squeezed.

"Tell me about your religion," he began carefully, as if clasping his own hands against possible misinterpretation. And when she clearly did not understand his use of the word, he talked around the subject until at last she said, "Oh, way of living! You should talk to Left Ear. She knows all about it." She tugged his wrist with her tail. "Come on, I'll introduce you." Kirk followed, only a tail loop behind.

Chapter Nine

Uhura had done as Brightspot suggested, and it was a good thing she had—Rushlight later said he would indeed have been angry had she not explained her own customs and agreed to abide by his. They spent their evening trading songs and learning about each other. He was almost as delighted by her earrings as she was to learn that he too had perfect pitch. He had not understood her joy in that until she explained that Chekov whistled off-key; at that, his tail looped and he said, "Think of him as welcome-homes. Deafness does not dampen his enthusiasm any more than it does Brightspot's." And she, smiling, had to agree.

By then, the hour was late. "Let us sleep on shared songs," Rushlight had said and, thinking it unwise to pressure him, Uhura had agreed.

When she awoke, to her dismay, Rushlight was nowhere to be found. Disturbed and disappointed, she sought Spock and, once again, he had given her the courage to persevere. She would keep at it; she would find a way to help Sunfall and Christine and all the others.

Uhura introduced herself to one of Chekov's budding shelter builders and asked the whereabouts of Rushlight. The child, CopperEye to-Srallansre, who came only waist high to her if one didn't count his ears, said, "He's hunting—will *you* sing me a song?"

His whiskers quivered so eagerly that she could not disappoint him. Drawing out her *joyeuse,* she obliged with a lively air popular with Eeiauoan children. He was more than satisfied, and she soon gathered a crowd of children, equally eager for songs. At the edge of the crowd hung one young adult, the "masked" Sivaoan Uhura had first spoken to; curiously, Jinx to-Ennien seemed afraid to join the rest.

At the end of the song, one of CopperEye's friends poked him with her tail. "Maybe we should give her something?"

"I don't know," said CopperEye.

"Seems right," said the other. "Go ahead."

CopperEye said shyly. "Should we give you something? Because you sang just for us?"

Uhura said thoughtfully, "I don't know what's proper in your customs. In my custom, I sing for the joy of singing. I don't even need an audience, but shared joy is doubled."

CopperEye's friend turned—reluctantly, it seemed—and called to Jinx. "Should we give her something, Jinx? Her custom or ours?"

Uhura waited for Jinx's answer. When it came, Jinx spoke so quietly she could barely hear. "Please, Jinx," said Uhura, motioning to her. "Come closer."

Jinx started to obey, but CopperEye said hastily, "She said 'Our custom—to be safe.' You really couldn't hear her?"

"No, my ears are not as sharp as yours, CopperEye."

CopperEye looked her over critically. He nodded, "Too small, I guess."

Uhura smiled. "That's a matter of opinion, CopperEye. Perhaps your ears are too large."

He flicked them back in surprise.

While he considered that, Uhura motioned once again to Jinx. "Please," she said, "it is apparent that I do not hear as well as you. But you're right—I should follow your custom. I am a guest in your camp. If you would be kind enough to explain what I must do in order to be polite, I would be very grateful."

CopperEye's friend jabbed him with a tail tip. "Not *Jinx,*" she whispered. Jinx heard the unmistakable emphasis as clearly as Uhura did and, whiskers and tail drooping, she began to slink away.

CopperEye said, "Stupid!" He cuffed his friend, who hissed and backed.

"Wait," said Uhura to the pair—and, more loudly, "Jinx, please don't go! *Please!*" To her relief, Jinx stopped, waited with frightened eyes. Uhura looked again at the two young ones. "Listen carefully," she said to them. "This is one custom of my own by which I *must* abide. I do not know Jinx, but she has never done anything to harm me. I don't know what she has done to hurt you, little one. . . ."

The little gray Sivaoan lashed her tail and said, with a sullen look at CopperEye, "Jinx hasn't hurt me!"

"Then *why . . . ?*"

"She's just Jinx," CopperEye said, as if that explained everything.

Uhura wondered if it did. "CopperEye, a long time ago— long before your grandmother's grandmother was born— people might have said that of me. There were people then who would, without even knowing so much about me as my name, have told me to go away because of the color of my skin."

That brought about the ears-back look of pure amazement from all of them. "But everybody has different-colored skin. Look!" He turned his palms up—so did the rest. One of CopperEye's palms was gray, the other pink. His friend's were pink with three black fingers. "That *would* be silly!"

"Yes, it would. And it would be just as silly for me to turn Jinx away because 'She's just Jinx.' I want to get to know her before I decide I don't like her." Uhura raised her head to address Jinx directly. "Maybe I'll find a friend."

Jinx's ears perked, then flicked back in surprise. "Will you come, Jinx, and tell me how to be polite in your custom?" She looked down at the two others. "Will you invite her, too? To share the joy of a song is to double it."

CopperEye looked at Uhura, at his friend and then at Jinx. "Come on, Jinx"—he nudged his friend with his tail—"Say something to her, SilverTail. It's your fault!"

"Is *not,*" said SilverTail, her tail lashing. But she too turned and said, "Please come, Jinx. I'm sorry I was stupid. Copper-Eye makes me say stupid things all the time."

The outrageousness of this got her cuffed again and ended

in a knock-down, drag-out fight between the two. By the time the fight had come to its natural end, Jinx had pulled together the courage to join the group. Some moved a little away from her, Uhura saw, but CopperEye—alternately washing his shoulder and SilverTail's—said, "You tell her, Jinx. She's a bard and she doesn't know she's a bard."

Uhura looked up at the young female who seemed so like Sunfall of Ennien.

"Among our people," Jinx began, "a bard is a very special person. Isn't this true among your people as well?"

"Yes," said Uhura, "but I'm not a bard, not professionally. I sing because I love to sing."

"Then, forgive me, but there's something wrong with the way you use the word—if you love to sing and you sing with such beauty, then by our standards you're a bard."

"All right," said Uhura, smiling. "What must I do—as a bard—to follow your customs?"

"You sang a song for CopperEye—at his request. Now he wishes to know what he may do for you in return."

Uhura spread her hands. "I have no idea what sort of return to ask, CopperEye. I don't know the fair return for a song on your world."

CopperEye said, "I can gather wood for your fire, or get water for your cooking pot, or—I know where the best silverberries are"—this caused a mild sensation— "and I could pick you a basketful."

Uhura turned it all over in her mind. The group waited breathlessly for her to choose. At last, she said, "Could you help me learn your language, CopperEye? Would that be fair?"

"But you speak our language!"

Uhura shook her head and explained the universal translator in the simplest possible terms. Then she turned it off to demonstrate. Amazement ran through their ears in great waves of movement.

CopperEye said something and Jinx translated in the Old Tongue, which Uhura did understand. "He says that's fair."

"Good," said Uhura. "Would you be kind enough to ask him how to say, 'What is that called?'"

Jinx did and CopperEye said something, pronouncing it

very slowly and clearly. Uhura repeated it, adding to Jinx, "Please, ask him to correct me if I get it wrong. I have no wish to learn halfway."

Jinx translated. CopperEye nodded at Uhura, solemnly.

Uhura turned the translator back on. "I will make the same agreement with all of you," she said. "I will sing whenever you ask me if, in return, you will all help me learn your language." She smiled. "I shall wander all over your camp, pointing and saying, 'What is that called?'—and I shall make a terrible nuisance of myself, I promise. I shall be worse than your brother or sister because I have to be told *everything*. And, probably, I shall have to be told everything three times. Are my songs worth that much trouble in return?"

"Oh, yes!" said CopperEye and, to Uhura's immense joy, there seemed to be general agreement on that subject.

"Good," she said. "Then you must first teach me how to ask for a song, so I'll understand you when you do. And then you will tell your names for different *kinds* of song, so I can sing one that will please you."

Uhura sang for hours and for hours the children taught her their language. Once, she asked Jinx to explain a word. Jinx looked at her in surprise. Uhura said, instantly, "I'm sorry, Jinx. I thought you agreed to the bargain as well."

Ears still back, Jinx said, "I didn't know I was included."

"Of course you are. I thought that was understood. Will you help me learn in return for songs?"

"Oh, yes!" Her silver gray tail looped in pure joy.

Soon the afternoon sun began to beat down, and they all moved to the shade of the forest. Several of the younger ones wandered off to do chores, to be replaced by others who, apprised of the bargain, readily agreed to join in.

"You have not eaten," Jinx pointed out at last. "We should give her a rest," she announced to the others. "Even the best bard's voice tires."

With all the expected reluctance of children, they agreed, and the crowd slowly dissipated back to camp. Jinx lingered behind.

Uhura put away her *joyeuse,* rose and stretched her cramped muscles. "What is it, Jinx?" she asked. The young female was disturbed about something. "What troubles you?"

"Would you—would you eat with me?" Jinx seemed to steel herself for a refusal.

"I'd be delighted," said Uhura. "It's very sweet of you to invite me." Jinx seemed so startled by this that for a moment Uhura was afraid she might bolt like a frightened deer. She didn't, so Uhura said, "Please, lead the way." Jinx did, her step light, almost dancing now. Her resemblance to Sunfall was even more marked in the supple grace of her movements. Uhura fought back tears at the thought.

By the time they reached Jinx's tent, Uhura had regained her control, but Jinx seemed to give her a questioning look nonetheless.

Jinx ushered her in and pointed to a camp stool. When Uhura began to thank her, she said, "Rest and eat first. We'll exchange news later, when your throat is soothed." She brought out brightly colored bowls and an array of fruits and smoked meat, untwisting the latter from ornamental strips hung to one side of the tent. She said, "This is all food you can eat without harm. Catchclaw and I both checked it with her sensors. But I won't be offended if you double-check."

"I'll take your word for it, Jinx." She smiled. "Evan says you and Catchclaw might grumble about our odd physiology, but you wouldn't do us any harm."

"First rule of good medicine," Jinx said, then, with an air of conspiracy, she added, "She had me show her emergency medical techniques for a Sivaoan, and she showed me what to do for you or Mr. Spock."

"That doesn't surprise me. Evan doesn't seem the type to pass up *any* kind of knowledge if it's available."

"She offers it, as well, I mean. You all do."

"People must learn from each other, Jinx. If that weren't important, why would there be so many differences in the universe?"

Jinx shook her head. "I don't know. . . . You aren't eating. Are our senses of taste so different that you find it bad?"

"Oh, no. I'm resting and thinking."

"Then eat while you rest and think."

Uhura smiled and obeyed. They ate together in silence and, the food gone—Uhura *had* been hungry and the food good—they sat awhile in the same comfortable silence. Uhura found it a pleasure to relax for a time.

At last, Jinx stretched. It was a lavish production, one Uhura had seen Sunfall perform many a time, and it involved each muscle in her body. Uhura watched Jinx's skin ripple with the pleasure. "A good stretch," Sunfall had once said, "will do as much for your body as a good song will do for your heart."

Jinx said, "I hope you will forgive me for asking—I don't know your people and their smells well—but contrary to your smell you seem unhappy. Do you wish to leave my company?"

"Oh no! I am more at ease here than I have been for a long time. I am sad only—only because you remind me so of a friend." She had to say as much but she did not say any more.

"Is that why you asked if I was 'of Ennien'?" At Uhura's nod of confirmation, Jinx hesitated a moment and then went on, "You said you brought news of my relatives. . . . Will you tell me?"

"I would like to very much," Uhura answered carefully, "but when I first spoke to you, Winding Path cuffed you. When Captain Kirk tried to speak of the matter, *he* was cuffed."

"I won't hit you. I give you my word in Old Tongue."

"It's not me I'm worried about. I have no wish to cause you trouble with your people."

Jinx grasped her tail and shook it. "StarFreedom, you have seen how my people treat me. In fact, aside from Catchclaw, you are the only person who has ever tried to help me. You can't possibly get me in any more trouble than I'm in for being Jinx. . . . Please tell me your news. I must know."

Uhura looked her up and down, from the tips of her quivering ears to her claws, sunk into the useful beneath her. She was in earnest and to deny her would hurt her deeply. To tell her might just help Sunfall. Captain Kirk had told her to use her own judgment and, to her, no other decision was possible. She reached into her utility pouch and brought out the photograph of Sunfall of Ennien. Tears filled her eyes and she wiped them hastily away. She motioned Jinx to her side.

Jinx took the picture she held out and looked. "She's very beautiful," she said.

Uhura opened her mouth to speak and the words caught in her throat. She took a deep breath and tried again. "Her name is Sunfall, Sunfall of Ennien. I don't know if you have seen yourself in a mirror or in a painting or reflected in a lake, Jinx, but you could be her younger sister. You have that same beauty. That's why I spoke to you and asked if you were of Ennien."

"She looks born to-Ennien," Jinx confirmed. " 'A tail so long it can be angry and delighted at the same time.' But you keep saying 'of Ennien.' "

"She lives on another world, Jinx, a long way from here. It is their custom to name themselves *of* Ennien, *of* Vensre. I suppose it's because they knew they could no longer go *to* Ennien or *to* Vensre, but they still wanted to remember this world in some way, even after two thousand years in exile." There—she'd said the word.

Jinx made no move to strike. She continued to consider Sunfall's photograph. "Odd," she said, "to think I have a relative on another world. . . ." She pulled a stool close by and continued, "I know there are other worlds, and it seems likely they'd have life too—especially since I've seen you and a Vulcan—but to have a relative on another world that I didn't even *know* about!"

She seemed unable to take her eyes from the photograph, even as she sat. "Why didn't she come with you?"

Again, tears stung Uhura's eyes. This time Jinx looked alarmed. "Your eyes!" she said.

Uhura wiped at her eyes. "Don't be frightened, Jinx. It's just something humans do when they are very unhappy."

Uhura looked at Sunfall's photograph and saw again in her mind's eye the Eeiauoan hospital. "Sunfall didn't come with us because she is dying. She may already have—" Her voice failed her completely. She clasped her hands in her lap and struggled for control.

Suddenly, she felt the warmth of Jinx's tail wrapped around

her waist. "I'm sorry," she said, "I don't mean to cry but . . . Sunfall and Christine . . . and god alone knows how many others by now . . . all dying. *All dying.*"

"That's why you asked for our help?"

Shakily, Uhura nodded.

"But if we can help, why aren't we?" Jinx's tail tip flicked once in anger, then gripped her waist again.

"I don't *know* that you can help. I only *hope* you can help—your medical science must have advanced a great deal since . . . the Eeiauoans left this world. It's just possible that your science has a cure. But we've been forbidden to speak of the Eeiauoans. Stiff Tail would have us expelled from camp if she learns I spoke of them to you."

"Tell me," said Jinx. "Tell me everything you know about the disease and its symptoms. *I* will ask Catchclaw for you." She thrust the portrait of Sunfall into her hands and added, "For my relative, Sunfall of Ennien."

She leaned close, and Uhura could feel her comforting warmth against her shoulder. Jinx said, "And I promise you in the Old Tongue that no one will ever hear how it happened that I am asking these questions."

"T—thank you, Jinx. Even if there is nothing that can be done, thank you for caring about someone you've never even met."

Jinx squeezed lightly with her tail. "I've met you," she said. "And you gave me songs and other worlds to think about . . . how can I fail to help?"

Jim Kirk found Left Ear a charming, matronly female—almost plump by local standards. Her fur was ginger banded, her eyes a brilliant shade of gold, her muzzle cream colored. As for her left ear, he could see nothing unusual about it.

Brightspot introduced the two and then said, "He wants to ask baby questions." She explained carefully what she meant. When she had finished, Left Ear said, "I understand, Captain. If it is of any reassurance to you, I am quite used to dealing with ignorance—you'll notice I don't say 'stupidity,' although I must admit I've dealt with that as well."

Kirk nodded. Recalling his conversation with Stiff Tail, he said carefully, "I do not speak the Old Tongue, Left Ear, but

I give you my word that I will not repeat whatever information you give me to anyone *unless* it is necessary to save a life."

Left Ear and Brightspot looked at each other. "Bless you!" said Left Ear. Her tail corkscrewed. "That is not necessary with me! Brightspot has mislead you!"

"I didn't mean to," said Brightspot, looking contrite.

Left Ear looped her tail around Brightspot and drew her close. "Of course you didn't, child. But when you tell someone our customs, you should also tell him the exceptions." To Kirk, she said, "You may repeat anything I tell you. I only ask that you repeat how it happened. Do not improve it."

"I'll be careful, Left Ear; you have my word."

"Fine. Sit down and ask your questions. If you wish, you may sit well out of reach of my strong right hand. . . ."

It was not a joke. It was a genuine offer, made to reassure him. It did—he sat down first and let her position her chair where she wished. He was mildly relieved to see that she chose a spot just out of arm's reach. Brightspot sat on her heels, with her tail curled contentedly about her toes.

Kirk phrased the question carefully. "We are—strangers to your world, Left Ear. We know nothing of your customs. It has been our experience on other worlds that sometimes we can learn only by making mistakes."

Left Ear nodded—*That expression is certainly getting around,* Jim Kirk thought—and she said, "As Brightspot says, you have to ask baby questions." Her tail looped up and her whiskers arched forward. "There are some things babies are taught only in a negative way. They are cuffed for their curiosity about some subjects. Is this true on your world, also?"

"I'm afraid so. But it seldom stops them from being curious, from wanting or—*needing* to know the answers to certain questions." He took a deep breath. "Yesterday, I believe my questions were of that sort. Perhaps I have, in my ignorance, trampled on a religious taboo. If I knew, if I *understood* what I had done, I might be able to ask my questions in a way that would not be sacrilegious." That was the best he could do without actually mentioning the Eeiauoans. He hoped it would be enough. He also hoped the distance between the two of them would give him ample time to duck if she swung.

Left Ear stared at him fixedly. The tip of her tail shivered with suppressed emotion. Suddenly, she was on her feet.

Kirk tensed, ready to leap to one side to avoid a blow, but she made no move toward him. "Brightspot—out!" she said.

Brightspot cowered but her eyes were bright with defiance. "I want to know too, Left Ear!"

Left Ear's tail lashed. She gave Kirk a fearsome glance, then turned again to Brightspot and repeated, "Out!"

This time Brightspot scrambled. She was out of the tent before the useful she'd been sitting on had a chance to drift to the ground.

Jim Kirk rose. "I apologize, Left Ear—" he said, placatingly.

"You sit."

He sat, so hard he jarred his teeth.

Left Ear very slowly sat down again, this time sliding her chair a little further out of reach. Her tail beat the ground with a steady, ominous thump. Her ears were almost flat against her head.

"What you speak of is not religious," she said.

He opened his mouth to exclaim at this, but she said, instantly, "Say nothing more! I warn you! You must not press this! Wait!" She took several deep breaths and her ears slowly began to rise to their normal position.

She said, with effort, "You speak of a shameful thing. If you and your people have met strangers before, you must know that the more shameful a thing, the more difficult it is to speak of to strangers."

He nodded. Better that than speak when she had forbidden it. It was clear that she was trying very hard to keep her temper; if she lost it, he might lose what chance he had at the information.

She went on, "We do not speak of this to our *own* children. Shall we tell it to the children of strangers?" She shook her head; she did not mean for him to answer that.

He had to speak. "To save lives," he said, "to save lives I would tell my own most shameful secret, Left Ear."

"I do not know. I do not know *you*. And perhaps I do not have your strength, Captain Kirk." Her yellow eyes bored into his and held them for an age. "I will think," she said, at last. "Leave now and let me think. When my anger is gone—when I can speak to you with my claws sheathed—I shall come to your tent and we shall talk further."

"Thank you, Left Ear." Kirk rose and walked to the tent opening. He knew he would get no further at the moment and, if he left it, he might have some chance later.

"Captain Kirk!" Her voice stopped him, and he turned to face her again. She said, "If I can speak of this, I will. But I make you no promise in the Old Tongue."

He nodded and stepped out into the clearing. *At least that's something,* he thought. And he had gained some information —even if it was only what Wilson called YNK.

He found himself in the shade of an ancient tree at the edge of the encircling forest and sat down to think. *Something you don't tell children . . .*

Something crashed through the upper branches and, still tensed from the encounter with Left Ear, he threw himself to the side. Brightspot scrambled down the tree trunk and leapt the last five feet to land on one knee beside him.

"Did she tell you? Are you all right? Did she cuff you? Shall I get Catchclaw?"

If nothing else, her enthusiastic questioning cheered him. He held up his hands. "Please! One question at a time!"

"Are you all right?"

"Yes," he said. "She never laid a hand on me."

Brightspot looked relieved. "She *scared* me. I've never seen her angry. She doesn't *get* angry. Well, she does, but not like that!" Brightspot seemed unable to relax. Her visible distress over Left Ear's behavior gave force to her assessment.

"Was she that angry when you asked her, Brightspot?"

Brightspot shook her head. "No. She flicked her tail a little and, like everybody else, said I should keep my tail out where it's not wanted." That seemed to reassure her. "She *wasn't* angry at me!"

"No, she was angry at me."

"So she didn't tell you anything."

"I think she tried, Brightspot, but she couldn't. Some things are very hard to talk about."

"Maybe she'll try again, then."

"I hope so."

They sat in silence in the shade of the tree for a long while. Kirk thought back to his childhood. How did he get information adults wouldn't give freely? *Of course!* "Brightspot, where's the nearest library?"

Brightspot said, "What?"

"Library?" he repeated, but it was painfully clear there was no equivalent word in Sivaoan. He stared at her a moment in sheer disbelief, then began the business of explaining 'library,' 'book' and 'reference work.'

"Enough!" begged Brightspot at last. "My *ears* ache!" and she apparently meant from the strain of constant amazement. In the resulting silence, she rubbed the muscles at the base of each ear. "You mean," she said finally, "you don't *remember* things?"

"I couldn't possibly remember *everything,* Brightspot!"

"Do you remember the night we first talked and you explained about the baby questions?"

"Of course. That would be hard to forget."

"Tell me how it happened." That seemed to be formula or ritual. Kirk told her all he could remember of the encounter. Making an effort to be as accurate as possible, he found himself recalling details he ordinarily would not have mentioned.

When he was done, Brightspot said, "But you don't even remember that! *This* is how it happened. . . ." She proceeded to give him her own version. It included every line of dialogue, no matter how unimportant, and descriptions of the eyes of the speakers—whether they were dilated or contracted—and of the position of her tail, claws and ears.

About halfway through, Jim Kirk turned on his tricorder and scanned for the rest of the conversation. Spock had recorded it for the ship's computers. Brightspot had missed nothing in her account.

Brightspot looked at the tiny image on the tricorder screen. "You store your memory in a *machine!?*" she said.

"It is more accurate than my physical memory, as you yourself noticed. Are all your people able to remember with that kind of accuracy?"

Brightspot thought. "Left Ear said to tell you about exceptions, too. No, not all. Sometimes a very bad fever or blow to the head . . . *that's* what happened! When Stiff Tail hit you, you forgot!"

"No, Brightspot, it's not that simple. I have a very good memory for my people. Ask Dr. Wilson or Uhura or Spock. Spock has a better memory than I have, but that's normal for a Vulcan."

She was on her feet and tugging at his arm with her tail. "Come, I must ask Evan!" She hurried him across the clearing where, just beyond Chekov's shelter, they found Spock improvising a table.

Wilson was assisting and, as she and Spock turned to greet them, Jim Kirk saw that she had not disappointed Fetchstorm. She wore the child's blue and silver useful wrapped twice around her waist, rising to cross her breasts on the diagonal, her arms and shoulders bare; the remaining length rippled behind her, emphasizing the bareness of her back. The colors made her blue eyes even bluer, but the eyecatching thing about it, he thought, was how accident prone it looked—then he remembered, and suddenly understood, her remark about surgical glue.

In any event, it certainly did not disappoint *him*, but Brightspot gave him no time to express his appreciation.

"Evan!" said Brightspot, "Do you remember the conversation we had about baby questions?"

Evan Wilson cocked her head slightly to one side. "Something's in dispute?" she asked, "Mr. Spock could check his tricorder records."

Kirk said, "Brightspot wants to check your memory, Dr. Wilson."

"Oh," she said, as if that explained everything. "Do you want the short form or the whole megillah, Brightspot?" "Megillah," of course, did not translate, but Brightspot got the gist of the expression.

139

"Tell me how it happened."

Evan Wilson closed her eyes and, like Alice, began at the beginning. . . . Her version was considerably more accurate than his own and she included facial expressions and descriptions of Brightspot's tail and ears.

Spock said, "You have a very good memory, Dr. Wilson."

Wilson shook her head sharply. "Only on short term, Mr. Spock."

Brightspot said, "Mr. Spock, will you tell me?"

"If you wish to test the accuracy of my memory, Brightspot, you would do better to choose another incident. Having just now heard Dr. Wilson's version of the events in question, I have been reminded—although I would offer some emendations and corrections to her account."

Brightspot caught her own tail and shook it in one hand. It seemed a gesture of strong impatience. "Tell me about the conversation we just had with Stiff Tail."

"In detail?" Spock asked.

"Tell me how it happened," said Brightspot. Spock took this to mean 'in detail' and did. Brightspot listened, ears and whiskers quivering with the effort. When Spock had finished, she caught her tail in both hands, wrung it and said urgently, "Wait here. I have to get Stiff Tail." She darted off, leaving Kirk to explain the conversation that had led to this.

"No books!" said Wilson. "No libraries! Elath!—no wonder I couldn't find out anything about medical references!" She sat and jammed her chin disconsolately into her palm. After a moment, she looked up, surprised. "No wonder they hold grudges so well!"

Kirk looked at her inquiringly, and she explained, "If you learn information from a book, you're free to interpret—if you learn it from a person, you'd be more likely to be influenced by the manner of its delivery."

"A very good point," said Spock, thoughtfully. "However, an oral tradition of this magnitude would seem to leave a great deal of scope for the transmission of accumulated inaccuracies."

"You wouldn't say that, Spock, if you'd heard Brightspot's version of our conversation. It did not vary from your tricorder's." Jim Kirk tapped the instrument for emphasis.

"Fascinating," said Spock. He did not continue.

Brightspot returned, with Stiff Tail in tow. She was talking at high speed to the older woman. As they came within range of the universal translator, Kirk realized that Brightspot was telling Stiff Tail *his* version of their conversation, including their refusal to tell Brightspot their urgent questions and the reasoning behind it.

Brightspot then gestured at Wilson and repeated *her* version. She finished with a rapid-fire repeat of Spock's version of the conversation with Stiff Tail. Spock's brow lifted higher and higher; he switched on his tricorder.

Stiff Tail pointed to the instrument. "This remembers for you?" she asked.

"Yes," said Spock, "when I wish to retain an accurate account for the ship's records, I record the proceedings in this manner."

"I would like to see," said Stiff Tail. "But first, I must hear with both ears your—mind's—account of our conversation."

"As you wish," said Spock. "I presume you require a verbatim account of the conversation that took place between us in your laboratory." She nodded, and he complied. Once or twice during his account, she gave him an ears-back surprised look, but she did not interrupt. He then played back their conversation as recorded. To Jim Kirk's ear, the difference between the two versions seemed minimal.

Finally, Stiff Tail said, "May I ask without insult—a baby question?"

Kirk said, "Go ahead, Stiff Tail."

"Is this inability to remember the result of an injury? I know of no local disease that could afflict the memory so noticeably—"

Spock said, "What you have heard, Stiff Tail, and I am under the assumption that Brightspot has relayed to you both Dr. Wilson's and Captain Kirk's versions of a single incident,

141

is a fairly accurate representation of the range of human and Vulcan memory."

"This is normal? Physiologically normal?"

"For our peoples, yes. Some other peoples, also members of the Federation, do have your people's ability for total recall, but we do not."

Stiff Tail," Wilson put in, "the memory is there, we just don't access it as well as you do. Mr. Spock could demonstrate. There's a Vulcan technique that enables him to read from another mind a fully accurate replay of a given event. My conversation with Fetchstorm, for example. Mr. Spock was not present, but *he* could tell you 'how it happened' even if I can't."

Whiskers quivering with interest, Stiff Tail said, "I would appreciate such a demonstration."

"Dr. Wilson," said Spock, "I must advise you that the process is often painful. The human mind gives up its secrets reluctantly."

Wilson frowned slightly and, for the first time since Kirk had met her, she seemed indecisive. At last she said, "I'm willing if you are, Mr. Spock." When Spock nodded, she added to Stiff Tail, "I assume Fetchstorm will be able to verify the accuracy of Mr. Spock's account?"

Stiff Tail said, "Fetchstorm has told me how it happened. I shall be able to verify the accuracy of the account."

After a moment of preparation, Spock looked inquiringly at Wilson, who took a deep breath and nodded her readiness. Spock reached toward her. The tips of his fingers barely brushed her temple, but she gasped with shock at the contact—then she closed her eyes and made no other sound while Spock told Stiff Tail how it happened between Wilson and Fetchstorm. . . .

Spock drew back his hand. With a second deep breath, Wilson opened her eyes and focused with effort on Spock. At last, she said, her voice unsteady, "Thank you for the experience, Mr. Spock." She turned to Stiff Tail. "Was he accurate by your standards?"

"He was!" said Stiff Tail, her ears amazed. Wilson nodded, drew out a medical sensor and began to take readings on

Spock. *Fully recovered,* Kirk thought. Stiff Tail said, "Is this also a part of the process?"

Evan Wilson shook her head. "I'm still finding out about Vulcans, Stiff Tail," she explained. "Mr. Spock, are you aware of any lowering of your body temperature when you do that, particularly in your fingertips?"

"No, doctor, I am not." Spock was clearly intrigued.

"It's like being spattered with a drop of liquid nitrogen, so cold it burns." She rubbed her temple and looked at him in surprise. "I guess I expected to find a blister. When we return to the *Enterprise* would you be willing to repeat the experiment with a few judiciously applied probes?"

"Indeed, Doctor, I should be most interested myself."

"I am also interested," said Stiff Tail. "When you perform your tests, I would like you to tell me how it happened." Her ears flicked back. "—But you *can't!*"

Stiff Tail caught her tail and wrung it; her distress was all too apparent.

"That's why we have recorders of all types—so you can see for yourself what happened during an experiment," Kirk told her. "Spock, didn't I see graphs in that laboratory . . . ?"

"Affirmative, Captain," Spock said, "but they are unlabeled. I had intended to ask Brightspot the reason for such unorthodox scientific notation."

"My people have no accuracy for things that must be displayed visually," Stiff Tail explained. "If I asked Brightspot to reproduce a graph from memory it would be—as inaccurate as your memory of our conversation. I keep the graphs here in the event that someone should ask me to tell how it happened that I came to some conclusion or other."

She and Spock considered each other at length. Finally she said, "Yes, I see why you developed machines to store information, but I do *not* understand how you handled the matter well enough to develop such a high level of technology."

Kirk could not suppress a grin. "That makes us even, Stiff Tail. *I* don't understand how you developed such a high level of technology *without* recording devices."

Stiff Tail twisted her tail again. "I am concerned by this, Captain Kirk. . . . Humans and Vulcans are more alien than I expected from your forms. I dare not make assumptions about you without further information."

Kirk nodded. "Just as we dare not make assumptions about your people, Stiff Tail. My people will tread as lightly as we know how—"

She interrupted with a flick of her tail. "One moment—you use the term differently now. Can a Vulcan be one of your people although he is not human?"

"Mr. Spock is my chief science officer—and he is my friend. In that sense, he is 'my people.'"

"Then you do not find him as alien as you find us?"

Jim Kirk had to smile. "I do indeed find Mr. Spock alien. Usually in the most unexpected ways. But that does not make him any less my friend."

"And you, Mr. Spock?"

"If I understand your question, Stiff Tail—yes, I am pleased to count James Kirk my friend."

"Although you find him alien?"

"His ways are often most peculiar, as are those of most humans I have encountered. I must often make an extreme effort to understand them. But Vulcan philosophy encourages such understanding, as we hold a strong belief in 'Infinite Diversity in Infinite Combination.'"

"'Infinite Diversity in Infinite Combination,'" she repeated.

Spock nodded.

"Your alien form of memory frightens me as I have seldom been frightened before. I would send you away—but I have seen Evan Wilson risk something as unknown to her as this is to me and be both interested and grateful for the experience, and Brightspot has told me that you would protect her relationship with me"—she looped her tail possessively about Brightspot's waist and continued—"and I have heard you call each other friend. My people can risk much for the sake of a possible friendship—and for the sake of 'Infinite Diversity in Infinite Combinations.'" She nodded at Spock.

She finished, "We must *all* tread lightly. I'll tell the others in camp." She walked slowly away. Kirk could see the tip of her tail still quivered from her emotion, but she did not call Brightspot away with her.

Brightspot said, "This is *exciting!*" and Jim Kirk laughed his relief.

Chapter Ten

Pavel Chekov was quite genuinely surprised at the number of Sivaoans who stayed to learn his techniques of construction rather than strayed to hear Uhura sing. They were mostly older, he thought, judging from their range of sizes; and each one tried each individual process involved. When they were finished, he was quite sure, each of them would be capable of duplicating this style of shelter.

Remembering what the captain and Mr. Spock had learned, Chekov had asked Distant Smoke the proper way to give them all permission to use the design whenever they wished and to teach it to others and give the same permission. This they accepted as joyfully as if he'd made them a gift. By their standards, he had, one that would have pleased his teacher back in Volgograd as much as it pleased the Sivaoans.

A short time later, there had been a huddle around Distant Smoke. Chekov, then occupied with the roof thatch, missed most of the conversation; from his vantage point, he saw only quivering ears and tails. Then three Sivaoans vanished into the wood.

He thought at first that they had gone to join Uhura, whose voice came to him in sweet snatches of song, but all three returned half an hour later laden with branches and leaves quite different from those he had been using. They explained, with much excitement, that Distant Smoke wished to improve his design; and they began a fourth shelter on their own, this time showing *him* how it was to be done. Not wishing to miss a single detail, Chekov turned on his tricorder and watched in fascination.

They certainly knew the local materials, he thought. Rather than basket-shape, this shelter was going up with the elegant sweep of a bird's wing—and it was not just its style they were improving. Using a more flexible branch to begin with—they assured him it would remain flexible for a longer time—they were weaving a more intricate and sturdy base.

Then came the covering of leaves: some four different varieties, each a different shade of green, ranging from almost black to a reddish to a pale creamy green that was almost white. Distant Smoke himself had brought an armful of plumed rushes. There was a second huddle as Distant Smoke explained what he had in mind, but most of this was lost to the universal translator, which had no referents for artistic descriptions.

They began at opposite ends of the structure and worked toward each other and, to Chekov's utter amazement, when they met in the middle a stylized flight of birds swept across the face of the shelter as if they rode it like a current of air. Chekov stared, openmouthed.

The two largest of the Sivaoans hoisted Distant Smoke up to place the plumed thatch, then they all stepped back to stand beside Chekov. After a long good look at their work, they turned inquiringly to Distant Smoke. Distant Smoke's whiskers arched forward and trembled. "Yes," he said, at last, in a satisfied tone, "That is what I meant," and much pleasure and mutual congratulations flashed through the group.

Chekov still could not quite believe what he saw. They had taken his general process, a purely functional design, and made of it a work of art no less beautiful than their own tents or the permanent building woven among the trees. At last he said, "It is beautiful, Distant Smoke."

Distant Smoke preened his shoulder, pleased. "Let's see if it works as well from the inside." Chekov followed; so did the others.

Inside, the sunlight filtered through the multicolored leaves and cast bright shadows on the floor. There was a sweet scent and a subdued rustling from the plumes overhead; Chekov was sure they been chosen for sound and smell as well as sight. "Wonderful," he said softly, "It's wonderful, Distant Smoke."

"Good," said Distant Smoke, "Your people have much individuality of manner, but none of style. I intended something as unique as you are. I'm pleased you like it; it's not easy to improve for someone from such a different culture." He twitched his ears to the rustle of the plumes. "For the time being," he went on, "I am satisfied with my work. As I learn more about you, Pavel Chekov, I may find this inappropriate —but then, that would hardly be surprising. Even with my own people, I find changes from day to day, from year to year. Don't think I mean that because you're alien. Until then I would be honored if you would use the pattern whenever the desire strikes you."

Chekov suddenly understood: Distant Smoke intended him to have the design as a gift. He was stunned. It was all he could do to say, "I hev no way to thenk you, Distant Smoke. No one hes ever made me such a gift before. To hev something so beautiful created for *me*—thet is something I never thought would heppen on any world!" Embarrassed by his own emotion and a sudden awareness of his own inabilities, Chekov added, "I hope I will not disappoint you—but I think I hed better warn you, I would not be able to duplicate your work."

Both pleased and astonished (to judge from his ears and tail), Distant Smoke said, "Perhaps I misunderstand. . . . Will you eat with me? We'll talk further. I'm curious to hear about your world and its customs. If you will try to explain, I will try to understand."

"I'd be gled to, both."

As Distant Smoke led him into the clearing again, Chekov took a last wondering look at the shelter. So beautiful! he thought again.

The gift of a personal design made him take a second look at the other structures around the camp, and he saw something that he hadn't seen before. They were the work of several artists—four, or perhaps five in all. He strongly suspected, now that he thought about it, that Distant Smoke had also designed the permanent building and one or two of the tents in camp. He asked, and Distant Smoke confirmed this, looking pleased.

"This one as well," said Distant Smoke, as he invited Chekov into what had earlier been identified to him as Stiff Tail's tent. "I have for some time been wanting to redesign it. Stiff Tail has softened through the years, and I wished to reflect that. And I have gained more skill and I wished to reflect that as well. But she"—he seemed amused—"says she is comfortable—that the design is an old friend." He spread his hands and added, "What is one to do with one's mother, after all?"

A brown tail thrust through the tent opening. "Send them in, Catchclaw, and good hunting to you!"

Four tiny creatures scrambled through the door, took one look at Chekov and froze in their tracks, tails bristling. Catchclaw stuck her head in, took in Chekov and made a harrumphing kind of sound. *Exactly like Dr. McCoy,* thought Chekov. Catchclaw fixed grave eyes on Chekov. "Noisy baby," she said. As this seemed to require some response on his part, Chekov shook his head and, grinning, said, "It won't bother me, if thet's what you're esking."

She stepped in and the four little ones instantly scrambled up her and clung to her back, peering at him from various vantage points over her shoulders and around her sides.

"Don't stare," Distant Smoke told them firmly; to Chekov, he added, "Forgive them please. They're very young."

"And I'm wery strange to them," said Chekov. "I wish I could sing them a song like Lieutenant Uhura did, but I suspect my woice would frighten them even more."

Catchclaw snorted and used her tail to peel one of the babies off her back. "Not frightened," she said, "just cautious." She dangled the little one in front of Chekov. "Take a good look," she said. "No claws to scratch you, no teeth to bite you, no fur to protect him from you. How dangerous can that be?"

The baby, the same brown shade as its mother, but with a pure white splash along its belly, stared at Chekov wide eyed and upside down. "No claws?"

Chekov held out his hands. The little one, still clinging, stared all the harder. "No teeth?" it said.

Chekov drew back his lips to show the child. The other three were easing down from their mother's back to approach him cautiously for a better look. They were very small, about as high as his knee. He leaned down to display his teeth for them as well.

The white-bellied one let go Catchclaw's tail and dropped to the ground. "No fur!" it said.

"Some fur," corrected one of the others. "Looks sick, Catchclaw. Can you make it better?"

"Yes, please?" interjected the third.

"He's not sick—have I interpreted your sex correctly?— that's normal for a human, or so I'm told. He's just different. Go ahead, he won't hurt you." Her look said clearly that he had damned well better *not*.

"My name is Pavel," he said, "What's yours?"

"Grabfoot to-Ennien," said the white-bellied one and feinted at his foot by way of demonstration. The others were TooLongTail (that he could almost see as well), WhiteWhisker (also self-explanatory) and EagerTalker (that one he didn't get at all—it seemed the quietest of the three). As far as sex went, he hadn't the vaguest idea, but he supposed it didn't really matter much at this age, especially since he had seen nothing to indicate sex roles in professions or chores.

Catchclaw harrumphed again and turned to Distant Smoke. "I hold you responsible, Distant Smoke."

"I accept the responsibility, Catchclaw, and I thank you."

That sounded like a ritual exchange to Chekov and he made a mental note to ask about it sometime—he realized he was saving a lot of questions for Brightspot. It seemed safer to ask her than to ask at random, no matter how friendly the others might appear.

Catchclaw went to the door and turned back to the babies surrounding Chekov. "You," she said, fixing them with a glower. "You take care not to hurt him. He has no fur for protection. As for you, Pavel Chekov, have the good sense to squawk if you're hurt."

He wasn't sure how to reply to that and, before he could decide what to say, she was gone.

TooLongTail looked at Distant Smoke. "Can we touch?"

"You ask him. He's a person, not a tree, and he understands you perfectly well."

"You mey touch," said Chekov, holding out his arm. For the next few minutes, he was explored at great length—patted, poked, prodded, sniffed and tugged at. EagerTalker very delicately extended one claw and drew it across the back of his hand.

It was a minor scratch and Chekov could see that she was experimenting so he did nothing to stop her. She peered closely at his hand and her ears flicked back. TooLongTail took a close look as well and turned and cuffed her soundly.

"Catchclaw said not hurt him!"

"Didn't," said EagerTalker. "Didn't squawk!"

The argument turned into a scuffle, with the two others joining in. The others seemed to take no sides but cuffed and bit and hissed at random.

Distant Smoke deftly moved a pile of bowls out of range of the free-for-all and gave them a general shove away from the embers of the cooking fire with his foot. He placed the bowls safely in some overhead netting, then bent to examine Chekov's hand. "You humans don't know enough to squawk when you're hurt," he said, and Chekov could almost hear tsk-tsking in his voice.

"It's only a scratch," he said. "I hev been hurt worse by the brenches in the forest." He showed Distant Smoke the cut on his other palm from the sharp-edged leaves.

Distant Smoke flicked his ears back. "You *are* delicate!" he said. "That's why you wear clothing on your feet!"

"Boots," said Chekov. "I should hope so—ef I went barefoot here, I would most likely be permenently lame."

The melee rolled toward them, a chaotic scramble of claws and lashing tails. Grabfoot bounced out and attacked Chekov's foot. Chekov, startled by the unexpectedness of the pounce, jumped. Distant Smoke cuffed Grabfoot and sent him (or her) rolling back into the free-for-all.

"Grebfoot didn't hurt me," Chekov said quickly. He knew the child had intended no harm; in fact, the pounce had seemed more an invitation to join the play. Chuckling, he said, "My boots are strong enough to protect me even from a Grebfoot."

"Are they?" Distant Smoke looked extremely interested, as if Chekov had said something entirely different.

Chekov thought of the little ones scrambling up their mother for protection and said, "I think Cetchclaw needs protection more then I do. Perhaps you would explain to me: how do the bebies climb her without clawing her to little pieces?"

There was a squawk from the center of the free-for-all and Distant Smoke instantly turned his full attention on the four children. Just as quickly, the fighting stopped. All four were suddenly a good two feet from each other, just beyond arm's reach, and were ignoring each other with a studied indifference.

Except for the shiver at the very tip of TooLongTail's overly long tail, one might never have known anything had happened among them. "Are you all right?" Distant Smoke asked. "Come let me see."

The child did, and the others crowded around as well, to look her over and to lick her rumpled fur. By the time they were finished, she looked five times as rumpled as when they'd begun.

"I thought," said Chekov, "thet you would lick the fur in the direction it grows, not agenst the grain."

"It would seem sensible, wouldn't it?" agreed Distant Smoke. "But, believe it or not, there's a good medical reason for licking it backward. It stimulates their circulation and warms them, which reassures them. Catchclaw says that's probably the reason for the instinct to lick anybody injured backward." He hefted the child and she scrambled onto his shoulder and clung there, now preening her own fur back into place the right way.

"As for climbing," said Distant Smoke, returning to the question the squawk had interrupted, "they use their claws, of course. But adults have a heavy tangled undercoat—those sharp little claws never reach skin." He offered his side to Chekov. "Go ahead," he said. "Feel for yourself."

Chekov did and found that he could readily hook his fingers into the undercoat. He gave a slight tug. "I see," he said.

"See what?" It was Stiff Tail. The four children scrambled away from Distant Smoke and climbed all over her by way of greeting.

She gave them each a good lick hello as Chekov explained, "How they climb you without scretching you to pieces."

"Oh," she said. She took what seemed to be a bouquet from a hook on one side of the tent. Having just eaten the same thing with Distant Smoke, Chekov knew it was dried meat of some sort, and very good if a trifle tough. She chewed thoughtfully and passed small pieces to the clamoring children. "Bet you don't eat like this at home," she told them, looping her tail in amusement. To Chekov, she explained, "Most children like to nurse as long as they can get away with it, so they only eat solid foods when they're visiting. . . . I think I'll tell Catchclaw on you." This last drew a minor storm of protest from the little ones until Stiff Tail assured them she was only pulling their tails. "But," she said pointedly, "it's not as if you don't have teeth!"

While the children concentrated on the meat, their ferocious chewing serving to confirm her observation, Stiff Tail turned again to Chekov. "I have learned something about your people that I must tell to Distant Smoke," she began. "Will it disturb you to listen?"

"I don't mind, unless *you* prefer to speak privately."

"I prefer to have your reaction and any corrections you might wish to make," Stiff Tail said. She told first of Wilson's fight with Fetchstorm. At Chekov's exclamation, she quickly reassured him that Wilson was fine, as far as Catchclaw knew, then added, "But your friend doesn't know enough to squawk when she's hurt!" She made it sound like the local equivalent of not knowing enough to come in out of the rain.

"They *all* seem to share that trait," Distant Smoke said, pointing to the mark EagerTalker had left on Chekov's hand.

Stiff Tail gave an exasperated sigh and said, "I have cuffed Fetchstorm for his disobedience."

"I'll bet the keptain cuffed Dr. Wilson, too." At her ears-back surprise, Chekov explained with a mock swing, "Not physically—with words."

"Is that effective?" Stiff Tail asked, and Chekov blushed, remembering a few times the captain had done it to him.

"Wery," he said.

Stiff Tail nodded thoughtfully. Then she said, "I have learned another very important difference between our peoples." She gave a very long recital, detailing their differences in memory. Chekov was astonished as she explained how it happened that she learned this. He himself could hear very little difference between Spock's version of the event and Brightspot's, but there was no doubt that Distant Smoke found the variance between them shocking.

When she had finished, Distant Smoke said, "Now I understand, Pavel Chekov. I thought it very strange when you said you had neither the memory nor the skill with materials to recreate my design, but you *meant* that, didn't you?"

Chekov leaned toward him, nodded, then said, "I want to be wery correct about this. You gave me the gift of a design, to use whenever I wish. I hev not the memory or skill to duplicate thet design. I do not wish to offend you by trying and failing—and to fail at such beauty would be terrible! But I want you to understand thet I eppreciate what you hev given me."

Distant Smoke said, "After what Stiff Tail said, I thought it impossible to make you a gift. . . ."

Chekov shook his head vehemently. He tapped his tricorder. "I hev taken pictures. When I return to the *Enterprise,* I will hev those pictures trensferred to paper so I can see them whenever I wish. They will be with me always—and they will remind me of you and your people and your kindnesses. They will always give me pleasure."

"Still," said Stiff Tail, "if you wish them to remember, you must ask them to turn on their memory machines. It is—unsettling."

Spock stared hard at his tricorder, as if by sheer will he might force it to tell him the answer to his questions. "Illogical," he said at last. It was the closest to an insult in his manner of delivery that Jim Kirk had ever heard him come. *Vulcan or not, Mr. Spock,* he thought, *if you had a tail, it'd be twitching right now.*

"We still have insufficient data, Captain. I do not understand this culture. . . . I beg your pardon, Brightspot, but confusion is often the result when two peoples as different as yours and mine first meet."

She had been watching his work with absorption. Apparently, it made no difference to her whether she looked at the screen right side up or upside down. She twitched her whiskers at him. "It's all right. I think you're confusing, too. I never met anybody who kept his memory in a machine." She looked down again at the tricorder. "Can't I help? I remember everything."

"Then you will remember that we have no wish to cause difficulty between you and your mother," Spock told her.

The tip of her tail swept up and quivered. "Yes, I remember—I was only hoping you wouldn't."

"Hoping to take advantage of our weaknesses, Brightspot?" Kirk grinned at her. *Children,* he thought, *would be quick to see the possibilities.*

She stepped to his side. "When you put it that way, it doesn't sound very nice. I guess it wasn't very nice, was it?"

"It's nice of you to want to help," he said, "even if you're devious about it. And some of my best friends are devious— isn't that right, Mr. Spock?"

Spock lifted an eyebrow. "I have no idea what you mean, Captain."

Brightspot's tail looped in amusement. She said delightedly, "You just pulled Mr. Spock's tail!"

"Indeed he did," said Spock. "May I ask how it is you were able to recognize that, knowing as little of our relationship as you do?"

Brightspot looked startled. "You said he was your friend. Is that a baby question?"

"I believe so."

"And the captain—did I use that right?—always pulls his friends' tails, even if they don't have any. Besides, your—" Momentarily without a word, Brightspot drew an arc in the air with the tip of her tail.

"Eyebrow?" suggested Kirk, pointing to his own.

"Eyebrow," she repeated in Standard, "went up—It's almost as good as a tail—and your smell changed." Spock's eyebrow lifted a second time. "Now you're very curious," said Brightspot with complete assurance. "That's a different smell."

A glance passed from Spock to Kirk. Kirk said, "I'm curious, too, Brightspot. Can you tell that as well?"

"It smells different on you than on Mr. Spock, but I can tell."

"Brightspot, I think I'm going to . . . shock you again. I can't tell when someone is curious by the way he smells."

She was indeed taken aback. "You can't?" she said. "Mr. Spock?"

"Nor can I," said Spock.

She fell silent to consider the two of them. At last she said, "I think you must miss a lot."

Kirk grinned, but it gave him an idea. "Brightspot, do you remember smells the way you remember words?"

"Yess."

That came out in Standard English, too; Brightspot was picking up their words as well as their expressions. He went on, "Do you remember the first time Lieutenant Uhura spoke to Jinx?" She made what was clearly a scoffing sound, and Kirk grinned again. "Sorry, I *forget* how good your memory is."

Her tail went into a virtual paroxysm and ended up wound once more around his wrist. When she had gotten herself under control, she said, "You mean, when Lieutenant Uhura talked about—the You-Know-Whos?"

"Yes. Tell me, what did you smell?"

"First," Brightspot began, then, seeing that Spock had turned on his tricorder, began anew, addressing her remarks directly to it: "First, I smelled *very* strange smells. I never smelled any human or Vulcan smell before, but I did smell that you had come through the stand of green velvet just outside the camp. . . . Do you want to know how my people smelled, too?"

"Please, Brightspot," Kirk said.

"Mostly curious, but some frightened," she said and added scornfully, "Catchclaw's babies ran away."

"That is a logical response for the young when confronted by an unknown," Spock interjected.

"I suppose so. Better that than stick their tails in a slicebill nest. But I'm old enough to walk," she said, clearly for the record. "*I* stayed."

"You did," Spock acknowledged, also for the record. "Continue."

"Well, when Lieutenant Uhura sang to Catchclaw's babies, most of the smell of fear went away, and it was only curiosity—*until* she mentioned the You-Know-Whos." Her ears suddenly flicked back. "That's odd!"

"What is?" Kirk asked.

She spoke slowly, as if thinking it through aloud. "Most of us still smelled curious, but Winding Path and Catchclaw and Settlesand smelled . . . guilty, ashamed. The way Fetchstorm does when he's been told not to do something but he's done it anyway. Stiff Tail smelled that way when she cuffed you—and that's not usually how she smells when she cuffs somebody—usually she smells angry! Left Ear, too!" She caught and shook her tail vehemently. "When I asked about the You-Know-Whos! Everybody I asked smelled either curious—or guilty!" She stared at Spock and concluded, "You're right, Mr. Spock; it is illogical. I don't understand it at all."

"Kagan's Law," said Kirk.

When he had explained that for Brightspot, she nodded and said, "I'm going to find out. I'm going to find out why I don't understand my own people. . . . Do you need any more baby questions answered right now?"

"No, Brightspot. Thank you, I think you've answered a big one."

"Okkay"—again she spoke Standard—"I'll see you later. *I* have some baby questions to ask." She walked away, the tip of her tail flicking behind her.

"Guilty," said Kirk, thinking aloud. That confirmed what Left Ear had told him. "After two thousand years?" He turned on Spock as if expecting an answer.

"The Eeiauoans still bear a guilt of their own," Spock said.

"How the hell do we fight two thousand years' worth of stubbornness, Spock?"

"As you pointed out, Captain, you yourself have considerable talent in that direction. Perhaps, in this instance, it may be of value."

"Why, Mr. Spock, I do believe you're pulling my tail!"

"I am merely stating a fact, Captain." Spock's expression was as bland as ever, and Kirk found himself wishing Brightspot had not left before she'd sniffed out the truth for him.

Uhura left Jinx's tent in a pensive mood. Jinx had not recognized ADF syndrome from her description of the symptoms. That might be a good sign; that might mean the disease had been wiped out on this world—or it might mean that ADF was a new disease for which the Sivaoans had no cure. Jinx had assured her Catchclaw would know, if anyone did. Uhura said a small silent prayer that Catchclaw *would* know.

The commotion of welcome-homes drew her from her thoughts, and she waited to see what new arrivals there might be. Making as much noise to announce their arrival as the welcome-homes had, a hunting party emerged from the wood. The eight of them, male and female, waved and shouted their triumphal return until they drew the rest of the camp from tents and trees to look. Whatever their catch was, it was certainly bright. She walked over for a closer look.

One had a fistful of something that looked like chicken-sized dinosaurs, complete with needle-sharp teeth. "What is that called?" she asked SilverTail in her best native speech.

"Grabfoots," he answered, indicating the teeth and motioning toward his ankles so that she would get the general idea what the word referred to, as well as how to pronounce it. "Grabfoots," she repeated. He nodded, mimed eating and licking his chops and said something more. She took it to mean 'Good eating' or 'Tasty' and repeated that as well.

Rushlight came toward her, with something large and four-footed slung across his shoulders. She turned the universal translator back on, very much afraid of being misunderstood in the general confusion.

"As we say, 'Take a bard and the hunt goes fast.' A good hunt, as you can see!" he said. He unslung the creature from his shoulders and dropped it onto the ground to stretch. "And I shall tell you what happened to ThreeTimes—we'll make a song about it, you and I." He blinked at her and suddenly said, "You're twisting your own tail. Is something wrong?"

Embarrassed, Uhura said, "When you left without saying a word, I was afraid I had done something to offend you."

He started. "Surely you smelled the hunting scent . . . ?"

That confused her still more. "I don't understand, Rushlight."

Rushlight considered her for a long moment, then his tail curled around her wrist. "I think I do: *that's* why your songs don't speak of smells. Next time I'll leave a message with one of the children." He reached up a finger and tapped her lightly on the side of the nose. "Remarkable," he said, "such long noses and no sense of smell at all!"

A handful of Sivaoan children sprang from branch to branch in the trees at the edge of camp, playing hide-and-seek. Staring up from below, Evan Wilson couldn't tell if rousting the welcome-homes was part of the game or purely incidental—it certainly added to the excitement, though. The game was much simplified compared to that of her own world, but it stirred a memory of her childhood and she smiled. An instant later, the smile turned to a puzzled frown. The memory *could not* be hers!

She hastily excused herself from Fetchstorm. She sought out Spock and found him alone with his tricorder. Having no wish to disturb his calculations, she sat down and tucked her chin into her hand to think. If Spock couldn't explain . . .

"Dr. Wilson." Spock had completed his task, and he now gave her his full attention. Once again the intensity of it disconcerted her. She blushed and, with some difficulty, she said, "I'm not sure how to put this. . . . Does your memory transfer technique work both ways?" Nothing in the literature I read even suggested the possibility."

"I do not understand."

"I have a memory that's not mine. If it's not yours . . ." She frowned. "It *must* be yours, Mr. Spock. There's no other possible explanation."

Spock's expression did not change. "May I inquire as to the content?"

The question startled her—it seemed too personal until she recognized the sheer foolishness of the feeling. "If it's your memory in the first place, there's no reason *not* to tell you," she said.

She described it to him as best she could, setting the richness of the game against the austerity of a desert world. It began with a challenge given and accepted, and it became a sort of hide-and-seek that required all one's skills, from computer programming to physical tracking. No one but the players knew the game was in progress. Yet, for all its complexity, the game *she* remembered playing held as much or more excitement as that of the Sivaoan children in the trees.

When she had finished Spock's raised eyebrow left no doubt that she had in fact been given one of his memories. "A child's practice on Vulcan," he said. He did not say "game;" and she understood him to mean a sharpening of skills. "Remarkable," he continued. "To my knowledge, there has been no previous mention of this phenomenon. Have you been tested for extrasensory perception, Dr. Wilson?"

"Meaning, was I reading your mind while you were reading mine? I've had all the standard tests: I come out average. I thought perhaps it was deliberate on your part—a kind of fair trade."

He shook his head. "I was unaware the possibility existed, Doctor. It too would be worth investigating when we return to the *Enterprise*."

"Yes, and meanwhile, it's a relief to know that I'm not completely off my rocker." She met his eyes and held them: "Thank you for the gift."

Caught in his continued scrutiny, she felt her face redden again. And this time Spock said, "Dr. Wilson, several times during the course of our conversation, your face has turned a distinctly darker shade of red. I believe humans refer to this as a 'blush.' I am unfamiliar with your culture. I apologize if I have inadvertently caused you distress. If you find it possible to speak further, I should appreciate knowing what taboo I have . . ."

Until that moment, she had not recognized the cause herself. She raised her hands. "No, no, Mr. Spock. Nothing like that. I'm afraid it's a cultural misinterpretation on my part. I've seen it happen more than once between Vulcan and human." It was easier to speak of it impersonally. "The kind of undivided attention a Vulcan gives as a matter of simple politeness is often misread as . . . sexual interest by a human."

"Fascinating." He fixed her with a long steady regard—experimentally, she thought—and her blush deepened. Smiling, she said, "Yes, you've done it again. In my book you just gave me the eye. If I were you, Mr. Spock, I'd try to tone it down a little. I'm sure I'm not the only one this happens to."

She glanced away and, to her relief, saw the tip of Catchclaw's tail disappearing into her tent. "If you'll excuse me? I have an appointment with the local physician." She rose and, as an afterthought, added, "Don't worry, Mr. Spock, I'll get over it."

She strode away without a backward glance. A moment later, Catchclaw's invitation to enter wiped the encounter from her thoughts: here was the problem she *had* to solve.

The Sivaoan glared at her from head to toe and growled, "What am I to do with a species that has a privacy taboo about removing its clothing?"

Wilson grinned. "We make an exception for doctors," she said, "and I'll satisfy your curiosity, if you wish."

"Thank you," said Jinx, giving a sidelong glance at Catchclaw, who arched her whiskers forward.

When their examination of both normal flesh and injured flesh was completed, Wilson rewrapped her sari. "Stay and talk," Catchclaw invited. "Jinx tells me you wish to find the cure for a disease. Will you tell me what you know of its symptoms?"

"That's the best question I've heard all day," said Wilson. She pulled up a stool, sat down and went to work.

Left Ear had come to speak with Jim Kirk with her claws sheathed, but to no avail. Try as she might—and he could see the effort it cost her—she could not bring herself to speak on the subject of the Eeiauoans. She skirted the topic, edging nearer and nearer, but she never quite got there.

He wished he could think of something to make it easier for her. Meanwhile, he kept his questions to areas she could talk about.

The only thing he had learned about the Eeiauoans was negative: They did not seem to have been exiled for religious reasons. How can you have a schism when each camp has its own god—and every plant and animal its own spirit? If he understood her correctly, the Sivaoans had not so much a religion as an ecology. There were limits to the number of animals of each kind that might be taken in a season, for example, and strictures that allowed land to lie fallow. It might have been fascinating had his mission simply been to establish contact.

Left Ear sensed his distress. Giving her tail a vehement shake, she said, "I cannot. I can no more tell you than I could tell Brightspot or Jinx or one of our own. You must try elsewhere, Captain Kirk. I am only wasting your time."

Kirk felt an enormous sympathy for her. He had seen the strength of taboos—he'd even had to deal with some of his own—and he knew the difficulty she must be facing. But he could not let the chance slip away. "Please, Left Ear. Keep talking. Talk around it, if you must. Tell me what it's *not* about, and perhaps I may be able to learn enough from that to get the help we need."

Her hackles rose, but she said mildly, "We will continue our discussion after dinner." Having little choice in the matter, Kirk followed her lead once again.

Stepping from her tent, he found himself in the midst of a festival, like something from a medieval costume drama. A cooking fire blazed before every tent, and exotic spicy scents filled the air. A welcome-home, tempted by the smells, ventured into the clearing; a handful of children chased it back into the trees and then threw it scraps.

They crossed to Stiff Tail's tent, where Distant Smoke and Chekov happily improvised dinner over the fire. Two small children clung to Chekov—one at shoulder height, peering over into the cooking pot, and the other clutching his head. A third dashed in circles, trying to catch his own tail and shouting excitedly. Distant Smoke jabbed a tail in the child's direction and said, "Noisy baby."

"It certainly is," Jim Kirk agreed with a grin.

"A little less claw there," Chekov said, turning his eyes up. "Hello, keptain. This is TooLongTail and EagerTalker,

Ketchclaw's children. They hev already discovered that I hev no tail to remove them with." He bent to taste the concoction in the pot.

Kirk saw that neither child was in danger of being dislodged —Chekov, however, was going to be a vaste collection of scratches and pinholes. "I don't recall assigning you pincushion detail, Mr. Chekov."

Chekov grinned back. "I ken't keep them away, sair. Perheps you want one? The other two are WhiteWhisker and Grebfoot—I respectfully suggest the keptain watch his toes around thet last."

On hearing Chekov's suggestion, Grabfoot forgot his tail and pounced for Kirk's foot. Kirk caught him up and held him dangling. "Hello, Grabfoot," he said. Grabfoot flipped in midair. Kirk, horrified he might drop the child, scooped him close.

Grabfoot's tail snapped around his neck and, for a brief moment, Jim Kirk was sure he was about to end his career ignominiously strangled by a small child. Then the tail flipped away and he felt Grabfoot's weight on his back. "Hello, Captain Kirk," said a voice very close to his ear. Except in the initial scramble, he hadn't been scratched; Grabfoot was using only enough claw to pierce his tunic.

Chekov reached up. "I beg your pardon, Keptain," he said, and he cuffed the child. "You do not," he said firmly, "wrep your tail around the neck of a human. Humans ken't breathe thet way."

"Didn't squawk," Grabfoot protested.

"He couldn't," said Chekov, "No air, no squawk." To Left Ear, he added, rubbing his Adam's apple, "The air intake on a human is much too close to the surface of the neck for comfort around these little ones. I'm gled they learn fast."

"Sorry, Captain Kirk," said Grabfoot, and something scratchy—the child's tongue—licked his ear by way of apology.

"No harm done, Grabfoot," Kirk assured him, "but be careful next time." If Kirk had thought their tails a strange sensation, he was now ready to admit their tongues were even more so. He didn't know whether to laugh or to evict the child from its perch.

After a few licks at his hair, Grabfoot said, "Smell nice, taste funny."

Chekov looked knowingly at Distant Smoke and said, "I suppose he'll hev to taste ewervone."

"Taste this," said Distant Smoke, indicating the stew. "Do you think it could do with some tail-kinkers?"

"Old Russian proverb," said Chekov. "You ken't spoil kasha with butter." When that didn't seem to translate, he explained, "It means you ken't spoil something good by putting something else good in."

"That depends on how *many* tail-kinkers," said Distant Smoke, looping his tail.

"New Sivaoan proverb," Chekov corrected: "You ken't spoil stew with a tail-kinker or two."

The universal translator's version of that was much more successful—all four children immediately took up the line as a chant, rocking to its rhythm. Kirk wasn't sure how much childish glee his tunic could survive. Fortunately, he did not find out, for Grabfoot suddenly stopped rocking and chanting to thrust his head forward and stare. The object of his intense scrutiny was Spock, who returned the scrutiny with equal interest, to Grabfoot's immense satisfaction.

"Grabfoot, this is Mr. Spock. Mr. Spock, this is Grabfoot, one of Catchclaw's children."

"Not touch Mr. Spock," said Grabfoot, then he added, "Ears?" Spock treated this as a request and turned slightly. "Good ears," said Grabfoot, with an air of decision.

"As to the matter of my ears," Spock told him, "I had little choice in their appearance. However, I am gratified that they meet with your approval."

Grabfoot's ears flicked back, brushing Kirk's cheek. Jim Kirk said, "He means he's glad you like them, Grabfoot."

"Indeed, Captain, Grabfoot understood me."

"Understood," said Grabfoot, distracted, but wanting to set the record straight. His attention shifted completely and he suddenly scrambled from Kirk's back. Two others scrambled down Chekov, nearly causing him to spill the stew, and another nearly ran Kirk down. All four gave Spock a wide berth. A moment later, they all swarmed up Catchclaw, and there was much licking and patting.

164

By the time their tails seemed inextricably entangled, they had begun to tell her everything that had happened that afternoon—and their memories seemed to be fully as good as Brightspot's, though limited to what they *chose* to notice. *Not* limited to what they comprehended, he noticed. They repeated things verbatim and demanded explanations. Catchclaw provided as many as she could.

They were chanting Chekov's 'Sivaoan proverb' for her when Evan Wilson tapped his arm. "Captain? Mr. Spock? May I have a word with you both in private?" Her face looked drawn, taut.

He nodded, and the two of them followed her a short way away. Dissatisfied, she motioned them still further. "You wouldn't believe how good Brightspot's ears are, Captain." She turned off her universal translator; the two of them followed suit.

"What's wrong, Dr. Wilson?" Kirk asked.

She looked up and her eyes passed from him to Spock. "Oh, *hell*, Mr. Spock," she said, but her voice was more tired than angry. Spock seemed to stare at something over her left shoulder; Kirk saw nothing to warrant his attention. Wilson went on, apparently still addressing Spock, "Don't go out of your way for me! Right now I could use a lift to my spirits—even a purely misinterpreted one."

Spock gave her his full attention.

"Thank you," she said, "I appreciate it." Then she was all business again. "We've got more trouble than we thought, Captain. Catchclaw doesn't recognize the symptoms of ADF syndrome."

Chapter Eleven

Leonard McCoy was waiting for results. Half of research is waiting for results, he thought, angry at his own impatience. The other half is interpreting them. Neither thought was of any use. He swabbed his eyes with a swatch of sterilized cotton. At least the serum seemed to be working . . . if his case of ADF had progressed much further he wouldn't be able to *see* the results, if there were any.

The whole thing was a damn long shot. Half a dozen of Micky's staff had checked out free of ADF and volunteered to undergo preventive treatment. Working in the quarantine wards, they were all at high risk anyhow. Three of them with relatives already in second-stage coma had volunteered to be infected with ADF, providing someone could find a way to do it.

That was the crux of the problem: They couldn't even infect a lab mouse, let alone a human volunteer. *We can diagnose it the minute the toxin starts being released into the bloodstream,* he thought, *but we can't spot the bacterium, the virus releasing it—the victims have nothing in common. What the hell is this thing?*

So they waited for results, and the only good results were negative. Every day that passed without diagnosis of ADF in someone undergoing the preventive regime was either a good sign or just a coincidence.

McCoy decided, after some thought, that he'd even settle

for the coincidence, as long as no new cases were reported. Even a single new case among his volunteers, however, would put an end to his hopes for a preventive. He said as much to Micky, the next time they spoke.

"Don't be an idiot, Leonard," said Micky. Her smile took the sting out of her words. "We've got close to two thousand humans, humanoids and Eeiauoans on the preventive regime. One case out of that doesn't mean it won't work and you know it. If it works for even one *species*, it's a victory."

"I know," he said curtly.

"And not even the old commonplace vaccines are 100% reliable."

"I know."

"So don't *I know* me with that look on your face, McCoy."

McCoy shook his head. "I don't want any . . . more . . . cases. Ever. I want it *stopped*." As he said it, he realized to his horror that he no longer believed the Federation could find a cure.

As for Jim's wild goose chase—might as well ask for a miracle one direction as another. To believe in the existence of a cure on the strength of a few lines of song—well, that took more energy than he could command at the moment—but he found himself hoping Jim and Spock could still believe in it. As long as they did, the *Enterprise* and its crew remained out of harm's way.

Catchclaw doesn't recognize the symptoms. . . . The words struck James Kirk like a physical blow. "You can't mean that, Evan!"

Evan Wilson gave him an odd look. "Catchclaw wasn't lying, Captain, and she has a reputation for being one of the best doctors on Sivao. . . . Sweet Elath! you don't think I mean there isn't a cure, do you?" She caught his wrist; although her hand did not quite encircle it, her grip was surprisingly strong and reassuring. "Listen to me carefully, Captain: I mean only that we must convince Catchclaw or someone else with medical knowledge to deal directly with the Eeiauoans. We can't just snap up the information and go."

"But if she didn't recognize the symptoms—!"

"Medical terminology relies on convention. A med student learns to recognize the symptom 'livid skin' by seeing a patient that has a disease with that symptom. The phrase, the *symptom*, means nothing to you. You wouldn't have the vaguest idea how to recognize it because you have no referents for the convention. If the universal translator can't help you, how's it going to help Catchclaw?" She released his wrist and raised her hand to rub her temple at the point where Spock had touched her earlier in the day. "Worse," she said, "Catchclaw diagnoses by body smell, by texture of fur; things that can't be conveyed by filmed medical records."

"Suppose ADF is of Eeiauoan origin." As much as the thought horrified him, Kirk had to say it.

Evan shook her head vehemently. "It's *Sivaoan*. I've heard Nyota's song and that's ADF, all right—no doubt about it."

"So what do we do now? Suggestions, Spock?"

"If, as Dr. Wilson suggests, Catchclaw might recognize ADF syndrome if confronted with an actual case of the disease, we must find a way to present her with such a case. It would seem, Captain, that our only course of action would be to force the Sivaoans, not only to acknowledge the existence of Eeiauoans, but to make—in Dr. McCoy's somewhat archaic terms—a house call on them."

Kirk looked grim. "That's not going to be easy, Spock. There must be another way."

"There is one other possibility," Evan Wilson said, "though I admit it's chancy. You see, Captain, natural selection operates among germs and among the peoples they infect. A disease is most virulent before it has a chance to adapt to its host and vice versa. Catchclaw may see a case of ADF every other day and not know that's the disease I mean."

"I don't understand," said Kirk. "You mean Catchclaw might be seeing a milder form of ADF, with milder symptoms?"

"You do understand. Exactly. But the most difficult part is that the symptoms may not just be milder—they may be altogether different. It's possible that the Eeiauoan form of ADF hasn't been seen on this world for two thousand years or more!"

"So we must get one of their doctors to Eeiauo," said Kirk. "Good God, how am I supposed to do that?!"

His outrage was addressed to the universe at large, but Evan Wilson suddenly looked up at him with that wicked grin of hers and said brightly, "I'd consider kidnapping myself. Why don't we give Catchclaw and her babies a tour of the *Enterprise?* I'm sure Mr. Scott would love an opportunity to show off her abilities under warp speed."

"Dr. Wilson," said Spock, "such a course of action would undoubtedly be considered extreme, if not actually criminal, by Starfleet Command."

Evan Wilson looked offended. "Mr. Spock, do you honestly believe I'd kidnap *babies?* I'm shocked, sir. I respectfully suggest that you look to your tail, sir."

Involuntarily, Spock followed her glance to where his tail would have been had he possessed one, and Kirk laughed, more from relief than humor. "Well," he said, "does anyone have any other suggestions"—he gave a quick glance at Wilson—"aside from finding a local doctor with no close family ties?"

"Eat first, talk later," Evan Wilson said, but there was a speculative look in her eye that surprised Kirk. *By god,* he thought, *she might just take that seriously! And, if worse comes to worst, I might give her the ship to do it with!*

Dinner was festive: Children moved from cooking fire to cooking fire in a vain attempt to taste everything, jokes and tales were swapped, children tussled and were cheered on by their elders. It lasted for several hours. Kirk found time to apprise Chekov of Wilson's meeting with Catchclaw, and to make sure he understood this was no cause for despair. Uhura already knew and understood the implications, a credit to Wilson's bedside manner.

Chekov introduced Wilson to Catchclaw's children and, apparently, gave her good instructions on the proper disciplinary techniques. She squawked and thumped one soundly for digging its claws into her sore back and, from then on, they took exaggerated care. Wilson draped her train over her shoulder blades and, drawing it a second time across her breasts, tied the loose end at her waist. The resulting cowl gave her back and shoulders a measure of protection and soon she was as laden with children as Chekov—one clinging to her trousers at the hip and a second sprawled in the hammocklike sling of the cowl.

Rushlight was called upon to sing. The translator couldn't manage rhyme or rhythm well, but the tune was a jaunty one and even Kirk found himself faking the chorus, which was all about pulling tails. The hero was familiar: CloudShape to-Ennien.

Then Rushlight turned to Uhura and asked her for a song. She shyly complied with a light tune in Swahili. The Sivaoans clamored for more, but Rushlight pointed out that Uhura had spent all afternoon singing for the children and—in fairness—ought to be given a rest. This brought a spate of apologies and an admission from Uhura that she was truly a bit hoarse. She would sing another night if they wished; and from the reaction, there was no doubt they'd wish it.

Rushlight sang a dozen other songs. By the time he finished a second song about CloudShape to-Ennien, Grabfoot had fallen asleep in Wilson's cowl. EagerTalker, sprawled like a cap on Wilson's head, said to Kirk, "Has CloudShape ever come to your camp?"

Kirk could only think of Harcourt Fenton Mudd, who didn't quite seem to fit the bill. "Oh, yes," said Wilson, with a smile.

"A great many times, EagerTalker," Spock said, "and under a great many names and guises: Raven, Coyote, Uncle Saunday." At Kirk's surprise, he explained, "The trickster is a common figure in folklore, Captain, a god or demigod who can change shape at will."

"A thief and a clown," Wilson added.

"All of those," Spock confirmed. "Each culture has a different name for him or her." To EagerTalker, he said, "On my world, CloudShape called herself T'kay."

"Will you tell me how it happened, Mr. Spock?" Eager-Talker said.

"Tomorrow," Catchclaw interrupted firmly. She began the process of disengaging the two children from Wilson's hair and clothing.

A tail, Brightspot's, curled around Jim Kirk's wrist.

"Please come," she whispered. "I have an idea." He followed her, away from the crowd and the music, and into the comparative peace of Left Ear's tent.

Brightspot said, "I told Left Ear how it happened that I learned about your memory and how you can keep it in a box. . . . This is the machine, Left Ear." She held up Kirk's tricorder and said urgently to him, "She can't tell me, and she can't tell you—but maybe she could tell your memory machine."

Left Ear said, "I might . . . be able to. I don't know, Brightspot."

"I'm not asking in Old Tongue," said Brightspot. "Just *try*. Can she try, Captain? Will you show her how it works?"

"Gladly," said Kirk, meaning it. He drew the strap from his shoulder and handed the instrument to Left Ear, who took it hesitantly. "It's all right," he assured her, "I'm not asking in Old Tongue, either. It's worth a try, though."

He showed her how to use both record and playback and watched as she tested it. She was startled at hearing her own voice. "That's not me," she said. Brightspot flicked her ears back and said, "It sounds just like you, Left Ear. It's my voice the machine doesn't get right."

Kirk explained the phenomenon; a good technical explanation distracted Left Ear from the ultimate purpose of the demonstration. The explanation seemed to satisfy Left Ear—intellectually, if not emotionally—and she tested it once more, pitching her voice at different levels. At last she said, "I will borrow your memory box, if I may, Captain Kirk. I will return it to you tomorrow."

"Yes, Left Ear. And thank you."

Left Ear bristled. "Go away, now," she said, "I have to think again."

Brightspot scurried. Jim Kirk lengthened his stride to rejoin her. "Thank *you*, Brightspot. That was a good idea."

"It better work," said Brightspot. Her voice was almost a growl. "I'm old enough to walk and I don't understand what's going on around here."

"If it's any comfort to you, Brightspot, I *am* an adult and *I* don't always understand why my people do the things they do. The only solution is to keep learning."

"And, I suppose, keep asking questions, even if they're baby questions?" The tip of her tail lashed briefly.

He grinned at her. "Sometimes even if you get cuffed for asking."

"How do you know you're an adult?" she asked, quite suddenly.

Kirk grinned again. "The Federation doesn't put children in command of starships," he said, "at least, not knowingly."

"Oh," she said, "oh. What kind of walk did you take?"

It was suddenly clear to Kirk that by *Walk*—this time he capitalized it in his mind—Brightspot meant some kind of rite of passage. "That's not our custom, if I understand you correctly. Being a legal adult in the Federation varies from world to world and culture to culture. . . . By my culture's standards, though, I'm a legal adult."

That embroiled him in an explanation of the term *legal adult* that lasted until they rejoined the crowd around Rushlight. "All ears" summed up the intensity of Brightspot's interest nicely, he thought, and when at last she settled down to listen to the singing, she still cast a thoughtful look at him from time to time. But she said nothing further on the subject.

The singing lasted long into dusk. In the fading light, with a last few quiet songs, the Sivaoans began to drift away into their tents. Uhura could just make out Jinx climbing into the trees a few yards into the forest; although she had free use of Catchclaw's tent during the day she apparently slept in a swagger-lair like an adolescent. Others made quietly for the trees as well, including Brightspot and Evan. Some few adults stopped to comment on Evan's peculiar style of climbing.

As Uhura put away her *joyeuse,* Captain Kirk paused to remind her that the rest of the crew would be in the new shelter. "Get some sleep, Lieutenant," he added. "We'll need all our wits about us tomorrow." He said it as if he expected something different to happen the next day, but Uhura knew he was only trying to lift her spirits.

When he had gone, Rushlight said, "I don't read your peoples' smells very well, Lieutenant Uhura, but from what Jinx tells me, I'd think you were unhappy. Should I have let you sing? I didn't mean to push you aside, you know. I only thought you deserved a rest."

"Thank you, Rushlight—it's not quite that—although singing always makes me feel better." She did not want to press the issue, so she said nothing more.

"Come then," he said, rising and taking her wrist with his tail, "you will sing as softly with me as you would alone, to lift your spirits. There are a great many songs that we may not sing in public; perhaps I will find a song to cheer a bard."

As they walked toward his tent, he said, "Your captain smells of anticipation. Is he so different from you that his anticipation distresses you? I ask because I have no way of knowing the range of variation of your people; I mean no offense."

"Anticipation?" she said. "You're right about my nose, Rushlight. I thought he was only being cheerful to keep up my morale; he's quite good at that. In other circumstances, I would have believed him."

"You may believe him now, if Brightspot's observations are accurate. And they usually are. He hopes for something good to come—and soon."

"I also *hope* for something good to come. . . ."

He gestured her into his tent and touched the small round object stitched into the fabric. Light sprang from it, a clear muted light good enough to read by. He said, "Something good has already come."

Uhura shook her head. She sat down on the soft pile of usefuls beside the banked fire, drew her knees up and stared into the embers.

"You don't believe me," said Rushlight. "You'll see: When two bards meet in one camp, the world can be changed. You have come farther than any bard I ever met. Between us, we will change many worlds."

She smiled sadly at him. "I want to believe that, Rushlight, but I'm not even allowed to speak of the changes I hope for."

"Then sing," he said quietly. "There are no restrictions on song."

"Is that true?!" A sudden wild hope sprang up in her.

"Of course. Even with your poor memory, you must recall how it happened when you first entered our camp. When you sang, we all knew you for a bard. Winding Path also took you for a nursing mother, but we have come to understand otherwise. . . ." She nodded and he went on, "You spoke of things that—are not often spoken of—but Winding Path didn't cuff you."

"I assumed that was because we were so strange to him that he didn't dare."

Rushlight looped his tail. "Winding Path dares a great deal. No, Lieutenant Uhura, not even Winding Path would dare cuff a bard or a nursing mother. We have a saying: Without children and song, there is no future. You may sing what you like; the only penalty you risk is being asked to leave the camp."

Uhura said, "But that's the same penalty as for speaking."

He sat beside her, his tail wreathed about his toes, and took up his stringed instrument once more. "*I* will not ask you to leave the camp, Lieutenant Uhura. Not for singing."

Like Jinx, Uhura thought. Then, *They're all trying to find a way to help us! As difficult as it is for them, they're all trying!*

She took up her *joyeuse* and adjusted the little instrument to Eeiauoan tuning. *Start simply,* she thought, and aloud she said, "I'll sing for you in the Old Tongue, Rushlight. My accent may be strange to you, but I think you will understand."

She began the version of "The Ballad of CloudShape" that she loved best, remembering, as she sang, the night so many years ago that Sunfall had taught it to her, and an afternoon in her quarters when she sang it to Captain Kirk. She wondered if she were breaking Sunfall's code of balladry, but Uhura had never heard Sunfall mention the kind of promise that she'd had to make to Rushlight concerning his songs. Eeiauoan-song was for everyone to sing, like Earth-song. The only restriction Sunfall had placed on the Old Tongue songs was that she not sing them before a Eeiauoan. This afternoon she had carefully reminded herself that these people were not Eeiauoans. She had sung her teaching song for Jinx, and again for Catchclaw, at Wilson's request. Neither had recognized the song, nor knew the missing verse that held the cure for the Long Death. . . .

When she came to the end of the ballad, she realized that

Rushlight was staring at her with widened eyes. She had never seen that kind of look from a Sivaoan before. His nictitating membranes slid briefly across his eyes. When they slid back, his pupils had contracted to their normal size. But, as he continued to stare, they began once more to widen.

"What is it . . . ?" she began.

Immediately, he looped his tail around her wrist. The grip was tight but reassuring. "I didn't mean to frighten you," he said quickly, "I swear it in Old Tongue. You don't know what you've sung, do you?" His ears flicked back in his amazement. "You truly don't know!"

She shook her head.

"Lieutenant Uhura, please!" His manner was so urgent it was almost as frightening as Stiff Tail's anger. "Do you have permission to sing that song in public? Tell me in Old Tongue!"

Having already thought it through, she didn't have to hesitate. She switched to Old Tongue instantly and said, "Yes, I have permission to sing 'The Ballad of CloudShape' in public. I've done so many times. I even translated it into my language to sing for Captain Kirk and the others on the *Enterprise*."

An enormous relief seemed to wash over him. Then he stood and turned his back to her for a long moment. His tail shivered with—excitement? Uhura could not be sure what he was feeling, but she was no longer afraid.

When he turned back, he said softly, "Lieutenant Uhura, 'The Ballad of CloudShape' was created by one of the greatest bards our world ever knew." He watched her closely. "You don't know the origin of the song, do you?"

"No," she said, "I only know the song. I don't even know the name of the"—she narrowly avoided saying *Eeiauoan*—"one who created it."

"Her name was Sunfall to-Ennien."

Uhura let out a small involuntary gasp, and he dropped to his knees beside her once again. "You recognize the name," he said, "and yet you don't know that is her song?"

Uhura shook her head and said, carefully, "It may be I learned the song from—a descendant of Sunfall to-Ennien." That would be one explanation for the similarity of names.

175

"Will you give me leave to sing the song in public?"

Uhura knew the look of someone wanting something with every fiber of his being, yet Evan said these people must acknowledge the Eeiauoans to help them. She said, "I'm very sorry, Rushlight. It's not mine to give. It is a song of—that people I am forbidden to name."

"I see," he said. He stood again and walked away, his tail dragging the ground. There was nothing she could say to console him. She had no wish to hurt him, but she had done the only thing she could think of to help Sunfall. . . .

His tail lifted slightly, and he turned. "Now I will sing you a bard's song, Lieutenant Uhura." He seemed to mean something particular by the phrase. When she inquired, he explained, "Another song to be sung only between bards, never in public." He took up his instrument and swiftly tuned it.

She felt compelled to reiterate her Old Tongue promise about the sanctity of his songs, but he stopped her before she could speak. "Say nothing. Listen," he said, and he began to sing in a very quiet voice, so low she had to lean toward him to hear.

He sang for a long time, not a single song but a cycle; the tune now angry and dissonant, now sad and pleading and finally ending with mingled chords of sadness and hope.

Uhura knew she had to remember every word, every detail. She concentrated so hard that, when he laid aside his lute, she was startled by the movement.

He asked if she had understood. Between her knowledge of the Old Tongue and the language lessons the children were giving her, she had not missed much. What little she had not, he patiently explained.

Then he said, slowly and distinctly, "You may not *sing* that song before anyone but another bard."

She could not miss his careful emphasis but, to show him she understood, she repeated the words: "I promise, Rushlight. I will never *sing* this song before anyone but another bard."

Without warning, he bristled, his fur standing out in spikes. "Your memory!" he said.

She knew she feared the loss of his attempt. She said in Old Tongue, "My memory is not as bad as you think, Rushlight. It would take me a dozen hearings or more before I could sing your songs, but I promise you I will *never* forget the content."

"Good," he said, his whiskers quivering with relief. "Now we'll dream on it. Tomorrow, when your voice is rested, I'll ask you to sing me what other songs you know in the Old Tongue." He rose, touched the light; it went out, leaving only the dull warmth of the embers.

Uhura slipped off her boots and wrapped herself in darkly patterned usefuls against the night's chill. With so much to think about and understand, she lay awake in the shadows for a long time before her eyes finally closed in sleep, to dream of an ancient world and a bard called Sunfall to-Ennien. . . .

It was a night that should have been dark. . . . Sunfall to-Ennien stood at the edge of the city and stared out longingly into the forests of her childhood, lit and changed to fantastic shapes by the Mad Star's light. When she could bear no more, she looked down at the shifting of her own shadow and thought, *Shadow by night, that's what I've become—what we've all become. So changed and changing that we can no longer share the forests of the world. We're leaving camp.*

It seemed so trivial a thing, to fold a tent and move on, but the camp they would leave was Sivao itself. Leave, move on, you've done enough harm here.

But where would they find a welcome?

Well, too late to wonder that. They'd already agreed, out of shame for the fifteen kinds of plants that would never grow in the world again, the four kinds of animals no child would ever learn to hunt. Out of shame for the death they'd found in their cities, as if they'd created it and carried it into the deepest forest like some horrifying song. The death stopped now, gorged full on rotting flesh, and those few remaining victims could be cured by Thunderstroke's treatment—but nothing could cure their shame. So they had agreed to go.

She wished for some other solution but saw only the flickering shadow of a predator, the ship that stood ready in the center of the city. Its flight would destroy much of what her people had built. The forest would, long years from now, reclaim the rest, hiding it from sight, though not from memory.

She could stay if she wished: A bard would be welcomed in any camp. Wish it she might, but she knew she would go—for the same reason she had come to the city in the first place—because her songs were needed here as much as they were in the forest. They'd be needed still more on the journey, still more on another world. So she said good-bye in her own way, with a last song, and turned to go.

And saw All Loops. He stood with his back to her, in song's range, his tail uncharacteristically trailing the ground. She waited silently as he composed himself. When at last he was able to face her, his eyes, his tail were pleading. "Your songs," he said.

That too had been a difficult decision, but it was the only hope she could hold out to her people in their exile. She said, with great sadness, "From bard to bard, All Loops, for remembrance of me." There, she had done it; her songs would be remembered only by the bards, never to be sung in public. Still using the ritual words, as old as any tradition she knew, she said, "Until such day as that one bard will come to my camp. On that day, I will free all my songs."

And now the ancient words took on a different meaning. That was all she had to offer her people in their exile, that her songs would be theirs alone until they could be reunited with someone from their homeworld. They'd no longer need them then—such reunion could only mean their shame and exile had ended. They'd have new, joyous songs to sing.

All Loops seemed to understand, even to accept, her decision. He stood quietly for a moment, then he said, "Neither of us will live to see that day, Sunfall. . . ."

She arched her whiskers. She knew. She also knew he was making no renewed plea.

He wrapped his tail around her waist and said, "Sunfall to-Ennien, I give you all my songs—to be freed wherever you make camp at last. You and the others may have need of them."

She didn't trust herself to speak. Instead she curled her tail around him. Then, in unspoken agreement, they released each other. All Loops walked silently into the forest. Sunfall turned and walked toward the heart of the city and the great ship that waited there. She did not dare look back, for her heart looked ahead.

Evan Wilson stirred restlessly at the snatches of angry sound that leapt from deep in the forest. She propped herself up on one elbow, desperate to blink the sleep from her eyes and shake the confusion from her head. Chilled, she pulled the useful tighter around her.

She was alone. The realization brought her abruptly awake and to her knees; just as quickly, her phaser was in her hand.

The sounds were louder now but no more understandable —an argument? It sounded too complex for something that simple, and Brightspot's absence made her extremely wary.

She edged to the side of the swagger-lair and peered out. She couldn't see anything, either. To make the jump to the access branch would be risky in the dark, but to stay here—where she was *expected* to be—was riskier. She trusted Brightspot, but not Brightspot's absence.

She eased silently toward the outflung branch that was her only handhold, paused to clip her phaser to her belt. As she did, a tail shot down from above and slapped across her mouth—Brightspot's tail!

Looking up, she saw Brightspot clinging to a limb above the swagger-lair. Then she remembered seeing the gesture used to hush noisy children. She nodded and the tail flicked away.

Soundlessly, Brightspot dropped her head until it was directly above Evan's ear. "Wait here," said Brightspot in a very low voice. "You're too noisy in branches."

Evan nodded a second time, and Brightspot scrambled to another branch, making no noise that Evan could detect, and leapt into the darkness.

Watchful, phaser back in hand, Evan waited nearly two full hours by her internal clock while the noises in the forest continued in fits and starts. The argument or threats at last died down to a mutter, and the mutter came closer.

Brightspot reappeared as quietly as she had gone. A thrust of her tail sent Evan deeper into the swagger-lair; then she rolled neatly over the edge of the roof to land without a sound beside Evan. She knocked Evan on her side and, again, slapped her tail across Evan's mouth.

The muttering party passed directly beneath them. Evan Wilson was able to pick out a few words among those in range and translatable: "Stupid fools. Stupid, stubborn fools." It was Catchclaw's voice. "Humans don't know enough to squawk when they're hurt; Sivaoans don't know enough to stop squawking when the hurt's over." Then, just before she passed out of range once more: "You'll be sorry, Stiff Tail. This time you've stuck your tail into a slicebill nest, see if you haven't."

Several others passed beneath, but Evan heard nothing else. At last, Brightspot released her shoulders; they both sat up. Brightspot said quietly, "It's okay to talk now if we're quiet. . . . You didn't fight me when I pushed you over."

"It's your world, Brightspot. If there's trouble, I have to rely on your judgment. Sometimes you have to trust people. Now, what's going on? Are my friends in danger?"

Brightspot flicked her ears back. "Of course not! I just didn't want them to catch me listening in! How else am I going to find out what's going on around here?" That last was almost plaintive. "You're not angry because I eavesdropped on the adults, are you?"

"I'm not your mother," Evan said, "and in my book you're old enough to take your own chances. Did you *learn* anything?"

"You said you trust me," Brightspot said. "I have to think and put things together. I have to talk to—*somebody*. What happened is nothing that will hurt you, I swear in the Old Tongue, but I have to know more about it before I tell you how it happened. Can you wait?"

Evan Wilson thought about that. "Brightspot," she said, at last, "I can wait a lifetime for the answers to all my questions. But there are people on another world who cannot afford the time. I ask only that you consider them as well. They are my responsibility."

"I think that makes them my responsibility, too," Brightspot said. "Will you be afraid to stay here alone?" She wrapped Wilson's wrist with her tail and explained, "You smelled afraid before."

"If it will help, I can live through it," said Wilson.

"Good. Get some sleep. I'll wake you when I'm done." Once again, Brightspot flung herself out into the darkness and vanished.

Evan Wilson lay down and closed her eyes, but she did not sleep.

Chapter Twelve

Jim Kirk woke at the first pale rays of sunlight and, remembering Left Ear with hope, gave Spock a cheerful, "Good morning, Mr. Spock. I trust you slept well?"

"I did not sleep, Captain. Just after midnight there was considerable disturbance in the forest not far from here. I felt it best to remain on watch."

"You might have waked me," Kirk said.

"I might have, but I did not. I saw no further cause for alarm."

Damn Spock's literalness, anyhow. Short of a direct reprimand, there was never a way to tell him that his behavior bothered you. And, of course, there was no need for a direct reprimand. It was a very annoying habit of Spock's. "What sort of disturbance?"

"An argument, or so I would judge from the types of sounds I heard and from the behavior of various members of the camp this morning."

Kirk took in the few Sivaoans who were up and around. He saw what Spock meant: they greeted each other the way Brightspot greeted Fetchstorm, with the twitch of a tail tip. *I don't like that,* he thought.

Seeing his concern, Spock said, "I merely report the fact. I have no reason to believe we are the cause of the disruption or that we have anything to fear from it. I am, however, curious."

"Curiosity—" Kirk stopped in mid-sentence. He had been about to say, "Curiosity killed the cat"; he thought better of it. "Nothing, Spock. I suppose we'd better see to breakfast. Even curiosity has to be fed."

"I believe Mr. Chekov is preparing something."

Kirk grinned. "Mr. Chekov is certainly full of surprises. I may recommend that Starfleet Academy look up that teacher of his in Volgograd; the skills she teaches are remarkably useful planetside."

"They are indeed, Captain. And the attitude she instills toward 'primitive' people could be extremely valuable when dealing with native cultures that lack the high technology of this world."

"Good morning, Keptain," said Chekov. "Breakfest should be ready in a minute, sair." He brushed his hair back and wiped sweat from his forehead. Apologetically he added, "I thought we'd eat outside, es long es we hev the chence."

Kirk waved aside the apology and examined breakfast, a sort of shishkabob of various items roasted on a green stick. Chekov, brushing a sauce over them at intervals, said, "Local shashlik—Distant Smoke gave me his recipe."

Bemused, Kirk rejoined Spock and said, "Shashlik."

"I am unfamiliar with the term, Captain." Spock did not turn; he was watching the activity in the clearing with interest. Kirk followed his stare.

Across the clearing, a crowd gathered quickly around Catchclaw's tent. "Captain? I should like a closer look."

"Of course, Mr. Spock." The two of them walked across the clearing. Kirk searched the crowd for Brightspot—her interpretation might be useful—but she was nowhere to be seen. They pushed to the fore.

Catchclaw emerged from her tent carrying a pair of small, neatly wrapped bundles, dumped them on the ground and glared at the crowd. Her tail lashed. "Well?" she said. "Haven't you ever seen a to-Ennien move on before? Where are your manners?" All the ears in the crowd flicked back in amazement, then two Sivaoans leapt to her assistance. She gave a few sharp directions and they began to remove bottles and dried herbs from her tent, these they took across the clearing to store in the chem lab.

From the tent nearest Catchclaw's, Settlesand came out to look. She too flicked back her ears. She vanished back into her tent and, when she reappeared, she was carrying another pair of small, neatly wrapped bundles. She walked over and, without a word, dropped her bundles beside Catchclaw's. Catchclaw curled her tail briefly about Settlesand's wrist.

The four children were wildly excited. They bounced and bounded and poked all the bundles with their tails—and began making tiny packs in imitation of their elders.

Grabfoot, in his excitement, pounced on every foot in reach; Kirk could trace his route through the crowd by watching adults jump in reaction. At last, it was Kirk's turn. Grabfoot pounced, then swarmed up to his side and clung to his chest, staring nose to nose. "To Sretalles!" Grabfoot said, "We're going to Sretalles! You come meet us there! Catchclaw says!"

Kirk didn't know what to say but gave in to the impulse to scratch Grabfoot fondly behind the ears. Grabfoot looped his tail delightedly, then he climbed to a better vantage point on Kirk's shoulder to peer at Spock's ears. "Not touch Mr. Spock," he said, almost sadly. "You come to Sretalles! Maybe different there—maybe okay to touch! Tell how it happened CloudShape came to Vulcan. Good-bye for now, Mr. Spock!"

"Good-bye for now, Grabfoot," said Spock gravely.

Grabfoot scrambled to the ground and led his siblings in a mad charge across to say good-bye to Chekov.

There was a touch at Kirk's elbow. He looked down to find Wilson at his side. "Captain," she said, "have you seen Brightspot this morning?" There was a note of urgency in her voice.

He shook his head. "Mr. Spock?"

"Nor have I, Dr. Wilson. Is there some problem?"

She shook her head. "I'll tell you after I find Brightspot. And she should be here, dammit. She's missing Armageddon."

"I beg your pardon, Doctor?" It was just as well Spock asked, thought Kirk, it saved him the trouble.

Catchclaw pulled tent pegs. Now she reached inside and struck the main supporting pole. The tent collapsed in a flutter of bright-colored fabric—and a collective gasp ran through the assembled crowd. Catchclaw glared at them defiantly and, stripping the poles of their usefuls, began to roll up her tent. A moment later, Settlesand's tent collapsed with a soft whoosh.

Wilson, distracted, finally turned back to Spock and whispered, "Brightspot must have been right about Catchclaw. You'd think none of these people had ever seen anybody pack up to move before."

Spock said, "I see, Dr. Wilson. I agree with your assessment. Captain, it is our conjecture that these people have never before seen *Catchclaw* decamp."

"Armageddon," said Wilson darkly, "I told you. When scandalous people start behaving respectably, watch out!"

The two tents were packed in a remarkably short length of time. Settlesand brought two quickens. She held a muttered conversation with Catchclaw and shooed Catchclaw away from the work. Distant Smoke, ears still flattened in surprise, stepped over to offer his assistance, and soon he and Settlesand were at work loading the packs.

"Dr. Wilson," said Catchclaw, "I would like to check your wounds, for safety's sake." She motioned and Wilson followed.

"Interesting," said Kirk, watching where she led, "I'd say Catchclaw wants to make sure Stiff Tail knows she's going."

"She could hardly be ignorant of the fact, Captain, given the attention paid the event by the other members of the camp."

Kirk watched Catchclaw evict Stiff Tail from her own tent and usher Wilson inside. "Ignorant, no, Mr. Spock. But I'd say Catchclaw was twisting the knife." Stiff Tail paced outside her tent, her tail lashing. "Catchclaw could, after all, have examined Dr. Wilson's wounds before she struck her own tent."

"You are right, Captain. And Catchclaw need not have chosen Stiff Tail's tent for the purpose when we have our own shelter."

"Exactly. I'd be a lot happier if Dr. Wilson didn't look so grim."

"I fail to understand why Dr. Wilson's purely emotional response to such a situation should affect your own."

"Her instincts are good, Spock."

"While I agree with your assessment of Dr. Wilson's talents, I would object to your use of the word 'instincts.' It bears a strong resemblance to Dr. Wilson's own 'gut reactions.' And it is still my observation that—"

"I know, I know. That Wilson refuses to admit to logic. Spock, if she has a *logical* reason to be worried, I'm even more concerned."

Kirk caught a glimpse of a bright flash of fur through the milling crowd and moved to get a better look. Brightspot and Jinx stood in the spot where Catchclaw's tent had once been, staring down at the oval of blackened groundcover that confirmed a lengthy stay. Brightspot bristled her amazement; Jinx looked frightened.

Chekov brought his shashlik—the aroma made Kirk realize how hungry he was—and gave them each a skewer. "I hev some for Lieutenant Uhura and Dr. Wilson, too," he said. "It was just es easy to make enough for five."

Wilson and Catchclaw came from Stiff Tail's tent. Chekov started toward her, but Jim Kirk held him back. "I'm not sure you should interrupt them at the moment," he said; but when Wilson spotted Chekov, she gave an easy wave and came to collect her breakfast.

"Mr. Chekov," she said, "thank you. You have just saved a life. I'm ravenous." She demonstrated by tearing into the food. Aside from her thank you, she did not turn her attention from Catchclaw and Stiff Tail.

"Brightspot's here, Dr. Wilson," Kirk said. "You wanted to speak to her?"

"Where?" she said. He pointed, and she waved and called out. Brightspot immediately joined them. Jinx followed, her attempt to remain unnoticed making her seem clumsy; Jim Kirk had no doubt now that she was badly frightened.

Brightspot said excitedly, "Catchclaw's leaving!" and Jinx flinched.

Catchclaw and Stiff Tail were still having words with each other, tail tips quivering. When Catchclaw saw Jinx, however, she walked away from Stiff Tail and called the youngster to her. Jinx dashed to her; Catchclaw caught and wrapped her comfortingly in her tail.

Jinx brightened and straightened. Catchclaw said a few words to her, and Jinx arched her whiskers forward in assent. Tails still entwined about each other, the two walked toward the *Enterprise* landing party. Stiff Tail followed at a distance, tail twitching.

"Dr. Wilson," said Catchclaw, "I go to Sretalles. I hold you responsible for Jinx to-Ennien."

Whatever Wilson had been expecting, Kirk thought, seeing her startled expression, it wasn't this. She said, "By my custom, I must ask, Catchclaw, does this meet with Jinx's approval?"

"Keptain," said Chekov urgently, "she's esking Dr. Wilson to beby-sit!"

Jinx looked at Catchclaw, then at Wilson. "I don't mind," she said unsurely and then, as if realizing something, "No, I don't mind."

The other Sivaoans, to judge from their reactions, *did* mind. Stiff Tail's tail whipped. Ears were laid back all through the crowd and more tails began to lash. "Captain," said Spock in a warning tone.

"I see it, Mr. Spock," he said. "Stay alert, Mr. Chekov."

He called out, "Dr. Wilson, you can't accept the responsibility for Jinx. We have no idea how long Catchclaw will be gone."

Wilson did not turn. She regarded Jinx and Catchclaw gravely.

Catchclaw repeated, "Dr. Wilson, I go to Sretalles. I hold you responsible for Jinx to-Ennien."

"Captain," said Wilson, "I sincerely hope that wasn't a direct order. I accept the responsibility, Catchclaw, and I thank you."

Pandemonium broke loose. Stiff Tail rounded on Catchclaw, hackles bristling. "No!" she said. Half a dozen others in the crowd echoed her sentiments but no one made any move to interfere.

Catchclaw gave Jinx a lick on the forehead and released

her, nudging her toward Wilson. Jinx immediately wrapped her tail around Wilson's wrist and Wilson stroked the tip reassuringly.

Then Catchclaw groomed the fur on her right shoulder, the one facing Stiff Tail. The action was remarkably contemptuous, and Kirk was not the only one to think so: Stiff Tail raised her arm as if to strike. Catchclaw jerked her head back, her eyes wide, her ears flattened to her skull. A low growl went through the crowd and Stiff Tail, as if startled by her own actions, immediately let drop her arm. She stepped away from Catchclaw and turned her back. "No," she said again.

"It's done," said Catchclaw. Without a further word, she walked toward the crowd. It gave way before her and she stepped through, gathered up her children and plumped them on top of the packs. They clung and waved their tails; their excitement made them oblivious to the distress of the adults around them.

Catchclaw said, "Well, Settlesand. Are we going, or are we just planning to stand around all day with our tents packed?" Settlesand jumped and mounted. As they vanished into the forest, the welcome-homes set up a farewell racket.

Whatever protection Catchclaw had afforded Jinx and Wilson was gone. Kirk took advantage of the distraction and ran to her side. Spock and Chekov were right behind him. They made a small protective V around the two. "Phasers, Captain?" said Spock.

He hoped that wouldn't be necessary. "Not unless you absolutely have to, Mr. Spock. I want to avoid it if we can, but if we can't—" He saw Uhura through the shifting crowd. "Lieutenant Uhura," he called, "Here. On the double."

Uhura hurried to join them. "What happened, Captain?"

"I don't know, Lieutenant. Ask Dr. Wilson."

He had meant it as a reproach to Wilson, but Uhura took it literally. Wilson said—and Kirk could almost sense her shrug—"Catchclaw asked me to look after Jinx, and I said I'd be glad to."

Still the crowd made no threatening moves toward them. Brightspot padded over to Wilson and said, "Don't be scared. They're not mad at you."

Kirk said, "Are you sure, Brightspot?"

She flicked her tail tip at him. "Why should they be mad at you? Catchclaw did it. Catchclaw was right, but they don't believe that."

Winding Path crept toward Stiff Tail, making himself so small he almost groveled. He said, "Once to-Ennien is more tail than brain—and Catchclaw is *twice* to-Ennien." Stiff Tail whipped her tail twice; Winding Path shrank smaller.

Rushlight stepped in; and, unlike Winding Path, he made no attempt to minimize himself. "Tell me how it happened," he demanded, with a quick glance past Stiff Tail to Uhura; he seemed almost amused. Bristling, Stiff Tail gave him the details.

The longer he listened, the more his tail curled. Stiff Tail got angrier. When she had finished, Rushlight said, "Catchclaw does as she sees fit. *You* should know better, Stiff Tail."

That set her ears back, Kirk saw.

"Know better!" said Stiff Tail.

"You heard me," he said, and this time his tail stiffened to seriousness. "Look at them, all huddled together like a clutch of baby silverspots. . . . Smell for yourself!" Stiff Tail turned; her manner changed instantly.

As she started toward them, Jim Kirk tensed. She froze on the spot and thrust her tail forward, as if the group were surrounded by an invisible tent. He relaxed cautiously. "Come in, Stiff Tail," he said, hoping he was right. She took the fewest steps necessary and reached for his wrist with her tail.

"I apologize for frightening you," she said. "This was no fault of yours. You do not know our customs. Evan Wilson did not understand what she was saying, although she knew the correct words."

"Wrong," said Evan Wilson. Still holding Jinx's tail in her hand, she advanced on Stiff Tail fiercely. "I knew precisely what I was doing. I accepted the responsibility of looking after Jinx. I *accept* the responsibility and I will do it."

Stiff Tail drew her arm back to deliver a blow, but Wilson was fast—one arm shot up to block, the other to strike. Stiff Tail was so astonished, she froze. So did Wilson. It was just long enough for Kirk to catch Wilson's arm. Rushlight did the same to Stiff Tail, wrapping his tail around her wrist; he made the chuffing noise Kirk had come to associate with amused disapproval and said, "You see, Stiff Tail, you are caught in your own snare. You dare not strike if she truly does not comprehend her actions; and, if she does, you have no right."

His tail released her falling arm, then immediately looped up again. "Oh, this will make a fine song, Lieutenant Uhura. You'll see—you and your people will provide us with two night's entertainment for the next festival!" Uhura laughed; it was the sweet sound of relief.

Then Rushlight perused Wilson slowly, from the set of her feet to the tension in her upraised arm to the glare she fixed still on Stiff Tail. *"You* are a tail-kinker," he told her. "I hadn't realized that someone without proper claws or sharp teeth could be so fierce." Without taking her eyes from Stiff Tail, Wilson bared her teeth in acknowledgment.

"No fight," said Stiff Tail. With that, she simply walked away.

Brightspot happily looped her tail around Wilson's waist, entangling it with Jinx's. Wilson laid a small hand on the shoulder of each and exhaled a deep breath. "Elath bless me," she said, "I have never been so scared in all my life," and then she laughed too.

"You stood up to her!" said Brightspot, a little awed. "You offered to fight her!"

"Yeah—and for one awful moment I thought she might take me up on it! I didn't want to fight her, Brightspot; you should know that."

The crowd was slowly drifting away. Kirk realized there was no longer a threat and said, quietly, "People, I think perhaps we shouldn't be standing in the middle of the camp."

"I agree, Captain," said Spock, taking his cue. "We will attract less attention if we retire to our shelter."

Brightspot, Jinx and Rushlight took this as an invitation and walked along beside them. With two tails wrapped around her, Wilson was forced to coordinate her walk; it made the trio oddly triumphant. When they reached the shelter however, Wilson paused. "Jinx, Brightspot, you'll have to let go for a minute. I think the captain wants a word with me in private."

The captain certainly did, thought Kirk. He wondered how

he would have managed if she hadn't suggested it herself. "This won't take long, Mr. Spock. Keep your eyes open. And, while you're waiting, you might explain the concepts 'brig' and 'insubordination' to our friends here." He followed Wilson inside.

"I shall be happy to, Captain."

Why, thought Kirk, *do I always get the feeling Spock is not taking this seriously?*

Inside the shelter, Wilson stood at strict military attention. There was no mockery in her attitude, as there would have been with some; the stance signaled her full acceptance of her fate.

"At ease," he said, and she snapped into the formal at-ease pose, legs spread, hands behind her back. "Sir," she said crisply.

He looked her over, falling into the manner himself. "You will explain your conduct, Dr. Wilson," he said.

"No one treats me like a kid, *sir!*"

He was taken aback. "Explain yourself," he said and added, "Sit down, Evan, before you bring out the martinet in me."

She smiled. Reaching for a stool, she said, "I doubt that's possible, Captain, but . . ." She sat.

He pulled up a stool of his own and said, "I do want that explanation."

"Captain, when a person is much smaller than average, she often finds herself treated, consciously or unconsciously, as if she were a child. You might not notice, being the height you are, but I'm sensitive to it; and I've been treated as a child ever since I stepped into this camp." She shifted on the stool and jammed her chin onto her fist.

In that pose, she did look like a small, gravely serious child. Kirk stared back at her as he realized exactly what he was thinking. "I see!" he said, more in reaction to his own image of her.

She straightened instantly, as if the pose had been a deliberate demonstration. "I thought you would. At any rate, Chekov told me about the ritual for taking responsibility for a child. Only an adult can do it. When Catchclaw and I were in Stiff Tail's tent, she barely glanced at my back. She wanted to

tell me that she had thought of something that might help us."
Evan Wilson threw up her hands. "That was *all* she said,
Captain, and she said that with a grudging reluctance. . . ."

"Go on," said Kirk.

"The rest you saw. Catchclaw asked me to take the
responsibility for Jinx. Stiff Tail didn't want her to—and that
implied that she didn't think I was old enough or responsible
enough to handle the job properly. The only way I could
prove my maturity was to accept Jinx's care."

A small frown crossed her features briefly. "I don't know if
I did the right thing, Captain, but it *felt* right." The frown
became a rueful smile. "And yes, I would have disobeyed
even a direct order to refuse the responsibility." She offered
her wrists, as if for restraints. "Take me away, Captain. I
knew the possible consequences."

"No doubt," he said, not able to resist a slight smile. "You
also know I can hardly afford to return you to the *Enterprise*
for three days on bread and water, not when you're baby-
sitting one of the native children."

The sparkle was back in her eyes now. "The thought had
crossed my mind, Captain."

Kirk threw back his head and laughed. "I'll bet it did—tell
me, Evan, does Starfleet Medical Academy give a course in
insubordination to all its students?"

"Now why would you suggest that, sir?" The question was
innocent; her expression was not.

"I always thought Bones's tendency to insubordination was
a matter of personality; now I'm beginning to suspect that it's
generic to doctors."

She shook her head, still smiling. "I doubt it, Captain. At
any rate, I didn't learn insubordination at Starfleet Medical."

The thought of Bones had sobered him. Rising, he said,
"All right, Dr. Wilson. Wherever you learned it, I'll have no
more of it. . . . Evan, tread carefully. You weren't the only
one scared out there. If Stiff Tail had delivered her reprimand, the *Enterprise* would be short a doctor."

She chuckled. "A tail-kinker's small, too. The one real
advantage my size gives me is the element of surprise."

Recalling Stiff Tail's astonishment, he nodded. "I
understand—but that's not what I meant. I want you to be

careful, Evan; you're too valuable a person to lose. No more foolish chances, and that is an order I'll expect obeyed."

To his surprise, she turned a vivid shade of scarlet. With a defiant toss of her head that could not belie her blush, she said, "Captain, I never take *foolish* chances."

"I'll get the rest of the party," he said. Rather than call the rest in, he stepped outside; she needed time to regain her composure.

"You can't lock Evan up, Captain Kirk! You can't. You don't understand!" Brightspot bristled at the prospect. On a world where the ultimate punishment seemed to be throwing someone out of camp, that might well be frightening, Kirk realized.

"I won't, Brightspot," he reassured her, "but I did cuff her for causing so much trouble."

"Oh," said Brightspot, and her fur settled. "I have to— Jinx and I have to tell her something important. Wait," she added suddenly, as he gestured them inside. She turned to Jinx, "Evan says Captain Kirk is . . . is the person responsible for their camp."

"A camp within a camp?" Jinx asked.

"There is very little 'of course' when it comes to custom," Brightspot quoted.

Jinx appeared to think about this. When she had, she said, "Then maybe we should tell them all."

"Tell us all what?" Kirk asked.

The two Sivaoans glanced anxiously at Rushlight, who said, "Lieutenant Uhura, you also have things to *tell* your people. If you will excuse me, I will return to my tent. I have a song to make. You will be the first to hear." Tail still looped in amusement, he walked away. Jinx and Brightspot looked after him, obviously relieved.

Kirk repeated his gesture inviting them into the shelter. Jinx shrank visibly and said to Brightspot, "Are you sure you want me?"

The tip of Brightspot's tail twitched. "You are Evan's responsibility, and I am Evan's friend. I think I must be your friend, too." The two stared at each other hard for a long moment, then they simultaneously offered each other their tails. Thus entwined, Jinx shyly behind Brightspot, the two entered the shelter. Kirk and the rest of the landing party followed.

Jinx rushed to examine Wilson. "Looking for cuff-marks?" Evan asked, grinning.

Brightspot said, "Humans cuff with words, Jinx. Captain Kirk says he's not going to lock you up, Evan, so it's okay."

Evan nodded. "Brightspot, can you tell me now?"

Brightspot nodded back. "I—" She glanced at Jinx and corrected herself, "We figured out *why* we can't find out what's going on. And you can't either."

"We weren't sure," put in Jinx. "We were afraid to tell you the wrong thing, but you accepted responsibility for me from Catchclaw—"

"And when Stiff Tail got so angry, we knew we were right!" Brightspot finished.

Wilson raised her hands. "Slow down. I'm not following any of this. Sit down, take your time and tell me how it happened."

The two glanced at each other and Jinx deferred to Brightspot, who said, "Should I tell the captain?"

"Please," said Evan, "if you can."

The two were more at ease speaking to Wilson, Kirk saw; he said, "Tell Dr. Wilson, Brightspot, I'm listening."

Brightspot made an effort to slow her words but her report was breathless with excitement. "Evan, the problem with babies is that there are some questions they don't think to ask. They don't *know* enough to ask." Brightspot looked again at Jinx. "We had to walk it through. You see, in our customs there are some things adults don't tell children. So even if you ask, you don't get an answer."

"We have some similar customs, Brightspot," Evan assured her. "That's no real surprise."

"One of the things adults don't tell children here is about the you-know-whos—about the *Eeiauoans*," she finished defiantly. "If I ask them, they smell ashamed and guilty and they change the subject or tell me to stop sticking my tail in where it doesn't belong."

Brightspot flicked out her tail and made a brushing caress against Wilson's cheek. "All the angry noises last night

. . . The adults were having a real tail-twister of an argument about all of you." Her glance shot about the room, to include the entire landing party. "You and Captain Kirk say you're adults, Evan, and so do Catchclaw and Rushlight. Stiff Tail and some of the others say you're children, and they won't discuss the Eeiauoans with children. They're too ashamed."

Children! thought Jim Kirk, staring at his acting chief medical officer, *She's done it again!*

Evan Wilson said, "So that's why Catchclaw asked me to be responsible for you, Jinx?"

"I guess so. To make the rest see that you're an adult. Catchclaw . . . doesn't think adult has anything to do with ritual," she said somewhat defiantly to Brightspot. "She says I'm an adult. She asked my permission before entrusting me to Dr. Wilson because it was deceitful—she couldn't have done it in Old Tongue, she said. Not because of you, Dr. Wilson, but because of me."

"In that case, Jinx," said Evan Wilson, "you're on your own recognizance. I mean if I cuff you for no good reason, I expect you to cuff me back. I mean I rely on you to keep me out of trouble the same way I try to keep you out of trouble."

Brightspot shrank. Evan Wilson immediately gave the parti-colored Sivaoan her full attention. "What's wrong, Brightspot? Do my customs make you uncomfortable?"

Brightspot flicked back her ears. "What about me?"

"Oh," said Wilson, "and what happened to your wonderful memory, Brightspot? What did I say last night when you asked if I was angry at you for eavesdropping on the adults?"

"You said, 'I'm not your mother. And in my book you're old enough to take your own chances.'" Her ears pricked up. "That means the same thing! You treat me like an adult too! Thank you, Evan!"

"There's nothing to thank me for. You act like an adult, you get treated like one." She stood and laid a hand on the shoulder of each. "Now, how do we get *Stiff Tail* to treat us as adults? If that's why they won't discuss the Eeiauoans with us, we'd better do something to remedy it fast. There are too many lives at stake to leave the problem in the hands of children."

Jinx said, "Catchclaw may have done it. It depends on what Stiff Tail decides."

Brightspot's tail drooped. She said, "Then it didn't work, Jinx. Stiff Tail won't acknowledge it—believe me, Jinx—I *know* how she thinks. When her mind is made up, it stays made up."

"Inflexible," said Wilson. "Elath builds a universe on change, and then She gives us Stiff Tail. What a sense of humor!"

"Inflexibility," said Spock, speaking for the first time, "is as much a handicap to Stiff Tail as to us. If you will recall, Dr. Wilson, Rushlight referred to Stiff Tail as being 'caught in her own snare.'"

"Of course, Spock!" said Kirk. "If we play by her rules, she would be forced to talk about the Eeiauoans. . . . Brightspot, if *we* Walked would Stiff Tail consider us adults?"

"Oh, yes, she'd have to! Once you have your own name, she wouldn't dare treat you like children!"

"Then tell us exactly what we have to do to be legal adults in Stiff Tail's eyes. And be very careful." Kirk gave her a long, hard look. "That's a baby question. Anything we don't know could kill us—and a lot of others as well."

"Jinx," Brightspot said hesitantly, "I don't mean . . . I don't mean to hurt you, but you know more about the Walk than I do. And so many people depend on them. . . . Please, you tell them."

Jinx stiffened and stood. Without warning, she turned her back to them all. Brightspot said, "Please, Jinx." Jim Kirk opened his mouth to say something, but Brightspot's tail flicked up for silence.

At last Jinx turned. Making a visible effort to gather her thoughts, she said, "In your culture, we are both adults; in mine, both children. Either way, we're much alike. And an adult would act to save so many lives, no matter how painful. I'll tell you, if you wish to take the risk."

A child past puberty, Jinx told them, could not be denied his or her ritual Walk into adulthood. A group, in number anywhere from four to ten, went to the camp leader; they announced their intention to Walk by asking the name of another camp that needed their number of adults. They were given as their destination the name of a camp some five days' walk through deep wood.

They were allowed to take only a knife and usefuls to make shelter in the trees. They could, of course, make spears; and they all did. Everybody knew how to sharpen a stick into a spear even if she only used the skill once in a lifetime.

It was a survival test and yet it was also one last lesson, for if even one member of the party failed, the rest remained children—until they formed another party, tried and completed the Walk. It taught that adults relied on one another for their lives: that cooperation was the greater part of maturity. *A lesson*, thought Kirk, *that Stiff Tail had failed to learn.*

Jinx did not make light of what they would face: the deep woods were full of wild creatures, many of whom, like the slashbacks, traveled in pairs or packs and wouldn't hesitate to attack people. There were other hazards as well—treacherous rockfalls, flash floods. Her fur spiked and, as she paused to smooth it, Kirk suddenly knew she was speaking of things that had happened to her own party. Jinx had tried and failed; worse, she had been the sole survivor of her party.

And he understood Brightspot's attitude now. "Jinx" was not a name, it was an act of striking cruelty. Into the silence, Jim Kirk said, "I can't call you 'Jinx'!"

Her ears flicked back. "You're angry!"

"Of course I'm angry. I didn't realize the name was *meant*. I thought it was only . . ."

"Only sounds, like most of your names," she finished for him. "You must continue to call me Jinx, Captain. It's the only name I have until I earn my own." She touched his arm lightly with the tip of her tail and added as if consoling him, "When you say it, I will know that to you it is only sounds. That way it will hurt neither of us."

"Thank you," he said, for there was nothing else he could say.

Then he wrenched himself back to the job at hand. His people would be at twice the risk on a Walk—they had no long practice dealing with the hazards of the Sivaoan wilderness. He turned to Spock: "Mr. Spock, if Catchclaw's ruse hasn't done the trick, you and I will take a little Walk."

"Just a damn moment, Captain," said Wilson. She was on her feet, hands on her hips, her blue eyes blazing.

He looked at her and said sharply, "More insubordination?"

She snapped to attention; this time her body was rigid with anger. "Permission to speak, *sir!*"

"Permission granted."

"I should like to point out to the captain that, as a *child*, I would be unable to carry out my assigned mission to learn the information we need from the Sivaoan doctors. I respectfully remind the captain that I am acting chief medical officer and the bloody plague gives me the right to pull medical rank if necessary, *sir!*" She fairly spat the final words at him.

Spock regarded her with undisguised interest. "She is quite right, Captain, although I fail to understand the need for such an extreme display of emotion when the logic of the situation would have been sufficient."

"Enough," said Kirk. "All right, Dr. Wilson. If it's necessary, you will join us; you've made your point. But so, I hope, has Mr. Spock." He waited, watching her face; the anger went as quickly as it had come.

Still at attention, she struck a jaunty pose and said, "Mr. Spock, to a Vulcan I would make a logical appeal; the captain's human, so I thought an emotional display might be more effective."

Spock gave her a moment's consideration, nodded, then said, "I have known the captain to respond to logic, Dr. Wilson."

Giving Jim Kirk no time to respond to this, Wilson turned promptly back to him and said, with a hint of a smile, "I shall take Mr. Spock's observation into consideration for future reference, Captain. Thank you, sir."

"As you were, Doctor," Jim Kirk said. As she sat down, Kirk looked across at Chekov and Uhura and recognized their need as well. He said, "You both know how dangerous the Walk is, so I'm putting it on a voluntary basis. Those of you who do not wish to come may either remain here in camp or return to the *Enterprise*. Lieutenant Uhura? Mr. Chekov?"

"I'll come, sir."

"Aye, Keptain."

Jinx said, "I must ask you something, Captain Kirk." She tensed, so tautly that her body shivered. "Please, if you must take the Walk to prove to Stiff Tail that you are adults, will you . . . will you let me come with you?" She asked it of them all, her eyes wide with pleading. "If even one says no, I won't ask again. I don't want to endanger your Walk or your mission, but—*please,* would you at least consider it?" She sprang to her feet. "I'll wait outside," she said, "I'll—" And she darted from the shelter.

Wilson rose to follow. Kirk caught her arm, "Wait, Dr. Wilson. Brightspot, that was Jinx's party that got caught in the flash flood, wasn't it."

Brightspot nodded unhappily. "She tried the Walk twice. The first time, SharpTooth was killed by slashbacks. The second time . . . the second time, the flash flood—Jinx was the only one left alive. Now she has that name, and no one will go with her."

Jim Kirk said, "Do *you* think she was somehow at fault, Brightspot?"

"No," said Brightspot after a moment's hesitation, "But most people think she's unlucky."

Wilson snorted angrily. "I'll agree she's unlucky," she said, "but a bringer of bad luck? Never. I vote we take her if we have to go, Captain."

"Indeed, Captain," Spock added, "her knowledge of the terrain would be of great assistance to us."

"I agree, Mr. Spock. Any objections?" As he expected, there were none.

Brightspot said, "Then would you take me, too?"

Kirk was startled by the request. "What about your friends, Brightspot? From what Jinx says, you'd ordinarily go with people you've known for a long time."

"Friends are friends," Brightspot said, "whether I've known them for a long time or a short time. You're my friends, and . . . and 'Jinx' is only sounds. What do you say?"

"I say you should tell Jinx that—and we'd be glad to have you. Both of you." He released Wilson's arm.

"Aye, sir," she said and, grinning, she snatched lightly at Brightspot's tail. "We'll tell Jinx."

As the two of them scurried past, Jim Kirk thought, *Let's hope we don't have to do this. Let's hope we have to find another way to help . . . Jinx*—and find it he would, he promised himself.

Left Ear returned the tricorder. Brightspot's suggestion had been a good one. Between the information Left Ear provided and what Uhura had learned from Rushlight, Spock was able to put together a sketchy history of the Eeiauoans' exile.

The nearby nova had caused widespread upheavals in the Sivaoan ecology. By the time, some hundred years later, things had begun to return to normal, the Sivaoans found they had two very different cultures: one nomadic, the other city based. Along with vast technological changes came the city diseases. It was a familiar pattern, Wilson assured him; cities gave disease a chance to spread rapidly.

Here on Sivao, however, the two factions had faced each other down, and the nomadic, being the traditional way of life, had the edge. To worsen the situation, the city dwellers felt guilty—for the plagues, for the species that were now extinct because of their failure to follow nomadic ecological practices. The city dwellers had been told to return to the old ways or leave camp; only this time the camp was Sivao itself.

They had the technology to leave their world, and they did. Because of the species' unusual way of transmission of data, however, and because of their strong feelings on the subject of ownership of information, it seemed the Eeiauoans took the art of space travel with them. The Sivaoans had never attempted it again.

"Sunfall to-Ennien took her songs as well, Captain," Uhura said. "Here they may only be sung between bards."

When she had explained, Spock said, "Perhaps the bards have retained the knowledge of space-going techniques as well?"

"I have no idea, sir. Sunfall *to*-Ennien"—she always made

the distinction very clearly—"hoped that the loss of her songs would eventually lead to a reunion between the two cultures. She had no reason to believe the techniques of space travel would be lost."

"Or deliberately forgotten, Uhura," suggested Kirk. "It seems to me that, on a world where memory is the only way to store knowledge, it would be quite easy to forget something forever. Perhaps the one person who had the information simply didn't pass it on. And yet, the Eeiauoans have books, haven't they?"

"They do, sir."

Spock said, "Do the Eeiauoans appear to have the same type of memory as these people?"

Uhura shook her head. "I don't think so, sir. I was often astonished by Sunfall's ability to recall things she had only heard once, but she did not have the ability to—to *record* as Brightspot does."

Kirk said, "Perhaps the Eeiauoans for some reason lost that ability? That would explain why they have books when the Sivaoans don't."

"That is one possibility, Captain," said Spock. "The other is that they adopted the technology of printing from the new cultures they encountered and no longer needed such a highly developed memory."

"Stubborn people," said Kirk. "To forget an entire technology but remember a slight for two thousand years."

"Memory—even such a highly developed memory—can be exceedingly selective, Captain."

"I know, Spock. I just wish their choices had been better."

Wilson said, "They're trying, Captain. As . . . ashamed as they are, Left Ear and Rushlight and Catchclaw—they're all trying to help us. If they have to find a loophole to do it, well, at least they're out looking for loopholes."

"It won't do us much good if they don't have the cure for ADF," said Kirk.

"They've got it," said Wilson. "They just don't know it." She stood and paced. "If only Catchclaw hadn't left . . . I understand her reasons—it was a good try—but given a few more days I might have been able to convince her to come with us. Jinx would come, I think, but she says she simply hasn't the experience. So we've got to find another doctor and start all over."

Spock said, "What is the local ritual, if any, of leave-taking?"

"None," said Wilson. "Pick up and go. Brightspot says you only give your itinerary to someone you'd like to see again." She stopped pacing abruptly, gave Spock her full attention. "That's odd."

"Yes," Spock agreed.

It was clear the two of them knew what they were talking about. Before Jim Kirk could question them, Evan Wilson said, "Damn! I'm a fool! Captain, Catchclaw left in a huff, but she made sure everybody knew where she was going. You told me yourself the last group didn't give a destination at all."

"You were to look after Jinx," Kirk said, "I assume she wants Jinx returned to her."

"That's the point—what if Catchclaw expects us all to follow her to Sretalles?"

"Grabfoot!" said Kirk suddenly. "He said, 'You come meet us there. Catchclaw says!' You could be right."

"If you had a map, Mr. Spock, could you determine the coordinates?"

"I could approximate them, Dr. Wilson."

Wilson gave a curt, satisfied nod. "Come on, Nyota. You try Rushlight, I'll try Brightspot and Jinx. Somebody must know the way to Sretalles." And they were on the way.

Kirk was silent as Spock returned to his tricorder. When at last Spock looked up, Kirk said, "Well, Mr. Spock? Anything new to report?"

"I think it unlikely that the Sivaoans will be able to provide a map. Given their ability to remember and their highly developed sense of smell, they would hardly need invent such a device. I think it more probable that they would give directions; and that such directions would depend a great deal on the sense of smell."

"Meaning we couldn't even follow their directions without Brightspot or Jinx."

"Precisely, Captain." Spock folded his arms. "If Dr.

Wilson is correct, however, and Catchclaw did intend that we follow her to Sretalles, it would be logical to suppose that Jinx is capable of serving as guide as well as motivation. Given the oblique nature of the assistance the others have provided, for Catchclaw to employ such a . . . tactic would not be unlikely."

"So we might have to Walk, anyway. I suppose you're right. And it also wouldn't do for us to arrive before Catchclaw. We don't know what she has in mind, but she may need some time to prepare the way for us."

"Possibly. I should like Dr. Wilson's thoughts on the matter. Her unorthodox use of logic may be of considerable assistance to us."

Kirk couldn't suppress a grin. "Still theorizing that she uses logic rather than instinct, Spock? Then I'll give you another item for your collection: She took responsibility for Jinx because she was tired of being treated like a child." He explained in detail, thoroughly enjoying the bemused expression on his science officer's face. He ended his account and added, "I give her a lot of credit. She's one of the few humans I've met who could resist saying 'I told you so.'"

"Such a statement would be quite unnecessary, Captain."

"Spock, you've worked with humans long enough to know that simply because something is unnecessary doesn't mean it isn't done."

"Indeed, Captain, I have." He continued to look thoughtful. At last he said, "However, Dr. Wilson is quite beyond my experience. I should be interested to know her world of origin."

"Check her transfer dossier, Spock." Kirk said it for something to say; he was rather surprised at Spock's reaction to Wilson.

"I have, Captain. I find her records somewhat perplexing."

"Perplexing? In what way?"

"They are the records of a career bureaucrat, with a history of sheltered posts on highly civilized worlds only."

"A desk jockey, Spock? That doesn't sound a bit like her."

"Precisely my point, Captain. As for her world of origin, Telamon is given."

"And why wouldn't it *be* Telamon?"

"Telamon was colonized in the very early days of Earth's interstellar expansion by religious dissenters who, to this day, consider their monotheistic god to be male. Dr. Wilson swears by 'Elath'; it is an ancient Earth term meaning 'Goddess.' A Telamonite—"

Kirk grinned again and interrupted: "That's no mystery, Spock; that's pure contrariness—another human trait you should be familiar with by now."

"I am, most certainly. However, that alone would seem insufficient to explain the observed facts of the case."

Kirk shook his head, still smiling. "Don't let her pull your tail; she enjoys it too much." *And so do I,* he added to himself. *It's been a long time since I've seen Spock set back on his heels by human behavior.*

"Captain Kirk?" A voice called from outside the shelter and a tail thrust in. Kirk recognized the markings; he gave Spock a significant look and said, "Come in, Stiff Tail."

She entered with Distant Smoke at her heels. With no preliminary courtesies, she said, "Distant Smoke has agreed to accept the responsibility for Jinx to-Ennien."

Kirk knew Catchclaw's attempt had failed, but there was no point to giving in without a fight. "Catchclaw made Evan Wilson responsible. Even a human could tell you how it happened."

"That is not possible," she said.

"Tell that to Evan Wilson."

She gave him her ears-back amazed look. "From what Brightspot tells me, you are in some sense responsible for Evan Wilson—"

She takes it to mean like an older brother, he thought and said instantly, "Not in the sense you mean."

"In any sense," she said, "I speak to you. Evan Wilson does not understand our customs, and I wish to avoid injury to her. I had hoped you might be of assistance."

From the risen fur at the back of her neck and the lash of her tail tip, he knew this was no idle warning. "I'll do what I can, Stiff Tail," he said at last. She nodded and left, Distant Smoke following dejectedly at her heels.

Kirk turned to his first officer. "If Jinx isn't willing to make an issue of her adulthood, the penalties must be severe. I won't have Evan taking on Stiff Tail, even if she is willing."

"Then may I suggest that you inform Dr. Wilson of your decision in the matter before she has occasion to make her own."

"Good lord, you're right, Spock! I'll see to Wilson. You tell Scotty we're going for a Walk." Kirk was on his way before Mr. Spock had opened his communicator.

Outside, he paused to scan the clearing and spotted Wilson deep in conversation with Jinx and Brightspot. He crossed to join them.

Wilson rose to greet him and, once again, he was painfully aware how tiny she was. That was enough to confirm his decision in his own mind. Having seen Wilson's temper—and the sort of risks she was wont to take—he chose not to give her an option. *I have no idea,* he thought, *how she defines a foolish risk.* "You were right, Brightspot," he said. "Stiff Tail won't let Catchclaw get away with it. We're still children."

Wilson bristled almost as visibly as Stiff Tail had.

"So," he said, before she had a chance to respond, "we Walk. Dr. Wilson, would you be kind enough to inform the rest of our party? We must make our formal statement of intent to Stiff Tail."

Wilson turned to the two Sivaoans. "What do you say, Jinx, Brightspot? Shall we take a stab at it?"

It took both of them a moment's time to understand what she was asking, then, with a bravado it was apparent they did not feel, the two said in one voice, "Yes, we'll Walk."

"Okay, then you find Chekov and Uhura. We'll meet you outside Stiff Tail's tent." The two hurried off, talking at rapid fire to each other.

Kirk said, "I thought I'd assigned that job to you."

"A good officer always knows how to delegate authority. I don't want them to have a chance to start worrying, Captain."

"How about you?" he said pointedly.

"I never worry about things I can't change."

"You could, Evan."

"No," she said, "and stop pushing, Captain. Neither can you."

So she'd caught him out. In spite of that, he gave one last try. "I thought you said you never took foolish risks."

She favored him with her wicked grin and asked, "Can you honestly define this as a foolish risk, Captain?"

He had no recourse but the truth. "No," he said soberly, "I can't. It's the only chance we've got."

An hour later, the full party assembled before Stiff Tail's tent. Brightspot or Jinx must have spread the word of their intentions, because the remainder of the camp had turned out as well.

Jim Kirk, rehearsed by Jinx in the full formalities, called Stiff Tail to the opening. "We wish to leave your camp, Stiff Tail. We ask the name of a camp that has need of seven adults. We will begin our Walk tomorrow at dawn."

Her ears shot back. "Seven?" she said. That was not a ritual question; there was a subdued growl from the assembled crowd. Stiff Tail steadied herself and began again. "How are the members of your party called?"

That was acceptable. Jim Kirk identified himself, then he stepped back and gestured the others forward. Spock, Chekov and Uhura each identified themselves. "Jinx to-Ennien," said Jinx next with an air of defiance. The crowd made a low noise, whether approving or disapproving, Kirk couldn't tell; certainly, Jinx's inclusion caused a mild sensation.

Then Brightspot did the same, with the same defiance. Stiff Tail fixed her daughter with a glare. "Brightspot to-Srallansre," she said bristling, "you are still young. Do you truly wish to Walk in this company?"

Again, Stiff Tail had broken ritual, and again the crowd reacted with a low growl. Kirk started forward to argue that it was Brightspot's right, but Evan Wilson stopped him, shaking her head in warning. "Her fight, Captain," she whispered. "Let her make her own decisions."

Brightspot bristled back at Stiff Tail. "I choose my own time," she said, "I choose my own friends to travel with." That put an end to it, as far as the crowd was concerned, but Stiff Tail continued to glare at Brightspot.

Wilson said, "Doctor Evan Wilson, Acting Chief Medical Officer, U.S.S. *Enterprise,*" and then it was Kirk's turn again.

"We ask the name of a camp that has need of seven adults," he repeated. "We begin our Walk tomorrow at dawn."

Not taking her eyes from Brightspot, Stiff Tail said, "I have heard that Sretalles has need of seven adults. . . . May you Walk in safety and arrive in maturity." She turned on her heel and vanished, tail lashing, back into her tent.

The crowd closed in around the party, to wish them well on their journey and to offer an overabundance of advice. Afraid he might miss something important, Kirk switched on his tricorder.

Through the forest of ears, he caught a brief glimpse of Rushlight at the entrance to Stiff Tail's tent. When Stiff Tail did not respond to his politely thrust tail, Rushlight called out his name. A reluctant growl from within at last granted him permission and he entered.

"Sretalles, Captain," said Wilson, cutting deftly through the jostling elbows of natives to join him. "Do you suppose that's serendipity or setup?"

Jinx heard the question and pushed to his other side. "She gave us a close one," she said. "She thinks Brightspot's too young to Walk, but she can't stop her from going. So she did the best she could to help."

"That's the best answer we're going to get to your question, Dr. Wilson," Kirk said. "Let's see if we can get this expedition organized, shall we?"

Jinx said, "You'll need weapons. I'll get the wood." She flicked her ears back abruptly. "You don't have knives!" she said. "Or usefuls!" Before Kirk could respond, Jinx snatched at Distant Smoke and repeated this.

His ears too flicked back and he, in turn, grabbed two others. Kirk could see the word spread through the crowd. Moments later, the rest rushed to and fro, gathering items from their tents and piling them onto an outstretched useful Distant Smoke provided.

Leaving Jinx in charge, Distant Smoke vanished briefly himself—to return almost immediately with Rushlight and Stiff Tail in tow. Stiff Tail had lost none of her anger, but she appeared to have regained her control. She called the crowd to quiet. "We must come to a decision," she said. Distant Smoke undercut her by dropping his burden noisily into the pile.

She showed him her teeth but went on. "Some of the members of this traveling party are unfamiliar with our world and our customs," she said. "This leaves them at a disadvantage we would do well to redress. I ask that they be permitted to retain some few technological items on their Walk."

"What items?" demanded a voice from the crowd.

"First," said Stiff Tail, "because they have no protective fur, I ask that they be allowed to retain their clothing and their boots."

"Seems fair," said the same voice, "if only because they'd frighten the children in Sretalles with their lack of fur." Tails looped on all sides.

"Agreed?" asked Stiff Tail. There was no dissent so she continued, "Secondly, I ask that they be allowed to retain their translation devices. One cannot cooperate without communication."

Kirk tensed. Stiff Tail was right: without the universal translators, the trip would be impossible.

There was discussion of this, and Jim Kirk sweated out the decision. At last Rushlight put in, "A bard is nothing without a song to sing. Let them have their bard and her words."

"Agreed?" asked Stiff Tail, snatching at the opportunity Rushlight provided. Again there was no dissent.

"Third," she said, and a ripple of disapproval went through the crowd. Two items, they might agree to, given the extraordinary circumstances, but a third . . . Kirk knew she was asking too much. He doubted they'd allow phasers under any circumstances. This was, after all, a test of their ability to survive without such supports.

"Third," she repeated, "I ask that they be allowed to retain the devices that permit them to contact the others of their kind."

"On what grounds?" demanded Winding Path; his tail whipped twice.

Kirk, who had kept contact with the *Enterprise* as discreet as possible, started. *That* he did not like at all. If it was cheating to carry communicators on the Walk, it was cheating in the line of duty. He had no wish to be cut off from the *Enterprise* for any extended length of time.

"On the grounds that their families may worry about their safety," Stiff Tail said.

Winding Path scoffed. "And you won't worry about Bright-spot, Stiff Tail? Every mother worries about her child's Walk—often for years before they take it. If the traveling party is in constant communication with their families, it might be tempted to rely on the advice of others. That is no Walk, Stiff Tail. I say no to this request."

Rushlight said, "Will you make no allowance for their unfamiliarity with our world, Winding Path?"

"They are familiar enough to wish to attempt the Walk. I have made sufficient allowances already." The two stood nose-to-nose, tails twitching.

"Enough," said Stiff Tail. Almost reluctantly, she asked, "What is the decision?" This time, Kirk could see, it was against them; that gave him grave second thoughts about the project. Stiff Tail said to him, "You will not be allowed your communication devices."

Evan Wilson said, "And my medical sensors, Stiff Tail? We have no way of knowing what foods are safe without them. Would you have us poisoned?"

Ears flicked back around the circle. "I had not thought of that," Stiff Tail said. She glanced around her as if expecting dissent, but Rushlight glared Winding Path silent.

"Medical supplies are okay," someone else pointed out and, to Kirk's relief, the rest agreed the sensors fit this category.

"But," said Winding Path, "we have had enough exceptions for one Walk."

Even someone as stubborn as Stiff Tail knows when to give in, thought Kirk. "Yes," she said, "we have had enough exceptions for one Walk. Who will carry our decision to Sretalles?"

I guess they like to tell the next camp to expect the kids, Kirk thought, as Distant Smoke volunteered and was accepted.

That way, someone will look for the injured survivors if they don't arrive within a reasonable amount of time. Injured survivors, he thought again and knew he needed a word with Spock in private. The loss of the communicators was a serious complication.

As the crowd began to thin, Stiff Tail fixed him with a stare and said sharply, "Captain Kirk, your people have no knives, no usefuls. As unprepared as you are, I cannot deny you the Walk. Do you wish to reconsider? Any one of you may." She avoided Brightspot's eyes.

"We have no other way of learning the information we need, Stiff Tail," he said carefully and, when she did not contradict him, "I must make the Walk. I leave the others to their own decision." He hoped that the loss of the communicators would deter some of them, but he should have known better. One by one, again, they agreed to the journey; and by the custom, he could not order them to stay behind.

Stiff Tail looked over the landing crew. "You are as stubborn as my own child," she said. "So—my people wish to lend you these things. You will need them." To each in turn, she and Rushlight gave a beautifully designed knife and a half dozen usefuls.

When she came to Wilson, she paused and said, "I have lost four of my children before they came of age. They Walked too soon or too often. Don't be angry with me, Brightspot. I do not mean to imply that you are unprepared, nor do I blame Evan Wilson for your decision: only you could have made it. I only mean to say . . ." She proffered knife, hilt first, and a neatly folded bundle of shimmering usefuls. "These belonged to one who took the other trail to adulthood. I wish to make you a gift of them. May they serve her memory and her blood and the friend of her blood well."

To Kirk's surprise, Evan Wilson made no move to accept. "The gift of a knife?" she asked. And when Stiff Tail nodded, she went on, "I'm honored by your offer, Stiff Tail, but I cannot accept without a pledge that is, to me, as binding as any you might make in Old Tongue."

"What pledge? I will observe your custom if it is possible for me to do so."

"You must take the knife and make a small cut in your skin and in mine. . . ." As solemnly as any child, Evan Wilson proposed blood-sisterhood to Stiff Tail. Stiff Tail listened carefully and, when Evan was done, she nodded, laid aside the usefuls and made a knick in the heel of her thumb. Wilson offered her outstretched hand. Stiff Tail hesitated. "Please," said Wilson. "You must." Stiff Tail steeled herself and made the cut.

As the blood welled bright against Evan's pale skin, Stiff Tail jumped back, but Evan caught her hand and pressed their palms together, knife blade flat between their two hands. "This knife knows we are of one blood," she said. "This knife knows the taste of that blood. This knife protects that blood wherever it pulses. May Elath hear and strengthen us down the years and across the seas." She suddenly clasped and released Stiff Tail's hand. "It's done," she said. "Now I may accept your gift."

Matching Evan's dignity, Stiff Tail again extended the knife; this time Evan took it. Evan turned to Brightspot and said, "Daughter of my sister, would you help me find the proper wood for my weapon? I prefer a quarterstaff to a spear any day."

Brightspot swelled with pride at the new status conferred on her. "Quarterstaff?" she said. "I don't know what that is, sister of my mother."

"I'll show you—I'm sure it's legal. It's only a spear without a point."

Kirk, who continued to watch Stiff Tail, saw what Evan had done: she had promised to bring Brightspot through, safe and sound. *We all do,* he thought, *but she found a way to say so without being asked. Stiff Tail knows we're adults and she can't admit it publicly.*

Rushlight broke the silence. "Lieutenant Uhura," he said, "I would also like to make a gift. Does your culture require the same ritual?"

"No, it doesn't," said Uhura. "My culture gives and accepts gifts freely; and those between friends, with deep feeling."

"Then you will accept this with my deep feeling," he said,

pressing a similar bundle into her hands. "I have no child to give it to and it would give me great pleasure to think of you as my child who leaps from world to world."

Uhura took the knife and usefuls in one hand; with the other, she slipped her earrings from her ears. These she held out to him. "Because you like them so. We say"—she smiled brilliantly—"I suppose because our memories are *not* as good as yours—'I would like you to have something to remember me by.'" She took his hand and closed his fingers gently over the two gold rings. "I shall never forget you, Rushlight."

He looped his tail almost mischievously. "I'll see that you don't. You'll sing my songs yet, Lieutenant Uhura. Come, we still have much to discuss." He led her away.

Jinx said, "Spears."

Kirk nodded and said, "Spears. You and Mr. Chekov will see to that. Mr. Spock, I'd like a word with you in private."

The groups went their separate ways. Kirk waited until the others were well out of earshot, then turned off his universal translator as well. "Spock, I don't like traveling without the communicators. Any suggestions, short of canceling the whole trip?"

"One."

Spock was being exasperatingly literal again. Kirk said, "Then what is it, Mr. Spock?"

"With your permission, Captain, I shall modify one of Dr. Wilson's medical sensors. As they are tied to the ship's computers, Mr. Scott would be able to monitor our position on the surface of the planet."

"But we wouldn't be able to speak to Scotty—"

"It should be possible to devise a code to cover most circumstances, Captain, but Mr. Scott would be unable to reply."

"I'll take what I can get, Spock. See to it. And if Wilson gives you any trouble about it, tell her it's her sensor or no trip. No, cancel that: I'll tell her myself."

Kirk and Spock did not find Wilson for almost an hour, when she and Brightspot emerged from the forest. Kirk readied himself for battle. "Better the weapon you know," she said, by way of greeting, and brandished a length of stout wood. "Captain, you look positively grim." She pointed Brightspot toward Jinx and Chekov and nudged. "I'll be along in a minute, Brightspot."

Wilson held up a slim finger. "One minute, Captain," she said, turning off her translator, "before I forget—Mr. Spock, I'm not sure of the ethics of this, but I'd personally feel better if Scotty could find our remains." She opened her medical kit and handed him one of the sensors. "You can jury-rig this, can't you, so it'll at least transmit an S.O.S?" She turned to Kirk. "It's up to you, Captain, but medically speaking I'd prefer it, even if Scotty can't talk back."

"But your sensor . . . ?"

"Captain, there are *very* few medical problems that can't be diagnosed by eye, ear, finger and occasionally nose—and none of those are the kind that would be emergencies in the middle of a five-day trip on foot. I didn't give Spock the sensor that tells me the severity of a concussion, or lets me distinguish between a bruised and a broken rib." She gave him a fierce look and added, "I wouldn't."

"Thank you, Dr. Wilson," said Spock. "With your permission, Captain, I shall see to it." Only when Spock was gone did Jim Kirk realize he was not anxious to be left alone with Wilson.

"Captain," she said, "is something wrong?"

"I thought you played by the rules, Evan."

She chuckled. "I do: your rules, since you chose to impose them, not Leonard's, and not Stiff Tail's. Look, I *know* it's a technical violation, but neither of us wants to see anybody dead because of Stiff Tail's stubbornness."

He shook his head. "It's your damn talent for being one step ahead of everybody else."

"Captain?" A small, worried frown spread across her face.

He laughed, mainly at himself. "Spock had thought of it," he explained, "and I was gearing up to fight you for your sensor."

For once he seemed to have surprised her. She rammed the end of her staff into the ground and leaned her cheek against it, still looking up at him. At last, she said, "Sorry to have disappointed you, Captain. I'll try to live up to your expectations in the future."

He laughed aloud.

As they started over to join the others, he found himself saying, "One other thing, Evan. I'd be pleased if you'd call me Jim from time to time, as the occasion suits."

"Seems unmilitary of me," she said. "Suppose I get the wrong occasion? You may have noticed that I don't deal with all this red tape and rank terribly well."

"Professional hazard," he said, thinking of Bones. "What's gross insubordination in Engineering is SOP in the medical ranks. And you did say you liked to call people what they wished to be called."

"I did. That's the problem." She smiled slightly and did not elucidate.

A strange tapping sound distracted them both before he could bring himself to question her. They turned to see Chekov, surrounded by an audience of assorted Sivaoans, banging rocks together. At least, that seemed to be what he was doing. Wilson hurried on ahead for a closer look.

By the time Kirk worked his way through the crowd, Wilson was standing behind Chekov, devoting her full attention to his project. Deftly, and with great determination, Chekov chipped away at the stone in his palm with a second stone. Finally he stopped and made meticulous scratches; and, grinning boyishly, he held up the finished object for Wilson's inspection.

"Mr. Chekov," she said, "you can be in my lifeboat anytime! Why did you add your initials? I'll grant them out of justified pride, but it doesn't seem likely your work would be mistaken for anyone else's on this world. They've obviously never seen the like!"

"Hebit," said Chekov, flushing. "Et home, if I didn't scretch my initials on them, they turned up in collections— once in a museum!"

Wilson laughed delightedly. She tossed the object to Kirk. "Have a look, Captain. There's something you don't often see—a brand-new, freshly chipped neolithic point. What kind is it?" The last was directed at Chekov.

"Ectually," he said, looking somewhat embarrassed, "it's a Chekov point. I could make you some other kind, if you prefer?"

"A Chekov point?"

"Yes, sair. We held a contest to see if we could improve the technology. . . ." He trailed off and concentrated again on his work.

The object Jim Kirk held in his hand was a flint spearhead, something he'd only seen in museums. Jinx took it from him, considered it from all angles with awe and proudly fixed it to the end of her stick. Wilson went on, "No preference, Mr. Chekov. You're the expert, and I'd just as soon take your recommendation." She searched behind her, found another stool and pulled it up. "Show me," she said, "if it won't interfere with your work."

He shook his head and picked through the pile of stones at his feet to find several more suitable ones. When he looked up, he said, "Jinx says they're legal, Keptain. Enything we make with our hends and our knives is ecceptable technology."

"That anthropology teacher of yours ought to be teaching a course at Starfleet Academy. Remind me to put in a recommendation to that effect when we return to the *Enterprise*," said Kirk.

Chekov looked enormously pleased. "Thenk you, sair. I will." He began to chip away at a new stone.

Wilson watched him carefully and copied the procedure with fierce determination. Soon Jinx had also taken up stones, and the air rang with the sound of their industry. But before Kirk could try his hand at stone knapping, a dark hand touched his elbow. "Captain," said Lieutenant Uhura, "Rushlight would like to speak with you. I don't know what it's about, but I—think you should listen."

"Lead on, Lieutenant. Our weapons officer seems to have things well in hand. Carry on, Mr. Chekov." Chekov scarcely nodded.

Kirk followed Uhura to Rushlight's tent, well outside the main encampment. Rushlight greeted Uhura with a curl of his tail. To Kirk, he said, "Lieutenant Uhura tells me you make decisions for your group, Captain Kirk. I'd like to offer you some further assistance. I too leave for Sretalles tomorrow. If you wish, I will carry that equipment you are not permitted with me; that way, your devices will be waiting for you when you arrive."

Kirk had planned to have Scotty beam the extraneous equipment back to the *Enterprise,* but this would be a better solution. If—he didn't like to think of the possibility but he had to be prepared for every contingency—if they did not reach Sretalles, Scotty would have a fix on the location of the camp in order to beam down a search party. As friendly as Rushlight seemed, Kirk was not about to entrust him with phasers. He compromised: the phasers would go back to the *Enterprise;* the rest would travel to Sretalles with Rushlight.

"We'd be grateful for the helping hand, Rushlight," he said, "and I know the Lieutenant would be glad to see you again." Uhura smiled and nodded.

"That was my reason as well," said Rushlight. "There is one other thing, Captain. If you will teach me the use of your communicator, I will report your progress to your companions on your starship. We would do no less for the relatives of our own children on a Walk."

"You keep watch on children during their Walk?" said Kirk. Neither Brightspot nor Jinx had mentioned that— perhaps they didn't know!

"I did not say that, Captain." Rushlight's tail curled around Uhura. "I would not give such information to children on the eve of their departure."

"Of course," said Kirk, "I understand." So they watched, he thought, but he doubted they'd intervene. Jinx had Walked the last two days alone after the rest of her party had been wiped out by the flash flood. The watch seemed purely for the benefit of the relatives back home.

"Any help will be cheerfully accepted," Kirk said. He flipped open his communicator to show Rushlight how it worked. Minutes later, he was introducing the bard to his chief engineer. Scotty made an immediate hit; as he and Uhura left Rushlight's tent, Kirk could hear Rushlight speaking quietly to himself in a rhythm and intonation that was unmistakably Scotty's. Something of that brogue had made it through the universal translator, Kirk knew. "I have a feeling, Lieutenant," he said with a smile, "that your friend is going to call Scotty just to hear him talk."

"Yes," she said, smiling back, "you heard too, Captain?"

"How could I not? Before you know it, you'll be singing a song that will make you sound exactly like Scotty. And I thought the import limit on that accent was one to a ship!"

By the time they all sat down to the last meal of the evening, once more at Stiff Tail's invitation, the party was thoroughly equipped. Evan Wilson ceremoniously traded Spock a spear in return for her sensor. "Your weapon, sir," she said and was clearly delighted at his reaction to the point. Chekov looked at his feet as she explained the origin of the innovation over burnt and sharpened sticks.

While Spock examined the blade, Wilson turned to Kirk. "Don't worry, Captain," she said. "Everybody's spear is equipped with the top-of-the-line Chekov point." She grinned. "Mine don't come out nearly as sharp." She pulled a sample from her medical kit to show him. "That takes a lot of practice and not a little talent. Believe it or not, Mr. Spock, Mr. Chekov can chip out one of those in fifteen minutes flat."

Spock examined hers as well. She said, "I ruined three before I got the hang of it. Jinx and Brightspot caught on a lot faster, and theirs are almost as good as Chekov's."

"Fascinating, Mr. Chekov," said Spock. "I should like to observe the process at some future time."

"Wait a day or two, sair," Chekov said. "I'll be heppy to show you when the cremp is out of my fingers. I em out of prectice, I suppose."

"Out of practice," said Wilson with mock disgust. "I can't stand it, Captain. Tell him to stop bragging."

"You heard the lady, Mr. Chekov."

"Aye, sair," said Chekov, happily embarrassed by it all.

Brightspot confided to Jinx, in a tone just loud enough to be overheard by everyone around the fire, "Captain Kirk just pulled Mr. Chekov's tail." Jinx looked startled and Brightspot immediately added, "Don't worry he does that to people he *likes!*"

217

"Pull the captain's tail a little, Brightspot," Wilson suggested. "Ask him if he plans to sleep in a tree with us."

Kirk said, "A tree? *Me?*" He overplayed his reaction considerably, and Brightspot, charmed, looped her tail into a tight spiral. "No, Brightspot," he said, "you'll have to teach me how to throw together a ground tent. I don't mind a tree with a lot of branches, but these . . ." He gestured vaguely into the forest and finished, "I never was much at climbing the greased pole at the county fair." And that required enough explanation to keep him talking through dinner.

After dinner, it was Brightspot and Jinx who did the talking and the demonstrating. Wilson, who had already had the course (both on the ground and in the air, Kirk learned), settled down to finish her quarterstaff to her liking. Within the hour, the rest of them had learned to put up and strike a tent using two usefuls, a handful of broad, sashlike ties and any convenient tree. Satisfied they would have no trouble with shelter, Kirk stood and scanned the area where he had last seen his acting chief medical officer.

He spotted her at last, dancing beside Distant Smoke's cooking fire, alone. Then he caught the flash of a blade and realized she was not dancing but dueling an imaginary opponent. He watched, fascinated. Although he was no judge of knife-to-knife combat, it seemed to him that she was quite good. She was most certainly a pleasure to watch.

And, he noted with amusement, *it's nice to know that some . . . esthetic pleasures are not entirely wasted on Spock.* The Vulcan, arms folded, seemed totally absorbed by Wilson's graceful demonstration.

"Now I understand her need for ritual," said a voice beside him. It was Stiff Tail. "It should have occurred to me that a species like your own, so lacking in claws and teeth, would have learned to fight with imitation claws."

"Dr. Wilson is an exception, Stiff Tail," Kirk felt compelled to say. "We're peaceful beings under normal circumstances. That's not a common skill where I come from."

"Nor on Telamon, Captain," Spock said, so pointedly that Kirk could only laugh and repeat his earlier conclusion.

"Pure contrariness, Mr. Spock."

Wilson had replaced the knife in her belt. Now she took up the quarterstaff and set about familiarizing herself with its weight and surface. Once again, without warning, she faced an invisible enemy. She thrust, withdrew—feinted, then thrust from a different angle—

The welter of powerful movements took only a few seconds to complete. Kirk could almost see her opponent go down beneath the onslaught. Triumphant, she rested on her staff, smiling to herself.

She stiffened her back, grimaced; only then did Kirk recall the wounds Fetchstorm had given her. Stiff Tail started toward her; Kirk and Spock followed.

"What is that designed for?" Stiff Tail asked.

Wilson raised the staff but caught herself instantly. "Sorry, Stiff Tail; I live a rich fantasy life. This is for bashing things I wouldn't touch with a ten-foot pole." She had to explain the reference.

Although Spock was as interested as Stiff Tail in the weapon, Kirk had to cut the conversation short. There was one last detail to clear up before they began their Walk, and then he wanted his crew to have the best possible night's sleep in preparation. They left Stiff Tail and the three of them walked toward the shelter.

"I am intrigued," Spock began, as if he were making conversation—a human habit Spock had never acquired— "by your skill at knife combat, Dr. Wilson. Is that a custom on Telamon?"

She gave him a shocked look. "Mr. Spock, someone's been telling you *tales* about Telamon! Elath, no! That's hardly the sort of thing you'd pick up on Telamon. How to make a public prayer and look down your nose at the fellow who doesn't, perhaps. The knife fighting I learned from a trader on Tangle."

Kirk gestured her through the door to the shelter first. It was more than courtesy. "Enough, Spock," he admonished with a frown. From Spock's expression, that was not the end of it, but Spock said nothing more on the subject as they entered.

Kirk flipped open his communicator and hailed the *Enter-*

prise to outline their plans. Scott said, "Ye can't mean it, sir. W'out phasers or communicators!"

"We haven't any choice, Scotty. It's the only way to find out what we need to know. Spock wants to check you out on a simple distress code—but you're not to beam us up unless we specifically request it. I won't have you jumping the gun and pulling us out before we've had a chance to finish the Walk."

"Aye, Captain," he replied grudgingly.

Spock confirmed to his satisfaction that his one-way communication device did work, then instructed them all on the code.

With further reluctance, Scotty beamed up the phasers.

"Captain?" Wilson held out her hand, "Could I speak to him for a moment before you sign off?" He passed the communicator to her. "Hey, laddie," she said.

It was hardly the proper form of address for the acting captain or the chief engineer of the *Enterprise,* but one would never have known it from his cheerfully returned, "Hey, lassie. Wha' can I do for ye?"

"First, you'll spare me the bottle of Jubalan rum you've got stashed away for emergencies. I declare an emergency—and I'll replace it with something a little better when I get back."

"It w'd have to be an emergency." Scotty sounded shocked. "That stuff's nae fit for drinkin'. W'dna ye rather I sent ye somethin' w' a wee more style?"

"Only if it comes in a plastic bottle. I don't know what drugs they'll let me carry, but I'm sure I can get away with alcohol. This is for medicinal purposes, Scotty. Whatever its taste, you'll have to agree Jubalan rum will kill just about anything."

"Aye, that it will. You wait just a minute while I send someone down t' my quarters." The communicator was silent, presumably as Scotty turned away to deliver instructions, then Scotty said, "It'll be w' ye in a moment. What else can I do for ye?"

"Well, I hesitate to ask. It's a bending."

"Try us ennaway, lass. It's not as if we have a lot t'

do—seein' how far we can bend a regulation might keep us out o' trouble. Besides, I'm sure the captain'll have a word t' say if it's nae all right."

"I'm sure the captain will," said Kirk, making sure Scotty heard him. "Go ahead, Dr. Wilson."

"If you'd have somebody have a look at *Jamie* for me, I'd appreciate it. She's got a flux in the Bodner lines that I can't pin down. It's been driving me crazy, and I could use a second opinion."

"Jamie?" said Kirk.

Spock said, "I believe the reference is to the doctor's skiff, the *Dr. James Barry*, in which Mr. Scott has shown considerable interest." Wilson smiled up at Kirk and, for confirmation, made grabby motions with her free hand.

"Captain?" Scott said, and Kirk could hear eagerness in the question. It might keep him out of trouble at that, and it would certainly keep his morale up. "Be my guest, Mr. Scott," he replied.

Scotty's voice sounded more cheerful again. "I'd be delighted to, lass."

"Elath bless you, lad," said Wilson, grinning, "that's all. Drink me a toast tonight, and I'll talk to you sooner than you think." She started to return the communicator to Kirk, but Scotty's voice said, "Ye canna get away sae easy, Evan. I'll have a promise ye'll take good care."

"By Elath, I promise." In mild protest, she added, "I'm looking for answers, not trouble."

"Then I canna understan' why it finds ye so often. . . ."

Wilson laughed. "Neither can I, Scotty. Here's the captain."

Kirk said, "There's one last thing, Mr. Scott: about Rushlight, the Sivaoan who'll be keeping in contact with you. You may find he calls in just to hear you speak." The communicator made a puzzled noise and Kirk explained, "He likes your brogue. Humor him, will you? He's a bard, and that gives him a lot of status here."

"That gi'es him a lot o' status where I come from too. Dinna ye worry, I'll nae disappoint a bard."

"Thanks, Scotty. Look after the ship for me, will you?"

"Aye, an' ye take care, now. I still dinna like this."

"We'll speak to you soon, Mr. Scott. That's a promise. Kirk out."

"En'rgizing now," said Scott—and in place of their phasers, two bottles of liquor twinkled in. Wilson gave a delighted laugh as Scott said, "T' yer health, sir. Scott out."

"Ah, laddie," said Evan, almost to herself, as she picked up the two bottles, "I think I'll be a Scot in my next incarnation. You're a lovely people." She held out the glass bottle to Kirk and said, "He gave us his best, captain."

"Scotty always does, Doctor." Jim Kirk could see she took that the way he meant it. "I believe this calls for a ceremonial drink. Why don't you round up the rest of the party, Evan, assuming that won't harm a Sivaoan?"

She shook her head. "It won't harm them, but they don't appreciate it. The smell of alcohol to them is like skunk to a human. Even the Eeiauoans used it only for chemistry; you should have heard Leonard grouse. I'll go round up a couple of people who will appreciate Scotty's thoughtfulness, though."

Spock clasped his hands behind his back, his face thoughtful. "There is one other discrepancy, Captain," he began when Wilson was out of earshot. "Upon her arrival to the *Enterprise*, she docked her skiff in the shuttle bay without need of assistance."

"Scotty didn't have to use the tractor beams to bring her in? That's good piloting."

Spock nodded and finished, "—And yet she professed to know nothing of pulsars."

Evan's question to Sulu, Kirk thought, *Just her way of taking some of the presssure off Uhura. She beat me to my diversion. And speaking of diversions . . .!* "Mr. Spock," he said, "if you must be suspicious, I suggest you be suspicious of that convenient flux in the Bodner lines."

That startled Spock. "Captain? Am I to understand that you believe Dr. Wilson to have lied about the condition of her vessel?"

"Lied? Lord, no! Scotty'd spot a lie like that in a minute, the way he knows engines. No." Jim Kirk grinned. "But I wouldn't put it past her to have *arranged* a flux in the Bodner lines. If I know Scotty, he'll give Evan's skiff a complete overhaul while he's waiting to hear from us. That's a lot less time he'll spend worrying—and the doctor couldn't have ordered a better tranquilizer for the acting captain!"

Chapter Thirteen

The dawn sky had an ominous overcast as the party assembled for departure. Spears aslant, bright packs tied to their backs, equally bright improvised sashes to hold their knives in easy reach, they looked like a handful of children hard at make-believe, Kirk thought. *We,* he corrected; his own sash and spear made him feel like a pirate chieftain. Dignity seemed impossible under the circumstances but, striving for a certain gravity, he called them to order. Brightspot and Jinx snapped to attention with the rest. *They're following our "customs,"* he thought. *That may simplify things.* "At ease, people," he said aloud. "Brightspot, Jinx, since you know the way to Sretalles, suppose you begin by giving us directions."

Brightspot said, "Mr. Chekov has a—what did you call it?"

"A mep," said Chekov.

"Mep," she repeated dutifully.

"What's this, Mr. Chekov? I thought these people didn't use maps?"

. Chekov pulled another brightly colored swatch of cloth from his sash. "They don't ordinarily, sair. I think Distant Smoke inwented the idea for us. And I don't know how accurate it will be."

He unrolled the fabric. It looked more like a work of art than a conventional map, but Kirk could recognize stylized rivers and lakes and well-traveled trails. Here and there were tiny, delicate drawings of plants and what seemed to be water droplets. Chekov indicated one of these last, explaining, "Thet means we will smell water in the air—"

"At least, Jinx and Brightspot will," Kirk said ruefully.

Chekov nodded, went on, "And he traced us two routes, Keptain. This one is easy but, he says, tekes twelve days. . . ."

"And the other?"

"Five, sair, but he warns us it is more dengerous." They all considered the map as Chekov traced first one, then the other.

"Time is what we have the least of, Mr. Chekov," said Kirk.

Jinx and Brightspot stared at the map, still trying to grasp its basic concept. At last, Jinx touched the fabric with a single extended claw. "Sretalles!" she said in sudden comprehension. She retraced the route Chekov had shown them. "I understand!"

"Do you know this route, Jinx?"

She nodded and the fur at the back of her neck rose.

"What would you advise?" he asked.

She fixed her copper-colored eyes on him. "Both ways have killed. . . ." She could not complete the phrase. After a long moment, she said, "Time kills those who wait for your people, does it not? I choose the short route. I . . . know it well. Perhaps my misfortune will be of some advantage."

"Are we agreed?" The rest nodded, and Kirk continued, "Is there a ceremony for leave-taking, Jinx?" No one had come out to see them off. But for a few wisps of smoke above the tents, the camp would have seemed deserted.

"We go. Nothing more."

"No good-byes?" said Kirk, surprised.

Jinx said, "They hope only for hellos in Sretalles."

"So do I, Jinx," said Kirk fervently, "So do I. Well, let's see how far we can get before we have to contend with the rain as well, shall we? Jinx, since you know the territory, you and I will take point. Spock, Brightspot: bring up the rear. And keep your eyes peeled, people." (Uhura interjected, "He means listen with both ears, Jinx.") "Now let's get this show on the road."

The party moved warily into the forest. High above their

heads, the welcome-homes set up a racket, and Jim Kirk smiled briefly. At least they gave a cheerful sort of send-off, he thought and felt a little better.

Leonard McCoy felt like hell. As he rose from the computer console, every muscle in his body screamed a protest. *Must try upping the dosage of Wilson-Chapel serum,* he thought, *see if that does any good.*

Pessimistically, he assumed that it wouldn't. All the serum did was slow the progress of ADF. It did not halt it. Nor did it work in every case: two more humanoids had died. As Micky had been quick to point out, this was always a possibility—and both had been in what, for humans and humanoids, was the terminal stage of ADF syndrome. Christine Chapel was still holding her own, which was no small comfort to McCoy.

And to add to his relief, the morning brought no new cases among the volunteers at high risk; as of today, the preventive regime still seemed to be working. Tomorrow might be different, but he held on to the hope from day to day.

What disturbed him now were two reports from Starfleet Medical Command of humans who had died within five days of contracting ADF. Both victims had the same HLA factors. It was an indication that some people had a genetic predisposition to react more quickly and more violently to the disease. Micky had immediately checked the medical records of everyone on her staff. Luckily, no one had the risky HLA factor. McCoy passed the word to Starfleet to do the same with anyone working in close proximity with victims of the disease. They were to be isolated from the wards and given high dosages of Wilson-Chapel serum. Those in the general population who had the same factor would also be given the preventive treatment; he hoped it would give them time.

McCoy found himself mentally running through the medical records of the *Enterprise* personnel: Jim, Scotty, Uhura, Sulu, all of them were safe. He had no way of knowing about Spock: that human-Vulcan mishmash of his was always a problem, medically speaking. As for Wilson, he didn't know offhand; he'd have to check her—

Chekov! That was what he had been trying to pin down. Pavel Chekov was in the high-risk category! McCoy slammed his hand angrily against the console. There was no way to warn the *Enterprise* about the wildfire version of ADF. He didn't even know if any of the crew had contracted the disease. He was suddenly furious with Jim for having taken off like that, where he couldn't keep at least half an eye on his friends.

He caught himself. Maybe Chekov is safer there, he reminded himself, wherever they are.

The adrenalin shot of anger momentarily pushed the pain from his muscles. Perhaps, he thought, if people with a certain HLA factor are a higher risk than the rest of the population, then some other HLA factor might offer some protection. If he sorted the victims by HLA factor and by severity of disease he might find a new angle of attack. He sat down and once more threw himself into the work.

Jim Kirk pushed through a tangle of thick vines and found himself wishing for a machete. The party had been climbing slowly but steadily for the past two hours and the undergrowth was thick enough to make every step an effort. At least the rain seemed to have bypassed them. That was one small point in their favor.

Against them, however, was their ignorance of the local flora and fauna. It made the members of the *Enterprise* crew twice as tense and twice as wary as the Sivaoans. They started at sounds that Brightspot and Jinx took as a matter of course. That level of tension, Kirk knew, could not be sustained for long periods of time without exhausting them on a physical and mental level. He found himself watching Jinx and taking his cue from her reactions.

With the shaft of his spear, he pried aside a tangle of vines to let Uhura and Chekov through. Surprised at Uhura's endurance, he remembered with effort that she had gone through the same survival training at Starfleet Academy as the rest of them. *It's that she seems so quiet, so gentle,* he thought. *She's not the kind of person you find in a barroom brawl on shore leave.*

Chekov stumbled; Kirk caught his arm and was shocked to find his face so drawn. "Are you all right, Mr. Chekov?"

"Fine, sair," said Chekov, working his way through the

vines, "A little stiff. I em not used to sleeping on the ground, sair."

"It's going to get worse before it gets better," Kirk warned.

"I'll be all right, sair."

"I think we're all in need of a rest, Mr. Chekov. What do you say, Jinx," he called ahead, "find us a good spot to rest and eat?"

"Not far, Captain," she called back. "Good eating ahead. Turn right and follow the smell of grabfoots."

Spock caught the vines on the shaft of his own spear. "I have them, Captain. You may continue. I should not like to rely on a human nose for direction."

"Nor would I, Mr. Spock." Kirk pushed on to remind Jinx of his limitations as Spock saw Wilson and Brightspot through the obstruction. Behind him, Wilson said with a chuckle, "Save your strength, Mr. Spock; Brightspot and I are small enough to wiggle through spaces like this. We won't hesitate to let you know if we need help, but we hardly expect gallantry from a Vulcan."

"Gallantry, Dr. Wilson? Am I to understand that you place an emotional interpretation on my assistance?"

Wilson laughed. "No. I'm merely pointing out that you're acting on a faulty assumption. I only meant to make a joke of it."

"I see," said Spock. "In future, I shall take your size into consideration."

Shortly the party reached a small outcropping of bare rock. Jinx sniffed, pointed into a dense growth of bushes. "Grabfoots," she said, "We'll catch a couple for our evening meal, and there's fruit here for Mr. Spock."

"I think we'll all start with fruit," said Kirk. He had not taken into consideration the fact that the party would be hunting its own food. Rest periods would have to begin while they were still fresh enough to hunt. *No wonder Chekov looks so tired,* he thought. "Stay put, ensign," he said, "I'll see to provisions this time." Chekov only nodded.

The fruit was simple enough. Brightspot climbed a broad-leafed tree and shook a hail of ripe black fist-sized fruits down on them all. Whatever they were, they met with the approval of Wilson's sensor and Kirk found them amazingly good. But then, four hours' walk might make anything taste that good. His hunger satisfied, Kirk said to Jinx, "Now we'll see about that evening meal. Mr. Spock, you'll stand guard here."

"Mind if I come along, Captain?" It was Wilson. "I'd like to see how it's done." *She seems to be enjoying this,* he thought, looking at her scratched face and her rakish smile. He nodded, and the two of them pushed through the bushes behind Jinx and Brightspot.

Moments later the dense growth gave way and they emerged into gray light overlooking a rocky incline. Brightspot and Jinx started to pick their way down; Kirk followed. The footing was bad, and the spear made his work more difficult. Bushes and trees were few and far between here—little to hang on to—but the loose rock was covered with layers of dead leaves.

Wilson, digging in with her quarterstaff, said, "What are we looking for, Brightspot? I know what grabfoots look like, I saw the ones the hunting party brought in, but where do they live?"

"You really can't smell them?" said Brightspot.

"Really can't," said Wilson.

Brightspot told her, "They live underground, mostly on hillsides like this. We have to be careful because it smells like a big colony of them."

"How do we find them?" Kirk asked. His foot slipped on some mossy plant, and he narrowly avoided falling by catching a nearby shrub.

"We don't," said Jinx. "They mostly find us."

As if the words were some potent magic charm, the dry leaves around them exploded outward. Something small and brightly colored shot toward him; it sank vicious teeth into his boot. Still grasping the bush, Kirk swung to spear the creature. It hissed once and went limp, teeth and claws still locked on his boot.

He scraped the grabfoot from his point just as two more flashed from cover to attack. The first he speared; Wilson slammed aside the second with her staff. Suddenly there were dozens of the vicious little creatures on every side of them.

"Too many!" shouted Jinx. "Climb up!"

The advice may have been good for a Sivaoan—both Jinx and Brightspot scrambled easily up the hill, slapping away grabfoots with either hand as they climbed—but Kirk had claws neither for traction nor for defense. He reached for a spur of rock to pull his way up and sharp teeth sank into his wrist. He let go, swung hand and creature against the outcrop of rock and shattered the grabfoot's head.

Wilson slipped and went down; a dozen of the creatures attacked her. She raised her arm to protect her throat and face and, dropping her staff—it was useless at such close quarters—fought back with her knife in silent fury.

The grabfoots tugged and dragged, pulling her relentlessly down the slope. Kirk saw to his horror that still more awaited them.

Kirk fought through to her, spearing as many as he could on the way. He grabbed at a tree trunk to secure himself— knowing that if he went down too neither of them would get up again—caught her upper arm and yanked her to her feet. She came up with a gasp, staff once again in hand, to slam two more before they reached his ankles.

Suddenly Brightspot and Jinx were beside them. The two—apparently realizing the trouble humans had climbing the incline—had returned. Taking the humans by the arms, they flung grabfoots aside with their tails. Together the four scrambled up the hill.

They had only gone a few yards when Jinx and Brightspot slowed and relaxed. The attack had ceased as unexpectedly as it had begun.

"It's okay, Evan. It's safe now." Brightspot wrapped her tail reassuringly around Wilson's waist.

"Safe!" said Wilson in disbelief.

"They won't come up this far," Jinx explained and, proving beyond doubt that she believed what she said, she sat down to catch her breath. "Grabfoots go down, not up." As if it were an everyday occurrence, she drew her knife and jabbed at the head of a dead grabfoot which still clung to her ankle. It took her only a second—obviously she knew from long experience which muscle to cut—to release the jaw and pry the teeth from her flesh.

Brightspot, who seemed unscathed, drew her own knife and tackled a grabfoot on Wilson's arm.

Wilson said, in a barely audible voice, "They tried to drag me down." She was shaking violently. Kirk realized that he still clasped her arm convulsively but, instead of releasing her, he jabbed his spear into the ground and caught her other shoulder as well. His own hands were none too steady.

"That's how they catch big things to eat. Grab its feet, pull it down where all of them can get at it," said Brightspot. Her tail bristled to twice its original width. "Jinx and I made a terrible mistake, Evan. We didn't think it through for you—and you didn't know the right questions to ask. You climb trees so well, it never occurred to me you'd have trouble with hills."

Jinx cut away the first of three dead grabfoots that clung to Kirk and added darkly, "We didn't think to tell them to go *up*, either! We're dangerous to you, Captain!"

"No," he said sharply, "listen to me, Jinx, Brightspot. We're none of us badly hurt—"

"Pure luck," said Jinx. Her tail twitched grimly; she stabbed at a second grabfoot.

"Yes," he went on, "but more luck than you think. Your world let us off with a sharp warning. If we've learned our lesson well enough, *all* of us, we have a better chance now than we had before."

She plainly did not understand. He said, "Think. If we asked you about the grabfoots now, what would you tell us?"

"Everything I could think of to tell!" said Jinx, and Brightspot nodded violent agreement and affirmed, *"Everything!"*

"Good," he said. "Remember that when we ask about something else."

"You're right, Captain." Evan's voice was steady now; she took a deep breath, stopped shuddering. He released her shoulders. "We'll ask better questions next time," she added, then she sat down and glared at the dead grabfoot with its teeth in her calf: "Now show me where to cut this sucker, in case I ever have to do it myself."

By the time they had pried loose the remaining grabfoots,

they'd piled up nearly a dozen—and she and Kirk were both bleeding in as many places. Kirk, wincing, dabbed at the wound on his wrist. "Let it bleed, Captain," said Wilson, "It'll clean the wound. Puncture wounds like that can be a lot of trouble if they infect." She shook a gaudy corpse. "I'm going to enjoy eating *you*, you nasty little sucker," she told it with feeling.

Kirk laughed. "Is that how you always hunt them, Brightspot—using yourselves as bait?"

Brightspot took the remaining grabfoot from Evan, threaded it onto a tent tie with the rest, then she looked at him morosely. "Usually, we hear them coming. We bash them and throw them up." From her gesture, she meant up the hill. "And they don't usually come in such *big* colonies. I've never seen so many in one place."

"Me neither," said Jinx. "I don't know how we're going to get down this hill. . . . They just weren't here the—last time I was."

"First," said Kirk, "we're going up this hill. We're going to sit down and let you tell us *everything* about anything else dangerous in this forest. Then we'll worry about how to get past the grabfoots."

Brightspot draped the string of grabfoots across her shoulders and rose. Jinx rose with her, and together they waited to assist their clawless friends.

Jim Kirk offered his hand to Wilson; she accepted it, and he drew her to her feet. He had not had time to be surprised at her lightness of weight before; now it came back to him as almost a shock. Something of his surprise must have shown in his face, for she said, "Captain . . . ?"

He had no wish to make an issue of her slightness of frame, so he grinned instead and asked, "You don't mind gallantry from a human?"

She cocked her head to look gravely up at him. "That was a good deal more than gallantry," she said, and he knew that she referred to the moment he had pulled her from the onslaught of grabfoots. "Thank you, Captain."

"You're welcome, Doctor," he said.

Then she turned to Jinx and Brightspot. "Thank you," she said again, with the same deliberateness.

Ears flicked back. "For what?" said Brightspot.

"For coming back for us. If you hadn't, we might never have made it out of there alive."

From their expressive ears, it was clear neither of the two had thought of it that way—they'd been too intent on blaming themselves for endangering the humans in the first place. Kirk leapt to the opportunity to reinforce the message. "Give us a hand the rest of the way, will you? If we're going to be shaky, we might as well all be shaky together."

The two Sivaoans gave eager assistance all the way back to the rest of the party, where an outburst of shocked exclamations greeted their return.

Kirk sat down to explain in detail what had happened, while Wilson doused their respective wounds with Jubalan rum. As she recapped the bottle, Spock said, "I beg your pardon, Dr. Wilson, but you have done nothing to clean those wounds suffered by Jinx and Brightspot." Brightspot glanced up from licking her heel and, tongue still protruding between her teeth, curled her lips back.

Wilson laughed. "They've done it themselves, Mr. Spock. If I am to believe Catchclaw—and I do—their saliva contains a better antiseptic than Jubalan rum. Anything I could do would be superfluous—and would make their fur taste awful."

"I see. My apologies."

"None necessary, Mr. Spock. I'd rather be reminded unnecessarily than risk forgetting something important because I wasn't."

Spock gave her another of his extremely close looks. It occurred to Jim Kirk that Wilson's ego was not as fragile as Spock assumed, or at least not fragile in the accustomed places. Under this scrutiny, Wilson reddened. Spock, to Kirk's amazement, turned away. "Captain?" he said. "Are you sufficiently recovered to continue?"

Kirk shook his head. "First," he said, "we're going to sit here and listen while Brightspot and Jinx tell us—in great detail—about any other hazards we may expect to meet."

Montgomery Scott stepped into the engine compartment of the *Dr. James Barry* and stopped so abruptly that Ensign

Orsay nearly ran him down. Her startled "Sir—?" brought her back to Scotty's awareness. The thing to be said for Marie-Therese Orsay, Scotty knew from experience, was that she loved a good ship as much as he did. Delighted to have someone to share the sight with, he stepped aside.

She did not disappoint him: her mouth formed a small *o* and, after a long moment, she said, "Now that's what I call beautiful!"

"Aye," said Scotty, "that she is. *Jamie*, I'm happy to have ye for a landsman! Dinna ye worry, lass, we'll find out wha' ails ye." He touched the machined surface of the engine casings with a reverent hand, then turned to examine the dials and sensors.

Watching over his shoulder, Orsay said suddenly, "Am I imagining things, or is this little skiff capable of warp five?"

Scotty turned to her and grinned happily. "Ensign, ye c'ld squeeze warp ten out o' this if ye put y'r mind t' it . . . *and* land her neatly as ye please on a planetary surface."

She grinned back. "Then if you don't mind my saying so, if I had a skiff like this, I'd be tempted to desert Starfleet and turn space pirate . . . *sir*," she added pointedly.

"Aye," he said, as pleased as if she had complimented him personally. "And if ye've a mind t' d' it, ye'll tell Evan Wilson that and gi' her the joy o' hearin' it said o' her *Jamie*."

Leaving Ensign Orsay agape, he turned once more to the engine and said, "We'll have ye in shape in n' time, *Jamie*." He began a series of tests on the Bodner lines, and Orsay recovered enough to call readings to him.

Three-quarters of an hour later, having stopped only once to shake his head with worry for the landing party, he got the flux reading Wilson had complained of. "Aye," he said, almost to himself, "that w'ld make ye tear y'r hair. Let's see what we c'n do for ye, lass."

Brightspot and Jinx, with many interruptions and additions to each other's thoughts, spent some two hours cataloguing what they might expect from the forest. Kirk considered the time well spent—it might save their lives when trouble came, whether in the form of grabfoots or slashbacks.

Now he stood overlooking the incline and presented the

immediate problem. "We seem to have two choices: either we detour around the grabfoots or we find a way through them. Suggestions, Spock—anyone?"

Jinx said, tail drooping, "There are too many of them, even for all of us. It would take two, maybe three, extra days to circle around them. And I don't know that area well—we could find worse things than grabfoots."

"There aren't even enough trees to swing over them," Brightspot said, "and you can't swing very well anyway." She looked apologetic for having mentioned it.

"Dr. Wilson," said Spock, "do the grabfoots find human flesh edible?"

Wilson shuddered. "They seemed to think so—but I take it you mean something else."

"Yes," said Spock. "We have all been in close proximity with Brightspot and Jinx and the others of their species. Perhaps you and the captain were attacked only because of the grabfoots' failure to distinguish between the Sivaoan scent and your own human scent."

"An interesting theory," Kirk said, "but one I can't say I'm anxious to test."

"Your reluctance is quite understandable, Captain," Spock said. "However, I had no intention of proposing such an experiment involving human life."

"I hope you don't intend to try it yourself, Spock. The only thing that would tell us is how edible they find a Vulcan."

"Hardly," said Spock, with some asperity. "I believe there to be a much less dangerous way to examine my theory. By your report, the four of you killed a great many more grabfoots than you carried back with you."

"What of it, Mr. Spock?"

"I see no dead grabfoots remaining in the area of the burrows. I would conclude that they scavenge their own dead as well as those other species on which they prey."

"Then we could test with a grabfoot carcass!" Kirk said. "But that still doesn't tell us how they react to human scent unadulterated with Sivaoan."

"That would be of no use to us unless we could somehow make Jinx and Brightspot 'smell human' as well. However, it is not human scent to which I allude. As Dr. Wilson has mentioned, and as Jinx and Brightspot have confirmed by their reaction, Sivaoans find the scent of alcohol objectionable in the extreme. Perhaps the grabfoots share their aversion."

"You needed it for an antiseptic," Jinx said. "We didn't want to complain—"

"But you *still* smell awful," Brightspot finished. "Maybe the grabfoots would hate it too."

Wilson pulled out the bottle of Jubalan rum and handed it to Spock. "Sparingly, if you please, Mr. Spock. This is only the first day of our journey."

"Understood." Taking the bottle and a grabfoot carcass that Brightspot hastily untied from her booty, Spock proceeded with his experiment. He used only a few drops of Jubalan rum, but Jinx no longer attempted to conceal her distaste. "That's probably enough, Mr. Spock," she said, wrinkling her nose and twitching her tail. "*I* wouldn't eat it now."

"Then let us hope the grabfoots share your dislike," Spock told her. He started to pick his way down the hill.

"Just a moment," said Kirk firmly. "Jinx and Brightspot and I will accompany you. We will go only far enough to throw the carcass down to the grabfoot colony. Agreed?"

"Captain? I assure you I had no intention of approaching the burrows."

"That hill's slippery, Spock. You're not going without backup."

Jinx and Brightspot bristled briefly but made no opposition to the plan, and the four of them started down the hill. In a short while, Jinx said, "Stop here," and they all did.

Kirk pointed out the area of the grabfoot colony, and Spock threw the gaudy carcass to the point at which they'd first been attacked. Once again, leaves exploded outward. Jinx made a low moan in the back of her throat, and even Kirk could not repress a shudder.

A dozen grabfoots converged on the carcass—and stopped. Several of them hissed and jumped back. They milled around, intermittently hissing; first approaching, then jumping back. It was clear that they liked the smell even less than Brightspot and Jinx did.

At last one of the grabfoots gathered its nerve and attacked the carcass, sinking its sharp teeth deep into the body. Seeing it from this distance, with time to consider it, Kirk was nauseated by the creature.

It let go as suddenly as it had attacked, sat back on its haunches and howled, a chilling sound. Its fellows liked this even less than Kirk and the rest of the party did—they all promptly vanished underground, hastily pulling leaves over their burrows to hide. The remaining grabfoot continued to howl for a moment, then punctuated its distress with two sharp hisses, and it too vanished into its burrow.

"Mr. Spock," said Kirk with relief, "I believe your experiment is a complete success."

"It would seem so."

They rejoined the rest of the party at the top of the hill. Kirk said, "From the results of Mr. Spock's experiment, Doctor, I would say that you and I were already grabfoot-proof—but I should like to be very sure."

She nodded. "Ankles, wrists, throat and around the eyes then, for safety. Brightspot, Jinx, I hope you can stand this because it's got to be done. The captain isn't the only one who wants to be very sure." The two Sivaoans, with much bristling and twitching and wrinkling of noses, managed to hold still through Wilson's ministrations. She saw to Uhura and Chekov, then handed the bottle of rum back to Spock. "You'll have to do your own honors, Mr. Spock."

"I fail to see the 'honors' inherent in such a procedure, Dr. Wilson," said Spock as he followed her instructions.

"So do Brightspot and Jinx, Mr. Spock," Wilson told him, smiling. She looked at Kirk. "Ready as we'll ever be, Captain." The rest of the party nodded assent, and Kirk motioned them forward.

"Stay alert, people," he added. "There may be one or two determined enough to want to taste despite the smell."

They worked their way down the hill, choosing the gentlest of the slopes to follow. The nearer they approached to the burrow area, the more ruffled Jinx and Brightspot became—but the two youngsters stayed carefully with their human companions, now and then offering a hand or tail as the terrain warranted.

The grabfoot carcass still lay where Spock had thrown it. "Good sign," said Kirk. "They certainly haven't overcome their aversion to the smell yet." From a few feet away, Wilson grunted an affirmative response, but Kirk got a glimpse of her face: all the color was gone from her cheeks.

Chekov slipped. Kirk and Brightspot hastily scrambled forward to catch and lift him to his feet. As they did, the grabfoots attacked. *"Bozhe moi,"* said Chekov, not yet steadied. Kirk swung his spear, and Brightspot too struck out at the nearest—but both grabfoots jumped back, hissing angrily. "I guess it works, sair," said Chekov shakily.

The animals hissed and approached again and once again jumped back at the smell. "I guess it does, Mr. Chekov," Kirk said, not taking his wary eyes from the miniature dinosaurs. He called to the others, "Keep moving, people. Let's not give them the time to change their minds."

He and Chekov and Brightspot pushed forward, surrounded by more and more of the creatures as they continued. Still none worked up the nerve to sink its teeth. "Evan said Jubalan rum would kill anything," he said to Chekov and was rewarded by a grim smile.

Brightspot speared one that had gotten too close for her comfort. Uhura closed in toward the party.

"Dr. Wilson." The voice was Spock's, from somewhere behind them; there was a sharpness in it that made Kirk turn. Spock was well above him on the slope—and some twenty yards farther up stood Wilson and Jinx, surrounded by two dozen or more hissing grabfoots. Jinx was urging Wilson forward but the doctor did not move.

"Keep going," Kirk snapped to Uhura, Chekov and Brightspot; then, slapping aside a grabfoot that came within inches of his boot, he started up the incline toward Wilson.

He managed only a few steps when he saw Spock slip and land full length on the ground. The grabfoots instantly converged on him. *"Spock!"* Kirk scrambled upward, his feet slipping wildly on loose stone and other debris, desperate to reach Spock before the grabfoots did.

Wilson gave a sharp exclamation, brought her staff down hard on the head of the closest grabfoot and skidded down the slope toward him, Jinx hard on her heels. Together they batted and speared their way through the grabfoots that surrounded Spock and, while Jinx kept the remainder at bay with her spear, Wilson braced her staff for Spock to rise on.

Kirk neared them just as Spock regained his feet.

The Vulcan, a few feet farther down the slope and hence eye-to-eye with Wilson, said without expression, "Your hesitation, Dr. Wilson, endangered Jinx."

Wilson glanced sharply at the Sivaoan, then back at Spock. In a hoarse voice, she said, "Thank you, Mr. Spock." Immediately, she began to make her way down the hill; Spock and Jinx positioned themselves on either side of her.

Without a word, Kirk fell in with the party. Wilson was still dead-white but, as he held out a hand to help her over a crest of rocks, she said, "Never underestimate small things, Captain, they have to be meaner than large ones to survive."

She meant the grabfoots, he knew, but he said, "Even the fiercest small thing has its limits, Dr. Wilson."

Chapter Fourteen

They made their first night's camp some two ridges short of their intended goal. Although the incident with the grabfoots had delayed them, Kirk felt it best to accept the fact rather than risk traveling in such unfamiliar territory after dark. They saw to the business of fire and shelter, Jinx and Brightspot opting to remain on the ground with their human companions, and then settled down to eat. Roast grabfoot was, as Jinx had promised, a very good evening meal. His announcement that he, at least, would "eat with a vengeance" drew a wan smile, but no comment, from Wilson. She had said scarcely a word since the incident on the slope; her silence disturbed him.

The empty spaces in their dinner conversation were filled with Brightspot's grumblings over the lingering smell of the alcohol. "Unless you want to lick it off, Brightspot," Kirk said—and she shuddered and stuck out her tongue—"you'll have to put up with it until tomorrow. You can wash when we reach the river." That idea was clearly worse but did nothing to halt her complaints; she was still muttering translator-rejected words as she crawled into her tent for the night.

"Wake me for watch," said Wilson curtly and crawled in after her. Uhura sang softly for a while, then she too settled for the night; the others followed until only Spock remained.

"Captain," he said quietly, "with your permission I will stand Dr. Wilson's watch as well as my own this evening."

"She won't thank you for it, Spock."

"That is perhaps true. However, I should prefer it. I am concerned the incident with the grabfoots may have done her some hidden injury, and it has been my observation that an uninterrupted sleep often has a salutary effect on the human spirit."

Kirk smiled. "I've noticed that myself. As you wish, then."

"Thank you, Captain." Spock retired to the second tent, hands clasped behind his head, his spear to one side—well within reach.

Standing in the entrance, Kirk leaned on his own spear and said, "Tell me, Mr. Spock, for curiosity's sake: was it my imagination or did you use a somewhat emotional appeal to get Dr. Wilson moving again?"

Spock propped himself up with one hand. "Emotional appeal? Hardly, Captain. One might better say 'tactical'—while Dr. Wilson was not able to force herself through the grabfoots for her own safety, she would not hesitate to do so to assist another."

"I see: a highly logical approach to the matter."

"So I had intended."

"Sleep well, Mr. Spock," Kirk said and, smiling to himself, left Spock to his rest. He had not really expected to catch Spock out—he knew from long experience that Spock could invariably produce a logical explanation for any seeming emotional outburst on his part. One human trait the Vulcan did not lack was the ability to rationalize his own behavior. He wondered if Spock would find it so easy to rationalize his decision to stand an extra watch for Evan Wilson.

When Spock woke him, the sky was still gray and overcast. A steady drizzle made the camp fire burn fitfully. The usefuls, Kirk was glad to learn, shed water without absorbing a drop; he threw one over his head and shoulders and ventured from the tent. "Just what we needed," he said.

Spock raised a startled eyebrow at him. "Sir?"

"Irony, Mr. Spock," Kirk explained. "I'll wake the others; you see if you and Lieutenant Uhura can find some dry wood to build up that fire. We've a lot of lost time to catch up today and I want us off to a good start." He strolled over to yank the tail that protruded from Brightspot's tent. "Up, up!"

There was a flurry of motion within, and Brightspot faced him, eyes wide and teeth bared. She blinked once and said, "Oh . . . oh, that's right." And, glancing over her shoulder, "It's only the captain, Evan, you can put your knife away." To Kirk, she confided, "Evan wakes up mean!" She seemed to think this an admirable trait.

Under the circumstances, Kirk agreed, adding, "You didn't look terribly sweet yourself. I forget how sharp your teeth are."

Her huge yawn gave him a more than adequate reminder. "You forget a lot," she said, as she stretched herself awake.

"Now you're pulling my tail," he told her.

Evan crawled from the shelter, glanced up at the sky and said, "Oh, hell." She drew her cowl over her hair, then narrowed her eyes at Kirk. "And just who decided I needn't stand watch last night?"

"Spock." Jim Kirk was glad she'd phrased the question as she had: it gave him the opportunity to deny all responsibility in one word. She was fully as angry as he'd expected her to be.

Brightspot said, "I didn't stand watch, either."

"You'll get a chance tonight, Brightspot," Kirk said. "Not everyone was needed."

"But I'm willing to bet Mr. Spock stood a double watch," Evan growled. He wondered how she had known but nodded confirmation. She scowled, glared about the campsite and, zeroing in on the returning Spock, stalked toward him.

Brightspot made a hissing sound. "Evan's really angry," she said. "Is she allowed to cuff Mr. Spock?"

"Technically, no," said Kirk, but from the way Wilson advanced on Spock, he was not sure that would stop her.

Spock knelt, stirring the fire back to flame. Evan Wilson planted herself beside him, hands balled into fists and jammed to her hips. *"Mr. Spock,"* she said; her tone was anything but kind.

Spock finished his task, then he rose to his feet. As if completely unaware of her anger, he said, "Yes, Dr. Wilson?"

Had Spock been anyone else, Kirk would have been moved to intervene on Evan's behalf. Standing, the Vulcan was almost twice her size. The discrepancy in their heights, which would have led humans his own size to reconsider the wisdom of such a confrontation, made no impression on Wilson. It meant only that she glared *up* at him. "Mr. Spock," she said, "why the hell didn't you wake me to stand watch?"

"It was unnecessary, Doctor."

"I suppose it was necessary for you to stand a double watch?"

"Necessary? No, it was not. Had I felt the need for additional rest I would have awakened Brightspot or Mr. Chekov—not you, Dr. Wilson. You had more need of sleep than the others. I am quite pleased to see you have recovered your spirits." From anyone else that might have been mockery; from Spock it was merely an observation, and Kirk knew from experience just how infuriating Spock's observations could be.

Evan Wilson raised a small fist. Kirk winced in anticipation and started forward to rescue his first officer. Evan Wilson's burst of laughter stopped him in his tracks. "Damn you, *sir!*" she said, to Spock's and his own complete amazement. Her hands dropped to her sides and she threw back her head to laugh again.

"I beg your pardon, Doctor," said Spock.

She made an effort to control her laughter. Finally she gasped out, "It is—impossible to work up a satisfactory anger at someone who so steadfastly refuses to reciprocate. You win, Mr. Spock; I give up. After all these years, I've finally found somebody I can't bully." She shook her head and gave another delighted peal of laughter. "I still owe you a watch, though. Don't you dare forget it."

That was the first thing she'd said that Spock understood. "You are under no obligation for my decision, Dr. Wilson. I fail to understand how my actions place you in my debt. . . ."

The situation had gone far enough, Kirk decided. He said, "Never mind, Mr. Spock, Dr. Wilson, you'll take Mr. Spock's watch tonight. That should satisfy you." Before she could reply, he added, "That's an order."

She gave him her wickedest grin. "Standing Spock's watch or being satisfied, sir?"

"Both," he said, grinning back.

Their second day's journey was—thankfully—uneventful. They camped by a small stream and finished off the grabfoots, rubbed with tail-kinkers from a tree that Brightspot had sniffed out. Spock dined on berries and fruits they had picked along the way.

The drizzle had not abated, but Kirk still considered them lucky. The roiling, muddy stream told him that up country it was raining hard.

From Brightspot's reaction whenever he suggested she wash the alcohol from her fur, he had expected the Sivaoans would avoid rain if it was at all possible, but the drizzle bothered them less than it did the humans. They objected only when they could not avoid a puddle and were forced to get their feet wet. The rest of the time, they scarcely noticed it, fluffing their fur against the slight chill and shaking free the few droplets that clung to them.

This time, the party made a single large canopy over the fire. Kirk pored over Distant Smoke's map with them and made plans for the following day. Uhura sang a few songs before they retired; it had already become a traditional way of ending their day. Despite the acrid smell of smoke, they all slept beside the fire; the warmth was comforting.

Evan Wilson woke him in the morning with a cheerful, "Rain's let up, Captain."

"So it has." He rose and stretched with as much attention as Brightspot or Jinx would have devoted to the process. "I take it you had a quiet watch?"

"Aside from a lot of thunder and lightning upstream, I've got no complaints." She threw some more wood on the fire and poked it into flame.

"Satisfied?" he asked with a smile.

"As the captain ordered," she said, smiling back. She proffered a handful of sharpened green sticks and together the two of them began to skewer fruit for roasting.

Kirk said, "Then satisfy my curiosity . . . what did you

mean when you told Spock you'd found someone you couldn't bully?"

"I'm not sure I want to give away trade secrets, Captain." She paused in her task and gave him a long look. "Well, I suppose there's no harm. It works on an unconscious rather than a conscious level."

The first roasted fruits had begun to spit and sizzle. Kirk turned them over. When he looked up again, Spock stood behind Wilson. He said, "I too would be interested in an explanation for your words, Dr. Wilson."

She craned up at him. "For your edification then, Mr. Spock; it certainly doesn't work on you. You're aware, Captain, of the disadvantages I suffer by being so small in comparison to the average human. What I seldom point out are the psychological advantages I can take when faced with somebody twice my size." She pulled a shishkabob from the fire and handed it to Spock, then she went on, "The first advantage is surprise. People do underestimate me."

"Stiff Tail most certainly did," Spock said. "She did not expect you to retaliate if cuffed."

"That was also because kids don't hit adults back, Mr. Spock, so I'm not sure that counts as a good example. It says more for her culture than mine."

"Indeed. Please continue."

"Please *eat*, Mr. Spock. I won't have it said I delayed our start." Spock obeyed. Wilson handed a second skewer to Kirk and passed one to Brightspot, who had just joined them.

"The second advantage," Wilson said, "is the Machiavellian advantage. I can walk up to a ten-foot-tall Horrovan in any bar in the universe and tell him his father was a Tullian *and walk away unscathed.*"

"That would seem difficult to believe, Dr. Wilson, given the belligerent nature of the Horrovan society and the severity of the insult you describe."

"Nevertheless I could do it, and the Horrovan wouldn't dare lay a hand on me. Instead he would politely correct me, attempt to placate me, and, if that failed, he'd drink up and find another bar." She shook her head, smiling. "You don't get it because it's illogical, Mr. Spock. How about it, Captain?"

Kirk considered the image of Evan Wilson insulting the Horrovan and suddenly recalled his own mixed feelings when she had confronted Spock. He laughed, and she looked pleased. "Yes," she said, "I see you do. Then I'll let you explain it to Mr. Spock, while I roust the rest of these slugabeds."

Spock waited expectantly, and Jim Kirk explained, "Even with all that provocation, our hypothetical Horrovan wouldn't attempt to harm her. If he so much as raised a paw to threaten her, every human and every other Horrovan in the bar would rise to protect her." He laughed again. "And every one of them would begin with the challenge. 'Why don't you pick on somebody *your own size,* buster?'"

"I believe I have seen such an encounter as you describe. Mr. Scott and Dr. McCoy both used just those words—however . . ."

"Something puzzles you, Spock?"

"Yes. Neither Mr. Scott nor Dr. McCoy was an equivalent height or weight to the human they challenged."

"It's the thought that counts. I would assume they were both larger than the person being threatened? Yes—so they were simply reminding the larger antagonist of the cultural strictures against his actions."

"Fascinating," said Spock, "although I fail to understand why Dr. Wilson should wish to, as she puts it, bully me."

That deserves an answer, Kirk thought, sought one and saw Leonard McCoy in his mind's eye. "For the same reason Bones does," he said. "He's always trying to bully you—or at least goad you into an emotional reaction. You must admit you make the temptation almost irresistible."

"As I do not understand your meaning, I can admit nothing of the sort."

"He means if you hang your tail from a tree branch, somebody's going to pull it," contributed Brightspot. "Right?"

"That's not quite how I'd put it, Brightspot, but that's very close to what I mean. Human beings, and Sivaoans too, it seems, have a bad habit of wanting to perturb the unperturbed—or the unperturbable," Kirk said and, with a sidelong glance at the returned Wilson, "in any event, being bullied is the least of your worries, Spock. From what I've seen of her, if bullying won't work on you, she'll stop bullying—"

"Exactly," she said, with a shrug that was deliberately comic. "Why waste time and effort? It would be illogical."

"—And try something else," Kirk finished. "If I were you, I'd worry about her next tactic."

Spock and Brightspot took point for the early part of the day, and Kirk brought up the rear with Evan Wilson. Talk was relegated to meals: the terrain took too much attention and, more importantly, they had to listen with both ears for the warning sounds of any predators. But shortly after he had passed the word forward to Spock to find a spot for a breather, Wilson caught his arm and startled him by saying, in a whisper, "Captain, Chekov isn't ordinarily this clumsy, is he?"

"No, he's not. He says he's stiff from sleeping on the ground."

"That's what he told me, too." She scowled and inched along, devoting her primary attention to avoiding a stand of sweetstripes—or so he thought, until she demanded, "Is he? You know him better than I do. Could that be the cause?"

He had seen Chekov under worse conditions than these but—he thought of Chekov's drawn face—and he shook his head. "Let's hear it, Evan," he said, knowing from the expression on her face that he would not like what he heard.

"He walks like the Eeiauoans, Captain."

Kirk stopped to face her; a sapling he had pushed aside snapped back with a whiplike sound. "ADF? He said he had no contact with any Eeiauoan."

"That he knew," said Wilson. She hugged her quarterstaff. "What do you advise, Evan? Should we turn back?"

She shook her head vehemently. "Catchclaw's in Sretalles, Captain; so are the communicators. Even if I knew for certain Chekov had ADF syndrome, I couldn't do anything for him except quarantine him." She shook her staff suddenly, much in the manner of a Sivaoan twisting her own tail. "I can't even do that—we haven't got a code to cover it. We'd expose anybody who met us in the transporter room."

"Scotty . . ."

"Scotty," she confirmed grimly.

A halloo echoed through the forest; the rest of the party had gone on ahead. Kirk called an answer to reassure Spock, as the two of them, in silence, hurried to catch up.

They found the rest of the party in a mossy glen, sprawled or sitting, each on the softest spot he or she could find. Chekov shifted restlessly, as if unable to make himself comfortable. Next to him, Kirk found a little hillock and sat. "Mr. Chekov," he said, "is your back still giving you trouble?"

"Yes, sair." Chekov looked embarrassed. "I em merely stiff, Keptain. I hev no difficulty with the walking."

"Dr. Wilson, have a look, will you?"

He made the request as innocuous as possible, and Wilson matched his tone with an easy, "Sure thing, Captain."

Chekov made a mild protest, but Wilson gave him a wicked look. "Come on—it's not as if I'm asking you to chop wood!" and, when he stared at her in astonishment, she added, "You're not the only one who can quote old Russians. . . ." At that, Chekov could only laugh and acquiesce to her poking and prodding.

"How long has it been bothering you, Mr. Chekov?"

"I didn't really notice it until the day we left Stiff Tail's kemp, sair. I em not accustomed to sleeping on the ground."

"You and me both," she said, grinning, "I bet an *Enterprise* bunk would play the same havoc with Brightspot's or Jinx's back. Any trouble with your vision at all?"

Kirk saw Spock's head come up sharply at that, but the query only embarrassed Chekov to admit, "Sparkles, sair—I em out of shape. I hev not been exercising regularly."

She clucked her tongue at him, then pushed back his sleeves and ran her hands over his forearms. She made one final check, this time with her sensor; then, rising, she looked at Kirk and waited.

"Straight, Evan," he said, knowing it was the right decision the moment he spoke. "It involves all of us."

Evan Wilson again knelt beside Chekov; it was to him alone that she spoke. "Listen to me very carefully, Pavel. You may, as you say, be stiff from sleeping on the ground, be out of shape. But there's another possibility I have to consider: the possibility that you have ADF syndrome."

Chekov's head jerked sideways. "But, Keptain!" he protested. "I heven't been near eny Eeiauoans. I give you my word, sair!"

"No one's accusing you of anything, Mr. Chekov," Kirk assured him.

Jinx said, "He has the disease you're trying to find the cure for? The one all the Eeiauoans have?"

"I don't know, Jinx," Wilson said. "All I know about the damn disease is what McCoy knew the last time we spoke. I've no way of confirming diagnosis until the symptoms are fully developed, no clear idea of the incubation period necessary, and no way of telling under what circumstances it's contagious. I'm saying it's possible Mr. Chekov has it, and that I can't eliminate or ignore the possibility."

"You'd quarantine him if you could?" Again it was Jinx who spoke.

"If—and remember I mean if Mr. Chekov has it, we're all exposed; I'd quarantine us all."

"If I hev it," said Chekov, distressed at the thought, "I may hev given it to eweryone already."

Wilson snapped, "Don't get uppity, Mr. Chekov. Someone else may have given it to the *Enterprise* crew, including you—if you've got it."

"When will you know, sair . . . if I hev it, I mean?"

"Not for a week or so, if you follow the general pattern. That's about how long it took for Nurse Chapel and other humans to start losing hair. The blurring of vision comes sooner but, like the muscular stiffness, is no sure sign. Now that I've mentioned vision problems, you may even develop them as a psychosomatic reaction."

"Then I could finish the Walk?" Chekov said. "Keptain? You won't send me beck, will you, sair?"

"I can't, Mr. Chekov," said Kirk, "Remember the rules? Either we all make it or none of us does. It would cost us the two days we've already spent, plus an additional two days to return you to camp, and we'd achieve nothing by it. Our communicator is with Rushlight on its way to Sretalles."

Wilson added, "And Catchclaw is also in Sretalles. *If*

you've got ADF, Pavel, *I* can't do anything for you or the rest of us. I'm still hoping Catchclaw can."

"Mr. Spock: suggestions?"

"I see no choice, Captain. We must continue."

Kirk rose and faced the two Sivaoans. "Jinx, Brightspot? What do you say?"

"If Mr. Chekov can make it to Sretalles, we should go on," said Jinx. "If he cannot, we must return to our last camp."

Brightspot twitched the tip of her tail. Her pupils narrowed to slits as she stared at the to-Ennien. "Jinx, are you thinking of third time?"

Jinx bristled and then, almost as quickly, smoothed her fur. "No, I'm not, Brightspot; I swear in Old Tongue. I'm thinking how many people can die in four days." She gestured at the humans. "If Dr. Wilson is correct, we may have been exposed to this AyDeeEff. We must find their answer now; we may also need it."

Brightspot looked contrite. "I apologize, Jinx. That was a pretty stupid thing for me to say."

"If it was being thought, it needed saying," said Jinx. She arched her whiskers forward. "Yes, Captain. We're willing to go on."

Go on they did. They made camp at dusk and found themselves huddled beneath a smoke-filled canopy while sheets of rain swept over, rattling the usefuls and chilling them. Squinting in the firelight, Wilson examined Chekov again; she found no new evidences of ADF. Jinx, having asked and received Chekov's permission, did the same. Little was said; the storm passed up-country, and most of the party dropped off to a disturbed sleep.

Spock shared the dawn watch with Evan Wilson. She was quiet and thoughtful; and Spock, who found the time for meditation restful in itself, said nothing to distract her.

She took a handful of branches that had been drying beside the fire and threw them on. As they caught, Spock momentarily had a glimpse of her expression: it was the same dazed horror he had seen on her face when she had been surrounded by the grabfoots.

"Dr. Wilson," he said softly.

"Yes, Mr. Spock?" There was no hesitation in her response, although he had expected one. She seemed fully aware of her surroundings. That puzzled him, and he reconsidered what he had been about to say. But she so seldom conformed to what he expected that he judged it best to make the offer. "If the incident with the grabfoots continues to disturb you, Dr. Wilson, may I be permitted to offer a solution?"

She frowned at him, clearly not understanding.

He explained, "There is a Vulcan technique that would allow me to excise your memory of the encounter—"

"Do I look that bad, Mr. Spock?" she interrupted. Her smile was grim. "Never mind; I don't think I want that answered. It's not the grabfoots." She drew up her knees and, folding her arms around them, rested her chin. "It's not that," she said again wearily.

He waited. At last, she spoke again. "Suppose we've been wrong. Suppose this world has no cure for ADF?"

"I see no need to speculate on the matter," he said. "If our assumptions concerning the social strictures of the Sivaoans are correct, we shall learn the answer to that when we reach Sretalles."

"That's not what I mean." She rubbed her temple irritably. "I mean that, if Mr. Chekov has ADF, he could not have contracted it on this world—not unless he's unique in his response to the disease. Damn, even if he's unique, I haven't seen any native with anything remotely like ADF that he could have caught it from."

She straightened and looked directly at him. "No, Mr. Spock. If he's got ADF and the natives haven't a cure, then we've infected an entire world with the most deadly disease known to Federation science."

"You do not know that is the case, Dr. Wilson."

"I don't know it isn't," she shot back; there was anger in her manner and voice. Spock had seen similar outbursts from McCoy and assumed the anger was not directed at him but at the universe in general. It was not a logical response but neither was it unusual for human medical personnel. He waited once again. "Sorry," she said with sudden gentleness, "it's not you I'm angry at, it's me. I thought I had screened the *Enterprise* thoroughly enough to eliminate the possibility."

"As the parameters of the disease were unknown at the time," Spock said, "I fail to see your purpose in assuming the responsibility. As you yourself pointed out to Mr. Chekov, such an attitude would be 'uppity.'"

She laughed softly at his use of the word. "Yes, Mr. Spock, I'm sure you're right, but I've never known a doctor who wasn't uppity. And I took the responsibility the moment I set foot on the *Enterprise.*"

"Then may I suggest you set aside your speculation for the moment? It is of no value at this time and could, conceivably, be of considerable detriment to our mission."

"Detriment?"

"Indeed. May I ask why you stopped when you reached the center of the grabfoot colony?"

If the question surprised her, she showed no sign of it. She said, "I could see them pulling me down again—almost feel it. I froze." She sat bolt upright. Her expression was one he had seen only once before: triumph after her experiment with Snnanagfashtalli. "Yes, Mr. Spock! You're right! My fear of what *might* happen kept me from seeing what *was* happening. My speculation endangered both you and Jinx."

"I do not say you should not speculate," Spock said carefully.

"Only that I shouldn't let it stop me from doing what must be done. I understand. Thank you."

As she spoke the last words, Spock realized with something of a shock that she had given him her undivided attention. Such attention was, as she had pointed out, quite ordinary from a Vulcan; but he had seldom received it from a human. From Evan Wilson, he found it disconcerting.

She nodded to herself, as if that put an end to her horrified speculation, then she said, "Mr. Spock, are you aware that, given the conclusion of our conversation, you began it with a highly improper—even illogical suggestion?"

"You astonish me, Doctor . . . in what way illogical?" He leaned forward for a better view of her face. Perhaps this was an attempt at humor.

"You offered, if I recall correctly, to 'excise' from my

252

memory the incident with the grabfoots. If I had let you do it,
I wouldn't have been able to see the analogy between my
behavior at that time and my recent fears."

"Ah," he said, understanding. "Illogical in retrospect. I am
still somewhat puzzled by your use of the word 'improper';
has your culture some taboo—?"

She cut him short. *"Your* culture should have some taboo
on the procedure. To forget deliberately—! Someone deliberately forgot the last verse of Uhura's song, the verse that gave
the cure for ADF, and look where it's got us!" Her arm swept
the smoky tent; her glance fell on the sleeping Chekov.
"Even the old Russians Chekov quotes knew better: 'Not a
word can be omitted from a song,' he says. But somebody,
Eeiauoan or Sivaoan, deliberately forgot."

She leaned toward him. "Think, Mr. Spock. All I am is a
collection of memories and experiences; that's all I have to go
on as I meet *new* situations. So anything I remember may be
crucial to my survival. Can you sit there and blandly propose
to . . . rob me of what is most valuable to me, to steal a
portion of what defines me as a person?" Once again, she
treated him to her full scrutiny. Her blue eyes were remarkably piercing. "I know you meant it as an offer of assistance,
and I thank you for your intention. But I would rather walk
through another colony of grabfoots—without a dose of
Jubalan rum—than accept your offer." She tapped her temple. "That's all I have, Mr. Spock. That's all I *am.*"

Remarkable, he thought, lifting a brow; cultural misunder-
standing or no, he could not look away. At last he said,
"That, Dr. Wilson, is a great deal."

She reddened, blinked once, then rose and said, "It's
getting light. If you'll poke up the fire, I'll wake the others.
And I'll save my worrying for a more appropriate time, I
promise."

As he built up the fire, Spock looked up from time to time,
watching Wilson, thinking: It would be as ill-judged to put
her behind a desk as . . . to put Jim Kirk in such a setting.
And he found himself thinking of Evan Wilson as much like
himself, out of place in human society. *Perhaps Jim is right,
perhaps contrariness to a particular culture could account for
it.* He acknowledged—but within the privacy of his thoughts

only—that a great many of his own actions were dictated by a need to deny his human heritage; he knew how strong the motive could be.

Jim Kirk's cheerful "Good morning, Spock!" so startled him that he dropped the green stick he'd been using as a poker; a shower of sparks leapt up. He hastily snatched for another stick to retrieve the first. When he had raked it out, he said, "Good morning, Captain. I trust you slept well?"

Kirk reached into their sling of provisions and chose a fruit. "I did, very well, considering the situation. *I* trust"—and he grinned—"that Dr. Wilson has been giving you a hard time again."

"Sir?"

"Personally, I don't think you should be allowed to talk to her without a chaperon. It makes you clumsy, Spock, and I've never known you to be." He gave the fire a significant glance.

"Your approach startled me, Captain. I was thinking."

"Indeed." With affected nonchalance, Kirk bit into the fruit. When he had swallowed, he said, "And may I ask what you were thinking about that had you so absorbed?"

"It was of no relevance to our circumstances, Captain. I was merely considering something Dr. Wilson had said."

Kirk grinned again. "I rest my case, Mr. Spock."

Spock eyed him. He knew Jim was baiting him; he knew also that Jim missed little—there was a good deal of truth in the joke. Evan Wilson's return with Brightspot spared him from the need to formulate a response, at least to Jim.

The captain tossed a fruit to Brightspot, who caught it deftly with her tail, causing Evan Wilson to exclaim, "Oh, but I *want* a tail of my own!"

"I'd have thought your tongue was agile enough to serve," Kirk suggested. He tossed a second fruit to her. Whether deliberately or accidently, it went high over her head. She leapt, thrust up a hand and caught it easily. Smiling, she said, "I'll bite, Captain. What have I done now?"

"I'll thank you to stop puzzling my science officer, Dr. Wilson. You left him so distracted I think he burned his hand."

Wilson shot a quick, concerned glance at Spock. He shook

his head; he could think of no way to explain this manifestation of Jim's humor. But Wilson said, "You see, Brightspot? I have all the disadvantages of a tail and none of the advantages."

She sat down and added, "Take care how you pull, Captain, or I might just tell you why I *haven't* called you 'Jim.'" She devoted all her attention to eating, leaving Spock to see what the captain's reaction to this rather odd threat might be.

Jim Kirk watched Evan Wilson for a long moment. She paused in her eating long enough to raise an eyebrow at him. If Spock interpreted her expression correctly, she was daring him to continue. It did not make sense. From Jim's expression, it made no more sense to him but, to Spock's enormous surprise, Jim said, "Let's see that map, Mr. Chekov. We have a lot of traveling to do today."

Within the hour they were again on their way. Distant Smoke's map lead them up once more. Chekov complained that each branch seemed bent on slapping water in his face. Spock might have corrected this—one could hardly assign intent to a plant—but he knew from experience that a minor contradiction under such circumstances was more likely to add to the irritability of a human.

Jinx and the captain led. Spock kept a close eye on Chekov; the ensign was overtired, there was no doubt of that, but he continued to press on with a dogged determination that even Spock found remarkable.

Happily, they did not have to climb the mountain itself, which Spock recalled from their aerial survey as one of the highest on this part of the continent. They had only to cross a portion of the lower ridge at its base. Had they been in other circumstances—a desert walk, for instance—Wilson and the two Sivaoans would have been at a disadvantage. Here, length of stride made no difference. The slope was not steep but, in combination with the undergrowth, Spock could see that it was wearying to both humans and Sivaoans—and most especially to Chekov.

Wilson paused and leaned on her staff. "Brightspot," she said, "grabfoots in this area?"

Brightspot shook her head. "Wrong kind of trees. Not steep enough. Too dark. This is slashback territory—that's worse."

"I'm not sure I believe that," said Wilson, pushing on.

The slope was gentle but continuous. For several hours, the climbing and the need to be wary of slashbacks consumed both their energy and their attention.

"Listen!" said Brightspot suddenly. Wilson did but shook her head. "Mr. Spock?" Brightspot called. "Can you hear it?"

"The sound of a river in the distance," Spock said. He could just barely hear it ahead of them.

Brightspot said, "From now on, we can't get lost. Cross the river and follow the path right into Sretalles."

Wilson grinned at her. "Well, don't lose me, either of you, until I can hear it too."

From just ahead and to Spock's right, Chekov said, "Thet goes double for me."

From somewhere not far from them but hidden from sight by the arrowlike leaves thrust up about them, Kirk called, "Don't stop to chat, people. It's about to get easier—we've got a trail up here."

"Well!" said Wilson. "It's about time!" She and Brightspot scrambled forward; with Uhura, they gave Chekov a hand to help him the last few hundred yards.

They stepped suddenly into the sunlight and the ground beneath their feet flattened out onto a wide plateau that arced around a steep outcrop of rock. At the opposite end of the arc, Spock could see the trail Kirk spoke of: it began—or ended—here. He wondered why there was no trail in the direction from which they'd come.

A soft gasp from Evan Wilson interrupted his thoughts. "Oh, Elath! We must be overlooking this entire half of the continent! I had no idea we'd climbed this far. No wonder it feels odd to be on level ground!" He followed her wide-eyed look into the distance and found the answer to his question: from here there were many directions in which to travel, but only one to the bridge that Jinx described as the only safe river crossing.

"And a terrific place for a picnic!" Wilson said. "Let's eat."

Spock saw she looked at Chekov as she spoke; she and Uhura were all that kept him on his feet. "Captain?" Spock said. "I believe this would be a suitable place for rest and a meal."

Kirk voiced agreement, and Chekov sat down heavily and sighed his relief. Wilson took a last look at the view, then sat down by his side. "Mr. Chekov?" she asked.

"I'm all right, sair," he said, although the grayish hue of his face belied his words. "A little rest is all I need."

"A little food, too," she said. "That's an order."

Jim Kirk joined them. "You'll be happy to know, Mr. Chekov, Jinx says it's all downhill from here." Jinx confirmed his words with a nod.

Uhura massaged her ankles and said, "Mr. Chekov is not the only one who's happy to hear that, Captain!"

"Here, here!" said Wilson. "Human beings still aren't fully adapted for walking upright, and, at this very moment, my feet and back could give you ample evidence of that fact." Struck by a thought, she added, "Mr. Spock? Vulcans have been bipedal longer than humans, haven't they? Does that leave you better prepared for long hikes than the average human?"

"What you say may be true, Doctor, although I have seen no study on the subject. Judging from an extremely limited sample"—he indicated the assembled group—"I would say that both Vulcan and Sivaoan seem better adapted to a prolonged walk of this nature than are humans."

"Then I've changed my mind," Wilson said. "In my next incarnation I want to be a Vulcan, not a Scot."

"Why don't you be like us, Evan," Brightspot suggested, "then you'd have a tail." From the way her own tail looped, the idea pleased her.

Seeing that Brightspot had taken her words seriously, Wilson explained, "It's a joke. Federation science could give me a nice set of ears like Mr. Spock's, but it hasn't yet gotten to the point where it could give me his circulatory system. Or," she said, almost regretfully, "a fur coat of my very own and a handy tail like yours."

"You have no idea how glad I am to hear that," Kirk said. Spock recognized that tone—Jim Kirk was baiting a trap;

Wilson, however, did not, and she looked at Kirk question-ingly. Kirk explained, "Think how much more trouble you'd be if you could stick your tail into things as well as your nose!"

Evan Wilson frowned slightly and pulled at her lower lip. She appeared to be looking at something just beyond the end of her own nose.

Jim Kirk, obviously puzzled by her lack of reaction, finally said, "Evan?"

She looked at him as if surprised and said, "I'm *thinking*, Captain. . . . It sounds good to *me!*"

It was so seriously said that Jim Kirk was startled into laughter. Uhura too laughed, and even Chekov managed a smile. "Perheps you shouldn't give her ideas, Keptain," Chekov said.

"Perhaps you're right, Mr. Chekov. Dr. Wilson, you are incorrigible."

Wilson grinned. "Yes, sir, and you're invited to incorrige me all you want, sir."

Although Spock understood her intent, he could not help but raise his brow at her usage. Without warning, Evan Wilson leveled a finger at him and snapped, "Don't you point that thing at me, Spock—it might be loaded!" Spock stared at her, not quite believing he had heard correctly. Color rose in her cheeks, but she continued to glare defiantly at him. At last she nodded in a satisfied way. "That's better," she said; she seemed to be referring to the fact that he had lowered his brow. "See that you take more care in the future," she added. "I don't take kindly to being used as a target."

At a complete loss to understand the purpose of her peculiar outburst, Spock turned to Jim Kirk for assistance—and promptly received an explanation. The captain was almost doubled over in an effort to suppress his laughter.

Spock looked around him. Uhura was making no such effort at self-control, nor was Chekov. Brightspot and Jinx had their tails so tightly looped he was surprised they were not in pain.

He looked again at Dr. Wilson. She alone did not laugh. Very distinctly, but without a sound, her mouth formed the words, "Sorry, Spock—for them," and her eyes traveled over the group.

He nodded. If he understood humor at all, it was this use of it—to restore morale. As he could be neither offended nor amused, he was a logical subject. With full consciousness of the act, he raised his brow at her again; as he expected, she too burst into laughter.

Uhura caught her breath. "I'm so sorry, Mr. Spock!" she said. "The image . . ." She began to laugh again. "I . . . am . . . sorry!" She redoubled her effort at control and finally achieved some measure of it. Between gasping breaths, she said earnestly, "I could . . . almost hear the captain give the command: 'Eyebrow on stun, Mr. Spock. . . .'" That was too much for Jim Kirk. He could no longer suppress his laughter and Uhura, caught up by the wave of emotion once more, spread her hands in a helpless gesture of apology.

Spock waited patiently. When their laughter tapered off, they had a relaxed meal—punctuated by an occasional laugh every time Spock raised a brow—which he did with greater frequency than usual. At last Jim Kirk rose to his feet and they all followed suit. As they moved to resume their journey, Jim Kirk glanced his way and said, "At least they can't be set for *kill*. If they could, we'd all be in a great deal of trouble right now."

They started down the trail in single file, Kirk now in the lead. Spock found his way barred by Evan Wilson's quarterstaff; he stopped, seeing the concern on her face. "There is no need for apology, Dr. Wilson," he said, before she could speak. "It is quite sufficient to note that even Mr. Chekov's color has improved." Relief flooded her features. The quarterstaff snapped out of his way.

"Still," she said, as he started down the trail before her, "next time it's the captain's turn."

Behind her, Brightspot said, "You're going to pull the captain's tail, Evan? That I'd like to see."

"You will, Brightspot. That's a promise."

They fell silent. This, according to the two Sivaoans, was slashback territory—and Spock kept his spear at the ready and his attention on their surroundings.

Tactically, the party would have been safer from slashbacks traveling in pairs, but this was impossible: the narrow trail, winding steeply down around bare outcroppings of rock and sketchy vegetation, was scarcely wide enough for single file. Still it was in many ways the easiest traveling they had yet had.

The sound of rushing water grew louder. Spock glanced back at Wilson, and she nodded. She could hear it too, now. Soon Spock recognized the distant roar of a waterfall—to judge from the sound, a very large waterfall. The air misted with water vapor, and the rock trail became dangerously slick underfoot. The party slowed again as a precaution. A fall here could be deadly. As he watched, a rock dislodged by someone up ahead careened down the cliffside. Striking a ledge some fifty feet down, it shattered and showered fragments the rest of the way.

To his relief, they passed over the most dangerous of this terrain without mishap, and the trail led them back into forest, where they could travel with surer footing. The ground was damp—so was the air—but the layer of decomposing vegetation was safer to walk on than bare wet rock. If one slipped here, one would fall into bushes or at worst stickpins —not down an escarpment.

The vegetation had changed: the heavy concentration of water vapor thrown into the air by the waterfall had probably had deleterious effects on the usual forest plants, perhaps animals as well. Others had moved in to take their place. There was a steady drip-drip of condensing water from the upper leaves of trees that Spock found irritating; his Vulcan half was not adapted to this sort of environment.

"Mr. Spock!" Evan Wilson had to shout to make herself heard. She drew very close, careful not to touch him, and stood on her toes to say into his ear, "Can you slow your rate of breathing?" Rather than shout, he nodded back. "Then do it," she said. "Your lungs aren't designed to handle this much water vapor." He nodded again; she was correct. She dropped back into line behind him but not, he saw, until he had done as she suggested.

They drew closer to the falls. Spock wondered if there might be others farther down the mountain. No falls had been indicated on Distant Smoke's map, only the smell of water vapor. The tiny droplets he had drawn might mean falls or marshes, and there had been three other such indications further downstream. He made a mental note to question Brightspot when conversation became less difficult.

Forcing his way through a thick cluster of sharp-leaved bushes, he came to an abrupt halt. The entire party stood in a knot, looking up. Spock followed Lieutenant Uhura's raised finger and got his first clear view of the falls, from top to bottom. The mist made it difficult to estimate their true height, but he had never seen higher. Wilson pushed through beside him. "Oh, Elath!" she shouted exuberantly. "You do *good* work!"

Jim Kirk tapped her and shouted, "Keep moving, people. Save the rubbernecking for your next shore leave!" He urged them all back onto the trail, but Spock saw him take a final look over his shoulder at the falls too.

For the next mile, the trail paralleled the river at a distance. Through the trees, Spock caught glimpses of roiling muddy water, although not the torrent he had seen at the base of the falls. The ground leveled off, and Kirk took advantage of the easy travel to hasten them on. They planned to cross to the far side to make camp for the night. Jinx and Distant Smoke's map concurred—slashbacks seldom ranged the other bank.

Even this far from the falls, the air was thick and uncomfortable to breathe. Spock continued to check his rate of intake whenever it was possible to do so; but their rapid pace made it more difficult, and his attention to the unfamiliar dangers frequently made him neglect the more prosaic.

The trail turned abruptly toward the river and debouched directly onto the bank: they had reached the crossing. Brightspot stared at the churning waters and shivered, her hackles rising. Jinx too watched fearfully.

There was a suspended bridge, made of the ever-present usefuls and just wide enough for a single person at a time, dipping low over the water. Ordinarily, he thought, it must be several feet above the river. But the river was swollen with the recent rains and now and again it caught the bridge at the low point of its arc, swinging it ominously downstream and splattering muddy water high.

Kirk eyed this structure with distrust. "Suggestions, Mr. Spock?" he asked.

"I see no alternative, Captain," Spock replied.

"All right, Spock. Bridge it is."

"It will hold three at a time," Jinx said, "but larger people should spread out." Jim Kirk nodded at her and took the lead. The bridge swung with each shift of his weight, and it took him some time before he caught the rhythm of it and began to move with assurance. When he reached the center, Jinx started across. The added motion of her steps threw Jim momentarily off stride, a surge of water struck—the bridge veered wildly and Jim clung to the twisted cloth railings.

After what seemed an interminable time, the bridge swung back, and Jim resumed the crossing. At last he reached solid ground on the far bank. He wiped muddy water from his face, then motioned them to join him.

Jinx was halfway across now, and Chekov started hesitantly. His face had once again taken on a grayish cast.

Without taking his eyes from Chekov, Kirk held out a hand to Jinx and pulled her onto dry ground. She dropped back and turned, to guard against danger from the forest.

Uhura went next, but she had gone only a few yards when the counteracting motion she generated overwhelmed Chekov and he faltered. Uhura quickened her steps to reach and assist him. "Freeze, Uhura!" Wilson shouted, and she did.

From the opposite side, Kirk said, "Freeze, Mr. Chekov." Chekov too stopped where he was.

"Now," said Jim Kirk, "do exactly as I say. Drop your spear."

"But sair—" Chekov began.

Kirk said, "That's an order, mister."

Chekov obeyed, and Kirk went on, "Grab both railings and move slowly toward me. Lieutenant Uhura, stay put." Chekov awkwardly, almost blindly, worked his way across. Then Jim had him and was sitting him down on the safety of the bank. With a smile of relief, Jim Kirk glanced up and called, "Come ahead, Lieutenant. Don't keep us waiting."

Uhura did. "After you, Mr. Spock," said Wilson, and Spock stepped cautiously onto the end of the bridge. His added motion did not unsettle Uhura in the slightest—even as a surge drenched her with muddy water, she never hesitated. She stepped lightly onto the far side.

It was only then that Spock realized something was wrong. As he reached the midpoint of the bridge, there was no additional motion. Brightspot had not begun to cross. He turned to look back, but Wilson called, "Keep going, Mr. Spock! We're coming together!" He was close enough to hear her add, in a quiet tone of command, "I'm not going without you, Brightspot, so stop being an idiot."

Spock quickened his pace as much as he dared and, as he neared the waiting Jim Kirk, he said, "Brightspot is afraid to cross."

"So I see," said Kirk, stepping aside to let him pass onto firm ground. "Evan," he called, "shall I come back?"

Spock turned as Evan Wilson shouted back, "Stay put, Captain. I'll manage." He wondered how she could sound so sure of herself; Brightspot's fur stuck straight out—her tail was a good six inches in diameter—and it was pure fear.

Wilson tucked her quarterstaff into her sash, calmly took Brightspot's spear and did the same, then gave the terrified Sivaoan a casual shove toward the bridge. Brightspot did not budge. She said something to Wilson that Spock could not hear. Jinx said, "Brightspot says she knows she has to—all those people will die if she doesn't—but she can't get herself to move. She wants Evan to help."

Evan Wilson nodded, said something and, with visible effort, maneuvered Brightspot to within an inch of the head of the bridge. Jinx told them, "Evan says she's just as scared, but she'll get Brightspot across if she has to drag her."

"She can't," said Jim Kirk, stepping onto their end of the bridge. "It's too dangerous."

Hidden behind Brightspot, Evan Wilson made a swift snatching motion. Brightspot yelped and leapt forward. Before she realized what had happened, both her feet were on the bridge and Wilson was right behind her, blocking the route back to the near shore. "Go!" said Wilson. "Or, by Elath, we're no longer friends!"

Spiky with fear, Brightspot looked the length of the bridge. Jim Kirk held out his hand. "Come on, Brightspot. If I can do it, you can do it." And Brightspot began to inch across, Evan

Wilson pressed so close against her that she had no alternative but to go forward. Snakelike, her thickened tail coiled tight around Wilson's waist.

They made it to the midpoint of the bridge. Beneath their combined weight, it sagged deeper into the water, sending up a constant muddy spray. As they began to inch through, Spock realized that their combined weight could not possibly equal his—the water was rising!

Fed by the runoff of last night's thunderstorms, just now reaching the river, the water surged higher; and this was Jinx's flash flood area. Spock shot a look upstream. In consequence, he was the only one who saw it coming: a vast sheet of red water filled with debris. "Flood crest, Evan!" he shouted. "Hold on!"

He saw her look upstream and brace, heard her shout to Brightspot to do the same. The crest struck. The bridge swung so far to the side that their upstream shoulders plunged into the water, splashing their faces. Brightspot howled. Wilson cursed over the roar.

For a moment, he thought them safe—then an uprooted tree trunk struck the bridge. It caught briefly and, as it did, Spock could hear the sound of ripping fabric. Ever so slowly, the bridge tore apart.

That was the last slow thing that happened; what followed was too fast for the mind to grasp completely. The two halves of the bridge snapped downstream, Brightspot and Wilson clinging to the nearest. Then Brightspot went under, went limp. Wilson grabbed for her tail, and the current tore Wilson from her precarious hold. And they were both gone in a swirl of red water and black branches.

There was a flash of movement at Spock's side and, before Spock could stop him, Jim Kirk dived into the flood waters after the two.

Spock recovered in sufficient time to catch both Chekov and Uhura before they could duplicate the captain's error. The rush of their despair almost overwhelmed him, and he shoved them away—thrusting them downstream. "Follow—on land—that's an order!"

The four of them crashed through the undergrowth along the edge of the still-rising waters. They had lost the trail, but that was of no importance. They had to reach some area ahead of the three in the water; they had to catch them somehow, before they were swept on by. Jinx wailed as she ran.

The water washed over the bank, but they splashed on until a branch carried by the current struck Uhura in the ankle and threw her to her knees. Jinx pulled her safely to her feet, but the dangerous eddies forced them back from the riverbank, further into the wood. Spock caught a last glance of Wilson swimming fiercely with the current; of Brightspot, of Jim Kirk, there was no sign. They plunged on, slowed by tangled vines and stickpins. Slowed too much, Spock knew, and yet he kept on.

An immense wall of gray rock loomed before them and put an end to whatever slim possibility they might have had of rescuing Jim Kirk and the others. Forced aside, the river veered violently to the left. Like the river, they would have to turn aside—in the opposite direction—and still they ran until they could go no farther.

Uhura slammed her hands against the blank, unmoving mass of rock. Tears streamed down her cheeks. "Mr. Spock!" she said, and he knew from her voice that she asked a miracle of him. Jinx beat at the stone with the end of her spear.

"What do we do now, sair?" Too exhausted to demand more, Chekov asked only for orders.

"We shall be forced to go around, Mr. Chekov," he said, although it was stating the obvious. He knew from experience that his unwillingness to mourn their situation invited their anger but he had no time to invest in their morale. He scanned the obstruction for the shortest, easiest way around, then he turned to inquire of Jinx—

Teeth bared, ears laid back, Jinx stood poised to strike him, but Uhura clung to her upraised arm, forcing it down. It was clear that Jinx had no wish to hurt Uhura but, to Spock's surprise, Uhura slapped Jinx sharply across the side of the jaw. Equally surprised, Jinx blinked at her. "He doesn't care!" Jinx wailed; this seemed to be an explanation.

"He does!" Uhura said. "The captain is his friend! He *hurts,* Jinx, as much as we do!"

"He doesn't—"

"He *can't* show it," Uhura said. "He's trying to find a way we can help. *You're* delaying us, Jinx!" At that, Jinx lowered her arm. Uhura released her hold and, panting from their efforts, the two of them stared at each other for a long moment.

At last, still bristling, Jinx pointed and said, "That way, Mr. Spock, if we go that way, we can get around it."

Spock nodded. "Mr. Chekov," he said, "are you able to continue?"

Chekov was slumped back against the rock. Gasping for breath, he nodded without wasting any on words.

"Jinx, will you please assist Mr. Chekov?" Jinx gave Spock a last glare, lashed her tail, then went to Chekov. The moment she reached his side, her manner changed: her fur smoothed, her tail stilled. Spock thought, *How like Dr. McCoy—all other considerations fade when a patient needs his help.*

Jinx got Chekov to his feet but, once steadied, he waved her away and staggered without her help. Spock in the lead, they set off along the route that Jinx had indicated, over and around the obstructing rock. Jinx, keeping a close watch on Chekov, brought up the rear.

Uhura climbed with Spock. Together they tried to smooth the way for Chekov. As they pushed on, Spock said to Uhura quietly, "Thank you for your assistance, Lieutenant. Such a blow, even from a smaller Sivaoan, might have been fatal."

Lieutenant Uhura smiled slightly. "I'm rather glad she attempted it, sir. If she hadn't, I probably would have. And no one would have stopped me." She smiled again. "You needn't worry about being struck from behind. What I said convinced me as well as Jinx."

"That is hardly logical, Lieutenant . . . nor were your arguments."

"We agreed that I wasn't, remember?" Then she added, "But, Mr. Spock, I *do* know how you feel about the captain. I feel the same." He nodded; that was all he could do to confirm her assessment. It seemed to be enough. "We'll find him," she said, as if to reassure him. "We'll find them all. We must."

"Mr. Spock!" Jinx called from behind. "I smell slashbacks! We must find a place of safety for Mr. Chekov!"

Spock turned, saw that Chekov had fallen. Jinx struggled to pull him to his feet. Showering loose rock, Spock scrambled his way back to the two. Without a word, he reached down, caught Chekov around the waist and pulled him up—ignoring the mental charge of the contact. "Find us a place of safety, Jinx," he said.

Jinx led them upward. Nose wrinkled, she kept a constant check on the air, trying to pinpoint the slashbacks. They continued to climb. The pitch of the slope softened, and Spock was able to carry Chekov, speeding their ascent. Spears held ready, Uhura and Jinx stayed close, one on either side when the terrain permitted.

"No time," said Jinx suddenly. She pointed to a rift in the rock. "Put Mr. Chekov in there." Spock followed her instructions.

Chekov, barely conscious now, managed to crawl into the rift; there he pulled his knife. "I will be all right, Mr. Spock. I em just tired, sair," he said.

He was still muttering assurances when Jinx said, "They're coming!"

Spock turned and straightened. Uhura and Jinx had deployed to protect Chekov, Jinx with her spear gripped in unsheathed claws, Uhura bracing hers with both hands. Taking their example, Spock leveled his own spear and watched the jagged ridge beyond and above.

"Two," said Jinx, in an undertone, "one male, one female. Take the female first if you can—the males don't hunt without an escort." To prompt their memories, she added, "The females are usually darker colored. And don't let them get behind you, whatever you do!" She flicked up her tail to cover Uhura's mouth in a gesture for silence.

The three waited.

There was a slight stirring of bushes that crowned the escarpment, as if a breeze had ruffled them—then two creatures stood silently looking down at Spock. They were felinoid, perhaps distant cousins of the sentient species, but quadripedal. The larger and darker of the two—the female?

—he estimated to be about five feet in length, excluding the tail, and to weigh some three hundred pounds. It sniffed the air cautiously. Jinx said, "She doesn't recognize your smell. Maybe she won't attack. . . ." It thrust its head forward, sniffing again, then it crept into the sunlight.

"Sabertooth!" said Uhura. Spock did not correct her; the resemblance of the slashback to reconstructions of the ancient Earth creature was striking, and all the more so when the female opened her jaw and two foot-long canines came into sharp focus.

With a barking roar, immediately echoed by the male, the female slashback launched herself at Uhura. Uhura took one step forward to meet the charge with her spear, catching the creature in the chest. The impact threw her back against the stone embankment, but she kept hold of the spear, forcing the creature away from Chekov's refuge.

The male sprang at the same moment. Spock caught it a glancing blow with the tip of his spear. It leapt aside.

Jinx rammed her spear into the belly of the female that thrashed and flailed at the end of Uhura's spear. It howled and twisted, ripping the spear from Jinx's hands.

The male charged Spock again and, for a moment, his entire concentration was on the creature. His spear broke at the impact, head buried in the slashback's side. With all his Vulcan strength, he thrust at the creature with the splintered end of the shaft and swept the slashback up—into the air—and down the hillside. It struck rock with a sickening crack, convulsed once and lay still.

Spock drew his knife and turned to aid Uhura and Jinx. Uhura had her foot on the slashback's nose, forcing its mouth closed, and keeping it pinned with foot and spear. Jinx had thrown aside her ruined spear and was on the creature's back, tooth and claw sunk into its spine.

Circling around behind, Spock reached in, grasped the creature by the ear, and slit its throat. Blood gouted, spattering them all. A moment later, the slashback went limp.

Jinx, growling deep in her throat, gave the carcass a few final shakes to assure herself the slashback was dead. Then she rolled away and sat up, licking its blood from her shoulder. Uhura had a dazed expression on her face. She looked up at Spock, then focused again on the slashback. She took her foot from the slashback's nose and planted it next to her imbedded spear. It took all her effort to remove the spear—intact—from the animal's chest.

"Lieutenant Uhura? Are you injured?"

"I'll tell you in a moment, Mr. Spock. I can't . . . quite think right now, sir." She looked at him in a puzzled fashion and added, "I've never done anything like this before."

Spock understood. To give her the time she requested, he knelt to examine the slashback, working the jaw to see how it was hinged. The design was elegant in its efficiency.

"Mr. Spock?" Jinx sat beside Chekov, his wrist delicately encircled in her fingers. "We can't go on," she said, "at least, he can't at the moment. He needs rest. And we must make camp before dark."

Spock surveyed the three of them. They were his responsibility, and he could not leave them to search for Jim and the others. "Would you advise we camp here, Jinx?"

She shook her head. "There may be more. You don't ordinarily find slashbacks on this side of the river but—" She gestured at the carcass.

"Understood," he said. "Choose according to your own best knowledge, Jinx. I will carry Mr. Chekov."

Uhura said suddenly, "The captain—"

"We can do nothing for them at the moment, Lieutenant. Our own survival is now our primary concern." He held her eyes. "I believe you understand that."

"Yes," she said, her voice barely audible; then with visible effort she resumed her professional manner. "I am only scratched, Mr. Spock. Are you all right?"

"I am uninjured. However, yours is the only remaining spear. I suggest we recover our spear points, as Mr. Chekov is in no condition to fashion more."

"I'll see to that. Yours is somewhere in the other slashback?" At his nod, she went to cut his point from the dead male.

Jinx returned from her examination of Chekov and knelt beside the female slashback. She drew her knife and began to slice into it. "Mr. Chekov—and the rest of us," she said, "will need food. Slashback's not tender but it will do." She found her own spearhead, handed the bloodied object to Spock and paused as she did to add, "We'll pick fruit as we go along." There was something more in her eyes. He waited, and she said at last, "Mr. Spock, can Captain Kirk and Dr. Wilson swim?"

"The captain is skilled at the art. As to Dr. Wilson, I should estimate her abilities above the average." The last was no lie: *if Wilson could swim she would swim the way she did everything else.* He did not add that even a strong swimmer might fail against such a current, nor did he inquire about the possibility of waterfalls further downstream.

Jinx said, forcing the words out, "Mr. Spock, Brightspot *can't*—any more than I could. We've lost Brightspot."

Uhura held out a second bloodied spearpoint, still attached to a short length of broken wood. She said, "Evan knew that, Jinx. That Brightspot couldn't swim, I mean. If they had any chance at all, Captain Kirk and Evan Wilson would save her too."

"Oh," said Jinx, "please let it be true!" And, without a further word, she threw herself back into her task.

Chapter Fifteen

Jim Kirk burst to the surface, spitting muddy water. He made no attempt to fight the current, knowing it swept him in the same direction as Wilson and Brightspot—and Brightspot couldn't swim. He caught a flash of something white. His first thought was that it was too small to be Brightspot, then he recalled the childhood memory of a soaked cat. He drove toward it, kicking powerfully. Ahead and to his right, Wilson splashed fiercely in the same direction. His more powerful strokes brought him to her side.

"Brightspot!" she gasped. "Get Brightspot!" She dived to avoid debris and came up still swimming toward the Sivaoan. Kirk hesitated only long enough to assure himself she could hold her own, then swam past. A branch struck him hard in the side, but he ignored the pain. He had to reach Brightspot—

He could see her clearly now. She must be unconscious— perhaps she'd been struck by the tree trunk as it hit the bridge—for she made no movement. The current raced along, carrying her limp body wherever it went. A momentary surge flung him forward and flipped Brightspot face down. He redoubled his efforts—caught her by the tail, flipped her back. Holding her face out of the water, he swam for shore.

The current ran faster now, and crossing it, especially with a burden, was exhausting. The chill of the water was rapidly draining his strength. He focused on the shore, tried to ignore the ringing in his ears. The next time he looked back, Wilson had Brightspot's other arm.

The river made a sharp turn to the left, and they were forced to swim once more for midstream, for fear of being smashed against a vast wall of rock. Debris caught, spun, splintered against it. Evan Wilson went under to avoid a ricochet and came up gasping. He saw she still held Brightspot's tail in one hand.

He knew they had to get to shore. They were both tiring rapidly—soon they would be unable to fight the current to reach *any* shore. The ringing in his ears grew louder, and he suddenly recognized the sound for what it was: there was another waterfall ahead. "Shore, Evan," he gasped. "Now."

The two of them put forth all their effort and—after a time that seemed to last forever—Kirk caught the thick branch of a tree that overhung the water. Wrapping his legs around Brightspot's torso, he pulled her, hand over hand, to shore, and heaved her bodily onto the bank. He reached for Evan, just as her grip on the tree gave way. Had she not been holding Brightspot's tail, she would have been torn away by the current. He caught her by the wrist and landed her in a heap on Brightspot.

Evan pushed herself up on all fours, stared at Brightspot, then ripped the sodden pack from the muddied youngster and flung her onto her back. Turning Brightspot's face to one side, Evan straddled her and laid her hands one over the other at the base of her diaphragm. She gave a sharp upward thrust. Heimlich maneuver, Kirk recognized, modified to prevent the water from returning to Brightspot's lungs.

Water gushed from Brightspot's mouth—Kirk bent over her, ready to give artificial respiration if she needed it—and Brightspot gasped and breathed. While Evan checked the pulse at the base of her tail, Kirk slapped Brightspot lightly, trying to bring her around. He got no response; her breathing was extremely rapid, like panting, and irregular.

"Out of the water," said Evan, and the two of them, fighting their own exhaustion, dragged Brightspot further up the bank. "Give me your tunic, Captain, and build me a fire."

He was not sure he had heard her correctly. He stared and found fury in her face. "Your tunic!" she snapped, tugging at the useful she wore. "This won't absorb water worth a damn—we've got to get her dry and warm. She's in shock!"

He stripped off his tunic and twisted the water from it; she snatched it from his hands and began to towel Brightspot, pausing only now and then to wring more water from it. As she worked, she said over and over again, "Brightspot! Brightspot, listen to me! You're okay. You're on shore. Damn you, Brightspot! You're out of the water!"

Kirk fought the dampness of the wood and, at last, nursed a fire to life. He built it up to a roar, then helped Evan pull Brightspot close. He began to rub Brightspot's fur too—with his hands, as he had no cloth—talking soothingly to Brightspot in Evan's pauses.

"Against the grain, Captain," Evan said, "it stimulates their circulation." She tossed him his tunic to use while she reached for her medical kit. "No broken bones," she said, as if the sensor only confirmed her opinion. "No internal injuries."

His glance fell on the sensor Spock had modified. "It's not working anyway," she said. "We're stuck here, Captain." She pulled the pack from her back and spread its contents on the ground: fruit, comb, usefuls, pegs, her flint point. She found what she was looking for —a small leaf-wrapped package. She undid it, and a handful of tail-kinkers spilled onto her lap. Clumsy with exhaustion, she at last managed to smash several of them between her fingers and rub them just beneath Brightspot's nose. Then she pried open Brightspot's mouth. Kirk reached to assist her, holding it open while she smeared oil from the tail-kinkers on Brightspot's tongue.

Brightspot came to so abruptly that, had Jim Kirk not been holding her jaw, Evan might have lost a hand. "Evan?" said Brightspot weakly. "Did we make it across? Are you still my friend?"

Evan Wilson laughed and hugged Brightspot hard. "We made it," she said triumphantly. "We're safe on the opposite shore. No, don't wash!" she added firmly. "You can't afford to expend the spit right now. Lie still a minute." Too weak to nod, Brightspot arched her whiskers and obeyed.

When Evan returned, bearing fruit, she said, "Now I want you to sit up and eat something—Captain, give me a hand." Kirk helped her lift and hold Brightspot in a sitting position. Brightspot took a few bites of fruit and stopped. "A little more, if you can, Brightspot," Evan urged. "You need the liquid—you had a bad time of it there for a while."

As Brightspot ate, Kirk stroked her muddy fur. Suddenly he smiled and said, "That's what I call washing off the alcohol the hard way!"

Her pupils went wide. "Evan!" she said, "I remember! I fell in the water!"

"You were thrown in; the bridge was hit by a log. You're safe now, Brightspot, you're on land."

"You came in the water after me?" Brightspot looked at her with awe.

Evan laughed and shook her head. "Don't ascribe high motives, Brightspot. I got thrown in just like you." She nodded to Kirk. "The captain jumped in after both of us. It was not terribly bright of him but since it all turned out well I'm grateful. He pulled you out of the water, and me too."

"Thank you!" said Brightspot, turning to him. "I was so scared—I don't remember anything except the water—"

Embarrassed by the worship in her eyes, Kirk said, "You, Brightspot? *You* don't remember? I'm never going to let you forget you said that!" Brightspot's tail moved, looping ever so slightly.

"That's better," said Evan. "Captain, see if you can get her to eat a little more. And if you feel the urge to pull her tail again, be my guest; it's obviously good therapy." She rose. "I'm going to throw a shelter up around you before it gets too dark to see what I'm doing."

By the time she had finished, Kirk had coaxed Brightspot to eat two of the fruits. Evan tucked her in usefuls—"Sleep now," she said. "Doctor's orders." And Brightspot closed her eyes and was instantly asleep. "Daughter of my sister," said Evan Wilson softly. "Captain? How are you holding up? Could you manage to stay awake for half an hour more? I know Jinx said a fire would keep the slashbacks away, but. . . ."

He nodded. "I can manage half an hour, Evan, probably more." He was running on adrenalin still.

"Good," she said. "If I don't sleep *now* I will collapse. Wake me in half an hour. I'm not saying that to short myself—I want to check Brightspot then—so don't get gallant like Spock."

Kirk smiled at her, and at her image of Spock. "It's a promise, Evan. Half an hour."

"And have something to eat," she added. "Just save one for Brightspot when she wakes. She needs the liquid." She lay down, curled herself around Brightspot and fell instantly asleep.

Taking care not to disturb them, Kirk slipped from the tent to assess the situation. He had lost his own pack in the river, and his spear he'd dropped before he dove into the water. There was no sign of Evan's quarterstaff, though she still had her knife. He checked Brightspot's pack, laying its contents by the fire to dry. There was more fruit, mashed but still edible. No weapons except their knives, he thought. No map—but Brightspot had been told the route they were to take—given her memory they'd be all right on that score. Weapons, though. . . . Then he remembered Evan's spear point: it might not be as good as a Chekov point, but it would have to serve. He drew his knife and set about to cut himself a new shaft.

As he worked, he reassured himself that Spock would look after the other half of the party. They'd find each other in the morning—Spock knew better than to travel in unknown territory in the dark, no matter how the others pushed him. Spock was immovable when the logic of the situation demanded.

Throughout the long night, he and Evan Wilson alternated watches. Brightspot continued to improve, and when Wilson woke him just before sunrise, he too felt better. "Don't wake Brightspot yet," she said quietly, "I want her to get as much rest as she can."

He nodded and, pointing to the newly peeled quarterstaff in her hand, said, "I see we both had the same idea."

"Yes"—she smiled—"how's the food situation?"

He remembered she hadn't eaten the previous night. "Brightspot had fruit in her pack," he said. "One for each of us, and that leaves two for Brightspot."

She ate slowly, just as he had, savoring each bite. When she was finished, she said, "What's the game plan, Captain? Do we wait here for Spock, or do we go looking? I suppose I'm asking what he's likely to do."

"Can Brightspot travel?"

"If we take it slowly. I'd just as soon get her to Catchclaw anyhow."

Kirk gave it some thought. Then he said, "We're about two days from Sretalles. Spock would expect us to make for the trail if we could. We can't be too far from them, Evan. We may even be in hailing distance."

"Well, wait till Brightspot wakes up before you try hailing, Captain."

They sat silent for a while. Jim Kirk stirred the fire. "All right, Evan," he said at last, "*why* won't you call me Jim? Especially after all we've been through together?"

She laughed softly. "*Especially* after all we've been through together I wouldn't. I call people what they want to be called, even Jinx, and you want to be called 'Captain'— that's how you think of yourself, as captain of the *Enterprise*. Out here, that needs a little reinforcement. That's why I don't call you Jim, Captain."

Despite her smile, she meant her words seriously, and Kirk found himself thinking of those people who did call him by first name. Spock had, and from Spock, it was an enormous compliment. As for Bones—when Bones called him 'Captain,' it was generally meant as an insult, roughly along the lines of 'I don't like your orders, and I think you're a damn fool, but you're the captain, *Captain*.' "I see your point, Evan," he said. "Tell me, would you prefer I call you Dr. Wilson?"

She spread her hands. "Call me whatever you want. The name truly doesn't matter to me."

"You fought Fetchstorm over it," he said, surprised.

She shook her head. "I fought Fetchstorm over a derogatory term for human beings. That's different."

"Ah," he said, "then that makes sense." Without thinking, he added, "Where are you from, Evan?"

"Read my transfer file, Captain."

He chuckled. "I did. Spock disapproves of it."

Her eyebrow lifted in uncanny imitation of Spock. "'Disapproves'?"

"Let me rephrase that: He disbelieves them."

"Does he? Now why on Earth . . . ?"

"Because on Telamon you'd hardly swear by a goddess."

"You'd hardly swear on Telamon," she said, grinning. "I'm sure you've picked up a handful of outworld expressions yourself, Captain—what else?"

"And because of your previous assignments. Your papers make you sound like a desk-jockey."

"I know," she nodded and, as if she were inquiring his opinion of any curious phenomenon, one that had no bearing on her, she said, "What do you make of it?"

He laughed aloud. "Damned if I know, Evan." He waited for some further response, but she only stared back, a hint of a smile in her eyes, and finally he ventured, "And you're not going to tell me either."

She shook her head. "Maybe some other time, Captain. For now—well, Mr. Spock brings out the worst in me, I'm afraid. Tail from a tree branch, as Brightspot says. And the only way to keep him guessing is to keep you guessing." She rose easily to her feet.

"Then at least tell me how you got Brightspot onto that bridge."

"Wake her and ask her. If she doesn't remember that this morning, I'm going to be worried about that blow she took to the head."

Jim Kirk did but he did not need to ask the question, for Brightspot sat up and, fixing a long accusing look on Evan, said with the purest of pure outrage, "You bit my tail!"

Through Kirk's laughter, Evan said, relieved, "Well, you're all right then. I was afraid you wouldn't remember," which only added insult to injury.

Kirk hastened to explain, "She means because of the blow to your head, Brightspot."

"Oh," said Brightspot, and then again, "She bit my tail, Captain!"

"She got you onto the bridge."

"But only *babies* bite tails!"

Kirk eyed Evan with amusement and said, "Apparently not."

He handed her the last remaining fruit and she subsided to concentrate on eating. By the time Evan had struck the tent and he had repacked their gear, Brightspot's outrage had given way to a combination of amusement and wonder. "I was just so *surprised!*" she said finally.

"Just think of me as a tail-kinker in your food," Evan told her, and Brightspot's tail looped happily, proving that no permanent damage had been done it.

Kirk stowed Brightspot's pack and slung it over his own shoulder, despite her protest. "Save your strength for walking, Brightspot—you're our guide, remember?" He put just enough emphasis on his last word to curl her tail and noted with relief that today she did it easily.

"Try giving a yell, Captain, maybe they're in earshot."

Kirk did. They all waited, but even Brightspot's sharp ears could pick up nothing. "All right," said Kirk, "head for the trail, Brightspot. We'll see if we can pick up traces of them there."

He did not say that the lack of response worried him. He knew they'd been swept a long way down the river but it seemed to him that Spock would have followed—unless something had happened to the other half of the party.

Spock spent the long night on watch: although Jinx smelled no more slashbacks, he did not wish to risk the party to the protection of the campfire alone. And there was Chekov to consider. . . . He seemed to be resting peacefully now, but when Jinx checked him last, the simple act of pushing up his uniform sleeves scraped large patches of hair from his arms. Wilson's fears had proved correct: Chekov had contracted ADF syndrome, and he had contracted it in a more virulent form than previously seen in a human. Spock had read the medical reports himself and knew that Chekov's reaction to the disease was nonstandard. If it continued to progress at this rate, Chekov would be unable to continue the journey on his own.

The speed with which Chekov succumbed, however, made it quite probable that he had contracted the disease locally, even though they had seen no comparable illness in Stiff Tail's camp. That in turn increased the likelihood that Catchclaw could do something to help Chekov, if she could recognize the human version of the symptoms.

"Mr. Spock?" Uhura's quiet voice broke into his thoughts. "Do you think the others are alive, sir?"

"I must assume that the captain at least is unharmed, Lieutenant. From our previous experience, it would seem I maintain a mental link with him. I would judge him alive . . . yes. As for the others, I can only speculate; I must act on the assumption that they are well and have found shelter for the night as we have."

She knelt beside him. She was fashioning a new spear and, intent on fixing point to shaft, she did not look at him. But she said, "There's something you should know—about Jinx. This is her third try, her third Walk."

"That is of some special significance?"

"Yes, sir. Stiff Tail said one of her children had taken the other trail to adulthood. I asked Rushlight what she meant. He said the child committed suicide." She raised her eyes to his in an unspoken plea for his help.

"You believe Jinx might also commit suicide?" Although he knew the culture illogical in the extreme, he found the concept difficult to imagine.

"If anyone in the party has—died. Yes, I do, sir, because it would mean she had failed again. Will you speak to her?"

"To what avail is logic in such a situation?"

"Anything is worth a try." She frowned uncertainly. "I'm not thinking so much of logic but . . . you consider her an adult, don't you?"

He said, "I consider her to be quite capable of taking the responsibility for her own actions and, as she has shown by her care for Mr. Chekov, willing to accept the responsibility for others as well. It is difficult to assess the maturity of a person of another species or culture but, in my estimation, she is an adult. She is still, of course, young and inexperienced."

Uhura nodded. "I meant, Mr. Spock, that perhaps you could help her see that other worlds would find her life of value, even if her own world does not."

"I shall endeavor to do as you suggest, Lieutenant. I do not promise the result will be as you hope."

Her eyes shone in the flicker of the firelight. "Thank you, Mr. Spock." She returned to her task, as if he had somehow managed to lighten it.

An hour later, she went into their tent for a much-needed rest. Jinx took the next watch, greeting him with some surprise. "You must sleep too, Mr. Spock," she said, "you have had as tiring a day as the rest of us."

"Vulcans are capable of forgoing sleep for long periods of time without deleterious effect," he explained. "I would prefer that two remain on watch at all times."

"That's interesting," she said and added, almost wistfully, "I wish I could examine *you*. I'd like to see how different you are from the humans. . . . I have a question, maybe it's what Brightspot calls a baby question. Would you mind . . . ?"

"You may ask, Jinx. I will answer to the best of my knowledge."

"Dr. Wilson said we mustn't touch you, that it would cause you distress."

"Physical contact with another being facilitates my telepathic abilities. I find myself subjected to strong emotions; it is such raw emotion that I find disturbing."

"But you caught Mr. Chekov and Lieutenant Uhura by the river," she said, "and you carried Mr. Chekov."

"I do what I must. Had I been able to prevent the captain from diving into the river, I would have done so. You are all my responsibility."

Her ears flicked back. "But they're adults!"

He had wondered how he might open the subject with delicacy. He took the opportunity she provided. "Have you not assumed the same responsibility for us? To members of the *Enterprise* crew, I am highest in rank until such time as we rejoin the captain, yet I am quite aware that we cannot reach Sretalles safely without your guidance and your experience."

Ears back and eyes wide, she absorbed his words. When he finished, she said in a flat tone, "You speak as if I were an adult."

"So, I believe, did Catchclaw and Dr. Wilson. The legal definition of adult may vary from world to world but I have learned to rely on my own observations in matters of safety."

She was quiet for a long moment. Spock watched her but did not interrupt her thoughts. At last she turned to look at him again. "If you consider me an adult, does that mean you'll listen me?" Her urgent manner surprised him; so did the question.

He said, "Have I not done so already?"

She hesitated—nodded suddenly—and said, "Mr. Spock, we must get Mr. Chekov to Catchclaw immediately. I can't help him. Catchclaw went to Sretalles to ask the rememberers there about this AyDeeEff. Maybe she's learned something. Evan said . . . Evan said there was nothing *she* could do if Mr. Chekov had it." She caught her tail in both hands and twisted it tightly. "We can't stop to look for the captain and Brightspot and Evan," she said, "Mr. Chekov doesn't have the *time.*" She rose to her feet and turned her back to him. It was the Sivaoan expression of overwhelming emotional distress.

He said, "I had reached that same conclusion. If Mr. Chekov is to survive, we must rely on Catchclaw. Once we have escorted Mr. Chekov to Sretalles, I shall return with a search party from the *Enterprise* to find the others."

Jinx turned only her head. Fur bristling, she said, "Thank you, Mr. Spock."

"I have no wish to add to your distress," Spock said, "but there is a question I must ask before I choose such a course of action."

With visible effort, she smoothed her fur and turned to face him. "Ask it."

"What effect will this have on you, by your custom? I can scarcely credit Lieutenant Uhura's conjecture but it has been my observation that your people are indeed capable of the act of suicide." He found the word distasteful but pronounced it unhesitatingly; there was no other way to learn the information he sought.

She began to shiver, from tail tip to ear tip. "That's a baby question, isn't it?"

"Affirmative," he said.

Her eyes looked past him, into the darkened wood. "It is difficult to find companions for a third walk; for a fourth, it is not possible." It was as if she spoke of someone else, even as she went on, "You are right to say I have responsibilities to you: you can't smell slashbacks, you didn't know about grabfoots. I must see you safely to Sretalles before I take the other trail."

Spock said, "And by this you mean you will take your own life? Surely there are others who have, through no fault of their own, failed their Walk three times. Have they all taken what you call the other trail?"

"Not all. Left Ear said to tell the exceptions too. I have heard talk of people who lived out their life as children, and alone. I am not capable of that, Mr. Spock. I was lonely enough after the second failure. Had it not been for Catchclaw's acceptance, I would have chosen the other trail even then."

"Would she not still accept you?"

Jinx hesitated. "Y—yes, I think Catchclaw would—but no one else."

"I believe Brightspot would, although she shares your cultural background."

"Brightspot's dead!" There was anguish in her voice.

"That is a possibility," said Spock. "However, as the captain is not, I do not consider it a strong possibility." The words so startled her that she stopped shivering. He went on, "In any case, that is not relevant."

"Not relevant?" Her ears cupped forward, a vivid expression of her disbelief.

"My point is that there are many worlds beyond this one—worlds that would accept you and your gifts. Your knowledge of your people would be of great value to the Federation and to its scientists and its diplomats. The

Eeiauoans as well might welcome you; you are, after all, a distant relative of theirs."

She seemed to understand him, even to consider it. "But, Mr. Spock," she said sadly, "the Eeiauoans are not my people."

In many ways, he understood what she felt, although he did not share its emotional impact. He said, "Nor are humans mine, and yet I have found them capable of and deserving of great friendship and loyalty."

After a while, she said, "I—will think about what you've said, Mr. Spock."

"That is insufficient." He rose and stood, his hands on his upright spear. "You have made my decision a difficult one."

She blinked up at him, and he went on, "If we continue on to Sretalles without seeking the others, you may commit suicide even though we have reached safety. If we stop to search for the captain and his party, Mr. Chekov will surely die."

"But there's no choice, Mr. Spock. We have to get Mr. Chekov to Catchclaw—I thought you understood me!"

"I understand that you force me to choose between Mr. Chekov's life and your own."

"No, I—you're not responsible if I commit suicide, Mr. Spock!"

"By your own account, the course of action I adopt may well decide the matter, thus placing me in a position of responsibility. My own culture has no word for suicide; it is an irrational act and, as such, cannot be considered a legitimate response to our situation."

Her muscles went taut, her hind claws dug the ground. For a brief moment, he thought she might run from him, then just as suddenly her spasm of xenophobia passed. She fixed her huge round eyes on him and said, "I didn't know how different . . . no *word* for suicide!?" She blinked again. "Even when I learned about your memory, I didn't realize how different you are. I didn't, I swear in Old Tongue. Have I hurt you, Mr. Spock, by talking about—the other trail?" This time she made of the expression a euphemism.

He shook his head. "It is quite possible for me to discuss an irrational subject in rational terms. The prospect of contributing to such an act however—"

Almost to herself, she continued, "I must help you if I can." She looked up at him again and spoke more loudly, "Catchclaw would, so I must. If my life is that important to you—"

To his surprise, she turned from him and walked to the tent where, careful not to disturb Chekov, she shook Uhura awake. Uhura came, sleepy-eyed, to the fireside. "What is it, Jinx? Has something happened, Mr. Spock?"

"You must witness for me, Lieutenant Uhura," said Jinx. "Mr. Spock does not understand the Old Tongue and I must make him a pledge in it."

"All right," said Uhura. At her gesture, Spock turned off his translator, and Jinx began to speak. Uhura translated: "She says she swears she will not take the other trail to adulthood even if she fails her third walk. She says she will live out her life to its natural span, although this means she may spend that span in exile from her own people, her own world. . . ."

Jinx spoke again, and Uhura went on, "She wishes you to understand that she makes two exceptions to this: one, that she will still hazard her life to save another; and two, that she reserves the option of suicide should she contract a terminal or degenerative disease. Do you understand, Mr. Spock?"

Spock wasn't sure if the last question was Jinx's or Uhura's, but he nodded and said, "I understand. I cannot argue her exceptions."

This was translated back to Jinx, who spoke again in response. Uhura once again translated: "She says she takes this pledge for the sake of Mr. Chekov and—for you, sir—that you may be able to help Chekov without risking your own mental well-being."

Jinx walked away without a further word. She crawled into the tent, pausing only long enough to examine Chekov carefully, then she curled her body into a tight, anguished ball. Even when Uhura touched her shoulder and, in deep concern, asked if there were some way she could help, she would make no response.

Uhura returned to Spock's side. He said only, "She will

not commit suicide, Lieutenant. You yourself have heard her pledge."

"Thank you, Mr. Spock." Uhura meant the words, despite the concerned look she gave in Jinx's direction.

He shook his head: he had not given Jinx a rationale that would allow her to live despite the cultural weights against it—he had demanded of her the sacrifice of many years of loneliness. He could only hope that she would find them, contrary to her expectation, years of value and of friendship. When he focused his attention once more on Uhura, he found he too was an object of her concern. She said, softly, "I'll stand the rest of the watch with you, if I may, Mr. Spock. I would find it difficult to sleep now." This time, he nodded. He had not exaggerated to Jinx the comfort he found in the friendship and loyalty of humans.

The indicator remained dark. Scotty thumped the console with an angry fist, hoping to jar it alight, and said, "They musna be hurt. Rushlight w'ld ha' told us."

Sulu said, "Begging you pardon, sir, but I don't think hitting it will help much of anything."

"Only ma temper, Mr. Sulu."

The failure was not on board but at the source, a malfunction of the medical sensor Spock had modified, and Captain Kirk had given very strict orders that he not interfere. Scotty could beam down to their last known position but, if the landing party were not in danger, he might seriously damage their mission.

"Rushlight is calling, Mr. Scott," Azuela said, and Scotty's mood lightened as he returned to the captain's chair to accept. In the past few days, Scotty had grown fond of the voice from the planet's surface. The captain had been right, Rushlight seemed to call just to hear him speak. Scotty was flattered by this—but there was something more: in Rushlight he saw a good man to have at your side for a drink or a brawl. He had to forcibly remind himself from time to time that he was speaking to an alien who might enjoy neither.

He hoped Rushlight would have news. "Aye, Rushlight," he said, "Scotty here. Have ye enmathing t' report about the children?" Sulu's head shot up, and Scotty realized he'd fallen into Rushlight's manner of speaking of the landing party. *Wait t'l the captain hears about that!* he thought.

"Only tail-twisting, I'm afraid," came Rushlight's reply. "There's been a lot of rain up-country—the bridge is down, Scotty. I can't cross the river, and I have no way of knowing whether the children made it safely or not. It will take me six days' hard traveling to reach Sretalles by a different route and, by then, they will either have made it safely—"

"Or they won't," Scotty finished for him. Scotty didn't like it, and he had no intention of waiting six days. It meant that much longer before he could reestablish contact with the landing party at all. And, apparently, once they reached Sretalles, there was nothing to say he couldn't assist them there but his inability to make that contact. He had an idea though that just might help. "Can ye tell me, lad," he said, "is what ye're doin' moral?"

"You mean, is it right to keep an eye on the children while they Walk?"

"Aye," Scott said.

"Aye," said Rushlight back. "The children don't know we do it, but the adults expect it."

"Then ye couldna object t' a little help, could ye?"

"How can you help all the way up there? I do know you're in orbit around the planet, Scotty."

"We've the neatest little device ye'd ever hope t' see, lad. We could pick ye up an' drop ye on the other side o' the river in the wink of an eye." *That way,* he thought to himself, *you can tell me if the captain is all right, and I won't be disobeying an order.*

There was a moment's silence as Rushlight considered the offer. "The other side of the river," he repeated, "in 'the wink of an eye'? I'd like to feel that!"

"Well then," said Scotty, "if ye'll tell me the width of the river, I'll see it's done."

Rushlight said, "Width? I don't know. I could only guess."

"A wrong guess c'ld get y'r feet verra wet," Scotty said, "Can ye swim, Rushlight?"

"Not in *that,*" came the reply. If the waters had taken down the bridge, Scotty could very well see his point; he abandoned the thought of getting coordinates from the Sivaoan.

"I guess I'd better start for Sretalles," Rushlight said.

"Hold on a minute, laddie. W'ld y'r people object if I joined ye, just for a moment, t' have a look for masel'?"

"No, of course not—as long as you don't interfere with the Walk."

"Then wait right where ye are, lad. I'm on ma way. . . ." Scott was halfway across the bridge as he spoke. "Mr. Sulu, ye have command," he shot over his shoulder.

"Aye, sir. Shall I send security to meet you in the transporter room?"

Scott paused briefly. "I'll not be stayin' long enough t' need them, Mr. Sulu. Th' fewer th' tails we stick in, the better, is ma thought on the matter."

Sulu looked very startled but said, "Aye, sir."

Minutes later, Scott stood on the transporter platform. As a precaution, he set his phaser on stun, then said to Ensign Orsay, "En'rgize."

There was a brief moment of disorientation, then he found himself on the brink of a torrent—tons of water raged by, sweeping with it flood debris at dizzying speed. He took an involuntary step backward, turned and found himself face-to-face with the largest, meanest cat he'd ever seen.

He raised his phaser, and the creature countered, raising something that might well have been a weapon. Just in time, Scotty thought of Quickfoot. He said cautiously, "Rushlight? Is that ye, lad? I canna believe ye'd raise a weapon again' a man with a brogue, now."

"Scotty?" The creature was equally hesitant, but its voice was unmistakably Rushlight's. The tail reached forward, wrapped around Scotty's wrist. Scotty decided it must be the Sivaoan equivalent of a handshake and grasped the tip and squeezed it firmly.

"Aye, lad," he said. "None other." He laughed. "We probably scared each other out o' two years' growth. Here I was, thinkin' ye were a Scotsman like masel', in ma mind's eye."

"You came from nowhere!"

"I told ye it was a neat little device."

"That you did," said Rushlight and eyed him. "Scotty, I should have known you would look like the rest of your people, but except for the music in your speech you talk like a to-Vensre, and I'd pictured you the same way." His tail released Scott's arm but sprang into a spiral.

Scotty grinned. "If those 're to-Vensre whiskers ye're wearin', Rushlight, I wouldna mind a bit bein' thought o' that way."

Rushlight said, "Your Dr. Wilson envies our tails. I'm glad you appreciate fine whiskers when you see them." His long pink tongue flicked out to lick the whiskers with great pride, startling Scotty all over again.

Laughing at the way his own mind tricked him, Scotty clapped Rushlight on the shoulder and said, "We'll get along just fine. D'ye think ye're ready to try the trick y'rsel'?" He pointed across the river.

Again the tail caught his arm. "Wait, Scotty. Do you have a weapon?"

"Aye, an' I'm ashamed t' admit it—ye so startled me I raised it again' ye." He added hastily, "Wouldna ha' killed ye, lad, if that's what ye're thinkin'. Would ha' put ye t' sleep for a wee bit o' time, is all."

"That's not why I asked. I smell slashbacks." He pointed across the river. "Over there. They're big and they're dangerous and if you can really get us across safely we had better be prepared for them."

Scotty unholstered his phaser once more. "Ye're the expert . . . whatever ye say." With his other hand, he flipped open his communicator and read the two sets of coordinates to Ensign Orsay. Then to the Sivaoan he said, "Are ye ready, lad?"

Rushlight bristled a bit around the edges but replied, "Waiting won't make it easier. Let's go."

. . . They were standing on the opposite shore. Rushlight looked down at himself, caught his own tail as if to make certain it had arrived safely, licked his shoulder and said, "Well, *that's* something to sing about!"

Scotty chuckled delightedly. "If ye'll do me the kindness o' tellin' Dr. McCoy that, should ye meet him, I'd be grateful t' ye. He carries on so about usin' the transporter, ye'd think it had scrambled his mother."

Rushlight nodded. "Should I meet him," he agreed.

Then, sniffing the air suspiciously, Rushlight surveyed the edge of the river. Scott, following suit, caught sight of something too straight to be flotsam and yanked it from a tangle of reeds—a spear. He held it out to Rushlight. "Is it them? Can ye recognize it?"

"It could *only* be your children. No one had ever seen a stone point before Mr. Chekov made them." Rushlight took it from Scott to examine, then gripped the spear, spun and raised it. *"Slashback!"*

Scotty whirled and brought up his phaser in the same motion—just as something huge burst from the undergrowth. As the animal sprang at Rushlight, Scotty fired.

His first horrified thought was that he had missed—the slashback's trajectory carried it directly at Rushlight, who rammed home the spear with all his force. The impact knocked him to the ground but, to Scotty's great relief, the creature was still. Scotty rolled it off Rushlight and pulled the Sivaoan to his feet. "Are ye all ri', laddie?"

"Fine, Scotty, thanks." He poked at the limp slashback and, for the first time, Scotty got a good look at the teeth and claws of the creature. They were considerably more formidable than Rushlight's. "Male," said Rushlight, "separated from its female for sometime now, or it wouldn't have been desperate enough to attack on its own. What did you do to it, Scotty—is it dead?"

"If it's dead, it was y'r spear in the throat that did the trick. C'ld be it's only stunned."

Rushlight knelt. Grabbing the slashback by the ear, he jerked back its head to examine its throat, then he rose and pulled the spear from the wound. "If it's not dead now, it'll be dead in a minute. I got it in the jugular vein." He turned his back on the carcass as if it were an everyday occurrence to be attacked by a sabertooth. Perhaps it is, thought Scotty, and didn't like what that implied about the landing party's chances of survival, especially without their phasers.

Rushlight lifted the spear, this time to smell the shaft. "Captain Kirk's spear," he said.

"I'll take y'r word for that, lad, but why w'ld he leave his spear? I dinna like it."

While Scotty looked for other signs of the party, Rushlight

also nosed around. "Jinx has been here, but I don't smell Brightspot. I don't like it either, Scotty. I can't tell about your people, except for the captain"—he held up the spear—"because they all wear boots. They don't leave scent the way we do."

Scotty took in the remnants of the bridge, then the forest itself. He pointed to the right. "Something big crashed through there," he said. He led Rushlight to the spot. In the mud between the broken plants, he saw a single footprint that might have been Uhura's.

Rushlight sniffed the broken plants. "Mr. Chekov," he said, "Mr. Spock, Jinx, Lieutenant Uhura. Fear from Jinx. I don't recognize your people's emotions as well but Jinx was horribly afraid." He stood and stared at Scotty with terrible eyes. "They ran along the river—"

"Aye," said Scotty, "chasin' someone who had fallen in when the bridge went." *And the captain dropped his spear to go in after.*

Rushlight's tail gripped his wrist, reassuring in its curious way. "I'll follow their trail, Scotty. I'll let you know the moment I find anything more."

Scotty cocked his head, gauging his worry against the captain's wrath. The worry won: "W'ld ye mind a wee bit o' company—if it's legal, that is?"

"I don't mind," said Rushlight, "and even Stiff Tail would be grateful for your sharp eyes."

Scotty opened his communicator: "Scott here."

"Sulu here, Mr. Scott. Is everything all right?"

"I canna tell ye just yet, Mr. Sulu. I'm puttin' ye in charge while Rushlight an' I take a look."

"Is that wise, sir?" Sulu clearly did not think so.

"The captain'll not be pleased, but the captain'll not know for a while yet. I'll keep in touch, Mr. Sulu. Scott out."

Brightspot sneezed delicately, several times in succession. Evan Wilson said, "I hope head colds aren't dangerous to you, Brightspot."

"It won't kill me, if that's what you mean, Evan. I'll just wish it would." Aside from the cold, Brightspot seemed considerably better, in spirit and in body. And they had found the trail that led to Sretalles. That laid to rest two of his worries. As for the third: once again, Jim Kirk hailed Spock and got no answer. The roar of another waterfall close by might account for the lack of response—he hoped so, anyway.

Brightspot sniffed and sneezed again. "I'm sorry," she said, "I can't tell if they've been here."

She looked so apologetic that Kirk said, "Don't worry about it—neither can I. The best we can do is make for Sretalles and hope they catch us or we catch them."

"In case they're behind us," said Evan, "let's leave a note." She drew her knife, adding, "I apologize for defacing the local forest, Brightspot, but it's the best way I know to show them we've been here." Choosing a birchlike tree almost directly on the trail, she slashed a symbol and an arrow pointing to Sretalles in its bark.

"Press your hand on it," said Brightspot, "you too, Captain. Jinx can smell we've been here."

They did. Evan stood back to inspect her work, then returned to carve a *3* as well. "Jinx may be able to smell us, but Mr. Spock can't. That's to reassure the numb-noses. Don't laugh, Brightspot, you're the numbest nose of all." Brightspot sneezed again, but her tail stayed looped.

In the morning, Spock was relieved to find that Jinx had come to terms with her pledge. She behaved no differently than she had on previous days. Chekov remained her major concern, as he was Spock's.

Uhura, soothing Chekov during one of his semi-conscious periods in a very human manner, stroked his head—only to find, to her horror, that his hair fell away at her gentle touch. To her credit, she controlled herself so well that Chekov remained unaware of the condition. When Jinx examined his arms, she found the first lesions.

She motioned Spock out of Chekov's earshot and said, "He can't walk."

"Then I will carry him."

"No," said Jinx, "It would be better to build a travois, that way whoever pulls him will have her hands free to defend herself."

"Do you smell more slashbacks?"

"No, but that doesn't mean there aren't any more. They're not usually on this side of the river at all. . . ."

"A travois then," Spock agreed. The two of them cut saplings and stretched a useful over them and tied Chekov, who was once again unconscious, into it. Spock put the sash around his chest and lifted the end of the travois. He was surprised to find how little effort it required to drag behind him. Jinx was right, and she or Uhura would be able to manage Chekov in this manner, while only someone with his strength could have carried Chekov to Sretalles.

They started for the trail, Jinx leading, Uhura bringing up the rear. At times, it took all three of them to lift the travois and Chekov over or around some obstacle but, once they reached the trail, it became quite easily manageable.

They walked for some time, and the roar of a waterfall once again deafened them. This time, Spock did not check his breathing rate—the combined pressure of the sash across his chest and the amount of water vapor in the air made even normal breathing difficult.

There was no sign of Jim Kirk, Evan Wilson or Brightspot. The waterfall was a constant reminder to Spock of their possible fate.

Jinx halted and shouted above the noise of rushing water, "My turn!" Spock helped Jinx into the travois harness and took her place in the lead. As they started down the trail again, he realized that the pressure across his chest had not diminished. He attempted to slow his breathing to prevent more water vapor from entering his lungs but found he was now unable to do so. He knew then he was in danger—but there was nothing to be done. He said nothing and walked on. . . .

The party rounded a bend. On the lookout for slashbacks and like menaces, Spock almost missed it—but the stylized Vulcan IDIC leapt out at him. He stopped and pointed. "There, Jinx," he said. It was she who needed the reassurance most.

Uhura gave a little crow of triumph. "They're alive! All of them!" She pushed forward to touch her hands to the scarred tree trunk, as if she would believe her fingers even when her eyes lied.

Spock lifted the sash from Jinx's shoulders, and she put her nose to the trunk of the tree. Her tail looped up in happiness. "All three!" she shouted, "All three!"

She knelt to rouse Chekov—she seemed to feel it important that he know as well—but to no avail. Her tail straightened. Without another word, she stepped back and lifted the travois. "Let's *move!*" she shouted. "They're not far ahead of us—the smell can't be more than an hour old." They quickened their pace.

The noise of the falls was beginning to subside. Jim Kirk was sure his ears would take an hour to recover from the assault, until he heard a noise on the trail behind him. Brightspot spun around and unsheathed her claws. "Slashbacks?" he asked, bringing up his spear.

"Can't smell; can't tell," said Brightspot, then sharply, "Listen!"

The three did, tensing for whatever followed them.

Brightspot suddenly relaxed and, curling her tail with delight, said, "It's Lieutenant Uhura!" A moment later, he heard Uhura's shout too.

He shouted back, "We're here, Uhura! We're coming!" and the three of them raced back the way they had come.

He did not stop until he was face-to-face with Spock. "Spock," he said, "you're a sight for sore eyes!"

"I fail to understand, Captain, what bearing my presence could possibly have on the condition of your vision . . . but I am pleased to see you."

Kirk laughed with relief. Spock, at least, was his usual imperturbable self. . . .

Chekov was not. The ensign lay on the ground on a stretcherlike affair; Wilson knelt beside him, fingers on his wrist, her face grave. Chekov's appearance was shocking— huge patches of hair gone, lesions on his face and hands— even Kirk knew ADF syndrome at this late stage. Not wishing to agitate Chekov, Kirk gave no sign he was disturbed. "Well, Mr. Chekov," he said.

"Keptain," said Chekov weakly, "I'm gled to see you, sair. Is Brightspot all right?"

"Aside from the worst cold you've ever seen, she's fine. How are you?"

"Not good, Keptain, but I hev meneged to get a free ride."

The joke was feeble, but Kirk smiled and said, "I see you haven't lost your power over females—of either species."

Chekov gave him a wan smile in return, then he said, "Sair?" Kirk had to bend close to hear his words. "If Ketchclaw ken't . . . I wanted to say, sair . . . it's been en honor working with you, sair."

Kirk laid a hand on his shoulder. "I'll have none of that, mister. I intend to have your expert services for a long time—and your friendship, as well." But Chekov did not hear him; Chekov was unconscious.

"How often?" Wilson asked sharply, looking up at Jinx.

"More often unconscious than conscious now," said Jinx. "If that's AyDeeEff, Evan, I don't recognize it. Catchclaw went to Sretalles to find a rememberer, someone who collects old information no one is interested in anymore. She hoped maybe one of them would know something. That's why we didn't come looking for you; we had to get Mr. Chekov to Sretalles as fast as we could."

"Right," said Evan Wilson. "Let's go then."

Jim Kirk traded Brightspot's pack for the travois. They could no longer husband their strength. They hastened down the trail as if pursued by demons.

They took no stops to rest that day and only slowed to forage for fruits and berries to keep them going. Chekov had two more conscious periods. Wilson followed behind his travois at a brisk trot and kept up a reassuring line of patter. Jim Kirk hoped Chekov believed her; Jim Kirk didn't.

Spock paced him and said, "Captain, we must make camp for the night. We cannot traverse terrain of this nature without light."

"I know, Spock, but let's get as far as we can and worry about putting up shelters after dark." Spock nodded agreement, coughed slightly and suppressed a second cough.

Catching Brightspot's cold, Kirk thought and knew it would not slow the Vulcan any more than it did Brightspot. He glanced at the others and considered his own condition. They would all need rest soon. He hoped Chekov could last another half day of travel. He hoped Catchclaw would be able to help.

Night fell and forced the party to a halt. He and Spock built up a fire, while Wilson and the Sivaoans raised a shelter. Uhura sat with Chekov's head in her lap. She stroked his forehead and sang softly, as much to ease her own pain as his.

Brightspot roasted strips of slashback meat over the fire and they ate wearily.

Chekov could not be roused. Once again, Evan Wilson examined the lesions on his arms, then she dropped heavily to her knees beside Kirk. *Exhaustion*, he thought, seeing her taut face in the firelight. "Get some sleep, Evan. Mr. Spock and I will take the first watch."

In a voice almost too low to hear, she said, "I can't do anything for him, Captain. It shouldn't be happening this fast. It shouldn't be happening at all! 'Not a word can be omitted from a song,'"—Kirk could hear the quotation marks—"but they did, damn them for it. For all their perfect memories, they changed the one thing . . ." She finished with a glare at Brightspot.

Brightspot's tail wrapped around Evan's wrist. "Lieutenant Uhura improved *your* song," she said, "You didn't get angry about that."

"Improved my song," said Evan absently. She laid her hand over Brightspot's tail tip.

"The baby in the treetop," Brightspot explained. She nodded at Uhura. *"Rockabye Baby,"* thought Kirk—the lullabye Uhura had just sung to Chekov. Evan Wilson frowned slightly at Brightspot. "She doesn't sing it that differently, Brightspot. I'd hardly call it 'improving' as in what Distant Smoke did with Chekov's shelter design."

Jinx said, "Brightspot is deaf." At least, that was how it was rendered by the universal translator.

Uhura explained, "The Sivaoan word doesn't quite translate, Evan. She means Brightspot has a hearing defect, or what the Sivaoans consider a hearing defect—she doesn't have perfect pitch."

"The others," Evan began, jerking the point of her chin at Jinx.

And Spock said, "To have a specific term for the lack of the trait would be indicative of its rarity."

"Yes," Uhura confirmed, "all the others have perfect pitch."

"Perfect pitch and perfect memories," said Evan, staring at Spock; then she jerked her head back to look at Uhura. "Nyota, you have perfect pitch too, don't you?" Still stroking Chekov's forehead, Uhura nodded.

Evan Wilson shivered and drew in on herself as abruptly as dry leaves crumpled in the fire. Troubled by this, Jim Kirk said, "Evan—?" but she silenced him with an urgent wave of her hand. Kirk exchanged concerned glances with Spock.

Just as suddenly, Evan looked up at Spock. "Perfect pitch and perfect memories," she said slowly, "and nothing changes."

"That is not possible, Dr. Wilson. Life itself depends upon change."

"Indeed, Mr. Spock." She held his eyes. "But what if they don't recognize the change?" She swung on Uhura. "Nyota, when you sang the teaching song for Catchclaw and Jinx, you sang it in the same key you learned it in, didn't you."

But she did not need Uhura's nodded confirmation. Jinx said, "You wouldn't improve anything that important!"

"You would if the disease changed its characteristics," Wilson shot back. She rose and moved to kneel beside Uhura. "I remember seeing an interview with a composer who had perfect pitch. He said he enjoyed hearing a new arrangement of one of his songs because, in a different key, it sounded completely new to him—like a new song. *Is that true?*"

Uhura frowned up at her. "To a certain extent," she admitted, "but, Evan, it's still the same song—" Suddenly her hand shot out, caught Evan's wrist. "Possible," she said, "It's possible."

"Then make Jinx hear the possibility," said Evan.

Uhura turned to the Sivaoan and said, "Jinx, listen carefully. On my world, there are many ways to sing the same song. All variations of an essential tune. I'm going to sing the teaching song about the Long Death as many ways as I can. I want you to tell me if you've heard any version of it before."

"Perfect pitch, perfect memories," said Evan again. "Even the words may be different; just the tune, Nyota."

Uhura began in a wavering voice but soon sang with something close to her usual power: the same four lines, each time in a different key, now fast, now slow. Kirk watched and saw before him something like an ancient shamanist ritual: three healers intent on saving Chekov's life.

Jinx's ears quivered forward, never once flicking away as they normally did to catch sounds from all sides. Her great copper eyes never blinked. When Uhura was done, Jinx was silent for a moment; then she said, "Yes, I understand. To you,"—she sang the opening notes of Uhura's song—"and" —she sang the same notes in a higher key—"are the same."

Wilson, never taking her eyes from Jinx, said nothing. Taking their cue from her, the rest kept still. At last Jinx said, "I don't know. It seems silly to think—" She stopped, began again, "I don't know if it means anything—it's so unlikely. The words are different, but it's the same tune, I think, what you mean by the same tune."

"Sing it," said Wilson.

Seeming almost embarrassed, Jinx did. Even Jim Kirk, unfamiliar with Sivaoan music, could hear that what she sang was a variation of Uhura's song. This version was bright, almost cheerful; the verse fast-paced, the chorus leisurely.

If Jim Kirk had expected a revelation, he was greatly disappointed, and he understood Jinx's embarrassment: the song spoke only of a children's disease, neither dangerous nor remotely related to ADF syndrome. The symptoms described were completely unrelated to Chekov's loss of hair, lesions, intermittent coma—these symptoms were so innocuous, in fact, that the only treatment prescribed was to let the child set its own pace and sleep whenever it tired.

Evan Wilson's face showed her own deep disappointment, and Jinx turned away, twisting her tail over the failure. "I can't think of any other songs like Uhura's," she said.

"No treatment for it," said Wilson flatly.

Jinx turned back, surprised. "For that?" she said. "There's a treatment—it can be dangerous if an adult gets it. But most people get it as a child and then don't get it again ever." *Like measles,* Jim Kirk thought. "It doesn't help, does it," Jinx went on. "I've seen an adult who had it. It's nothing like AyDeeEff."

"The *tunes* are the same," Evan Wilson said. "Mr. Spock?"

"As you yourself pointed out, Dr. Wilson, the symptoms of a disease may vary in an extreme—even unrecognizable fashion—from population to population."

"Yes." Wilson turned back and said, "Jinx, did anyone in Stiff Tail's camp have the disease *your* song describes?"

"Grabfoot had Noisy-Baby," said Jinx, without hesitation, "and the other three were probably coming down with it. Evan, does that mean something?"

Evan Wilson took a deep breath. Ignoring Jinx's question, she said instead, "Jinx, can Catchclaw treat an adult with . . . Noisy-Baby?"

"Of course," said Jinx, "so can I."

A sound came from Wilson's throat that might have been a sob, but when she spoke, the words came out flat, toneless: "What would you need to treat it."

Jinx stared at her, wide-eyed, then swung around to point into the undergrowth. "That plant there," she said.

"Do it," said Wilson in the same flat voice.

Jinx's fur spiked. "You mean you want me to treat Mr. Chekov for Noisy-Baby? Evan, that's crazy! Even if—I can't! I'd have to get the medicine into his bloodstream and I haven't the tools to refine it to a safe consistency and I haven't a needle and—Noisy-Baby?!"

"Make your potion," said Wilson sharply. "Don't worry about the lumps. Spock, Brightspot, I'll need a hollow reed, or anything like it, about six inches long and narrow." Spock and Brightspot scattered to obey, and Wilson glared again at Jinx, who darted into the undergrowth and began stripping foliage from the plant she had pointed to only moments earlier.

The realization of what she was proposing to do brought Kirk to his feet. Shocked, he advanced on her angrily. "No, Evan!"

"Shut up, Captain," she said. "This is my patient's life we're talking about."

"That's what I mean, *Doctor* Wilson. You could kill him." Kirk stared down at her but saw Chekov—his lesions were visibly worse. When he pulled his eyes away to look at Wilson, he saw the truth of the matter in her face. Through their entire discussion Evan Wilson, fingers curled around Chekov's wrist, had been monitoring his pulse. *Second-stage coma. He's dying now. He won't make it to Sretalles,* Kirk thought; he did not have to hear the words from Evan Wilson. *It may be a totally different disease, or the treatment may kill a human, or Chekov may be too far gone for treatment—but Jinx is his only hope.*

He said, in as calm a voice as he could muster, "Yes, Jinx. Please do as Evan says. And please—hurry," and he saw with gratitude that Jinx had not awaited his order.

Chapter Sixteen

While Rushlight followed his nose further up the incline, Scotty stooped to examine the body of the slashback. The more he saw of the creatures, the less he liked them. To kill one with nothing more than a stone-tipped spear—!

"They butchered the one up here, Scotty. They've got food, at least." Scotty rose and climbed to join the Sivaoan and found him wrinkling his nose at a rift in the jutting rock.

"Ye're sure they're still alive, Rushlight?"

"Yes, there are fresh scents for all four—but I think Mr. Chekov is ill."

Scotty said, "Ill? Ye mean, sick and not injured?"

"It's hard to tell. As I keep saying, I don't know your range of smells. But I don't smell blood."

Scotty eyed his back suspiciously. "How d'ye know that one?"

"Your Evan Wilson bled when Fetchstorm clawed her." He returned to Scotty's side and jabbed his tail tip upward twice. "This way."

Scotty followed, saying, "Who's this Fetchstorm? An' why w'ld he claw the lass?" Rushlight's tail curled. Scotty, who had quickly learned the significance of the gesture, demanded, "What's sae funny?"

"Fetchstorm is a young troublemaker, who made the mistake of assuming that someone without teeth or claws to speak of would be an easy mark. So he took on Evan Wilson, and I got a fight to sing of."

"Aye, I see it now. Did she have her staff?"

"Staff? No—she bit his ear." The tail coiled tighter.

"The lass is full o' surprises," said Scotty. He hoped his words were still true, as he thought again of the raging river. *Aye, an' I hope she bit its ear too. An' that th' captain showed it a trick or two o' his own.*

"Get some sleep, Uhura," Jim Kirk said gently. "Evan and I will stand the first watch." He nodded at Chekov to tell her that he meant to watch the ensign as well. "We have a lot of hard traveling to do tomorrow. Brightspot, Jinx—"

Jinx said, "He's my patient."

Kirk glanced at Evan Wilson, who nodded and said, "Let her, Captain. She's right." Without releasing his wrist, Evan raised Chekov's head from Uhura's lap and eased it into her own.

Uhura rose and stretched stiff muscles and said, "You *will* wake me, Evan . . . ?"

"I will, if there's any change."

"You too, Mr. Spock," said Kirk. "That's an order." For once, Spock gave him no argument.

Kirk threw more wood on the fire. Now that the rest of them had retired for the night, there was nothing for him to do but watch the woods and listen for any sound of slashbacks. From what Spock had told him, Jinx's nose was a better indicator of their presence than any of his own senses, but he did not wish to rely on it, and he needed something constructive to do.

"Evan," he said at last, softly so as not to disturb any of the sleepers, "you're going to need sleep as well. Can't you and Jinx take turns monitoring . . . ?"

She shook her head. "Can't, Captain; either of us," she said.

He understood. He resumed his patrol, pacing the perimeter of the campsite. Better that than inquire into Chekov's condition every five minutes. That, he knew, would do no good. Minutes seemed like hours. After several subjective years, Evan Wilson motioned him back.

"His pulse is improving," she said quietly. Kirk gestured at the shelter where the rest lay sleeping. "Should I—?"

"Don't wake them yet. I want something more." And as she said it, Chekov stirred. Jinx quivered all over, whiskers and ears cocked hopefully. "Talk to him, Captain," said Wilson.

"Mr. Chekov—Ensign—can you hear me? It's Captain Kirk." Jim Kirk caught Chekov's wrist and Wilson's encircling fingers in one fierce grip. "Pavel?"

Chekov's eyelids fluttered. "Keptain? Where—em I, sair?"

Relief washed over him. "In a most enviable position, Mr. Chekov," he said, "with your head in Dr. Wilson's lap."

Wilson gave a delighted laugh. "Don't let him pull your tail, Pavel," she said—and as he attempted to push himself up on one elbow—"Don't you move, you need the rest. Do you think you could eat something?"

"Bozhe moi," he said, a look of real surprise on his drawn face. "I could eat a horse!"

Jinx ran to get the slashback meat they had put aside for him, and Kirk said, "No horse, Mr. Chekov, but I'm afraid you'll find slashback has the same consistency."

"I don't mind, Keptain," he said, and true to his word he ate voraciously. After a few moments, however, he tired.

"Save the rest, Captain. You'll eat more later, Pavel," said Wilson. "Now I want you to sleep."

Chekov nodded with effort. "Dr. Wilson? Is it—do I hev ADF syndrome, Dr. Wilson?"

"No, Mr. Chekov," said Wilson. "All you've got is a nasty case of Noisy-Baby that you caught from little Grabfoot. Nothing at all to worry about." She smiled down at him. He smiled back, reassured; and, still smiling, he closed his eyes and went to sleep.

"Jinx," said Wilson quietly, "wake Uhura and the rest just long enough to tell them—" She did not need to finish the sentence; Jinx darted off with an excited parting whip of her long gray tail.

Jim Kirk glanced down and discovered that he still clamped Wilson's fingers to Chekov's wrist. He opened his hand, drew it back. When he met her eyes again, he saw they brimmed with tears. "Is it a cure, Evan?" he said, and his own voice sounded husky.

"Ask me again tomorrow, Captain, or next week." With her freed hand, she caught the corner of a useful to scrub the tears from her cheeks. Her other arm crooked around Chekov, fiercely protective. She finished, "But he came out of a second-stage coma—and he's *alive.*"

Then she made a small angry noise of frustration—as she had pointed out only a day ago, Sivaoan fabric wouldn't absorb water worth a damn. Acting purely on impulse, Jim Kirk reached out, took her chin in his hand and gently wiped away the tears with his palm. Something of a liberty, he realized, a moment too late, but she brought forth the ghost of a smile. "Thank you, Jim," she said.

"Thank *you*, Evan."

Evan Wilson woke to Jinx's light touch on her shoulder. She stretched, waved a hello to Brightspot who sneezed one back and leaned over to examine Chekov. "Pulse good," she said, "and the lesions have dried! Jinx, they're healing over! Does he need a further dose of your potion?"

"If it really is Noisy-Baby, no—one is enough. But we don't know it is, Evan, and humans react so differently. . . ."

"We'll go by standard treatment," Wilson said and caught her tail as it twitched past. "Jinx, it's working! Why so angry?"

"It's the thought that so many people, the Eeiauoans and the other humans you told us about, could die from a children's disease! How is that possible?"

"Diseases and people adapt to each other. Any time a disease hits a group that hasn't been weeded by that disease over time it will hit hard. On Earth, the world Chekov grew up on, there are two large continents, with humans on both. For thousands of years, they had no contact with each other. When they finally did meet again, what one population considered a minor childhood disease could be fatal to the other." Evan laid a hand on Chekov's forehead. "In fact," she went on, "you're almost sure to find the same problem when your people get together with the Eeiauoans again. The recurrence of diseases in old unfamiliar forms is something you—and every other doctor—will have to keep in mind."

"We will," said Jinx. "I'll tell Catchclaw, too." Her ears flicked suddenly back. "You think I'm a doctor!"

Brightspot too flicked back her ears at Evan. Their combined amazement startled Evan Wilson. "You . . ." she began and spread her hand above Chekov to finish the thought.

"Evan, I've been apprenticed to Catchclaw for years. I know all her techniques. But I can't be a doctor until I'm an adult."

"Nonsense," said Evan Wilson. "You know what you have to do and you do it. You're considerably more adult than Stiff Tail. Begging your pardon, Brightspot. Correct me if I'm wrong—but Stiff Tail ruled us children so she wouldn't have to think about the Eeiauoans, didn't she?"

Brightspot sneezed, nodded, sneezed again and looked abjectly miserable, whether from the cold or from Evan's remarks about her mother, Evan couldn't tell.

"So who's more adult—somebody who works like mad to avoid a problem or somebody who works like mad to solve it?"

The two Sivaoans looked at each other. For a moment, neither spoke, then Jinx said, "I think you're right, Evan." And Brightspot nodded agreement.

"I think I owe Mr. Spock an apology, too." Jinx glanced again at Brightspot, hesitated, then said, "Brightspot, Vulcans don't have a word for suicide." Brightspot's ears shot back; she stared at Evan, who nodded confirmation of the fact, wondering where it lead.

Watching Brightspot anxiously, Jinx went on, "He said he wouldn't trade my life for Mr. Chekov's. He made me swear in Old Tongue I wouldn't take the other trail to adulthood even if we failed this third time. Brightspot, it was the only way I could get him to take Mr. Chekov straight to Catchclaw."

Fur rose in spikes at the nape of Brightspot's neck, and Evan felt the hair at the back of her own neck rise. Though the reactions might be similar, the causes were not. Spock had solved Evan's problem before she learned of it, but only Brightspot could solve Jinx's. She waited and watched, hoping to see a way to help.

Brightspot broke the uncomfortable silence with a severe fit of sneezes. When she finished, Jinx said, "Would you like something for that, Brightspot, or would you rather suffer?"

She's decided she is *a doctor,* thought Evan, and her respect for the Sivaoan doubled. Brightspot accused, "You sound just like Catchclaw."

"I'll take that as a compliment, and I'll tell her you said so," Jinx countered. "Have you decided?"

"Yes," said Brightspot, "I have. I'm glad Mr. Spock made you swear. You're my friend, Jinx, and I won't lose you. If you don't make it, I don't make it either; and I'll go with you as many times as it takes." She curled her tail around Jinx's waist. "Or be your friend even if you decide not to go again. Evan can be an adult without having Walked, so why can't you?" The lift of her chin was the ultimate defiance of all her customs.

Jinx wrapped her tail tightly about Brightspot. "Thank you," she said. "Thank you *both.*" Evan could scarcely contain her pride in the two of them, but the best of it was that neither needed her approval. She contented herself with a fierce grin.

Then something odd stirred in her memory. She frowned, trying to track down the source of the unease. At last she found it, not in her own memory, but in Spock's. The two Sivaoans exchanged worried glances. Evan shook her head. "Not you two. Jinx, thank Mr. Spock too. He knew what kind of a sacrifice he was asking of you. It could not have been easy for him."

"He didn't—" Jinx stopped abruptly. "He *can't* show how he feels; Uhura said so. When you were all lost, she said he hurt, even though he didn't show anything."

Evan nodded. "And I'm sure he hurt for you too. Of all of us, he most understands what it's like to be alone, the kind of alone he asked you to be."

"What do you mean?"

Evan steepled her fingers, unconsciously imitating Spock as

she explained, "It's best to treat Spock as Vulcan because that is how he wishes to be treated—and thought of. He was raised on Vulcan, to Vulcan culture and tradition. But the whole truth is that Mr. Spock is half-Vulcan, half-human: his human half is alien to the Vulcans he grew up with, his Vulcan half alien to the humans with whom he lives and works. There *are* no other people like Mr. Spock, and I'd guess the captain and Uhura and Chekov are the only real friends he has."

Brightspot said, "And us, Evan."

She shook her head, but softened the gesture with words. "Perhaps, Brightspot, but that takes a lot of time. The rewards, I suspect, are infinite, but—time. That's the one thing some of us won't have." It was herself she thought of; she shook her head. "Well," she said, "Jinx, you'd better get some sleep now."

"Let me fix Brightspot something first—if I don't, her sneezing will keep me awake all night."

Brightspot said, "Don't pull my tail, Jinx," and simultaneously looped her tail invitingly into range. Jinx looped her own tail at the joke, licked Brightspot's cheek once, then she walked away to forage for herbs. Soon she was preparing another of her potions.

Evan was still thinking of Spock, when Jinx said, "It must be difficult to treat Mr. Spock when he's ill."

"You're right. The combination of human and Vulcan makes it tricky. You should hear Dr. McCoy on the subject: you'd think Mr. Spock's physiology was devised simply to torment him."

"Do you know why his breathing has changed?"

"Spock's? He's got control of functions in his body that are strictly involuntary in the average human. He slowed his rate of breathing to keep all that water vapor from the falls out of his lungs."

"Not slowed," said Jinx. She glanced up from her task and her ears flicked back. "You can't hear the difference?"

"Tell me," said Evan, keeping her voice as level as possible.

"It's not the same as it was back in camp, which I took to be

306

normal." She waited for Evan's nod, then went on, "Now it sounds as if he's working hard just to breathe. Short. Fast. Shallow." Evan rose from Chekov's side, and Jinx finished sharply, "Evan, what is it?"

Evan Wilson expelled a deep breath and sat down again. "Damn you, Mr. Spock," she said, just as a general comment. "And damn me, for paying all my attention to Chekov. Have you heard him cough, Jinx, Brightspot?"

It was Brightspot who nodded. "I thought he was catching my cold. . . ." She paused to accept the finished preparation from Jinx and down it with a grimace that showed most of her teeth. "Is he sick, Evan? Can you do something for him?"

"Not here," Evan said angrily. "Not *here*. I've got to get him back to the *Enterprise*. He needs rest and he needs antibiotics—and I'm not equipped to whip something up out of local herbs."

"He's not going to get much rest either. It's still a full day's travel to Sretalles," said Jinx.

He knows what he's got and he knows I can only treat it back on board, Evan thought. *He also thinks he can make it to Sretalles on his feet. But he won't chance telling the captain, for fear the captain will send us on ahead to bring back help, when, to cover all the bases, we've got to walk into Sretalles as adults—so I can talk to their doctors, so Jinx hasn't failed.* The logic was impeccable but, if Spock had misjudged, logic might be the death of him.

"Yes," Evan said and nodded grimly. "We'll have to play this by ear." The image only bewildered the two Sivaoans, so she said, "As long as Brightspot's okay and Chekov continues to improve, we travel slowly, with frequent stops for rest for Chekov's sake."

"But—Mr. Spock?"

"If he'd wanted us to know he was sick, he'd have told us. If we stop for his sake, we might just get an argument," Evan said. "I'll stand his watch tonight; he needs the sleep more than I do. Besides—I don't weigh much at all—if *I* pass out from exhaustion, you two can drag me into Sretalles by the hair."

The two Sivaoans agreed. Jinx settled down to rest, and

Brightspot resumed patrol, her tail still curled, apparently, over the idea of dragging Evan by the hair.

Captain Kirk, however, was anything but amused when Evan waked him in the morning. "I thought," he said, "that you and Mr. Spock were even."

Evan shrugged. "Now we are," she said. He scowled, but that was not an expression the captain was skilled at, and Evan felt neither chastised nor repentant. While he woke the others, she concerned herself with Chekov.

In the early gray light, she could see that the lesions were indeed beginning to heal. Fragile scar tissue covered all but the deepest, and even those had begun to dry. When she tapped him lightly on the cheek, he stirred and opened his eyes. "Morning?" he said, his voice still weak.

She chose to take the question as a greeting. "Good morning to you, Mr. Chekov. Very nice to have you with us again." She leveled a forefinger at him. "And don't you dare get up."

"But, sair!" he protested.

Grinning, she countered, "You may get away with murder by rolling those gorgeous eyes at Dr. McCoy, but it won't work on me—I know all the tricks."

"Indeed, Mr. Chekov, I believe Dr. Wilson to be quite accurate on that account." It was Spock, and Evan Wilson looked up to find herself subject to the full strength of his scrutiny. "You did not wake me for my watch, Doctor." He merely stated this as fact, but Evan knew an accusation when she heard one. She felt the color rise in her cheeks.

"As you did not wake me for mine, Mr. Spock," she said.

The long lines of his face took on a thoughtful expression, then he turned his attention to Chekov. "Your appearance would suggest that you are in the process of recovery. How do you feel?"

"A little shaky, sair, but I could walk, I think . . . only Dr. Wilson won't let me up."

"Mr. Chekov," said Spock, "it has been my observation that it is best to obey the orders of those who outrank you—particularly those in the medical branch of the service."

"But, Mr. Spock—you and Dr. McCoy, sair—" Chekov began.

Spock cut him short. "Dr. McCoy is not known for his skill with a quarterstaff."

Kirk had been close enough to overhear the exchange. He laughed and, kneeling to take Chekov's hand, said, "Mr. Spock has a valid point. Welcome back, Mr. Chekov—but you ride the rest of the way to Sretalles."

And ride he did. *"Chort vozmi!"* he said once through his teeth. Each rough patch of ground they dragged him over made him wince, and the abrasion reopened many of his lesions. Evan could see how painful it was for him—but aside from the incidental Russian curse his only complaint was that she would not let him walk.

The frequent halts for rest drew complaints from Captain Kirk. She understood his impatience this close to their objective, it was difficult to slow instead of speed. She shared his frustration—but she kept close to Spock and now she could hear his labored breathing. There were no reasonable options. She had to get him back to the *Enterprise* but she could not risk exhausting him. Spock coughed covertly. She did not glance in his direction. "Okay, Captain," she called ahead, "time for a break. I want to feed my patient."

"Evan, can't that wait the two or three hours until we reach Sretalles?" His voice was almost pleading.

"No, it can't," she said and shot Chekov a look that caused him to close his mouth in mid-protest.

At the next small clearing in the wood, they paused. While Jinx raised Chekov's shoulders and fed him berries, Evan examined the reopened lesions. "Still look good, Jinx," she said. "The ones that aren't being abraded are definitely healing. Is there anything we can do to pad this a little?"

"Stuff it with silver moss," said Jinx. "It's absorbent, and it's as clean as anything we've got."

Kirk paced the clearing as they worked, impatient at the time it took for them to do the job properly. When they had at last finished, Evan rose to tell him they could be on their way—and found him staring down at the seated Spock. From his shocked manner, she knew he had just taken a good close look at his friend. "Mr. Spock?" he said. "You look terrible!"

"I assure you, Captain," said Spock, "that my appearance does not differ from yours to any significant degree."

Kirk glanced down at his own rumpled, muddied clothing and at his scratched, bruised hands. "Point taken, Spock," he said ruefully. And Evan Wilson thought, *Bravo, Mr. Spock, you do that like a master! Never lie when misdirection is enough.*

"Slashbacks!" said Jinx. She pointed back the way they had come. "Smell them, Brightspot?" Brightspot shook her head and tapped her nose. She no longer had a spear and drew in behind Jinx and Evan. Spock and Kirk instantly moved to join the protective circle around Brightspot and Chekov. "Three," said Jinx, "or as many as five."

"How far away?" Kirk asked.

"Could be as far back as the last place we stopped, Captain—slashbacks smell *strong*. Stop talking and use your ears."

Hearing nothing, Evan Wilson raised her staff against the very silence.

The captain was alive! The Vulcan IDIC slashed on the tree had done more to convince Scotty of that than Rushlight's assurances that the entire party was now accounted for—by smell. Scotty was anxious to confirm this with his own eyes, especially since Rushlight held to the opinion that Chekov was ill.

Having seen the lay of the land—and the teeth on the slashbacks—he wondered how the party could safely sleep at night. Scotty hadn't tried it himself. At Rushlight's insistence, he'd returned to the *Enterprise* for the night; he'd slept in his familiar bunk while Rushlight spent the night in a tree.

"Freeze, Scotty," said Rushlight. Scotty froze, his phaser raised and ready. Rushlight took two noiseless steps down the trail and sniffed. "More slashbacks," he said in a whisper. "We're still upwind; they don't know we're here yet."

"D'ye suppose they're after the children?"

Rushlight nodded. "There are a lot of them—the rains must have flooded them out of their usual territory. Too many for the children to handle. If we can get close enough, we can even out the odds a little without ever letting on."

"I'm in favor o' that, laddie! Lead the way."

Rushlight veered from the trail into the undergrowth toward the river. The big Sivaoan's silent grace made Scotty feel both clumsy and noisy but, when it came to looking after the captain and the rest, he was game for anything.

A moment later, he regretted his choice of words. "Be ready," said Rushlight, "they've heard us." Despite the warning, the attack came as a surprise.

The undergrowth before them split apart. Scotty saw only the long deadly teeth. He fired his phaser at the leading slashback, fired at the second before the first had time to crumple, with a flash of bright blue light and a crackle like a bolt of lightning. Rushlight dropped two others. Then he and Scotty waited, not daring to relax.

Jim Kirk remembered the details of Spock's encounter with the slashbacks and came to the conclusion that slashbacks might well be frightened away if something as unfamiliar as a human made a direct, unhesitating attack on them. Evan Wilson must have had the same thought. At the silent appearance of the slashbacks on the trail, he and Wilson, with almost identical war whoops, charged the creatures. Startled and fearful, the creatures froze in their tracks.

Evan Wilson was the closer. With a second howl, she rammed her quarterstaff into the female's face. As it jumped back, shrieking its pain, she swung at the male, clipping it along the side of the jaw.

The impact flung it toward him, and Jim Kirk caught it in the throat with his spear. As he fought to keep a grip on his spear through the twisting leaps of the creature, Brightspot yelled, "Up and in, Captain." Kirk braced, pushed and levered up; there was the nauseating sound and feel of something tearing. The creature gave a cough and began to spasm back and forth. The spear ripped from his grasp. Expecting the creature to renew its attack, he reached for his knife. "It's dead," said Brightspot. "Help Evan."

The female had maneuvered Evan around, cutting her off from the rest of the party. Spock moved in to attack it from the rear, but Evan snapped something at him in Vulcan and he stopped; and it was Spock's iron grip on his arm that held

Kirk from intervening. "Do not obstruct her weapon," Spock said. "Keep watch for others."

Kirk did, though his eyes kept straying back to Evan. She never took her eyes from the circling creature. She feinted with the end of her staff; as the slashback raised its claws to snatch the staff, she whipped the staff around and brought the other end down on its head with a resounding crack.

The creature fell back on its haunches and shook its head. Before it could rise, Evan Wilson swung her staff again and struck it three times in rapid succession. It fell. She dropped the staff across the side of its head and knelt, throwing her weight onto the canted staff to pin the creature, and drew her knife. She reached for its throat—and hesitated.

"If you don't kill it, Evan," Jinx said in a clear voice, "it will come after us when it recovers. The captain killed its mate." Evan plunged the knife into the creature's throat. She remained kneeling while the slashback spurted its life onto the mossy verge of the trail, then she rose, staff in hand.

"More coming?" she asked.

Kirk looked at Jinx to see her answer as well. Jinx shook her head. "Two of them ran away—you scared them, I could smell it! I think there are some others back along the trail, but they must have found some other prey. I think it's safe to move on now."

That sounded good to Kirk. "All right, people," he said, "Let's move on." He gestured Spock to the travois. Grim-faced, Evan Wilson raised her staff; the end brushed Spock's chest without actually touching him.

"My turn, Captain," she said, not taking her eyes from Spock. "If I don't work off the rest of this adrenalin, I won't be able to see straight."

In following the glare she gave his science officer, Jim Kirk saw that Spock's words had been falsely reassuring. *He is sick!* "All right, Evan," he said, as if humoring her. He waved Spock away and bent to help Evan adjust the sash of the travois comfortably around her. His lips close to her ear, he said, "Evan, Spock—"

"Shut up, Captain," she snapped. Her voice was audible only to him, but the impact stunned him.

I hope you know what you're doing, Dr. Wilson, he thought. Aloud, he said, "I'll take the next turn, Evan. Let me know when that adrenalin runs out." Some of the tension drained from her face. She nodded, and he laid his hand lightly on her shoulder. She started down the trail, dragging the travois behind her. Kirk motioned Spock to follow; he wanted Spock where he could keep an eye on him.

Two more slashbacks burst from the bush. This time, Scotty and Rushlight made short work of them. Even before Scotty could catch his breath, Rushlight said, "I don't smell any more. I guess that's all of them."

"Then let's see t' the children," Scotty said. He grew more anxious about the landing party with each glance at the unconscious slashbacks.

"Let's take care of these, first," said Rushlight. He drew his knife and knelt by the nearest, "You said your weapon only stunned them?"

"Aye—Rushlight, wait! Are ye goin' t' kill them?"

Rushlight said, "Of course."

Scotty caught his arm, mildly surprised at the feel of soft fur over hard muscle. "If ye don't need them, I know a lad in Biology who'd dearly love t' have a close look at the beasties. I can beam them up t' him, if ye'll let me."

"Scotty, you can't have a thing like that running around loose on your ship."

"I didna say anything about loose," Scotty assured him. He pulled out his communicator and, making sure Security stood by for safety's sake, had Ensign Orsay beam up the stunned slashbacks. It took no more than a moment's time.

"All caged and carted off, Mr. Scott. No problems," said Ensign Orsay from the communicator, "Dr. Irizarry wants to know what they eat, sir."

"People," said Rushlight, speaking directly into the communicator.

Scotty said, "I wouldna recommend Dr. Irizarry feed the rest o' the staff to the creatures now. Tell the lad they eat meat, an' they like t' catch their own. I wouldna want t' spoil the fun he'll have learnin' about them."

"I'll tell him, Mr. Scott," said Orsay. "Orsay, out."

"Scott, out," he confirmed and, snapping closed the communicator, he gave a nod to Rushlight. The two of them started down the trail again.

Just half an hour later, they found the bodies of two more slashbacks. To Scotty's great relief, there was no sign that any harm had come to the children. Rushlight gave the area a thorough nosing to confirm this, the curl of his tail reassuring Scotty even before he spoke. *"All* safe," he announced, "and Mr. Chekov is better. Now we have to hurry, Scotty, if we're to be in Sretalles to greet them."

"Ye're sure they're safe."

"Aye," said Rushlight, speaking the initial word in Standard English, "I'm sure. And there's little trouble they can find between here and Sretalles."

"Then if it's all the same t' ye, Rushlight, I'll leave ye t' go alone. I wouldna like the captain t' think I'd been checkin' up on him."

Rushlight's tail curled in vast amusement, then coiled about Scotty's wrist. "I see your point, Scotty. Go ahead. It's been a pleasure traveling with you. You smooth a trail as well as any bard."

"Thank ye, laddie." Scotty gripped the end of the tail. "I'll be talkin' to ye, soon enough." He pulled out the communicator and arranged for transport. Then he looked again at Rushlight. "Ye take care, now, lad. I wouldna want t' miss the chance t' drink"—he remembered just in time the Sivaoan's dislike for alcohol—"t' brawl w' ye in some place a wee bit more friendly."

In the near distance, Jim Kirk heard the noisy racket of welcome-homes and, for the first time, appreciated the name they'd been given, even though it was not yet his party they welcomed. "Hear them?" shouted Jinx, walking backward for a few steps to share her excitement with those who followed. "We're almost there!"

Brightspot sneezed—Jinx's medicine must have worn off—and said, "Somebody stepped off the trail to pass us a few minutes ago."

"Pass us?" said Kirk. Brightspot fell back to trot along

beside him and explain, "Nobody's going to interfere with a Walk; people would go around." She made the explanation seem obvious, then Kirk remembered Rushlight. Perhaps that explained why the slashbacks had not attacked in force? He suddenly hoped that Rushlight had not been in any danger—and not only because Kirk wanted to find his communicator waiting for him when he arrived.

Chekov had made no reaction to the news, and Kirk could not twist far enough in the travois harness to tell if the ensign was unconscious or merely asleep. "Evan?"

She drew up close and, without his need to ask, she said, "Chekov's fine, Captain." Then she dropped back into place beside Mr. Spock. He was not certain he had heard her place a light emphasis on the word *Chekov*—

Suddenly the trees around them shook wildly and welcome-homes burst into full voice. The trail turned and widened, and without a word the party regrouped to walk into Sretalles side by side. The clamor of the welcome-homes was immediately drowned out by shouts of greeting from fifty or more waiting Sivaoans. Through it all cut Evan Wilson's sharp command: "Sit down, Spock—or *lie* down!" Spock did neither.

"Let's make this fast," Kirk said to Jinx, who nodded and helped free him from the travois sash. Together they laid the travois gently on the ground. He stooped, relieved to see that Chekov was stirring. "Give me two minutes of your time, Mr. Chekov," he said, "and then you can rest as long as you want." Chekov's eyelids fluttered open. Jim Kirk smiled at him and shouted over the noise of the crowd, "We made it. State your name, rank and serial number: that's all they need to make it official!"

The crowd hushed. Chekov looked up at the faces bending over him and said, "My name is Pavel Andrievich Chekov. Ensign, U.S.S. *Enterprise*. Serial Number SD710-820."

Kirk laid a hand on his shoulder. "That's fine, Mr. Chekov. . . . Spock?"

Leaning heavily on his spear, Spock took his cue. "Spock," he said, "Science Officer and First Officer, *Enterprise*." His voice was extremely hoarse. "I do not believe they are concerned with serial numbers, Captain."

He nodded to Uhura, who said, "My name is Nyota Uhura. Chief Communications Officer, *Enterprise*." She turned to Brightspot.

Brightspot glared into the crowd—Kirk's look followed hers and found Fetchstorm and Stiff Tail—and said, "My name is Brightspot to-Ennien. Do I hear any objections?" Evan Wilson glanced momentarily away from Spock and crowed her delight. Brightspot looped her tail around Evan's arm and said, "I guess there are none. Your turn."

Evan Wilson thumped her staff once on the ground and said, "Tail-Kinker to-Ennien." All around her, tails curled delighted approval. She nodded to Jinx.

Jinx said, "My name is Another StarFreedom." She paused, took a deep breath and finished, "to-*Eeiauo*." Shock ran through the crowd, but Jinx ignored it. "Captain . . ." she said.

Kirk stood and said, "My name is James Tiberius Kirk. I am captain of the Federation Starship *Enterprise*."

All hell broke loose at once.

Grabfoot scurried up his side and perched on his shoulder, crowing, "James Tiberius Kirk to-*Enterprise!*" Close enough, thought Kirk, already regretting having given his full name.

Catchclaw shouted, "Get back, you fuzz-brains! Back, back!" and punctuated her words with ear-ringing swats. "Can't you see there are injuries?! Back! Grabfoot, down!" Kirk jumped as Grabfoot clawed a tender spot in his eagerness to obey. Jinx—*Another StarFreedom,* he corrected himself, drew Catchclaw down to examine Chekov.

Evan Wilson charged Rushlight. Wresting the pack of their possessions from his grasp with little courtesy, she rummaged through them, snatched up the kit of hypos and medicines and fairly leapt at Spock.

Seeing her haste to get to Spock sent Kirk straight to Rushlight for the communicator. He flipped it open and was so relieved by the words, "*Enterprise* here, Captain," that he scarcely heard the remainder of Scotty's hearty greeting. "Stand by transporter room, Scotty," he said, as he went to join the two.

Evan Wilson had her hypo in hand. Spock made a move to

protest, but she said, "Don't be a dope, Spock. It's tri-ox. If I remember correctly, your people invented it." The hypo hissed at his shoulder. Immediately, she prepared a second injection. "Can your Vulcan half handle a broad-spectrum antibiotic?" Spock glanced at the vial she held up and nodded. The hypo hissed a second time.

She snatched the communicator from Kirk's hand. "Two to beam up, laddie, into full quarantine. Tell Dr. M'Benga." To Kirk, she said, "Chekov stays here, Captain: Catchclaw and J—Another StarFreedom can take better care of him than I can. I go with Spock."

"That is quite unnecessary," said Spock.

She glowered up at him. "Mr. Spock," she said sharply, "I want you in sick bay now. I do not wish to complicate your condition with a skull fracture, but, by Elath, I will if you don't cooperate."

As if mildly surprised she had misunderstood, Spock raised an eyebrow at her. "I merely meant that your presence can be of more use to Mr. Chekov. Dr. M'Benga is well versed in Vulcan physiology."

It was clear to Kirk that Evan Wilson knew as much, and equally clear that she was reluctant to entrust Spock to someone else's care. She continued to glower . . . but raised the communicator. "Scotty, put Dr. M'Benga on."

"He's listenin', lass."

A second voice followed closely on Scott's: "Dr. M'Benga here, sir. Do you have further instructions?"

"I'm sending you a sick Vulcan, Doctor: aspirant pneumonia is my guess. I've given him tri-ox and . . ." She lapsed into a spate of medical jargon that Kirk was hard put to follow. M'Benga replied in the same language. *Too bad we can't put the universal translator to work on that,* thought Kirk ruefully.

"And the quarantine?" asked M'Benga.

"For ADF," she said, "I don't know about the Vulcan half, but I'm damn near sure the human half's been exposed."

When M'Benga had completed preparations to receive Spock, she said gravely, "Thank you," then, "One moment." She turned her face upward to Spock again: "Mr. Spock, I want your word that you will do everything necessary to recover as quickly as possible."

Again he raised his brow. "I assure you, Dr. Wilson—"

She waved a hand, cutting him off. "I take this as you took the promise you extracted from Another StarFreedom when she was Jinx," she said. "I will stay here to help with Chekov only if you will agree to abide by Dr. M'Benga's strictures."

Spock searched her face. "Agreed," he said.

She raised the communicator. "Spock to beam up, Scotty." She and Kirk each took a step back out of range.

"En'rgizing now," said Scotty and Spock vanished slowly, to the stares of a great many Sivaoans. There was a short pause, followed by Scott's announcement, "He's arrived, safe and sound."

"Well, safe anyhow, lad," said Evan.

"He went along with Dr. M'Benga as meekly as ye please. That's hardly like Mr. Spock. What did ye do t' him, lass?"

"Shook my stick at him, Scotty."

"Aye, that might do it. C'ld ye put the captain on?"

Kirk took the communicator she handed him and said, "Problem, Mr. Scott?"

"I dinna know for certain, sir. The lass said, 'quarantine.'"

Kirk wondered what Scott was leading up to. "She did, Mr. Scott. We're not sure, but Mr. Chekov may have caught ADF from one of the local children. What is this about, Mr. Scott?"

"Captain, I'd rather not be tellin' ye this, but I've been t' the surface of the planet mysel', w' Rushlight."

"You've *what?*" Kirk said.

Evan leaned forward to speak into the communicator: "How long were you with Rushlight and when?" Scotty told her. When he had finished, she said, "I'll see what I can find out from Catchclaw. In the meantime, confine yourself to your quarters, Mr. Scott, on the double. Think of it as your own private quarantine ward—no contact with anybody else."

"You heard her, Scotty." Kirk thought it best to reinforce her words with his authority. "Mr. Sulu has command. Ah!" he said as a thought struck him, "You will not, repeat, *not* inform Mr. Spock of this situation." He didn't think Spock would break quarantine but preferred not to take the chance; and his precaution surprised neither Scott nor Sulu. "Kirk out," he finished and, as he closed the communicator, he said to Evan Wilson, "Just how much trouble are we in?"

She shook her head. "I don't know. Let's go find out." She pointed to where a family-sized tent had been thrown up to shelter Chekov.

"Hello?" called Kirk into the opening.

"Come in, James Tiberius Kirk to-*Enterprise*," said a voice. He had a feeling he was going to get very tired of hearing all that, and very quickly. He gestured Evan in and followed.

Uhura rose and said, "Mr. Spock—?"

Evan said, "He'll be fine. Once Dr. M'Benga drains his lungs, all he'll need is rest and antibiotics."

"Drain his lungs?" said Kirk. "I thought you said pneumonia!"

"Aspirant pneumonia, Captain." She immediately looked contrite. "I'm sorry. I thought you understood: Spock's whole body is adapted for desert conditions. He inhaled all that water vapor and his lungs just aren't prepared to deal with it. He will be fine, I promise."

"All right, then," said Kirk, "what about the ADF, Evan?"

Brightspot hissed. *"Tail-Kinker,"* she corrected, her tail twitching angrily. Rushlight, Catchclaw and Another Star-Freedom bristled at him.

Wilson put her hands on her hips. "Brightspot, names don't mean the same thing to me as they do to you. I hereby grant permission to all the members of our Walk to call me whatever name feels most comfortable to them, including Dr. Evan Wilson and variations thereof." She glanced from Catchclaw to Rushlight. "However," she said, "I shall expect the rest of the camp to follow your own custom, and I shall take it very much amiss if they do not."

"Understood, Tail-Kinker," said Catchclaw, and Rushlight arched his whiskers forward in agreement.

"Good," said Evan, and she sat beside Chekov. "Another

StarFreedom, is there any way you can confirm that what Mr. Chekov has is actually Noisy-Baby?"

The Sivaoan formerly known as Jinx said, "If Pavel Andrievich Chekov will permit me to take a blood sample."

"I knew it," said Chekov. "All doctors are wampires."

In the end, it was Wilson who played vampire—the Sivaoans had no idea where to draw blood from a human—and Another StarFreedom who, with her own exotic instruments, performed what seemed a simple test. Looking into an eyepiece, she said, "Yes, it's Noisy-Baby," and passed the instrument to Catchclaw.

"It's Noisy-Baby all right," Catchclaw said, after her own look in, "although I don't think I'd have believed it if I didn't see it with my own eyes. . . . The rememberers knew the name of Thunderstroke, Nyota Uhura to-*Enterprise*. They assured me the only possible connection on this world with your disease was Noisy-Baby." Her tail bristled. "Had I known it could act so quickly and so devastatingly on a human, I would have stopped your Walk. . . ." Her voice trailed off; she raised her eyes to meet those of Another StarFreedom. "Yes," she said, "even though it was your third time."

Instantly, Another StarFreedom reached out with her long silver-gray tail, to encircle Catchclaw's arm. "You would have been right to," she said firmly, "simply because a thing is custom does not always make it good or right."

Catchclaw arched her whiskers forward and wrapped her own brown tail around Another StarFreedom's waist, then she handed the instrument to Evan Wilson. "See the cells stained bright pink? Pavel Andrievich Chekov did have Noisy-Baby. He will be immune to further exposure now."

"And the rest of us, Catchclaw?" Kirk asked.

"Brightspot and Another StarFreedom both had Noisy-Baby as children. But the rest of you had the same exposure to Grabfoot that Pavel Andrievich Chekov had. We'll need a blood sample from each of you."

Evan Wilson thrust out a slender arm—scratched and discolored with mud and bruises. "You saw how I did it, Another StarFreedom," she said. "I can't very well take my own blood sample. Go ahead." Another StarFreedom did, and stained and examined the resultant specimen.

"Yes," she said, passing the instrument to Evan, "Now you can see the live ones—the dark pink cells."

As she stared into the instrument, Evan frowned. "But that's a very ordinary bacteria in human beings. . . . That *couldn't* be the cause of such symptoms!"

"No, no," said Catchclaw. "Only some of the cells are pink—*those* are the affected ones." She gave a sidelong glance at Another StarFreedom, flicked the tip of her tail and said, "I hope that translator of theirs works on this. Tail-Kinker, what causes Noisy-Baby is a bacteriophage."

"Do you understand, Evan?" Another StarFreedom asked anxiously, and Evan Wilson began to laugh quietly. She nodded at Another StarFreedom and again at Catchclaw. "I understand," she said.

"*I* don't," said Jim Kirk.

"It's an impostor, Captain," she said. "It's a thing like a virus that attacks some ordinary-looking bacteria in your body, stuffs the nucleus full of its own genetic material, and starts sending out different orders. No wonder we couldn't isolate the cause: it probably uses a different cover in a human than it would in Eeiauoan!" She turned again to Catchclaw and Another StarFreedom. "It's the waste product of the phage that does all the damage?"

Catchclaw said, "Yes, Tail-Kinker," and added, "Don't worry, though. That's what Another StarFreedom did for Pavel Andrievich Chekov. The remedy is twofold: neutralize the waste product and kill the phage so it won't produce any more. In your case, we can stop its progress before you lose any fur."

"Can you *prevent* it?"

Another StarFreedom said, "Yes, and in the case of humans it would probably be a good idea to see you all vaccinated, if you aren't already infected, for safety's sake. It hits you too hard to risk waiting."

An enormous grin spread across Evan's face. Her eyes sparkled. "Now there's a pretty word," she said and gave it loving repetition: "*vaccinate*. What do you say, Captain?"

For answer, Jim Kirk grinned back and, pushing up the sleeve of his uniform, offered his bare arm to the two Sivaoan doctors.

The blood tests proved him the only one free of the phage. Evan Wilson lifted her eyes to meet his. "Captain?" she said, "you are aware that this makes you our guinea pig?"

"I know," he said, "the vaccine might not work on humans."

"Worse," she said, swabbing his arm with antiseptic and reaching for the hypo Another StarFreedom had prepared, "it might give you the disease—and I've a philosophical objection to that sort of thing."

"Go ahead, Evan. If I come down with Noisy-Baby, Another StarFreedom can always mix up another batch of antidote—although I will insist she use a hypodermic to administer it."

"Having it blown up your nose is too undignified?" Evan asked, mischief in her eyes.

"Let's just say I have a philosophical objection to that sort of thing."

"Okay," Evan agreed, "stop fidgeting and let me get on with it."

He doubted he had been "fidgeting" but he made no objection. She went ahead with her work. When she had finished the injection, she sat back on her heels and said, "Elath, but I hate all this waiting!"

A tail tip thrust through the entrance to the tent. "Company, Evan," he said, "maybe that will take both our minds off the waiting. Come in."

It was Stiff Tail. With her, she had brought several other members of her last camp, including Left Ear. The newcomers crowded just inside the entrance, and their manner spoke of some hesitation other than a desire to avoid contagion. *Of course,* thought Kirk, *they all had Noisy-Baby when they were children too; they have no reason to be afraid of it.*

Bristling slightly, Stiff Tail began, "It is my understanding, James Tiberius Kirk, that you may speak for all of your people?"

"For my crew, yes," he said. "I would not be so presumptuous as to speak for Brightspot or Another StarFreedom."

Brightspot said, "You speak for me as well, Captain."

Another StarFreedom added, "Me too."

Adult they might be officially, he saw, but they were not yet ready to confront an adult as formidable as Stiff Tail unless it was absolutely necessary. "All right," said Kirk, "What do you want, Stiff Tail?"

She was taken aback. "It is what *you* wanted," she said. "We've come to speak to you about"—she took a deep breath—"the Exiles."

Jim Kirk folded his arms across his chest. "Don't stick your tail in something that doesn't concern you, Stiff Tail." Stiff Tail hissed; and all around him, Sivaoans—including Brightspot and Another StarFreedom—bristled. Evan Wilson laid her hand nonchalantly on her quarterstaff.

Her tail a spike of rage, Stiff Tail said carefully, "That is something we say to children, James Tiberius Kirk. . . ." She did not raise a hand to strike, but he saw claws unsheathe, saw the tremor in her arm, knew the effort she made in such restraint.

"Yes," he said, making it very plain, "to *children.*"

Stiff Tail took one step toward him—and Evan Wilson's quarterstaff barred a second. Stiff Tail turned on Wilson, but found no open threat, no challenge, in her stance, only a statement of fact: that far, no further. And with a massive effort, Stiff Tail lifted her ears erect and smoothed her fur. She stepped back.

"I do not understand your actions, James Tiberius Kirk," she said at last. "Do your customs permit you to explain . . . ?"

Kirk said, "Two thousand years ago, Stiff Tail, your people exiled the Eeiauoans. Now you are ashamed of that action—ashamed that you did not find some other solution to the problem. Am I right?"

Stiff Tail nodded. She shrank in size, just as Grabfoot did when he wished to go unnoticed. "I see," she said. "In your eyes, our treatment of the Exiles was childish."

"You don't see," Kirk said. "Your solution to the problem

323

of the Eeiauoans at the time may have been correct—or not—*but that doesn't matter!"*

Stiff Tail's eyes went wide, her ears flicked back: "Then why—?"

"The only thing that matters is what happens to the Eeiauoans *now,"* he said. He spread his hands. "Stiff Tail, you are so ashamed of something that happened two thousand years ago that you were willing to let an entire people die rather than discuss them. That kind of evasion of responsibility is hardly the act of an adult." He swung and pointed. "Brightspot, Another StarFreedom—they were the real adults in your camp. Time after time they tried to help, despite your customs, and despite ours."

He turned back to her. "We made the Walk to become adults in your eyes, Stiff Tail. Now you must make a journey to prove your maturity to us: you must accept what was done in the past and live with the consequences. The Eeiauoans need all the help they can get—and that includes yours."

Stiff Tail jerked back as if bitten. "You'd force us to go with you to Eeiauo?"

Jim Kirk shook his head sadly. "I can't force you to do anything you don't want to do, Stiff Tail—least of all grow up."

She turned on her heels and, tail lashing, pushed past the crowd and out of the tent. Her companions followed. *Well,* he thought, *I gave it my best shot.*

"Keptain?" said Chekov, a plaintive note in his voice. "I don't understend, sair. I thought we did all thet so we could talk to them . . . ?"

"We did all that to get their help, Mr. Chekov. If we can take a few extra hands back to Eeiauo with us, so much the better. Particularly if they know what they're doing."

"How many do you need, James Tiberius Kirk?" It was Catchclaw who spoke. "You must know that Another StarFreedom has already chosen to accompany you. She is a capable physician, despite her youth."

"I said all the help they can get, Catchclaw. I meant just that," said Kirk.

Her ears flicked sharply back. "How many will your ship hold?" she asked.

"In a pinch, several hundred," he told her.

"Oh!" said Brightspot. "Then I'm coming too."

"And I," said Rushlight. "It would be a trip to sing about."

Catchclaw curled her tail, amused at Kirk's surprise, and advised, "Never turn down the company of a bard, James Tiberius Kirk: songs ease a trail.—I and my four will join you too." It took him a moment to realize she meant to bring her children. Under the circumstances, she could hardly leave them behind—and he could not turn down the services of a second doctor.

"Thank you," he said simply. "All of you. And Catchclaw, I'd appreciate it if you and Rushlight would just call me 'Captain' like the rest." He was not about to listen to 'James Tiberius Kirk' all the way to Eeiauo.

"As you wish," said Catchclaw. "Your name is now your own choice, Captain."

Only then did he realize the implication of his request. When he looked over at Evan Wilson, she wore her sweetest smile. She said not a word. The tilt of her head was enough to say it for her.

Chapter Seventeen

Jim Kirk stepped from the transporter with a sense of elation. "Welcome aboard, Captain Kirk," said Ensign Orsay from the instrument panel. Her face was a study in mixed reactions: half delight to see him and half an attempt to conceal her horror at his appearance.

"Thank you, Ensign. It's good to be back." He needed a status report from the bridge, a shower and two days' sleep—in that order.

As the medical team Evan Wilson had requested helped Chekov onto a stretcher, she thumped her quarterstaff on the deck to spur them. Amid all the clean lines and austerity of the transporter room, she looked wilder than the Sivaoans. Brightspot, Another StarFreedom—each carrying one of Catchclaw's babies—stood frozen to the arrival platform, staring about in ear-straining amazement.

"Brightspot," he said, "you'll have plenty of time to see everything. Now clear the space for the next contingent. . . ." He motioned, and they stepped hesitantly down.

Kirk nodded to Ensign Orsay who said, "Energizing." Another StarFreedom gave a quiet shout, almost a cheer, as Catchclaw with Grabfoot, Uhura with TooLongTail, Rushlight, Knots (a rememberer) and Brave Tongue (another doctor) materialized. They too had to be motioned from the transporter platform.

Two more parties arrived, but Jim Kirk looked in vain for Stiff Tail. "I guess she's not coming," said Brightspot, whiskers drooping in disappointment.

"I guess not," Kirk said. "I'm sorry, Brightspot. I had hoped . . ."

"That she could grow up, too," Brightspot finished for him. "Me too. Maybe next year she'll be old enough to Walk."

"Maybe next year," Kirk agreed.

There was a horrible screeking sound at his feet, and Kirk looked down to see Grabfoot testing his claws against the deck plates. The child, ears almost flat against his head, said, "Catchclaw! All rock! No place for a tent! We'll get all wet!" He shook himself in disgusted anticipation.

"The whole ship is a tent," Kirk told him. "I promise you won't get wet unless you want to. Mr. Riley, would you see our guests to their quarters? You'll have to explain most of the equipment to them, but you'll only have to do so once. They'll remember it."

Brightspot brightened and curled her tail impudently at him. Uhura said, "If you don't mind, Captain, I'd like to do that myself."

"Of course, Uhura, but then see you get some sleep," Kirk said. "Evan, that goes for you too."

"First things first," she said. "After I get Mr. Chekov into sick bay and have a look at Mr. Spock, I want to see if I can spring Scotty. He must be chafing at the bit by now."

He nodded his permission, then added, "I'll be on the bridge if you need me."

She raised an eyebrow. "You need sleep too, Captain."

"I know that, Doctor, but I assure you it can wait until we're underway."

"That's what I meant," she said, and he realized it was so.

Excusing himself, he eased his way through the crowd of Sivaoans. Grabfoot, now perched on Catchclaw's shoulder, eyed him as he passed and said, in scathing tones, *"Want to get wet . . . !"* Jim Kirk laughed but continued on his way.

He did not stop until he reached the bridge. Sulu rose from the command chair, his formal salute and grin of welcome marred only by a startled blink. *Perhaps I should have taken the shower first,* thought Kirk ruefully, as Sulu said, "It's good to have you back, Captain."

"It's good to be back, Mr. Sulu."

He waited a moment as Sulu took his customary station, cheerfully displacing the crew member who had filled in. Sulu no longer hobbled; Wilson would no doubt be pleased to see him recovered from both her ministrations. Jim Kirk settled back into the command chair and did what pleased him—"Set course for Eeiauo, Mr. Sulu," he ordered, and added, "Let's not keep Dr. McCoy waiting."

"Aye, aye, sir!" came the reply. It was echoed with enthusiasm from all sides. Seconds later, Sulu said, "We're on our way!" And, while Jim Kirk luxuriated in the quiet surge of power beneath his feet, a soft cheer went up around him.

At last he swung the chair toward his communications officer. "Ensign Azuela," he said, "as soon as we are within range of a Federation relay beacon, I want to speak to Dr. McCoy—the sooner, the better." Reluctantly he rose. "The conn is yours, Mr. Sulu; I'll be in my quarters if anything comes up."

As the turbolift doors hissed open, he took one last look around the bridge, gave a contented sigh and headed for his quarters.

He awoke feeling better than he had in weeks, showered a second time, dressed—reveling in the feel of clean clothes— and opened the intercom to the bridge. "Scott here. Glad t' have ye w' us again, Captain."

Kirk chuckled and said, "And you too, Scotty. I take it you don't have a case of Noisy-Baby?"

"Noisy-Baby, sir? It was ADF syndrome the lass was checkin' on, I thought."

"Never mind, Scotty. I'll explain later. How's Mr. Spock?"

"Ye can see for y'rself, Captain. Dr. Wilson moved him back int' sick bay—where she can keep a closer eye on him, if ye take my meaning." That drew a full-throated laugh from Kirk.

"I do, Mr. Scott, I do!"

"Mr. Chekov's there as well. The lad looks a sight but he's in good spirits."

"I'll go have a look," said Kirk, "and, Scotty, make sure you inform me as soon as you get through to Bones."

"Aye, that I will." When Scotty had signed off, Jim Kirk rose, stretched and headed for sick bay.

A line of crew members stretched from the doors and halfway down the corridor, and he paused to greet each as he passed by. At last, he eased his way in and found havoc—a carefully controlled havoc, but havoc nonetheless, as doctors took blood, tested blood, barked records into the computer and generally inoculated everyone in sight.

A hand and a tail caught him firmly by the arm and steered him to a chair. "Hey, Brave Tongue!" called Evan Wilson, "Not him—he's already been done!"

Ears flicked back, Brave Tongue scrutinized his face and said, "Sorry, Captain. I'm getting carried away." The tail whipped away, and Brave Tongue added, "How big a crew do you *have?*"

"Over four hundred," Kirk said.

"Oh," he said, clearly startled.

"Cheer up," Evan told the Sivaoan. "At the rate we're going, it'll only take us two more days. Then we get some rest before we have to start in on the *real* problem. I'm looking forward to it —the rest I mean. I'm just about frazzled."

She did look shockingly tired, but Kirk saw with relief that her eyes still held a hint of merriment. "Evan," Kirk said, "have you had any sleep at all?" "Enough," she said. "Barely enough," he corrected.

She shrugged, then gave him a nudge in the direction of the next room. "Spock. Chekov. Morale," she said and, when he hesitated, added, "The sooner you stop bothering us, Captain, the sooner we'll be done—and the sooner I can get that sleep." She made shooing motions.

He did as he was told. He found both Spock and Chekov sitting up. Spock held a computer link, obviously absorbed in some task. Scotty was right: Chekov looked a sight. His face and arms were covered with scars and most of his hair was gone—but the lesions had visibly healed and Kirk could see the stubble of new growth. Chekov glanced up. "Keptain!" he said and laid aside the book he had been reading to sit at attention.

With a smile, Kirk said, "At ease, Mr. Chekov."

Spock lifted a hand to indicate that he did not wish to be distracted from his computer for the moment. Kirk took this as a sign that Spock was recuperating nicely and said to Chekov, "Have you two been behaving yourselves?"

Chekov grinned. "Wouldn't you, Keptain?" he said, and he pointed: Wilson's quarterstaff stood prominently between the two ward beds.

"Point taken, Mr. Chekov," Kirk said, grinning back.

There was a sudden burst of music and Spock's head jerked up. The sound seemed to come from his computer link. With a quick look at his startled science officer, Kirk strode across the room and keyed into the central computer from one of the medical terminals. The central computer replied as it normally did—but, softly underlying the mechanical voice, Kirk heard the same tune that came from Spock's link. It was difficult to repress a shudder; they'd had problems with the computer before— "Mr. Spock?" he asked, hoping to hear a simple explanation.

"I have no idea," said Spock, and Kirk said, "I don't like to think about it, Spock—another malfunction like the last time. . . ." This time he did shudder.

"No malfunction," said Evan Wilson. She stepped into the room and paused, arms folded across her chest, to consider Spock. Then she turned to the medical computer and said, "This is Dr. Evan Wilson."

"Dr. Evan Wilson, acknowledged," said the mechanical voice.

"Enough is enough," she told it.

"Enough is enough," the mechanical voice responded— and the music ceased as abruptly as it had begun.

She turned to face Spock once more. "Mr. Spock," she said, "if you're sufficiently recovered to be sticking your tail in where it shouldn't be, then you're taking up bed space under false pretenses. You are released from sick bay."

Except for the raising of an eyebrow, Spock made no move. Wilson's face went crimson, and Spock looked suddenly down at the computer link in his hands, as if seeing it for the first time. Wilson gave a fleeting smile and said, "Or am I to understand that your inability to spot the flag is an indication that you need further rest, Mr. Spock?''

At that, Spock rose with almost indecent haste for a Vulcan. "Indeed not, Dr. Wilson," he said.

"Fine. Now get him out of here, Captain, before I take a stick to him."

As if they had already obeyed, she stepped to Chekov's side and focused her attention completely on him. "Let me see your back, Mr. Chekov." Chekov leaned forward to comply, and she ran a gentle hand over his skin. "Looks good," she said. "Any pain?"

"No, sair—but it *itches!*"

"Enjoy it," she said. "That's the best news I've heard in days. We'll have you out of here in no time."

Kirk said, "I'm looking forward to that, Mr. Chekov. I want you back on the bridge as soon as Dr. Wilson says you're able."

"Yes, sair," said Chekov happily; and Wilson smiled her thanks for Kirk's contribution to her patient's morale.

Then her eyes once more sought Spock. "In the future, Mr. Spock," she said softly, "please be more discreet."

"I shall, Doctor, I assure you."

As he walked along beside Spock, Kirk frowned at his science officer. He knew from personal experience that Spock could be something of a . . . nuisance, to put it politely; and, once inside the relative privacy of the turbolift, he said, "All right, Spock. What was that all about—flags in the computer?"

"Apparently, Dr. Wilson set a flag in the central computer's programming to alert her should certain information be sought." He paused, as if to examine his own behavior, then added, "As I did not notice the anomaly, she is perhaps correct to say I am not yet fully recovered."

"And just what *sort* of information did she flag, Spock?"

"Information on the Telamonite culture, Captain."

"Good lord, you're not still working on your theory about the 'discrepancies' in her records!"

"Merely indulging my curiosity, Captain. I had a great deal of time to spend and very little to occupy my mind."

"And that exchange—that you be more 'discreet'?"

"If I understood her correctly, she wished to know if I planned to continue my investigations."

"I see—and you told her you would." Jim Kirk laughed suddenly. "Mr. Spock, I think you've been set up." Spock raised a brow, and Kirk added, "Sorry. My fault, really." He went on to relate his conversation with Wilson on the subject of the "discrepancies" in her dossier.

Once he had begun, he found himself caught up in Evan's mischief, enjoying the mystification of his science officer as much as she seemed to. ". . . So you see, Mr. Spock, why I'd be willing to bet she set the flag just for your benefit," he finished, as they reached the bridge, "You had your tail pulled." He settled into the command chair, smiling at the double take his choice of expression drew from Sulu.

Spock paused at his side. "Negative, Captain. The subtlety of her work would argue against such an interpretation of the data. Dr. Wilson has not had sufficient time to spare since we returned to the *Enterprise*."

"Then she spotted you coming before we left Eeiauo. The subtlety of her work would certainly permit that."

"That is a possibility. I shall be interested to see what other information she has flagged."

"Spock!" That was going well beyond "nuisance," Jim Kirk thought, and he said, "I think I'll have to find something else to occupy you—Evan has enough trouble on her hands for the moment."

Spock clasped his hands behind his back. He said, "If your interpretation is correct, I would most certainly be expected to continue my investigations." Kirk glanced at him obliquely but he could read nothing in Spock's expression.

"Mr. Spock," he inquired at last, unable to keep a note of amusement out of his voice, "are you suggesting that you wouldn't want to disappoint her?"

"I merely note the contradiction between your theory and your response."

"Of course." He nodded, a half smile on his face. Regrettably, Spock was right: if this was Evan's idea of a joke—and he was sure of that now—she would be disappointed not to have it sprung. "All right," he said aloud, "Your logic defeats me, as usual. Investigate away, Spock—though I trust you will use somewhat more discretion from now on."

As luck had it, Jim Kirk was once again on his way to sick bay to see Mr. Chekov when Uhura paged him. He opened a com link in the corridor and said, "Kirk here, Lieutenant."

"I have Dr. McCoy, sir," she said, and he could hear the triumph in her voice.

"Put him through to Dr. Wilson in sick bay, Uhura. I'll be right there."

He arrived on the run and pushed through the thinning crowd. Dr. M'Benga pointed him into McCoy's office. There he found Wilson seated before the screen, transmitting the specifications that would enable McCoy to synthesize both the remedy and the vaccine for ADF syndrome. Bones was turned away from his screen, watching the data as they came in and nodding gravely as he did. "It's related to the palliative we worked out," he said. "Blast! A little closer and we'd have had it!" He looked up and brightened. "Jim!" he said.

"Don't let me interrupt, Bones—but it's good to see you."

"Not half as good as it is to see you." McCoy grinned and, ripping off the printout, held it up, "—and this. Thanks, both of you. Now get the hell out of here and let me work."

"One more thing, Leonard!" said Wilson. "Take a good look at that last item—the HLA factor. It may be, at least I've reason to think, that people with that particular factor get hit harder and faster than—"

"*Chekov*," said McCoy, "Is Chekov all right?"

"Scruffy-looking but recuperating nicely," she grinned at him, "and everybody else is as healthy as a horse."

"I'd have said 'a Vulcan,'" McCoy told her, grinning back his relief.

"He's recovering nicely too, thanks to Dr. M'Benga," said Wilson.

McCoy's reaction was almost a parody of surprise. Then he shook his head as if to clear it. "You can tell me all about it when you get here. I've got work to do. McCoy out."

As the screen went blank, Evan Wilson snapped on the intercom: "Nyota? Dr. McCoy tells me that Christine Chapel and Sunfall of Ennien are still alive—and that he and Dr.

Mickiewicz will deliver our findings to them personally." A sharp indrawn breath was the only acknowledgment. She went on, "Would you make some sort of general announcement to that effect? I know a lot of people are concerned."

This time the reply was heard all over the ship, as Uhura switched immediately to public address: "Now hear this! Now hear this!" The rest of her joyful words drew cheers from the next room.

Evan Wilson turned her chair to face Kirk. "That's done," she said; then she sighed and closed her eyes briefly. "It's over." Kirk nodded and, because he felt it too, recognized the source of her dissatisfaction.

"Those are the hazards of modern communication," he said. "I admit it would be considerably more satisfying to charge in on a white horse and *hand* Bones the cure in person. As it is, he'll have most of the problem mopped up before we reach Eeiauo."

"I know. But the two weeks we just cut from our time may have saved a lot of lives. ADF syndrome kills humans. Elath bless Leonard McCoy: he bought them all time with his palliative. Now we'll have to wait and see if Another Star-Freedom's remedy will work at that late a stage in the disease." She sighed again, then she stood and stretched as thoroughly as any Sivaoan. When she had finished, she leaned back against the desk to study him: "You'd look pretty good charging in on a white horse, Captain."

"So would you," he said.

She shook her head. "Make mine an Appaloosa—spotty suits me better." But her smile faded as swiftly as it had come and, as the silence between the two of them lengthened, Kirk knew again what she was feeling.

"So there's nothing to do but wait," he said. The words came out more glumly than he had intended.

"Are you off duty?" When he nodded, she went on, "Good. I hear you're a better-than-average swimmer. How'd you like to volunteer for hazardous duty?" She took him lightly by the arm. "You and I, Captain, are going to drown-proof some Sivaoans. . . ."

"Watch me, ccaptain! Watch me! *Want* to get wet!" shouted

WhiteWhisker from the diving board. Treading water, Jim Kirk looked up. "I'm watching," he assured her with a smile. The child bounced twice and cannonballed into the pool, splashing half a dozen of the onlookers. She came up with a shout of triumph and paddled toward him, using her tail for extra speed. For a brief moment, she clung to his arm with both hands and tail, then the tail shot up, shot down, splashing water in his face. "Hey!" he protested, but she had already kicked off and was swimming away, shouting, "Ccatch me!" Kirk laughed and stroked lazily after her.

Hazardous duty, he thought. Evan had not been joking. It had taken all the patience and persuasion the two of them possessed to coax the panicked Brightspot into the water. She still lacked the confidence to join Catchclaws's four in their games, but now she paddled earnestly back and forth in the shallows.

"Duck!" shouted Evan. He did, and a red and blue ball missed his head by inches. He caught it and tossed it back to Grabfoot, who caught it with his tail and fielded it to WhiteWhisker. TooLongTail lunged for it at the same moment and the customary free-for-all followed. Kirk swam over to referee. He had no intention of letting the little ones drown each other in their enthusiasm.

In some way, Jim Kirk wished he weren't having so much fun. He knew Bones wasn't. *Well,* he thought, as he grabbed a tail and pulled WhiteWhisker to the surface for a breath of air, *When we reach Eeiauo, we'll have plenty to do. I might as well enjoy this while I can.*

As tired as he was, Leonard McCoy had never felt better: Two of his patients had already come out of coma! And his own vision had cleared, the pain in his joints eased—Jim Kirk had once again done the impossible.

From all the indications, he'd have good news for Uhura too. Although Sunfall of Ennien had not yet recovered consciousness, her condition was so improved that McCoy took the liberty of having her moved so he could keep a personal eye on her until she did.

Having administered the Sivaoan remedy to all the most critical of his patients, he sat down at the communication screen. It would only take a minute to call the *Flinn,* and he had to know how things were working out there.

Micky greeted him with a grin. "Just the man I wanted to see—I've got somebody here who wants a word with you, Leonard," she said, and the screen shifted to show him a patient in a ward bed.

"Hello, Dr. McCoy." The voice was weak and the patient did not lift her head to speak, but McCoy recognized her then. "Christine," he said softly, "it's good to hear your voice."

She gave him a faint smile and said, "It's good to hear yours too. Is the captain all right—and Mr. Spock?"

"They're just fine, Christine," he said, reassured and reassuring. "And they'll be mighty glad to hear that you are too."

She nodded, almost imperceptibly; then Micky interposed herself to say, "All right, Leonard, that's enough. I'll thank you to let my patient get some sleep."

Affronted, McCoy growled without thinking, *"Your patient!"*

It fazed Mickiewicz not at all. "My patient," she repeated. "You always were grabby, Leonard."

"Grabby!" he said, softening. "I resent that."

"Resent it all you want," she said, amused, "but go away. And get some sleep yourself. You deserve it."

"Oh, I deserve it all right, but there's still a lot to do. Sleep will just have to wait." He smiled, "But I am goin' to take the time to give Jim the good news."

"That would be 'Jim' as in Captain Kirk of the *Enterprise?*" and at his nod she went on, "Then I want an introduction when you get a chance. A remarkable man, your captain."

"That," said McCoy, "is an understatement. But ask for an introduction to Spock as well. That pointy-eared menace to mental stability is probably half responsible for the success of the *Enterprise*'s mission. I'd bet on it."

"Then we owe them both three cheers."

"Address your cheers to the *Enterprise* crew," McCoy advised. "Jim will appreciate that a lot more."

Having given the matter a good deal of careful thought, Spock had come to the conclusion that his initial failure to spot Wilson's flags stemmed not from any temporary mental impairment his illness might have caused him, but rather from her own very considerable skill at programming. While he had found and skirted some dozen other flags, he was both impressed and intrigued. If it were a joke, as the captain suggested, it was one he could appreciate on a purely intellectual level.

He studied the back of Jim Kirk's head, wondering if he should be informed. It surprised him somewhat, knowing the scope of the captain's curiosity as he did, that the captain had not asked—had not so much as alluded to, in fact—his investigations into the computer since giving him permission to resume them. This too was puzzling.

"Mr. Spock? Starfleet Records, sir. They say they have some information you requested?" Uhura glanced across, mild surprise on her face. He had made the request himself, not through her—nor did he wish to explain the reasoning behind his action.

"Thank you, Lieutenant," he said. "Kindly transfer the information to my quarters. I shall take it there. With your permission, Captain?"

Jim Kirk swung the command chair to look at him. Spock did not completely comprehend the expression on the captain's face—it seemed to combine exasperation and amusement—but Kirk only said, "You're relieved of duty, Mr. Spock. Enjoy yourself."

"Sir?" he said, lifting a brow.

"Never mind, Spock. Go on don't keep Starfleet waiting." Spock went.

Once in his quarters, he found himself hesitating before the computer console. Perhaps Jim Kirk was right, perhaps it was nothing stranger than the everyday strangeness of human behavior that baffled him. There was only one way to find out. He sat and keyed in the command that would screen the information he had requested: Dr. Evan Wilson's comprehensive Starfleet dossier. As the first image flashed onto the monitor, Spock knew that her protective flags had been no joke, but he read the records through. Then, in defiance of all logic, he read them through a second time. . . .

He sat back and put the tips of his fingers together, as if contemplating the next move in a game of tri-dimensional chess. The decision took him only a moment to reach but somewhat longer to implement.

First, he transferred the entire dossier to his private file. She might, he realized, be sufficiently skilled to access anything that did not require a retina scan. The possibility intrigued him and in consequence he devoted a considerable amount of time and energy to devising a flag of his own, to notify him if she did.

Then, returning his attention to the central computer, he sought out the flag he had so arduously avoided when requesting Evan Wilson's dossier. He tripped it.

Nothing happened.

He had expected another burst of music but there was only silence. Wondering if he had made an error, Spock frowned slightly at the screen. Then he saw it—a tiny starburst in the upper right-hand corner. It might have been a minor flaw in a tape, but Spock knew it would appear in every image on every screen until she saw it—

Kirk's voice from the intercom put an end to his speculation for the time: "Sorry to interrupt, Spock, but we're now in standard orbit around Eeiauo. Will you join me in briefing room A at your earliest convenience?"

"On my way, Captain."

When he reached the briefing room, it was filled to capacity with officers and Sivaoans. Uhura pushed through to his side and gave him a delighted smile. "Sunfall is conscious, sir! Dr. McCoy says she and Christine are both fine!"

"That is most gratifying," Spock said. Her smile faded, and he knew he had disappointed her, but he did not understand how.

"Never mind, sir," she said. "It is only that I feel good— and I wish you could share my joy." Her smile was wistful.

Spock considered her and said at last, "Thank you, Lieutenant. While I do not share your emotion, I do appreciate your intention." This time he had chosen the correct response —her smile brightened again.

"People!" Jim Kirk's shout cut through the noise and brought quiet. "People, I realize the current circumstances would seem to warrant a rousing cheer or two, but we still have business to attend to. If you'll be seated, Dr. McCoy has a few words. I suggest you all listen."

"Thanks, Jim," said McCoy from the triangular screens at each table. "First—for those of you who haven't heard— Nurse Chapel is recovering nicely. There seem to be no permanent effects, mind or body."

"All right!" said Sulu enthusiastically; then he added, "Sorry, Dr. McCoy. . . ."

McCoy grinned. "I know how you feel, Mr. Sulu. Don't apologize. Jim, I've notified Starfleet Command and they've agreed: the quarantine only applies to people who haven't been vaccinated for ADF syndrome. Since Dr. Wilson saw to all of you, you're welcome to beam down. I can still use a lot of help—and I don't mean just trained professionals, I mean any pair of hands I can get."

From the other side of the table, a pair of hands shot up promptly, and Kirk chuckled, "At ease, Dr. Wilson. I wouldn't dream of spoiling your fun. I think you've got as many as you need, Bones." There was a murmur of assent.

McCoy nodded, pleased, then he went on, "Jim, I'd appreciate it if you'd stop by and see Christine. Tell her she did a fine job, and pat Evan on the back for me too if you can do it without gettin' yourself thrown across the room."

Jim Kirk laughed. "I will, Bones. Without Evan, we'd have never grown up."

"I don't know what *you're* talkin' about," said McCoy, "but *I'm* talkin' about the Wilson-Chapel serum. All I did was complete the line of research the two of them worked out, and I'm damn well goin' to see credit given where it's due."

Kirk raised his head. Wilson was hidden from his view by the monitor. He said instead, "Tell her yourself, Bones. She's right here," and keyed the computer to show him.

Spock, standing, had a clear view. He saw Wilson shake her head once, then lean back to consider McCoy's image. "I'll be right there, Leonard," she said. "Meanwhile, I want you in bed and resting." McCoy's jaw dropped—but, for one of the few times in Spock's experience, he seemed at a loss for words.

"Dr. Wilson?" said Kirk; he too seemed surprised.

"Take a good look, Captain," she said. "He's obviously recuperating from ADF himself. That makes him a patient in my book."

McCoy found his voice. "Now see here—"

Caught between the two, Kirk appealed to Spock with a glance. Spock said, "She is correct, Captain."

"Yes, I had ADF," McCoy said, "but I'm fine. Blast, I can't just desert my patients, Evan."

With the flick of a switch, Kirk commanded McCoy's full attention. "You won't have to, Bones. I'm sending Dr. Wilson down with the first group of volunteers. *When she arrives*"—and this proviso cut short any further protest—"you are to consider yourself relieved of all duties. I'm sure she'll take good care of you."

Having resolved the problem to everyone's satisfaction, Kirk ended the call and turned to the Sivaoans. "Another StarFreedom," he said, "Catchclaw, the Federation diplomats would like to have a word with your party."

"Diplomats?" said Catchclaw. Apparently the word did not translate; and to Spock the amusement engendered by the captain's attempt to explain did seem somewhat excessive. At last, Catchclaw said impatiently, "These 'diplomatss'—are they sick, Captain?"

"No, but . . ."

The tip of her tail flicked her annoyance. She said, "If they're not sick, they can wait. I'm going to get my sensors. I take it we're to meet in the transporter room?"

Quite logically, Kirk chose not to argue her decision. He nodded and said, "The briefing is ended. Dismissed."

As people began to file out, Kirk stopped Uhura momentarily. "Lieutenant," he said, "I believe you would like to be in the first party?"

"Oh yes, Captain! Thank you, sir!" She left beaming.

"Evan," Kirk said, and Wilson paused at the door, pushed her way back to look up at him. He said, "About that pat on the back . . ."

"About being thrown across the room," she countered. "Not now, Captain, I have a lot to do."

"All right," he said, smiling, "then take good care of Bones, will you? I warn you, it won't be easy getting him to rest." She chuckled and said, "Believe me, Captain, I know. Doctors make terrible patients. I'll take my stick."

Spock glanced at the now-darkened computer screen. It seemed highly unlikely that she had missed the starburst, but he said, "Tail-Kinker to-Ennien." Jim Kirk favored him with an odd look as Evan Wilson paused for a second time on the threshold. Spock said in explanation, "It was the name she chose for herself, Captain."

"Yes, Mr. Spock," she said.

"The central computer—" he began, without thinking how he might end that sentence.

She smiled and made it unnecessary. "You put it there, Mr. Spock," she said. "*You* get rid of it. I have work to do." She turned, took a step and the doors hissed closed behind her. Spock stared after her, perplexed.

"Another flag, Mr. Spock?" Spock turned, to find Jim Kirk smiling at him almost indulgently. Kirk said, "Well, at least it's not a noisy one. I think she's right, and I must say I'm a little surprised." The smile changed to a slight frown of concern, as he added, "How are you feeling?"

"I am quite recovered, thank you, Captain."

"If that's true, how is it you're tripping Dr. Wilson's flags—or they're tripping you? I thought you were the resident computer expert around here."

"I am unable to explain, Captain." It was not a lie: Spock had no wish to involve Jim Kirk in his decision. "I admit I find her behavior most baffling."

"I could say the same for yours, Spock. What do you know that I don't?"

The question was totally without precedent in Spock's experience. He raised an eyebrow and said, "Captain?"

Kirk looked at him for a long moment, then laughed and shook his head. "Never mind, Mr. Spock. When I think of a way to rephrase that question, I'll try again. For now, let's see to giving Bones the hands he needs."

The figure curled on the circular bed bore so little resemblance to the graceful, glossy-furred image in her memory that Uhura's first thought was, *That can't be Sunfall!* But she knew it was and, knowing that, found the sight almost unbearable. Rushlight curled his comforting tail around her waist, and Uhura stroked it absently. Then she stepped to the side of the bed, drawing him with her. "Sunfall?" she said hesitantly.

The Eeiauoan opened her eyes with difficulty; the nictitating membranes were still swollen and red. "Nyota!" she said. "Is that really you?"

Uhura blinked back tears, fought the catch in her throat and said, "It is, Sunfall. Oh, Sunfall, how do you feel?"

Sunfall lifted her hairless tail an inch or two from the bed. "Like CloudShape after she stole the lightning," she said. "You see? Even my tail shows it." With effort, she stretched out a hand.

Uhura caught her hand and hugged it to herself. "You will get better," she said. "I promise you." And she knew it was a promise she could keep—beneath her fingers, she could already feel the velvety growth of new fur.

Arching her few remaining whiskers forward, Sunfall said, "I'll do my best. I wish I could thank someone. After all these years and all the deaths, your people found the cure we couldn't."

"It was Thunderstroke's cure. The songs you taught me. . . ." Uhura said softly, then, "Don't be angry with me, please, Sunfall. I had no choice. I couldn't let you die."

Sunfall's eyes narrowed to slits. "You promised, Nyota. You promised not to mention them to an Eeiauoan." She bristled, and the sparseness of her fur made her distress terrible to see. But her eyes were turned to Rushlight.

Uhura, reminded of his presence, said quickly, "But he's not, Sunfall. I'm sorry. He's *not* Eeiauoan and he doesn't understand your language." Uhura said, this time speaking not modern Eeiauoan but Old Tongue, "Sunfall of Ennien, this is my friend Rushlight to-Vensre."

"*To*-Vensre?" Sunfall said suddenly. She struggled to rise, but Uhura gently pushed her down again. "*To*-Vensre?" she said once again, this time to Rushlight. "How is that possible? Why would you come after all this time?"

Rushlight cocked his ears, and the gold earrings in them sparkled at the movement. As he lifted his lutelike instrument for her to see, his eyes held a sparkle brighter still. "I came to keep a promise: to meet a bard named Sunfall and to share songs."

"After all this time . . . you've come at last," Sunfall said. "Thank you, Nyota."

Uhura laid a gentle hand on her cheek. "Rest now, Sunfall. We'll talk later. Rest," she said again, and she began to sing a lullabye, softly so that only Sunfall would hear. Rushlight lifted his instrument and, just as softly, followed Uhura's lead. Sunfall of Ennien let her eyes drift from one to the other, then she gave a contented sigh and let sleep close them.

With the first party of volunteers, Jim Kirk beamed aboard the medship *Flinn*—and stepped from the transporter platform directly into the sharp-eyed scrutiny of a woman no taller than Evan Wilson. She had the face of a cherub, haloed by short curly black hair, but her Starfleet Medical garb glittered with stripes almost to her elbows. "Atten-*shun!*" she said, and Jim Kirk instinctively snapped straight. Around him, medical personnel of all ranks turned to face him; with broad grins, they too snapped to attention. The colonel, now grinning as broadly as the rest of her personnel, continued, "Captain James T. Kirk, prepare to receive honors on behalf of the crew of the U.S.S. *Enterprise*. . . . Hip, hip!"

"*Hooray!*" responded her team.

Had she directed the three cheers in his behalf, Jim Kirk would have been embarrassed, but for his crew he was proud and delighted. "Thank you," he said gravely when they had finished, "on behalf of my crew." With that, the epidemiological team went back to business at hand. The colonel stepped toward him and he said again, "Thank you, Colonel Mickiewicz—"

She cut him off. "Thank *you*," she said, "and call me Micky. Any friend of Leonard's is a friend of mine, especially you. You'll want to see Christine Chapel—follow me." Following his glance to the crew members he had brought with him, she added, "Dr. Dziedzic will put them to work, believe me."

Christine Chapel, he found, looked much like Chekov, and the sight of fading lesions on her face and hands did much more to reassure him of her continuing recovery than did her manner. She seemed uncomfortable with his presence. He stayed just long enough to make her understand how proud he was of her work on the serum, that had saved so many lives.

Outside the ward door, Mickiewicz glanced up at his approach and said, "I'll walk you back to transport—and you'll deliver some specimens to Leonard for me." She held up a small case and set off at a brisk walk, adding as he followed, "Don't worry, Captain. When Chapel's up to it, we'll give her a rousing send-off."

"Good," he said, smiling briefly, "she deserves it. But that's not what worries me—I think she would have preferred not to see me."

"The other way around, Captain: she'd have preferred that you not see her. She'll get over her shyness once her hair grows back. It's only vanity, and it happens to the best of us." Pausing in mid-corridor, she brushed her dark curls aside and displayed a dozen artfully hidden bald patches on her own scalp. "I was luckier: the Wilson-Chapel serum left me enough hair to leave me my pride. But I suspect caps and scarves are going to make an abrupt comeback in Federation style for the next few months."

Picturing Chekov and Chapel, Kirk had to admit the possibility and added speculatively, "I wonder how many of the top brass got Noisy-Baby?"

She looked up, with a slight smile, questioning; and Jim Kirk realized to his embarrassment that he knew of at least one. The smile turned to a grin, and she said, "Never mind, Captain. You're thinking of new uniforms, topped with a cap." He nodded confirmation. Thrusting the small case into his hand, she pointed him onto the transporter platform. "Take my word for it," she said. "The way Starfleet Command moves, it will be fifteen years before it's implemented and by then they'll have forgotten the cap. . . . Energize," and with a wink and a grin, she vanished like the Cheshire cat.

Jim Kirk arrived on the surface of Eeiauo with a Cheshire cat grin of his own. He stood facing the low attractive building that served as this area's hospital. To his right, on the tree-filled grounds, he saw a handful of brightly colored tents. Catchclaw and the rest of the Sivaoans had clearly had enough of indoor living. A handful of Eeiauoans, exercising limbs made stiff by the effects of ADF and weeks or months in bed, had stopped to stare in mingled wonder and disapproval at TooLong Tail and EagerTalker who swung by their tails from a branch and stared back in much the same manner. It took him a moment to recall that the Eeiauoans considered it vulgar to use a tail other than . . . decoratively. *I'd better warn Catchclaw about that,* he thought, climbing the long low stairway to enter the hospital.

Inside, he found Spock at the receptionist's desk, pieces of some delicate medical instrument spread before him for repair. "Captain," he acknowledged, as he continued his work, "I trust Nurse Chapel is well?"

"As well as can be expected. How's Bones—and where is he?"

"As he was asleep when I arrived with the third landing party, I was not permitted to speak to him," Spock said. "Dr. Wilson would like a word with you before you wake him."

"If he needs sleep that badly," Kirk said, "I'm not sure I should wake him."

At that Spock looked up, fixed him with a piercing look and said, "Dr. Wilson thinks otherwise."

Kirk spread his hands and, grinning again, said, "Who am I to argue with a woman with a quarterstaff? Carry on, Spock; I'll find Evan myself."

It was not long before he found her, monitoring the pulse of a Eeiauoan in the first ward. She jerked sharply toward him and growled, "You're supposed to be Catchclaw." There was little response he could make to that, and her wariness kept him from questioning it.

He looked more closely and recognized her patient: Quickfoot, the Eeiauoan doctor who had given Spock the last piece of his puzzle and then, because of this 'treason,' had attempted suicide. Kirk suddenly understood. Quickfoot was about to come out of her coma, and Evan was afraid this time she might succeed.

As Quickfoot began to stir, Catchclaw arrived in a scrabbling skid of claws. "Tail-Kinker? What's so important that it can't wait five minutes?"

"I can't explain, Catchclaw, but I need you here when Quickfoot wakes. You're in charge but make a point of introducing yourself with your *full* name." She relinquished her place to the Sivaoan and, catching Kirk's arm, drew him along as she stepped out of Quickfoot's line of sight. Asking no further explanation, Catchclaw took Quickfoot's head in gentle hands. The patience of her waiting was so complete that, had it not been for idle movement in her tail tip, Kirk would have thought her a statue. Minutes went by, and only the tenseness in the fingertips on his arm told Kirk of Evan's fears. He laid his hand over hers and the fingers convulsed—Quickfoot's form jerked.

Catchclaw said, "Quickfoot? Gently, Quickfoot, you still have a good deal of healing to do."

Jim Kirk could barely hear Quickfoot's whisper of disbelief: "Healing? The Long Death . . . it's the Long Death."

Evan Wilson clenched one hand on his arm, the other behind her back. Catchclaw said, "I'm Catchclaw to-Ennien. I came to help."

"*To*-Ennien? *To*-Ennien?" Quickfoot said, struggling to sit up. Catchclaw was not about to allow that.

"To-Ennien," she confirmed. "Now behave yourself and rest, and you'll be up and around in a week."

"Why would you come? How could you have forgiven us?"

"Forgiven you? . . . Oh!" she said with sudden comprehension. She took Quickfoot's hand firmly between her own and went on, "We forgave your ancestors a long time ago. It was ourselves we couldn't forgive. Captain told us we were all acting like children. So here we are, trying to grow up." Her tail looped in amusement.

Quickfoot stopped struggling and said, "I don't understand . . . but I'm glad you came. You *can* help? You can stop the Long Death?"

"Yes," said Catchclaw. "Now rest, Quickfoot. We'll talk later when you're feeling better."

Quickfoot arched her whiskers forward and said, as if it were the most wonderful word in any language, "Later . . ." She closed her eyes.

The small hand on his arm loosened, and Kirk released it from his grip. "Thank you, Catchclaw," she said softly. Then, turning to him, "She'll be all right now, Captain. Come on, I'll take you to Leonard."

He followed her outside and down a long corridor with rows of windows overlooking the grounds, sorry now he had let go her hand. He wanted very much to offer her a hug—not for purposes of demonstration, but for the sheer good spirits of it. Because he could not say what he wished, he said, "Is he awake, Evan?"

"No, but you can wake him. It'll do you both good."

He had to ask, "Then why didn't you permit Spock—?"

"I need that sensor fixed, Captain, and Spock hardly needs an emotional pick-me-up."

"I see"—he smiled—"and I do?"

She glanced up, faintly surprised. "Don't you? Besides, you're most likely to give Leonard the lift he needs." She stopped before a door. "In there," she said, "and do me a favor? Give him a long, highly detailed account of everything you've done since you last saw him."

"And make it good enough to keep him in bed?" Kirk suggested and read confirmation in her smile. "I'll do my best, Evan." He opened the door, stepped through and eased it quietly closed behind him.

Hidden among the boxes of medical supplies was a cot. On it sprawled Leonard McCoy; curled in the crook of his elbow was Grabfoot and, at his feet, WhiteWhisker. All three were sound asleep.

Jim Kirk hesitated to wake him. Even in sleep his face seemed drawn with weariness. He had lost a great deal of hair, but only the faint traces of lesions remained. He too was healing.

Reminding himself that Evan had put him in charge of McCoy's morale, he touched his chief medical officer on the shoulder and shook him gently. "Bones," he said, "Bones." McCoy stirred with a groan. Kirk grinned and said, quietly but in a tone of command, "Status report, Dr. McCoy."

McCoy's eyelids shot open. "Jim!" he said.

Kirk put a finger to his lips and indicated the two sleeping children.

Propping himself up from his cot on one elbow—not the one Grabfoot was using as a pillow—McCoy said again, more quietly but with no less passion, "Jim, it's good to see you!"

"Good to see you, Bones. No," he added, as McCoy eased Grabfoot's head from his arm, "don't get up. That's an order."

McCoy made a huffy sound, almost identical to Catchclaw's chuff of exasperation, and pointed to Grabfoot and White-Whisker. "I'm supposed to be watching them," he growled, but he kept his voice low to avoid waking them. "D'you know what I think? I think they're watching me!"

"That wouldn't surprise me in the least," Kirk told him.

"So it hardly surprises me that she's got you in on it too," McCoy continued. "D'you know she told me she'd let me make rounds once a day, *if* I stay in bed the rest of the time? She'll 'let' me! She threatened to send me—" He stabbed a finger at the ceiling, presumably in the direction of the *Flinn* and, still smoldering, he added, "I tell you, Jim, that woman, as small as she is, has all the makings of a tyrant!"

Kirk grinned at him. "You sound better already, Bones."

The scowl gave way to an answering grin, as McCoy lounged back on the cot. "I feel better, Jim. Lord, it's good to see you!" he said again. "Don't just stand there: pull up a chair and tell me everything."

Unable to resist the line, Kirk said, "Just what the doctor

ordered," and was rewarded by McCoy's startled laugh of comprehension. As Kirk reached for a small folding chair, he realized he was still holding the specimen case in his hand. "Micky sent her love," he said, "and some specimens you wanted. I should have given them to Evan."

"Specimens from Micky? Don't you dare." McCoy eased Grabfoot's head from his arm, and Kirk somewhat reluctantly turned over the case. McCoy opened it. "Ah," he said with a sigh. "She gave you your three cheers, Jim?" He looked up for the answer.

Kirk nodded. "For the *Enterprise* crew," he said, as he sat. "What's one got to do with the other?"

"That's Micky," said McCoy. "Always a woman of her word." He turned the specimen case slightly so Kirk could see the contents: a bottle of Csillag brandy and, nestled in tissue paper, a single glass. He unpacked them both. "There ought to be another glass in one of those boxes, Jim. Get one and we'll drink to the lady."

"Are you sure, Bones?"

"Is it medically advisable, d'you mean?" McCoy glared at him and went on, "It was prescribed by one of the finest doctors Starfleet Academy ever produced, and I ought to know—we shared a cadaver."

There seemed little Jim Kirk could say to that. He found himself a glass. "Sorry, Bones. I wouldn't dream of questioning the lady's judgment."

"Good," said McCoy curtly. "Sit down, drink up"—he poured—"and tell me all about it." He raised his glass and, touching it to Kirk's, said, "To Micky, McCoy and Macbeth." He downed the brandy, then sighed contentedly.

Kirk complied with the toast then asked, "Why Macbeth?"

"He was the cadaver. The report that came with him listed coronary infarction as cause of death, but he'd been run through with a sword. We never did find out the circumstances. And Micky never could resist a good alliteration."

From the foot of the cot came a sneeze, and WhiteWhisker sat up, tiny face contorted, nose working furiously. Before either could give the child a greeting, she hissed and bounced once on Grabfoot, who woke with an identical grimace. As

McCoy poured himself another glass of brandy, Grabfoot leaned gingerly closer, sniffed and jerked back as if he'd been slapped. With a shout to WhiteWhisker, he charged for the door and out; WhiteWhisker was right behind him.

McCoy peered into the amber liquid. "Never underestimate the power of a good brandy," he said, and this time sipped it slowly. "How's Chapel?"

"She's fine. Her morale's low, but Micky says it's the . . . esthetic loss." At Bones's look of incomprehension, Kirk pointed to the bald patches on Bones's own head. "She'll get over it when her hair grows back."

"I think I know how she feels," McCoy growled.

They were both silent a moment, appreciating the brandy and the company. At last, McCoy set his glass on the floor and lay back once more. "All right," he said, "now you can tell me all about it. Doesn't seem right, you know."

"What doesn't?"

"While we all work ourselves to exhaustion here, you wander off and find the cure to ADF—for a song!" His smug expression told Jim Kirk that he had been waiting for a chance to use the line for some time now.

Jim Kirk grinned back at him, spread his hands and countered with the line *he* had been saving for just this occasion: "It was child's play, Bones."

Captain's Log, Stardate 2962.3:

Vaccinated volunteers continue to arrive on Eeiauo from all over the Federation. Soon there will be no need of our extra hands and the *Enterprise* will be free for reassignment. Most of the crew has already returned to the ship. With the arrivals of Nurse Chapel and Doctors McCoy and Wilson, the ship's register is almost complete.

Personal Log, James T. Kirk, Stardate 2962.3:

. . . which leaves us little to do but write reports for Star Fleet. And a formal report has no heading for "Chief Medical Officer, Characteristic Entrance Of."

"Welcome back, Bones," Jim Kirk said, as McCoy sparkled onto the transporter platform.

"Jim," he said with a smile. He glanced down to confirm that all of him had arrived safely and, fixing a steely eye on Scott, he growled, " 'Scrambled my mother', Mr. Scott?"

Scotty looked momentarily bewildered—then, with dawning comprehension, he said, "Oh, *Rushlight!* He didna warn me about his memory. . . . I didna expect him t' tell ye the tale . . . !"

"Obviously not," said McCoy acidly, as he stepped down.

Evan Wilson, hopping lightly off the platform behind him, said, "Is *that* where Rushlight got the idea for his 'Scramble Song'? Don't grouse, Leonard, it's a great success with the children. You should be pleased to have contributed."

McCoy growled at her, "Some day I'm goin' to take you over my knee. . . ."

"I wouldn't advise it, Bones," Kirk said. "She's smaller than you are," and Evan rewarded him for it with a brilliant smile.

Rather than explain the remark to McCoy, she said, "I'm on my way to sick bay; I want to say hello to Christine."

"Tell her I'll be along in a minute," McCoy said.

"I'll tell her you're picking on Scotty, and I'll sing her Uhura's Standard version of the 'Scramble Song,'" said Wilson and scrammed before McCoy's amiable swat in her direction could connect.

When he turned back to Scott, McCoy was grinning. "I'm in too good a mood to be bothered, Scotty," he said, "but don't think I'll let you forget it."

"I wouldna do enna such thing, Dr. McCoy."

McCoy, pleased, nodded, then said, "I'd like to see Chekov."

"On the bridge," Kirk said and, leaving Scotty to supervise transport of the few remaining stragglers, accompanied him down the corridor.

"As for you," McCoy said, "you didn't tell me how Evan got the Sivaoan solution into the boy—I had to read her reports to find out. Are you gettin' fustidious in your old age?" He chuckled. "Blew it up his nose! Lord, you should have heard Micky laugh. And wait until Starfleet Medical reads that one!"

"And here I was thinking Starfleet misses all the good parts. . . ."

"Not that one, they won't." McCoy gestured him into the turbolift, said, "Bridge," then, "How's Spock, Jim?" As surprised by the question as by the seriousness of his tone, Kirk stared; and McCoy added hastily, "I don't mean medically. I mean, how does he seem to you? Noticed anything out of the ordinary?"

"Out of the ordinary," Jim Kirk repeated and thought immediately of the one bright afternoon he had found Evan Wilson and a double handful of children, Eeiauoan and Sivaoan, all sitting on the hospital steps, all listening with rapt attention as Spock—*Spock!*—told them the adventures of T'Kay, the Vulcan trickster. The memory brought a smile. "As in telling stories to the children? I didn't know he had it in him."

"Neither did I. Evan threatened to have his pointy ears if he didn't keep his promise to tell EagerTalker about T'Kay." He grinned. "I got the full story from EagerTalker, and not just 'How it happened when CloudShape came to Vulcan.' "

Then he shook his head and went on, "That's not what I mean, Jim. He's been doin' some sort of research—his idea of fun, I suppose. And Evan gets the fastest response from Starfleet on a reference search I've ever seen. All I did was suggest he take advantage of her connections, whatever they are—and he practically bit my head off!"

"Spock? I don't believe you for a minute."

"All right, I'm exaggeratin' . . . but for Spock it was a snap. That haughty affronted look of his"—McCoy demonstrated, overplaying considerably—" 'I am quite capable of conducting my own research, Dr. McCoy, and should I require assistance, I doubt that Dr. Wilson's would be appropriate.' "

"That's a snap, all right," Kirk agreed, "but then, you don't know what she's been doing to his pet computer. In fact, *I* can only guess. . . ."

By the time the lift drew to bridge level, Jim Kirk had filled him in on what little he knew of the flags in Spock's computer.

"D'you know," McCoy said, "the way he's been watchin' her, I was half expectin' her to jump up and go 'Boo!' at him. So here you are tellin' me she already has, . . . Well, that explains his behavior, but I'm sorry I missed seein' it."

"Cheer up, Bones. Maybe he hasn't found all her surprises yet."

The doors hissed open and they walked onto the bridge. McCoy reveled in the welcoming hellos and came at last to Chekov, who doffed his rakish nonregulation cap and offered a jaunty smile and a stubbly growth of new hair for his examination. "You're a lucky man, Mr. Chekov. You'll be back in shape in no time," McCoy told him and added, chuckling to himself, "Blew it up his nose. That woman should have cards printed: 'Dr. Evan Wilson, Imaginative Medicine A Specialty.'"

Sulu grinned at him. "Speaking of imaginative," he said, "is there really such a thing as the organ of Zuckerkandl, or have I been had?"

"The organ of Zuckerkandl? I'd say only one doctor in fifty even knows it exists. Am I bein' tested, Mr. Sulu?" McCoy eyed him suspiciously.

After a long, equally suspicious look back, Sulu said to Chekov, "It could be a conspiracy. I wouldn't put it past her to con Dr. McCoy into confirming it for her. . . ."

From his console, Spock said, "Your conspiracy theory, Mr. Sulu, is unfounded. While it is a difficult reference to locate, the Starfleet medical library computers also confirm the existence of such an organ in the human anatomy."

"Evan," said McCoy and, smiling broadly at Spock, he added, "I see why you didn't want her assistance, Spock. Any computer she queries is automatically suspect. At least, that's what I hear from Jim. Put her in the one-in-fifty category and leave it at that."

"Your estimate, Doctor, is conservative almost to the point of inaccuracy."

McCoy raised an eyebrow. "If I were Evan, I'd take that as a compliment. Bein' McCoy, I'm goin' to chalk it up as one of your usual slurs, Spock."

"Captain," Uhura cut through, "I have Starfleet, sir. New orders."

"On the screen, Lieutenant."

Kirk listened with a growing sense of satisfaction: first came the general commendation his crew so richly deserved; second, the announcement of three weeks' much-needed shore leave, also richly deserved; third and best . . .

". . . You are to report back to Eeiauo, to pick up and transport a Eeiauoan delegation to Sivao. A list of delegates follows."

They would all welcome the chance to see the outcome of the meeting between the two worlds, he knew. The name Sunfall of Ennien topped the list of delegates, and Jim Kirk could feel the radiance of Uhura's smile without turning.

When the screen blanked and he did turn, he found her smile had diminished. Pressing her earpiece to her ear, Uhura said, "Additional orders coming in from Starfleet Command, sir, for Dr. Wilson," then she held up her hand for a moment's grace. Spock stepped to his station and scrutinized his computer. It was odd, Kirk thought, but no odder than most of Spock's behavior concerning the doctor, and he let it pass without comment. Uhura lowered her hand and, frowning slightly, said, "She's to report to Laurel Station immediately."

"Immediately?" he repeated, taken aback, and McCoy muttered, "Starfleet," as if it were a word not used in polite company. Kirk said, "That's hardly fair. Ask them if they can wait three weeks."

Uhura brightened and returned to her console. But before she could translate his words into a formal request, Spock said, "One moment, Lieutenant," and she paused, startled by the command implicit in his tone. Spock went on, "Captain, if you will permit an observation? I believe Dr. Wilson has been anticipating these orders for some time now. She would no doubt appreciate your intention, but she would hardly consider the result a kindness."

McCoy studied him, then grinned to lighten the question: "Tryin' to get rid of her, Spock?"

"No, Doctor."

Kirk could read nothing in his face. *I trust his judgment,* he thought, and, waving a hand at Uhura, he said, "Let it go,

Lieutenant. Pass the orders on to Dr. Wilson." Then he thought, *I'm not so sure I trust his judgment on this one subject however,* and added, subduing McCoy with a stare, "If she squawks, I'll place the request."

But she did not squawk. Shortly thereafter she announced herself ready for departure. Jim Kirk eased his way through the thinning crowd of well-wishers on the shuttlecraft deck and found her, like her skiff, poised for departure. *Spock was right,* he thought, *she's been waiting for this.* "That anxious to leave us, Evan?" he asked, voicing it for the rest.

She shook her head; the smile she gave him was rueful. "No, Captain, not that. I haven't had so much fun in a long time, or met so many people I liked all in one place." She clasped both hands on her quarterstaff, the one that had served them all so well on Sivao, and leaned her cheek against it. "But you don't need me anymore," and glancing up at Spock, she once again produced that wicked grin of hers, and added, "And even a Vulcan's patience won't last forever."

McCoy guffawed. "All the more reason to stay, Evan—give us somethin' to look forward to! From what I've seen, you might just be the person to get through that stubborn front. . . ."

Evan Wilson laughed and held out the quarterstaff to him. "For you, Leonard, in case you ever have to contend with a Vulcan patient." McCoy hesitated, taking the offer as a joke, but she pressed the staff into his hands. She hugged Uhura and Chapel, kissed Scotty and Sulu each on the cheek.

Chekov doffed his cap and held out his hand. Reddening self-consciously under the stubbly scalp his gallantry exposed, he said, "Good-bye, sair. We'll miss you."

"I'll miss you too, Pavel," she said. "May I give you one last bit of medical advice, for safety's sake?"

Surprised, Chekov said, "Of course."

She leaned conspiratorially close to say: "Please take care when you get planetside. Women are going to be lining up to speak to you—and a great many of them will not be satisfied with speaking. Just be sure you get some rest between times."

With that, she took his extended hand, pulled him toward her and gave him a kiss on the cheek as well. Chekov ducked his head, at once flustered and reassured.

"Don't I get a kiss too?" McCoy protested, "Seems to me a quarterstaff is hardly a fair trade. . . ." Laughing, Evan stood on her toes to kiss him. "That's better," said McCoy, looking smug, then he added, "How about Jim? He could use a lift in morale, too, Doctor."

Jim Kirk grinned in anticipation as she turned his way. But, once again, he got the unexpected. Evan Wilson snapped to attention, saluted crisply and said, "Captain, it's been a pleasure to serve with you." Her blue eyes were bright with mischief. He returned the salute in kind and said, "The pleasure was mine, Dr. Wilson," and waited to see what she would do next.

She turned to Brightspot and said, "Hug?" Brightspot coiled her tail and cautiously embraced Evan, while McCoy gave her an outraged look on Kirk's behalf. Then Evan held Brightspot out at arm's length and said softly, "Don't forget, Brightspot."

Brightspot wrapped her tail around Evan's arm. "I won't, Tail-Kinker; I *don't*. I'll see you at Ennien."

Evan Wilson nodded—and came at last to Spock. He stared down at her, the look on his face unreadable. It was a long moment before she spoke and, when she did, it was as if she took refuge in the formal language: "I regret we had no time for our experiments in the physiological effects of the Vulcan memory reading process. I have left detailed notes of my experience in the medical log. They are subjective, of course, but they may be of some use in suggesting an approach to formal research. Perhaps you and Dr. McCoy might—" She broke off suddenly but did not take her eyes from his face.

"Perhaps," he said, "although you would have been the better subject."

"I like that, Spock," said McCoy acidly.

Uncharacteristically, Spock made no response to McCoy. Still looking at Wilson, he said, "Thank you, Tail-Kinker to-Ennien. I have learned a great deal from our encounter."

"So have I," she said. "Next time I'll be ready for you." The silence drew out between them, but no one dared to speak. "Mr. Spock," she said again, "Thank you for . . . everything. I owe you." Reddening suddenly, she looked away. "Clear the deck, people! *Jamie* and I have to be on our way!" She started for the skiff.

Last to the hatch in his reluctance to see her leave, Kirk paused before clearing the shuttlecraft deck. And, as he turned for one final glimpse of her, Evan Wilson shouted, "Hey, Jim!" and raced toward him. He was so surprised when she leapt to throw her arms around his neck that he caught and held her purely by reflex. She kissed him soundly on the cheek. Then, laughing, she lowered herself to the deck, much like one of Catchclaw's children scrambling down, threw her head back to look challengingly into his eyes and said, "I'll see you again, Jim—you may not see me, but I'll see you!" She gave one last wicked grin, turned again and darted back to her ship.

"*Much* better," said McCoy, lounging smugly just outside the hatch. He and Kirk exchanged grins.

"A proper good-bye," agreed Kirk.

From the airlock of her skiff, Evan Wilson yelled, "Hey, Leonard, shut the door! Were you born in a barn?"

"Yeah," McCoy yelled back, as Kirk stepped hastily past him, "and every time I hear a donkey bray, I get homesick!" At that, Evan crowed with delight and blew them each a kiss.

Kirk himself dogged the hatch, then followed the others to the observation bay to watch as the *Dr. James Barry* slipped from the shuttlecraft deck and sped away. Scott said to Sulu, "Y'see, laddie, Orsay didna once touch th' tractor beams. She's a fine captain, is th' lass, as b'fits her *Jamie*."

Kirk, who had been treated to a loving description of "her *Jamie*," knew high praise when he heard it, but he saw that her performance only bewildered Spock further. Quietly, he said, "About the pulsars, Spock, I can explain that—later."

"Indeed? I should be most grateful."

Something in Spock's expression made Jim Kirk look twice. Had it been anyone but Spock, he'd have thought him in need of cheering. Illogical or not, he found he could not shake the peculiar sensation and, as he walked to the lift beside his first officer, he acted on it, deliberately drawing from Evan Wilson's bag of tricks. "Well," he began, "I guess that wraps up all the loose ends but one. I never found out the answer, and now I suppose I never will."

He waited for Spock's query, got it. "Nothing important, Spock"—he waved his hand nonchalantly—"just a . . . riddle she posed me." He had Spock's full attention now, so he laughed and set the final hook: "I had intended to ask you, to see what you could make of it."

"By all means, ask. I would be most interested to hear this 'riddle.'"

"The first time we met, I asked Evan why she had taken up saber as a hobby, and she said 'for the same reason I took up quarterstaff and eating with chopsticks.' Make any sense to you, Spock, or is it as illogical as it sounds?" But as he asked, he realized the answer lay in her willingness to learn anything and everything, from Sivaoan emergency medicine to chipping out a spearhead.

"Illogical, Captain? Hardly," Spock said.

Kirk was taken aback: Spock clearly saw the riddle as a riddle and had found his own solution. "You mean there *is* some connection I'm missing? Saber, quarterstaff, chopsticks?"

"There is."

Kirk waited for him to expand on that. When he did not, Kirk eyed him warily and, in the time-honored tradition of the riddle, patiently repeated his query, "All right, Spock, I'll bite: why would she take up saber, quarterstaff and eating with chopsticks?"

"To extend her reach."

Chief Engineer Montgomery Scott found himself looking forward to his extended shore leave with somewhat mixed feelings. He had hoped to do a great deal of carousing with McCoy and Wilson—and to introduce Rushlight to the delights of their company. But Rushlight had remained on Eeiauo, looking after his newfound kin. Well, they had more need of a bard; Scotty could hardly begrudge them that. He did begrudge Starfleet's decision to transfer Evan without giving her leave, though, and he much resented being deprived of her company.

He answered the door absently and found himself staring at Uhura.

"May I come in for a moment, Mr. Scott?"

"O' course, lass. Sit down. What can I do for ye?"

She remained standing, shyly. She said, "You did it already, Mr. Scott. It was your idea to use Sunfall's songs to find Sivao. I . . . I wanted to thank you."

"Lass," he said, admonishing, "ye did all th' work: ye an' Mr. Spock. . . ."

"I still—" She broke off, began again. "Mr. Scott, were you serious when you said you'd like to hear me sing those songs? The ribald ones, I mean?" she added.

Scotty understood her immediately. He was at once enormously flattered and somewhat shocked by her offer. He said quickly but firmly, "Ye're a lady, Lieutenant. I wouldna ask . . . I know it wouldna be half th' joy for ye I'd find it. I'll not encourage ye, but I'll thank ye w' all my heart for the thought."

She said, "This is for you, Mr. Scott." She held out a small wrapped package and pressed it into his hand. "Thank you." With grave dignity, she turned and left, leaving Scotty puzzling over the item she'd given him.

When the door had closed behind her, Scotty sat down and unwrapped the package. It was a tape. He turned it over in his palm, as if this visual inspection would give some clue to its contents. When it did not, he slipped the tape into the computer and struck the play button.

At once, his quarters were filled with music. He recognized the *joyeuse* immediately, though it took him somewhat longer to place the second instrument as Rushlight's lute. Uhura's voice rang out from the tape, and it startled Scotty into a peal of laughter. He could hardly credit his ears. It was as ribald a song as he'd heard on any world—and twice as merry, for he'd never heard such a thing sung by someone with so clear, so full a voice.

By the time Uhura reached the chorus and her voice was joined by Evan Wilson's, Rushlight's and what could only have been Sunfall's, Scotty was roaring with joy and stamping his foot in time to the music. *Aye,* he thought, as his own private chorus began a second song, *ye're a lady t' y'r fingertips, Uhura, but ye've the heart and th' style of a bard.*

Scotty took out the bottle of Tau Cetiian verguzz with which Evan Wilson had, over his protests, replaced his Jubalan rum and poured himself a drink. The *Enterprise* might well be forty-eight hours from the nearest port for R and R, but shore leave was off to a rousing start.

Jim Kirk laid aside his finished report and frowned. In a few hours, the *Enterprise* would be in orbit, the first shore leave parties would be beaming down, and he would be expected to relax and enjoy himself. He was not looking forward to it. He had planned to spend a good deal of time with Evan, and now . . . He rose from the desk in his quarters and, without really thinking about it, headed down to sick bay.

In comparison to the last few times he had been there, the place seemed deserted. He glanced around for McCoy and, as he did, his eyes fell on a handful of sensors heaped on top of a cabinet. *Odd that Evan and Spock never got around to those experiments,* he thought. Given their mutual interest in the subject, the omission seemed almost deliberate. *Certainly not lack of time. She had a gift for using time to her advantage.* He smiled ruefully to himself and added, *I wish I'd done that.*

From McCoy's office, a voice, sounding much harassed, called: "They're right where you left them, Spock. Be my guest."

"If you're looking for Spock, I think you'll find him in briefing room A. Brightspot cornered him with some physics questions."

"Lookin' for him," McCoy snorted, appearing at the door of his office. "Not me! Good kid, Brightspot, I hope she has a lot of questions. . . . Y'know, Jim, that's probably the only good thing Starfleet Command has done all year—lettin' us sign her on as supercargo till we head back to Sivao."

Thinking, *They might have left us Evan,* Jim Kirk nodded abstractly. McCoy appraised him from head to toe and said, "Exactly as I thought," in a tone of voice that caught his attention where the scrutiny had not.

Surprised, he said, "Problem, Bones?"

"You," said McCoy, "Spock," as if that said it all. Then, because it did not, he added, "I want you both in the first shore leave party."

"I don't think—" Kirk was about to say that shore leave was not what he needed, but McCoy reached to one side and drew out the quarterstaff Evan had given him. He advanced on Kirk, waggling the staff, and repeated, "I want you in the first shore leave party." There was nothing Kirk could do but laugh and acquiesce.

McCoy's expression softened. "Well, how about that?" he drawled. "It works!" He gave the staff an experimental swing and struck himself in the ankle. "Ow! Maybe I'd better practice up before tryin' it on Spock."

"Maybe you'd better," Kirk agreed and, thinking of Evan, he added critically, "The expression could use some practice too. I've seen fiercer."

"For Spock, I can manage. He's been drivin' me to distraction."

"That's normal."

McCoy raised an eyebrow. "Not this way, it isn't. He's been in and out of sick bay a dozen times, lookin' over Evan Wilson's log notes as if he expected to find somethin' new added each time. And I have had to answer some of the damndest questions about human behavior you ever heard!"

"Bones . . ."

"It's hardly my imagination, Jim! If you don't believe me, ask Scotty. He got the third degree from our Vulcan friend on the subject of 'her *Jamie*' and then spent another twenty minutes tryin' to explain why Evan would take Orsay's wish to turn space pirate as a compliment!"

That brought a smile to Jim Kirk's face. "Poor Spock! Just when he thought he had human beings all figured out. . . . Evan said Spock brought out the worst in her. You'd have enjoyed it—I believe she actually bedeviled him more than you do."

"She did a damn sight more than bedevil him. I think she's got him bewitched." Put in those terms, the idea clearly pleased McCoy. But then, sobering, he added, "All I know is that he doesn't often ask my opinion—not Spock. M'Benga assures me he's completely recovered from his pneumonia, so I can't attribute it to that. If it weren't Spock doin' it, I'd take it for broodin'—the same way you're broodin'. I don't know what to make of it."

"I'm not sure I'd call it brooding," Kirk said, somewhat defensively. But seeing that McCoy's concern was serious, he gave the matter some thought and hit upon the obvious solution. "I'll tell you what, Bones—if it doesn't insult your professional pride, why don't you ask for a second opinion?" He waited expectantly.

It took McCoy only a moment to catch on, then he laughed. "Evan Wilson," he said.

"Evan Wilson," Kirk confirmed, and he gestured McCoy toward the communications screen in his office.

"Just a minute, Jim. What about Spock?"

Kirk shook his head. If McCoy were really worried about Spock, he wanted Evan's genuine opinion, and he wouldn't get it if Spock were present. "Let's speak to Evan first," he said. "If she wants Spock, she'll ask for him. She's not shy."

"Hardly—but it wasn't Evan I was thinkin' about." At Kirk's look, McCoy finished, "All right, Evan first."

He led the way back into his office. While he pulled up an extra chair and—thoughtfully—brought out some brandy and glasses, Kirk had Uhura arrange the call. Several minutes went by, more slowly than usual, and just as he had decided his anticipation was coloring his judgment, Uhura said, "I'm sorry, sir. I can't seem to clear the interference—I have no idea what's causing it. It looks like some sort of jamming, but it's not strong enough to disrupt communications."

"Never mind, Lieutenant. If it's good enough to speak, carry on. We can worry about what's causing the problem later."

Within a moment, she said, "I have Dr. Wilson's office, sir."

"I'll take it here." He had no intention of exposing Spock to the kind of crew rumor McCoy's queries might launch.

The screen brightened. The interference pattern she complained of was distracting, to be sure; it spread across the entire screen like a glittering stylized star. He understood her puzzlement: it seemed too regular not to be deliberate, yet the image behind it was clear.

He saw a typical Starfleet sick bay, somewhat larger than the *Enterprise*'s own. Smiling out at him was a tall slender black man dressed in a uniform identical to McCoy's. "Captain Kirk," he said. "This is an honor, sir. Forgive me for speaking from here," he gestured broadly around him, "but we're still cleaning up the last of the ADF cases—but you know all about that! What can I do for you, sir? Name it and it's yours!"

There was definitely something of Evan Wilson's manner in him. Almost sorry he didn't have a request to match the enthusiasm of the young man's offer, Jim Kirk shook his head. "Nothing so earth-shaking," he said, "I only wanted to speak to Dr. Evan Wilson."

The young man grinned, sketched a bow. "Well," he said, "here I am—and I repeat the offer."

It was as if Jim Kirk held in his hands an antique Chinese puzzle, and with those words, the last piece snapped into place and he saw the whole. He heard again her responses as Spock questioned her background. He had the sudden and most surprising thought that she had never once lied, only misdirected.

McCoy said, "Damned interference is affectin' the sound, too. Better tell Uhura." He reached for the intercom.

Jim Kirk caught his hand. "Sit still, Bones. That's an order." His intentional sharpness stunned McCoy into silence. "I apologize for the static, Dr. Wilson," he said smoothly, to the stranger on the screen. "This mission has been something of a strain"—he smiled—"and I'm afraid my crew is still blowing off steam."

The young man shook his head. "Don't apologize, Captain. I wouldn't dare tell you what *I* intend to do once I get all these vaccinations finished—but I assure you blowing off steam is the least of it!"

"Then I won't keep you long, Doctor." Kirk sought a plausible explanation for his call and found one: "This is something of a spot check—to convince Dr. McCoy that the Sivaoan solution is still working."

"Elath, yes!" He glanced slightly to Kirk's left. "Dr. McCoy?"—and when McCoy nodded in a disconcerted fashion, he went on, "I've got about a hundred patients that owe you and the Wilson-Chapel serum their lives, sir. As for the Sivaoan solution—damn, but you people are good!—it's nothing short of a miracle!" He lapsed into medical jargon that kept McCoy nodding for some time. Only someone who knew Bones well could have told that his interest was feigned.

When the image on the screen had finished, McCoy thanked him politely; so did Jim Kirk. The young man shook his head vehemently: "Don't thank *me*—let me thank *you!*"—again he sketched a bow—"You people did all the work! Keep me in mind, Captain, Dr. McCoy, if there's *ever* anything I can do for you. I owe you big!"

Having assured him they would, Kirk terminated the conversation. The screen went dark, but Jim Kirk continued to stare at it for a long moment. He found himself grinning because a Telamonite had sworn by a goddess—and wondered if the young man also used a quarterstaff. That he thought somehow unlikely, but he wished he could have asked.

"Just who the hell is *he?*" demanded McCoy, rising indignantly to his feet, "and where's Evan? Call Starfleet Command, Jim, and tell them they've got an impostor on their hands!" Jim Kirk opened his mouth, but could think of nothing to say, and closed it again. McCoy glared at him, then snapped, "Well, if you won't do something about him, I most certainly will." Once again, he reached for the intercom.

"You believe him an impostor," said a voice from behind them. "Fascinating." And they both turned, McCoy distracted from his intent, to find Spock watching them with open interest. Beside him, bristling with alarm, stood Brightspot. There was no way to tell how long they had been there, but Jim Kirk knew their presence was much more than coincidence.

"What would you call it, Spock?" McCoy growled. "I grant you, he does it well—even sounds a bit like her—but he's certainly not in her league."

"Oh lord," said Jim Kirk, without meaning to, "you can say that again!" Spock raised an eyebrow at him; and, inordinately pleased to have so surprised his first officer, Kirk went on, "You tell him, Spock. I don't have the heart."

"You're tryin' to say there's some other explanation? Then let's hear it, Spock. I'm waitin'."

Spock said evenly, "I believe Brightspot is prepared to offer one, Doctor."

That explains the odd interference pattern, Kirk thought, *Another flag—one designed to be easily seen by a Sivaoan eye.* Brightspot's tail shivered, and Kirk said reassuringly, "Don't be afraid, Brightspot. Just tell us what you know."

"You ccalled Dr. Evan Wilsson. . . ."

"We did, dammit," said McCoy. "We didn't get her." He was dangerously near another explosion, and Brightspot bristled more noticeably.

"Take it easy, Bones," said Kirk, firmly enough to interrupt the momentum of McCoy's outrage. "Don't scare her."

"I have no intention of scarin' her. I just want to know what this is all about. Now, will somebody please get on with it?"

"Ccaptain—?" Brightspot began again, hesitantly. "Tail-Kinkker ssaid you wouldn't be angry at me—"

"No one's angry at you," Kirk said soothingly, and she paused to preen her shoulder. While her fur settled, Kirk kept a wary eye on McCoy to prevent a further outburst.

At last Brightspot said, "—But she ssaid you'd probably be very angry at her. Ccaptain, don't be, please." Her tail rose hopefully.

"I promise you I'll do my best. Tail-Kinker is my friend too, *remember?*" He smiled.

The small joke reassured her more than anything else he might have done. She straightened herself to attention, took a deep breath, and said, "I have a message from Tail-Kinkker to-Ennien to those who ccalled Dr. Evan Wilsson." Her unblinking stare surveyed them all; her tail shivered once more.

When she spoke again, her voice held something of Evan's intonation: "I knew you'd ccatch me out eventually—Mr. Sspock has a to-Ennien tail. I've left a tape. Mr. Sspock will know where to find it if he gives the matter a little thought. All my love, whether you want it or not. Tail-Kinkker to-Ennien."

"Well, Spock?" Kirk said, "*Do* you know where to find this tape of Evan's?" He had nothing else to call her; unlike Brightspot, he couldn't think of her as Tail-Kinker.

As if to justify her words, Spock did give the matter a moment's more thought. "Yes, Captain," he said at last, "I believe I do." He stepped to the console—Kirk and McCoy right behind him—and spoke to the central computer. The odd interference pattern still glittered across the screen. Kirk watched over his shoulder as Spock accessed a private file.

The interference pattern vanished. "Fascinating," said Spock, eliciting a sputter from McCoy.

Kirk said, "What is it?"

"The file was for my eyes only, Captain. Tail-Kinker to-Ennien not only gained access to it but, in so doing, circumvented the flag I set to signal any such attempt. A remarkable display of programming sophistication."

"I'll give you a remarkable display of something if you don't get on with it, Spock," McCoy growled. Brightspot hissed a warning and edged away. Kirk caught her tail and stroked the end of it, but she kept him between herself and McCoy.

"Calm yourself, Doctor," Spock advised. "This may take some time. She has, to all appearances, set another flag of her own."

"Trip it," Kirk said. "I want to hear this and I want to hear it now."

"As you wish." Spock keyed the computer. It responded with a sudden fanfare of trumpets, causing Spock to lift his brow and McCoy to purple.

The screen sprang to life with an image of the *Enterprise*'s own Evan Wilson. "Hello, Mr. Spock." Her eyes were merry. "You do nice work: it's taken me three hours to beat your flag, and I enjoyed every minute of it."

Spock's brow shot up again. "Three hours," he said, almost to himself.

McCoy growled again, "Quiet, Spock."

The image on the screen continued, "A few explanations are in order—but only a few." She gave that wicked grin and Kirk caught himself grinning back. "If you're watching this, the chances are good that you've just spoken to the real Dr. Evan Wilson. Don't pick on the man. It's not *his* fault I liked his name. His Starfleet dossier is appended to the tape, and I think you'll find he's as good at what he does as I am at what I do."

A strangled sound came from McCoy.

The face on the screen turned solemn. "Mr. Spock, I don't know if this is important to you . . . but it is to me. I take what I do seriously, and I've done nothing to jeopardize relations between the Federation and the Sivaoans. Ask Brightspot if you don't believe me. And, transfer dossier aside, I only lied to you once—because it seemed the truth to me at the time."

She hesitated, reddened as if she could see the long thoughtful look Spock gave her image, then said, "If you will recall our conversation regarding possible misinterpretations between the Vulcan and human cultures . . ." As if in direct response, Spock nodded, and the image went on, "I said I'd get over it. Now I find I'm just contrary enough to appreciate the effect. There's small harm in that under the circumstances, so I might as well enjoy it."

She raised her hand in the Vulcan salute and said a few words in Spock's harsh native tongue. Spock returned the gesture.

Rising from the recording console, she took a step backward and Kirk saw that she no longer wore the uniform of a Starfleet doctor. She was dressed instead in a lace shirt over flowing blue trousers tucked in turn into knee-high boots.

Like an illustration in a fairytale, Kirk thought and then, *It suits her.* At her waist, beneath an elaborately embroidered vest, she still carried the knife Stiff Tail had given her. He understood it to mean that she would honor her pledge to the Sivaoan.

"You see, Brightspot?" she said. "I promised you'd be there when I pulled the captain's tail. Tell him, my hat's off to him and to the crew of the U.S.S. *Enterprise.*" She bowed low, sweeping the floor with her plumed hat. Without meaning to, Jim Kirk laughed out loud. "Tail-Kinker to-Ennien out," she finished, smiling out of the screen.

A Starfleet Command personnel dossier appeared, the picture of the real Dr. Evan Wilson replacing that of the spurious. Spock glanced at him; Kirk shook his head and Spock turned to cancel the rest of the file.

"Oh, good," said Brightspot, "you're not mad at Tail-Kinkker."

"I guess I'm not," Kirk admitted with a grin. "What about you, Brightspot? Do you understand what that meant?" He need not have asked: her tail was so tightly curled that it might well have been painful—the Sivaoan equivalent of laughing until your sides hurt. *A happy ending for her at least,* he thought, but had the good taste not to say it aloud.

"I understand," she said, "I didn't know Sstarfleet had people like CcloudShape. I'm *glad* for you." She arched her whiskers forward. "I'm glad for me too; I never met a real one before!"

McCoy exploded, "Never met a real *what* before?" and Brightspot jumped back, to peer at him from behind Kirk.

"Trickster," she said. "Is that the right word, Mr. Sspock?"

"I believe the term is accurate in this instance," Spock said.

McCoy glared at Spock, glared at Kirk. "What the hell are you all talkin' about?"

Very gently, Kirk said, *"She's* the impostor, Bones."

"She's a doctor, dammit, not an impostor!" McCoy glared at them all again.

"The captain did not say she was not a doctor," Spock pointed out, "only that she was not Dr. Evan Wilson."

This mollified McCoy not at all. He poured himself a glass of brandy, downed it and resumed his glaring. Jim Kirk studied his old friend with considerable amusement and no little sympathy. Then he said, "What about that call to Starfleet Command, Bones? Still want to make it?"

His mind still bent on outrage, McCoy did not at first grasp the import of the question. When he did, he looked shocked. "Lord, no, Jim!" he said. "Are you out of your ever-lovin' mind?" His eyes narrowed suspiciously. "Unless, of course, you intend that as an order, *Captain.*"

Jim Kirk laughed and raised his hands in surrender. "No, Bones, no!" he protested. "There's no need to take my name in vain! Although this does raise certain problems."

"Such as what?" McCoy's manner was still defensive.

"Such as how I request a commendation for someone who wasn't officially here."

McCoy dropped his defensiveness, chuckled. "I see what you mean, Jim. Y'know, you mentioned somethin' about commendations for Brightspot and Another StarFreedom. Seems to me Tail-Kinker to-Ennien is just as deservin'—and what Starfleet assumes is up to Starfleet."

"Misdirection," said Kirk thoughtfully, and McCoy stared back at him with such innocence that he couldn't resist adding, "I might think she'd been a bad influence on my senior officers, if I didn't know them as well as I do."

His innocence clearly injured by this, McCoy said, "I have a report of my own to write." His southern accent flared up, as it so often did when he was planning some mischief: "Just makin' sure there are no discrepancies. . . ."

"No," Kirk said smiling, "I don't foresee any discrepancies. Do you, Mr. Spock?"

"Oh, Lord," groaned McCoy, "I forgot: Vulcans don't lie!" He advanced on Spock—and Kirk braced himself for one more diatribe on the heartlessness of Vulcans. Instead McCoy said, "Your behavior's been a bit unusual lately, Mr. Spock. How are you feelin'? Why don't I just check you into

369

sick bay—don't worry about your report, Jim can take care of that—so I can do a few tests. At a guess, I'd say you're not fully recovered. . . ."

Spock froze him with a glance. "Your concern is unnecessary, Doctor. My report mentions Dr. Wilson only in the capacity of acting chief medical officer."

"Well," said McCoy, "so far so good. But suppose somebody asks him, Jim? What then?"

Kirk looked at his first officer's unreadable face and knew, with a sudden surety, that Spock had tripped the last of Evan's flags deliberately, to warn her that he was aware of her imposture, and that he had kept silent even when Evan ignored his warning to finish what she had started. "Even a Vulcan's patience won't last forever," he quoted. There was no change in Spock's expression. Kirk went on, "Don't worry about it, Bones. Starfleet won't know the right questions to ask—will they, Mr. Spock?"

"It would seem unlikely, Captain."

"*I* didn't even ask the right question." Jim Kirk folded his arms across his chest and, smiling, said, "Let's have it, Spock. What do you know about . . . *our* Evan Wilson that I don't?"

"Very little, Captain, and it is at most conjecture."

McCoy's jaw dropped but all that came out was the single word, *"Spock!"*

Kirk said, "I'm willing to entertain conjecture, Mr. Spock. Continue."

"Your own speculation, Captain, led me to investigate the history of the Bodner lines. Your intuition proved correct."

"Bodner lines," said McCoy, "aren't they something in the *Enterprise* innards?" He eyed Spock warily. "I don't get it, Jim. What's this got to do with Evan?"

Kirk said, "Evan asked Scotty to check out the Bodner lines on her skiff. I don't get it either, Spock."

"Bear with me a moment. The Bodner lines, doctor, were developed five years ago to replace the older, much less reliable Wascoli lines. They are called Bodner lines because their design drew heavily on the computer simulation work of Martha R. Bodner. It is a curious fact, however, that during the development of the lines that bear her name, Lieutenant Martha R. Bodner of Starfleet Science Division was elsewhere, engaged in a quite different project."

"Are you seriously suggesting that our Evan Wilson also designed the Bodner lines?"

"I am, Captain. I took the liberty of speaking to Lieutenant Chris Megson, who assisted on that project. I have every reason to believe that our 'Evan Wilson,' as you put it, and his 'Martha Bodner' are one and the same."

"Good grief, Spock! Let's not tell Scotty—I have no idea how he'd take it!"

Spock fell silent. For a moment the silence lengthened, then McCoy said, "That's all? All that time you were doin' research and that's all you found out? You *are* slippin', Spock!"

"Bones . . ."

"Dammit, Jim, now he's got me curious!"

Spock said, "I shall of course continue my investigation."

"You'll do nothin' of the sort!" McCoy said.

And Spock raised a brow. "Really, Doctor, I find your abrupt change of attitude most illogical. First you berate me for my lack of information—and now you insist I discontinue my investigations?" He turned to Kirk for assistance.

Kirk said, "I'm as curious as you are, Spock, but Bones is right—there's too much risk to go poking around in her background." Brightspot's ears flicked back, and he added hastily, "I mean, risk to Evan, Brightspot. We may not be angry at her, but I couldn't say the same for Starfleet Command if they found out what she's been up to."

"Oh!" said Brightspot and a ridge of fur at the nape of her neck rose briefly, then smoothed. Solemnly, she said, "I'll tell it only with my tail," and her tail corkscrewed.

"I take it that's a promise," Kirk said smiling. "Spock?"

"Captain, you yourself suggested I should not wish to . . . disappoint her."

"I thought she was pulling your tail. I didn't realize she was pulling mine *and* Starfleet's," Kirk began.

McCoy, who had been watching Spock, interrupted: "What d'you mean, Spock?"

"You do not speak Vulcan; consequently, you assume—as she no doubt intended you to assume—that her last words to me were 'Live long and prosper.' They were not, as your own medical log would verify if you so desire it."

"Medical log," McCoy repeated.

And Spock clarified, "Specifically, that portion of it describing the memory that Tail-Kinker to-Ennien drew from my mind."

"I read the damned thing three times," growled McCoy, "tryin' to figure out what you were lookin' for."

Kirk too had read Evan's report. He seldom heard anything in the way of personal memories from Spock and his curiosity had gotten the better of him. To Brightspot, he explained, "Mr. Spock taught Evan a kind of Vulcan hide-and-seek. . . ."

He straightened suddenly and, with dawning amazement, stared at Spock. Twice he had heard the formal words that began the game: once in Evan's meticulous description, and the second time—the second time, only moments ago, as she raised her hand in the Vulcan salute. "Oh lord, Bones," he burst out, "She dared him to find her!"

"She dared him . . . !" McCoy began—and finished, gaping.

"The word *dare* is hardly appropriate," Spock said. "The phrase is rather an invitation or a declaration of intent." He looked thoughtful, added, "Given her manner, however, I do find it understandable that a human would interpret this as a challenge."

McCoy beamed at him and drawled, "And you're goin' to take her up on it." Brightspot, echoing his good humor, wrapped her tail around his arm. He patted it jovially. "Well, well, Mr. Spock . . . I believe there's hope for you yet!"

Spock stared back at him with utter incomprehension, and Jim Kirk knew that any explanation of his own or McCoy's delight would only serve to baffle him further. "Never mind, Spock," he said, "You may continue your investigation. Keep it discreet, and keep us posted on the results . . . informally, of course."

"Of course, Captain."

It was so seriously said that Jim Kirk could not resist adding, with a smile, "Far be it from me to spoil your fun." And to his great surprise, for once Spock made no objection to his choice of words.